PRAISE FOR *THE ANTIQUITY AFFAIR*

"What a thrilling adventure with sisters at the heart of it. When Tess and Lila take the reins—of horse and camel—their stories take off, brimming with cases of mistaken identities, cat-and-mouse chases, booby-trapped catacombs, first loves, encrypted clues, and a long-lost treasure that all want to get their hands on. A rousing, page-turning romp across Egypt!"

—**JENNI L. WALSH,** author of *The Call of the Wrens*

"A deliciously entertaining, swashbuckling adventure, *The Antiquity Affair* gives readers a mystery to unravel, romances to swoon over, and a sister story to tug at the heart. An absorbing, heart-pounding page-turner."

—**LORI GOLDSTEIN,** author of *Love, Theodosia: A Novel of Theodosia Burr and Philip Hamilton*

THE ANTIQUITY AFFAIR

THE ANTIQUITY AFFAIR

A NOVEL

LEE KELLY AND JENNIFER THORNE

HARPER MUSE

Published by Harper Muse, an imprint of HarperCollins Focus LLC.

This book is a work of fiction. The characters, incidents, and dialogue are drawn from the authors' imagination and are not to be construed as real. Any resemblance to actual events or persons, living or dead, is entirely coincidental.

Any internet addresses (websites, blogs, etc.) in this book are offered as a resource. They are not intended in any way to be or imply an endorsement by HarperCollins Focus LLC, nor does HarperCollins Focus LLC vouch for the content of these sites for the life of this book.

Library of Congress Cataloging-in-Publication Data

Names: Kelly, Lee, author. | Thorne, Jennifer, 1980- author.
Title: The antiquity affair / Lee Kelly and Jennifer Thorne.
Description: [Nashville] : Harper Muse, [2023] | Summary: "Two estranged sisters must band together to solve a puzzle three millennia in the making in this female-heroine take on Indiana Jones"--Provided by publisher.
Identifiers: LCCN 2023001767 (print) | LCCN 2023001768 (ebook) | ISBN 9781400240630 (paperback) | ISBN 9781400240647 (epub) | ISBN 9781400240654
Subjects: LCGFT: Action and adventure fiction. | Novels.
Classification: LCC PS3611.E443255 A84 2023 (print) | LCC PS3611. E443255 (ebook) | DDC 813/.6--dc23/eng/20230124
LC record available at https://lccn.loc.gov/2023001767
LC ebook record available at https://lccn.loc.gov/2023001768

Printed in the United States of America
23 24 25 26 27 LBC 5 4 3 2 1

*To our fathers, who truly taught us we
could be anything we wanted to be*

MRS. LANGLEY AT THE HOME OF HER
ESTEEMED SON-IN-LAW, DR. WARREN FORD,
REQUESTS THE PLEASURE OF YOUR COMPANY

ON THE OCCASION OF THE DEBUT OF

Miss Lila May Ford

SATURDAY EVENING
THE SIXTEENTH OF MARCH
NINETEEN HUNDRED AND SEVEN

AT TEN O'CLOCK
IN THE EVENING

CHAPTER 1

LILA

Riverside, New York City

LANTERN LIGHT GLITTERS AGAINST THE GOLDEN object in my hand. Such a curious thing. So small to contain such power.

My palms are dampening. It's time.

Our lady's maid awaits. I deposit the treasure into her outstretched fingers.

This comb was one of Mother's few effects to survive the great sell-off. She wore it at her first ball, and I shall do the same tonight to honor her memory, formally accepting the mantle of debutante, object of notice, sole hope of untangling the Gordian knot wrought by a series of fiduciary errors that have compounded of late into ever-tightening debts.

Margaret places the comb in my hair. Its spokes scrape against my scalp before settling in, frame shining and shell gleaming in the mirror, and there I am beneath it, porcelain skin, periwinkle dream of a gown, milky half-moon bosom, swan neck, brown hair swept up like a chocolate drop.

I look like a confection. Which is to say, exactly as ridiculous as all the other young ladies who've gone on to marry rich in the past few seasons. Whether I am comfortable in this costume, whether I feel it is truly me reflected in the mirror, is immaterial. I am picture-perfect. I have to be.

Grandmama sighs with approval behind me. Her plump figure has been buttoned over-tight into her gown, but far be it from me to point that out. I reach back to clasp her hand, setting my chin to the ideal nine-degree tilt. Practicing.

"Dear Lila." Her eyes crinkle. "You look so much like her."

I know I do. I only wonder how Father will react when he comes home. After the Pyramid of Cheops, the palace at Knossos, the wonders of Pompeii, will the sight of me register? If he does find shades of Mother in me, tonight may force him to remember a time before his life became bent upon the pursuit of fortune and glory. If, that is, he even turns up in time to present me.

"Where is Tess?" I stand carefully.

Margaret waits beside me in case a curl falls. "I've not seen her, miss."

"That girl is as bad as your father," Grandmama tuts.

I take my sister's absence as an excuse to break for the bedroom window. I open it a smidge for a breath of air.

From the garden below, I hear men's laughter and then: "Pay up, gents!"

Mindful of my coiffure, I crane my neck out the window and stare, aghast, at my little sister—not so little anymore—squatting in the muck of the alley beside the string quartet we've engaged for the ball, collecting cash from their outstretched hands.

Gambling. *Tonight.* My indignant squawk echoes against the garden walls.

Tess looks up, her mouth falling open. "Hell's bells, it's not time already, is it?"

The musicians scramble inside, my sister flying in on their heels.

I wind myself back into the room. This family of mine. I could positively scream.

"I've located Tess," I say. "Margaret, see to her, won't you? She'll need to rush."

And rush she does, thundering up the steps like a stampeding cow. I glide from my bedroom to intercept her.

She has the cheek to grin when she sees me. "Look at you, Lila. You're a regular Gibson Girl!"

"Is there no end to your vulgarity, child?" Grandmama hovers behind me. "Don't listen to her. You look like a *true* Langley. An Astor. A Hendricks." She winks. "You were made for this."

Indeed, I was. Self-made. I have spent the better part of seven years devising and working toward a plan for financial absolution that entirely hinges on tonight—this place, this time. I've learned, despite my marked dearth of natural grace, to muster a waltz and a galop, perfected my posture, memorized every possible greeting from every possible guest, and crafted the most charming response to each, thousands upon thousands of equations.

In fact, the only variable I cannot solve for tonight is my family.

Tess lags in her progress up the steps, loath to come close. This is the way of things between us now. Back in the house on Madison, we shared a nursery. When she woke first, she'd slip into my bed for company, and when my mind whirred past control, she'd spin stories to send me to sleep. We were the Fearless Fords, intrepid adventurers, traveling the world, triumphing over foes. Now she's a world traveler, well and truly, and treats me like her foe.

I cannot think why. It's not as though I personally banished her to boarding school abroad. That was her choice. She could have traveled to her desert jaunts with Father from here, but no. By the age of ten, she clearly preferred his company to mine, so when he took a position at Oxford, off to England she went. And here she is again, after more than a year abroad, making a show of how very grudging this visit is.

"Quick, Margaret, kindly stuff this mud lark into a gown," Grandmama orders. "Can't have Mrs. Hendricks catching sight of her like this."

The mention of *the* Mrs. Hendricks—society maven, arbiter of good taste, and if all goes splendidly, perhaps even my future mother-in-law—doesn't do much to calm my nerves.

Grandmama's eyes glide down Tess's body as she continues down the hall. "One of the swan-bills from Paris, I think."

Tess opens her mouth, irate.

"It can be a weapon of persecution tomorrow." Unattractive archness creeps into my tone. "Tonight can you just let it be a corset?"

Tess fixes me with a leaden blink. "She was right. You could be mistaken for an Astor."

I don't have time to parse the insult.

"And you should be ready by now." I laugh lightly. Everything for the rest of the evening must be airy as a breath.

"The invitation said ten," Tess grumbles.

"There may be early arrivals."

She shrugs. "So don't let them in."

I breathe slowly, reminding myself that it isn't worth explaining the nuances of social etiquette to Tess. She's declared herself an archaeologist, like Father, eschewing polish and parlors for sweat and scholarship. She doesn't even seem to grasp what a luxury it is to be afforded that choice.

"*Ru kaba leiten shora,*" she says.

Our childhood language. *You really do look beautiful.*

I war between delight that she still speaks Fordish so fluently and irritation that she would bring up the past at the very moment I am attempting to usher our family into the future.

"Thank you," I reply. In English.

The front door chimes. We both lean over the burnished balustrade, watching newly acquired household staff two flights down hurrying to answer. The extras we've taken on for tonight's ball are a necessarily cut-rate crew, but in their numbers they do give the house an air of added wealth, essential for reeling in a husband who can actually provide said wealth.

A man's voice echoes from the entryway below and I abruptly regret the egg and cress sandwich I was persuaded to eat an hour ago. I press my hands to my cinched stomach, quelling my rising heartbeat, and turn to see Tess staring at me queerly.

"What?" I whisper, nudging her toward her room. "Go get ready! This will be Father. You won't want him to—"

"I suppose it could be," Tess says, turning oddly pale. She hastens to her room but can't resist tossing a comment over her shoulder. "I hardly think he'll care how quickly I can truss myself up like a Christmas goose," she says before Margaret shuts the door.

I peer once more over the railing, blinking away a wave of vertigo. It wasn't Father, just another servant. I wish he would get here so I can stop feeling as though lightning's about to strike.

When Tess arrived home this morning direct from school via the RMS *Lucania*, accompanied by a single chest of luggage, one dowdy Englishwoman who insisted on staying for lunch, and no signs of Father, I'd steeled myself for a public snubbing, but Tess reassured me. Father was coming from Cairo; they'd had to travel separately. No doubt he was exhausted from the sea journey and planned to unwind for a few hours at the Union Club. But today has ticked by without so much as a telephone call from the club, and I've had to keep reminding myself that it's not a slight; he is a busy man, a titan in the field of antiquities. Not that it helps one whit with our expenditures, but he did just discover a new tomb in the Valley of the Kings. It's in all the papers: "The Biggest Egyptology Find of the New Millennium."

Tonight it'll be me he's presenting to the world. It would be better, of course, if it were Mother—better all around if she hadn't died of a wasting illness eight years ago—and part of me wishes it were just Grandmama tonight. But the fact of the matter is, I do have a surviving parent, and it is proper custom for him to present me to society.

He does cut a presentable figure when outfitted in white tie. Perhaps he'll have cleaned his fingernails while he was at the club. And to be perfectly candid, his notoriety is more than likely the reason we've had quite so many acceptances to the invitations we issued for tonight's ball.

"Miss Lila." Margaret appears at my elbow to murmur low, "Your first guests have arrived."

I descend the helix of our steps to greet the two early arrivals, fellow graduates of the Veltin School for Girls. They clap and coo at the sight of my dress, and I offer them gentle hugs, like we're porcelain dolls at play.

I took care in selecting tonight's coterie of intimates. Minnie and Violet are already engaged, thereby posing no risk of siphoning the attention of the select register of New York bachelors I intend to captivate tonight, a list capped by a rather unexpected name.

No less a person than William Hendricks has traveled down from New Haven to attend my ball. Quite the coup. Grandmama might have been in the Four Hundred in her heyday, but the Hendrickses have had money since it was first dispensed in lumps of metal, which naturally positions young William as my greatest prospect tonight. We've never laid eyes on each other, as he spends most of his time at Yale and summers in Newport, but his extremely important mother has rather abruptly favored my grandmother with her friendship. One week ago, Mrs. Hendricks personally dropped in for tea and laughingly inquired why her son wasn't at the top of our guest list. Grandmama, dancing around the obvious—we are not, in fact, in the inner circles of Hendrickses and Astors—extended an invitation to William and his mother on the spot.

In the days that followed, they became practically inseparable. I sat with my stitching as they discussed what an ideal match the two of us would make, how I'm just the type of bride Mrs. Hendricks would choose for her only son. I pretended not to listen as a voice much like Mother's resounded in my head. *If you become a Hendricks, the fortunes of this family will no longer rise and fall with every sandstorm.*

Mother married for love. Died regretting it. I cannot make the same mistake.

"Do show us around." Minnie gives my ribboned waist a squeeze. "I've never been invited into a Riverside mansion."

"It's like a country retreat," Violet chirps.

My eyes espy the smug look that passes between them.

"A tour," I agree, and they brighten, following me from the entryway into the gallery, certainly the most impressive section of our otherwise underwhelming home.

And indeed, there are appreciative murmurs as the girls stop to take in what's displayed on our recessed shelves, the few finds of Father's that Grandmama determined were aesthetically neutral enough to have on display where polite society might peruse them. A carved Mehen board: supposedly mystifying, that ancient game, but compared to Carroll's *Game of Logic*, it was a laugh—goodness, I was seven, and it still took me only half a morning to suss out the rules. The stone falcon Father unearthed . . . in Greece, was it? A glass amulet from some unfortunate South American tribe, most likely. "Curiosities," Miss Veltin would call these objects, but only if you're curious about them, which I most resolutely am not.

The truth is, I find them wretchedly distasteful. Not the objects themselves but our possession of them. These are pilfered things, spoils of bald theft, snatched from peoples in no position to argue because they're dead or too poor or downtrodden or ensnared in political nets not of their own making to fight for what's rightfully theirs.

Oh, I know it's not correct for young ladies to dwell upon such things as politics, and I do try to keep my mind trained to the practicalities before me, but it proves such an effort at times to affect looking at the world through society's hazy lens when I can see it all so clearly: my father, the great adventurer, is no better than a common burglar, and every braggadocious item he adds to this collection only fortifies the case against him.

"Are any of these cursed?" Minnie whispers to Violet's giggles.

Had Tess been the one to make that joke, I would raise my eyebrows and volley choice words about falling prey to superstition. Instead, I laugh in just the right key, clutching my heart. "Heavens, I hope not!"

Bad enough that I have all these opinions. Far worse to actually voice them.

As we continue merrily onward, my eye catches on the news

clipping from last month, now proudly displayed on the wall, that photograph of clustered, dusty figures standing in front of a low tomb entrance. Father poses second from the right, foot perched on a crumbled pillar as if to claim it. The man of the moment.

Violet peers up as we pass the back stairwell while Minnie takes my arm and casually says, "Is your father upstairs? We're ever so eager to meet him."

I turn, surprised by the sight of color blooming on the décolletage of my two school friends. They look like the girls who gather outside Broadway stage doors hoping for a glimpse of George Cohan.

"He's getting ready at the club." I manage to keep my voice light.

"How unconventional." Minnie nods. "We'd expect nothing less."

We peek into the kitchens, study, dining room; observe our faithful old butler directing staff in white jackets to set the table with borrowed china. I lead the girls into the parlor, now cleared of furniture, the quartet setting up for the dance that will follow drinks and dinner.

"So small." Violet spins back to me. "An intimate gathering. Ever so much more fun."

Her ball was at Sherry's with three hundred guests. We could never afford something so lavish.

"You know me," I demur. "I'm not one for crowds."

"Sweet, simple Lila." Minnie beams. "Your moment has come."

"*Tapen ku leinen?*" someone drones from over my shoulder. "*Illa rette zit quu si shoon.*"

Simple and sweet? Not the sister I knew.

I turn to glare at Tess. She's gotten ready in extremely short order. Her evening gown is a darker shade of blue from mine, perfectly fitted over that new French corset. To her credit, she's hardly wincing, and her face is clean and powdered, hair dressed. Only girls who've entered society wear their hair up, and I find myself frozen with envy at the sight of Tess's, curled, spilling around her shoulders. I will always have to wear my hair like this now. A chocolate drop. No going back.

"*Zit runtle u shilla*," I whisper. *Don't embarrass me tonight.*

"What in the dickens are you speaking?" Minnie mutters.

I twirl back, willing away perspiration. "A bit of nonsense. Have you met my sister? Tess, everyone, everyone, Tess."

Yes, it is an appallingly insufficient introduction, but my nerves are showing and I need to race ahead of them. I must be serene, poised, effortless, or all this is for nothing.

"Shall we see if we can snare some champagne before the receiving line?" I offer more smoothly. "We have only a few minutes . . ." *before my famous father arrives and the world stops for him.*

The girls begin to chatter and lead the way. I start after them, but Tess grabs my arm so hard that when she lets go, white imprints remain. I stare at them in dismay.

"I need to speak with you," she says, edging deeper into the now-empty parlor.

"Now?" I press my lips together. "Father will be here any minute and—"

"I don't think he will, Lila." She swallows hard. "I don't think he's coming at all."

"You said he was at the club. Getting ready." My voice is hoarse. "Why—"

Her words become a flurry. "I said he *might* come. I have no idea. He's been too busy to even send me a telegram, just that chaperone, Miss Nutter. Can you think of a more perfect name for a paid spinster—"

I speak over her. "You've been covering for him. All day. You lied to me."

A defensive glint lights up Tess's blue eyes. "It wasn't a lie; it was a guess as to his whereabouts. But then the day went on, and my guess became less and less plausible, and . . . I didn't want to be the one to cause you worry. You put up a good front, Lila, but I know how much he means—"

"You know nothing of the sort." Something unfamiliar, filthy and cold, courses up my corseted rib cage. He's not coming. I'm nothing to him. Our family, our struggles, nothing here has existed to him for years, only his mad pursuit of glory.

Of all things, tears stab my eyes, threatening to spoil my powder. I smile them away.

Tess steps back, like we're dancing. "Are you all right, Lila?"

"'All right'? What a curious question. No one's here to see *me*, you know. They've come to gawk at Father, and he hasn't bothered to show up. But you'll do in a pinch." I reach for her puffed sleeve and clasp it tight, shaking her. "Do you want to give me away in his place? Go on. Change into a tuxedo. You're his puppet, aren't you? His instrument of chaos? Here to mess it all up for me."

Everything I'm saying is illogical, but it feels so good to say it, good and awful. To let it spill out, ugliness and all. Her eyes flare with temper.

"You call *me* a puppet," she snaps. "Look at yourself! All this needlepoint and gossip. You used to be smart; now you're just Grandmama's marionette, and it isn't you she wants, not a whit. She's painted you to look exactly like—"

I slap her. Without intending to.

I stare at my errant hand and start to cry, actual tears, impractical ones. Tess is cradling her face, but she still reaches for me. I swat her away.

Past the blur, I see carriages arriving outside. Throngs of voices rise in the front garden, a cheerful overture to the event. One hundred twenty-seven guests and I am not ready. I am standing here shuddering and snot-drenched and emotional. A debutante is not meant to be emotional.

"I shouldn't have invited you." I back away. "We both know you don't belong."

Violet steps into the doorway as I approach. "Lila? Mrs. Hendricks is here with her son and— Ye gads, what's happened to your face?"

I cover myself and run out of the foyer, into the servants' wing, through the side door into the cold March night, and around to the high-walled safety of the back garden, spooling myself back inward.

No one will find me here among the hedges. No one will see me swipe my eyes, rub my goose bumps, assemble myself into the shape of, yes, *Mother*, the person I've been working to become my entire life.

No. Not entire. There was a time when I wanted something else.

That doesn't matter. Father doesn't matter. This is the night I turn our fortunes around.

My fingers stop shaking. I have nearly gotten my smile to stick when I hear a peculiar sound, a dry whistling issuing from the bushes.

I spin and see a figure so incongruous that I wonder for a moment whether I'm dreaming.

I'd just resigned myself to him not coming. This is his house, even if it was bought with the very last of Mother's money, so why is he hiding in the bushes like a criminal, dressed in a patched wool jacket and dusty hat like some vagabond?

"Lila," Father whispers, breaking my stupor. "You have to come with me. *Now.*"

He stretches out his hand. And some perverse instinct compels me to take it.

CHAPTER 2

TESS

I AM COMPELLED TO TAKE THE STEPS TWO AT A TIME AS, behind me, Margaret pleadingly offers to "fix my face." As if her primping and fussing could fix any of this. Why do I even attempt to cover for our father, to endeavor patching the threadbare scraps of this family? Lila has made it abundantly clear, for the past seven years, that she'd prefer to discard the both of us.

Desperate for a sanctuary, I hurtle down the second-floor corridor, beelining for the open paneled doors of Dad's library. His study is my one solace in this house, the only corner where I actually feel at home, the sole room Grandmama hasn't transformed tonight in her quest to ensnare a rich husband for Lila.

My heart loosens when I glimpse his display shelves from the hallway. His teeming collection of glorious relics from decades in the field and countless expeditions. Proof positive of a meaningful calling, grand adventures, a life well lived.

Once inside, I pluck his whiskey from the cordial tray and

take a long, consolatory gulp from the decanter, though it does little to quell my flush.

To hell with society's rules. I snatch the tray's twin crystal stirrers and wrangle my locks into a hasty bun. Honestly, if my family cares so much about etiquette, why did Lila invite me to her ball? It isn't the done thing to include girls who are not yet out—all my hallmates at Queen's College confirmed as much. I'm sure Grandmama only wanted a scapegoat at the ready, should anything go wrong.

"Well"—I shrug—"at least I've finally fulfilled her expectations."

I turn, ready to recline on Dad's settee with the whiskey, when I see it—the new painting. A decadent, life-size, room-swallowing portrait of Lila, now hanging between the doorway and the portrait of Mother. And do my eyes deceive, or does the artist signature belong to the famed John Singer Sargent?

"Oh no. No, no, no." My one place, my only Lila-free sanctuary in this ghastly, suffocating house. Invaded!

I stomp toward the shelves, rooting past the Bes pectoral Dad received from the director of Egypt's Department of Antiquities. General Samy Pasha's gifted block statuette. The oil lamp, the ankh—until my fingers wrap around the relic I'm searching for.

Dagger from Thebes firmly in hand, I spin, thrusting my blade at the portrait in self-defense.

"Oh, don't flinch. I'd never really hurt you," I say, cheek still stinging from Lila's blow. "Though you obviously can't say the same."

Portrait Lila remains unmoved.

"Do you even know what this is?" I ask her, running my finger along the ancient bronze. "Silly question. Of course not. The only weapon you've ever wielded is a tapestry needle."

I stalk toward Portrait Lila until my eyes are inches from her cinched waist. The dainty parasol resting on her shoulder. Her custom Charles Worth gown's ruffled silk, cascading to the floor like a sky-blue waterfall. The same gown she's wearing tonight.

"I'll admit, once upon a time, I thought I wanted this too. Your grand society life. Grandmama's attention."

I gesture toward Dad's shelves. "But I've found far worthier pursuits than husband-hunting, thank you very much. Research. Discovery. Unearthing the past. I'm going to become a daring archaeologist, like Harriet Hawes and Marguerite d'Auteuil. Adventure is a far more valuable currency. What are you going to do with your life after you marry well, Lila? Play handmaiden to Mrs. Astor?"

I point the dagger like a fescue toward the highest shelf, the cornerstone of Dad's collection. His trio of limestone *talatats*: the tablets that launched his intrepid quest for the Serpent's Crown.

"I was there when Dad uncovered those stones. Mere steps away, with Alex, in the vestibule," I say. "Those tablets verified millennia of speculation; can you even comprehend the historical significance of that?"

A delicious shiver trills up my spine, as it always does when I reflect on the legends of the Crown. I can't help but set to pacing.

"The talatats confirmed that Pharaoh Akhenaten verily conquered the ancient city of Amarna. That the mind-controlling power of his Serpent's Crown was likely *real*. Akhenaten hypnotized thousands of people with the Crown—sparing only his mother, wives, and daughters, whom he assumed to be submissive already by nature of being women. But those clever Five Ladies managed to steal his powerful uraeus and hide it away."

My words come out in a squeal, so I steal a breath myself.

"The Crown's location was one of the world's greatest mysteries . . . until our father found these tablets, suggesting where the uraeus might be found."

I halt my pacing, frowning at Portrait Lila.

"You probably don't remember any of these stories, do you? And I'm certain you've forgotten all about the Fearless Fords too."

I swallow around the new lump in my throat, slowly turning away from her.

"Perhaps it's high time I let go of them as well. 'Make my own way,' as Dad says. Starting this instant, since you so graciously reminded me that I don't belong here with you."

After carefully tucking the dagger back into its position on the bottom shelf, I cross the room and search Dad's desk drawer for pen and parchment.

I scrawl a note:

Grandmama, Lila, I'm leaving tonight, returning to school.
That's how it's going to be. No more tears or dramatics.
I'll write when I'm back in London.

"I'm sure tonight's party will be a grand success," I murmur while I sign the letter. "I won't stand in the way of your happy ending. Your safe, small, dull, happy—"

"Miss Ford, I take it?"

"Good gods!" I whirl around at the unfamiliar voice, grabbing my skirts like an actress on Drury Lane.

I find a young man staring at me curiously, leaning against the wide doorframe to the library. "Could have sworn you were speaking to someone. I shall consider myself fortunate to have found you alone."

I blink. He's a few years older than I am, I'd wager. Twenty or so, with milk-white skin, ink-dark hair. The kind of boy one looks at twice, though I can't decide exactly why.

"William Hendricks," he says by introduction, not bothering to wait for my response. "I hoped we might skip past the debutante nonsense: my mother introducing us near the punch bowl, you pretending your dance card is full, the scores of fictitious competition, et cetera." He edges into the room with a pained smile. "Given the circumstances, I think we must all cut to the quick."

The young man archly raises his chin as he glances down the second-floor hall, flashing me his perfect silhouette. It's probably his square-cut jaw that reels one in. Along with his eyes; they're an indigo blue. That Cupid's bow is quite disarming too.

Not that a handsome face gives one the excuse to be so supercilious.

"Charmed," I say, attempting to slip past. I must start back to London before Grandmama catches me. Before Lila reads me the riot act for "making a scene."

I scramble to remember what the devil high society deems an appropriate exit when confronted with someone you have no desire to speak to. "Though you must excuse me, Mr. Hendricks, I'm not myself at the moment . . ."

Wait.

Hendricks.

Debutante nonsense, dance card . . .

Oh my gods.

This is William Hendricks of *the* Hendrickses. Whose name Grandmama has been repeating all day like a novena. A suitor who might deliver this family from financial and social inferiority if tonight goes as intended.

And who, for some reason, believes I'm Lila.

Despite everything, I can't help but thrill at being mistaken for my sister. We do resemble each other. If one squints, in fact, that portrait on the wall behind William could well be me. But I recall anew that it is *not* me, nor will it ever be, as Grandmama would sooner wear rags to the opera than commission a floor-to-ceiling homage of her least favorite granddaughter!

"I need you to come with me, Miss Ford," he says evenly. "I'll explain on—"

"The walls," sails out in Lila's airier tone.

William falters. "Pardon?"

"You wondered to whom I was speaking," I hasten to explain. "The walls. It's one of my favorite pastimes."

"The walls," William repeats, dubious.

"Indeed. My, ah, personality is so underwhelming, you see, that I prefer the company of inanimate objects. Makes me feel quite superior."

This is low. Very low. And yet likely no worse than slapping your sister.

"Why, even insects are stultified by the sight of me."

"I . . . Well, that cannot be true." William clears his throat. "In fact, I've been assured you have many wonderful qualities. Though not the time to discuss, as we must be—"

"I'm not being modest, believe me. This morning I tried practicing conversation with a housefly. Poor thing died of boredom in minutes." I gesture toward Dad's shelves behind me. "Though naturally I preserved its corpse. It's displayed with my family's other antiquities."

William's face remains stoic, though he now offers his arm with *barely* masked reluctance.

"So you have an interest in entomology," he clarifies pedantically as he leads me into the hall. "Odd passion, which my mother somehow failed to mention, though I suppose it's not too far afield from your father's pursuits."

"Entomology and archaeology are hardly the same."

He bristles. "I know that, I was merely—"

"Perhaps you need a cheat sheet? So many -ologies, I fear you're overwhelmed."

"Miss Ford, please, I do attend Yale."

"My father and sister pursue the past; I pursue the pests." I wink. "Handy memory aid, in case you get confused again."

William reels back. "Are you poking fun?"

"I never joke." I bite my lip to squelch a laugh. "'Humor is the death of the soul,' as my grandmother says."

He frowns. "How pithy."

"I pray every night for a long, somber, lonely existence. Much like hers." I give an exaggerated sigh. "Talking to walls. Counting the threads in my needlepoint. Visiting my own attic, as a domiciliary conquest."

William hardly stifles his grimace. "What a future we have to look forward to."

Only then do I sober, remembering that I am playing with my very real sister's future . . . and noticing that we've somehow drifted toward the servant stairwell.

"This has been fun, but I do believe you're lost, Mr. Hendricks." I gently pull away from his grasp. "The main staircase is best to return to the parlor—"

"No, it's time to go. Discreetly. It's all been planned." He presses the small of my back, urging me farther down the steps.

"I don't understand—"

"I'll illuminate on the way."

"Do stop prodding me like a mule!"

A gruff voice rumbles from below, "Need assistance?"

I stop suddenly, straightening.

A tall, bald, shadowed man in a servant's uniform lingers at the bottom of the steps.

Thank goodness. I open my mouth to ask him to escort this pushy cad back to the ball. But the servant looks past me.

"Your father said half past ten," he says to William.

The Hendricks boy huffs a breath, stepping aside. "Fine, let's get on with it."

A bolt of dread shoots up my spine.

On instinct, I turn, careening up the steps toward the second floor, but the servant lunges like a wolf, catching me in two bounds. He hauls me off my feet, skirts falling over me, drowning me in ruffles.

"What the— Help—" is all I manage as a gag is hitched over my mouth, a blindfold thrust over my eyes.

The muted dark of the stairwell transforms into utter black.

"The back entrance," William hisses. "Go!"

They jostle me down the stairs. A thousand questions, thoughts, protests shriek through me. But it's useless.

I can't even scream.

CHAPTER 3

LILA

❦

I HAVE NO TIME EVEN TO SCREAM AS FATHER HOISTS ME over the garden wall and into the alley beyond. My mind is whirring so gyroscopically fast that I scarcely feel my feet leave the ground.

The facts at hand: Father is not dressed for a ball. One may safely assume his broad-brimmed hat, ragged jacket, and boots to be a disguise. It therefore stands to reason that some unwelcome individual may be looking for him. He's taking me with him: a posteriori, someone may also be after me.

"Lila. *Lila.*" Father's whisper grows in sharpness. He slouches until I'm forced to meet his eyes, still the same pale blue I remember, albeit more weathered now. "I've got a motorcar waiting."

Father has a motorcar? We see Mr. Schwab drive down Riverside in his from time to time, but we can barely afford to keep our coupé carriage in working nick, and Father goes out and buys a motorcar without so much as a how-do-you-do?

"Hide in the back while I find your sister."

Tess's face appears in my mind's eye, just as it looked after I struck her.

Father pulls me after him along the redbrick wall. "Step lively, princess. Come on now."

This cannot be good; he hasn't called me "princess" for eons. Another memory rises: Father slipping me and Tess sweets before one of his lectures at Columbia, letting us watch from the gallery. *"Sit pretty, princess, pea. I promise not to blather on too long."*

When we were girls, Tess could listen to him talk for hours about ancient civilizations, elaborate legends, precise methods of digging in sand. I found it rather more difficult. In fact, I can hardly remember a thing he ever said.

I wrench myself from Father's grip, ignoring the protest from my corset. "Is it the police you're running from?"

"What?" Father freezes under my glare. "No. Why—"

"You steal treasures from other countries. Dig up tombs. Pilfer from the dead."

"For the last time, Lila, it isn't theft; it's scholarship."

"Just tell me plainly," I huff. "Am I in danger?"

"Not if you stick with me," he says, eyes blazing with confidence under that ridiculous hat. "I came back to protect you and Tess, so follow my lead, and I swear nothing will happen to you."

Rather a broad promise, but I'm still too enervated to do anything but grip his arm and continue around the side of the house, along the service drive, my pouf of hair hidden behind a flowering hedge the gardeners finished planting in time for my party.

What on God's green earth am I doing? I should be in the receiving line. We both should.

Father keeps me crouching, the position excruciating in my fittings and stays, until we face Riverside Drive.

"Quick now. Head to the car while I go inside and get your sister." He points across the road, but I'm staring past him at the line of carriages stretching to our home, light spilling onto the pavement from the house as if from a waterfall, while elegant guests step out to await entry. And who is there to greet them? This is not the plan.

I search for Grandmama in the foyer, expecting to see her wringing her hands, addled with worry at my absence, but she's not there. The door is shut, damming up the river of guests.

A movement catches my eye in the parlor window. I get a fleeting glimpse of Grandmama before my view of her is blocked by a statuesque woman whose face catches the glow from a wall sconce. Mrs. Hendricks, the most powerful socialite in the city, is inside, holding Grandmama's hands. Both fretting over my scandalous absence, no doubt.

And yet . . . is Grandmama hugging Mrs. Hendricks? Laughing? My heavens. Either she's lost her marbles or doesn't even realize I'm gone.

Father freezes, cursing under his breath. My toes curl inside my slippers, primed to steal back inside and set all this to rights before he can snatch me, when instinctively I follow his gaze and discern yet another anomaly, a smudge on a perfect sketch.

Past the crowd, beyond the light, three figures, furtive in posture, hasten across the drive and into the park. Two are larger, male, gripping the third between them.

She's wearing a ball gown.

A chill trickles down my back that has nothing to do with the brisk March air. It could be anyone: neighbors, a sick party guest helped by good Samaritans.

At the edge of the grassy lawn, one of the men stumbles and the woman wriggles loose, cocking her foot back and landing . . .

A kick to the groin? "Tess!"

I reach for Father just as he races away, yelling at me, "Get to the car!"

I glance at the crowd, not one soul taking notice of the scene unfolding behind them, and back at Father, in pursuit of the group in the park. They're running now, full tilt. Their numbers seem to have grown by one. The bald man she kicked is limping, but even so, three against Tess.

It might not be her. My stammering heart says otherwise.

I stand, clutching the top of the hedge. They're headed for the river.

Calculations swarm me like pigeons: Father is quick, but his angle is wrong. They'll reach the river thirty seconds ahead of Father, ample time to board, say, a waiting boat.

Father appears to have reached the same conclusion. He doubles back as the four figures disappear off the river wall. I watch Father sprint like an Olympian toward the motorcar, scouring the darkness for me, and I hover in indecision, feeling my sense of reason strain and rip. I could slip right inside the house, feel the rightness of my plan click back into place, but he's going to chase that boat and save Tess and . . . I'm going with him. No question.

She's my sister. Everything I've done has been for her.

I've never ridden in a motorcar before, but as I run gracelessly across the road, I recognize the model as a Triumph. I do hope the name is prescient.

"When did you buy this?" I shout once I reach him, motioning to the chassis. "Is it—"

"Borrowed." A dark tone ripples through Father's voice. He jumps into the elevated front seat, then revs the rattlingly loud engine and swoops me in a wrenching arc into the tiny seat behind him. My toe bumps a physician's bag in the footwell. Sakes alive, is it possible Father stole this vehicle?

"Brace yourself," he says, and before I can interpret that, we are careening away with a *sputter-sputter-roar*, and I have to dig my fingernails into Father's seat to keep from falling out.

The party fades behind us within seconds and my eyes stream with tears from the wind; the loss; this absolute disaster; terror for my Tess, my little sister; grief for those things I said to her, how absolutely wretchedly rotten I was.

We're headed north.

"Where did the boat go?" I scream over the roar of the engine.

Father turns his head a quarter. "What?"

"Where are we going?"

"Sit down and hang on!" he yells back.

He might have the excuse of the motor this time, but this is a typical exchange for us.

I squeal as a bump in the road lifts my backside a good six inches. I plant my feet, turn as far as my corset will allow, and search the river for vessels. I see nothing, but leaning out, I hear an engine growl with a different pitch, issuing from the river ahead. They've indeed taken her in a motorboat; isn't this a modern abduction?

Father clips the curb and I tumble out the side with a shriek, halfway to the spinning tires, when Father reaches back to lend me enough leverage to haul myself back in.

"Dammit, Lila, I told you to hold on!" He swats backward.

"I am trying," I scream back.

In the blur, I spot a tiny light on the river, a pilot lantern heading for the wharfs. I grip Father's shoulder to point. He doesn't hesitate. He yanks on the steering wheel and then pulls up on the gear, sending us rocketing off the road and into the grass of the park.

The wharf itself is dark, the stalls and loading strips closed

26

for the night, but the boat light has stopped at one of the thin piers. We can catch them!

Father drives us onto the graveled ground, steering us so sharply between crates that my hair gets pulled loose from its pouf by a jutting nail.

In the moonlit distance, I see two men leap from the boat, each in a different direction. Beyond them, the boat pushes away from the dock and continues upriver. For all I know, my sister is still on it, lost to us.

Father yanks on the brakes. I tumble back, legs akimbo.

"Stay here," he barks, then jumps from the car and chases the slower of the escaping men.

I blink so convulsively in the aftermath of the wind, ears roaring with the still-running engine, that the scene unfolding before me looks like a magic lantern show: a stranger, fleeing; my father, unrecognizable, pursuing; both vanishing behind a dark row of shanties.

Time loses context. The motorcar's engine stalls, sputters twice, falls silent. All I can hear is my pulse, marking each approximate second in louder and louder beats.

Clink.

I spin to see a tuft-bearded man sitting woozily on a barrel, a green bottle in hand. His grin reveals several missing teeth. "Keer for a slug, miss?"

I whip back around, spine taut. "Thank you, but no."

He laughs like I've just told the funniest joke he's ever heard.

I heave myself, voluminous skirts and all, out of the car and onto the wet wharf ground, my silk slippers immediately soiled by a puddle of what looks like grease. I will mourn them later. Right now I need to find Father.

I creep dizzily across the wharf, careful to avoid coiled rope, broken glass, various boat parts I couldn't begin to name left leaning against crates as if at random. The disorder offends me, something deep in me itching not to get out of here but to arrange it all, tidy it in logical rows.

What I hear, however, as I force myself onward, away from the drunkard, past the row of derelict shanties, defies tidy rationality.

Father's voice, a low snarl, in duet with a plaintive tenor, someone seeming to plead with him. I see them in profile, a bald man, pinned low like the *Dying Gaul*, someone else above, landing punch after punch. It's Father, rendered grotesque.

I've always known he had a reputation for scandalous conduct, but imagining and witnessing firsthand are two different matters. As I watch, stupefied, my childhood image of Dr. Warren Ford, professor of archaeology, wearing linen and tweed, his feet on his desk and a pipe in his mouth, is blotted out by the real man before me, arms flying wildly, inflicting harm like some backstreet bruiser.

"Did they send you?" Father shouts. "What do they want from me?"

I can't look away from him. My father. His bloodied knuckles. Spots dance and gather in a pointillist circle around them.

"Oh dear," I say but don't feel myself hit the ground.

CHAPTER 4

TESS

❧

"SMMMNNNNE? ANNNNYWNNN? HHHHMMPP!"

I clench my teeth, growl, and kick once more in vain.

And then the world goes silent. The roar of the engine stops. We've stopped. The blindfolded night sheds a shade of its darkness as my stale-smelling mound of blankets is pulled away. Freezing, salt-laced sea air sears my neck, my limbs.

I'm righted to my feet and shiver so hard my teeth begin clicking.

"It wasn't supposed to go like this." William Hendricks's voice, most definitely. He exhales a frustrated huff as he unties my wrists. "But the worst is over, Miss Ford. You're safe now—*oof!*"

He groans as I hit him with a sharp right hook.

"Mother of—"

I elbow him hard, hobbling past him, blind, tied, but free.

"Am I such a miserable prospect that you'd run off a boat to be rid of me?"

The ground disappears just as my stomach bottoms out. My blindfold is pulled off. White light from the boat's pilot lantern shocks my eyes.

The haughty boy I met in Dad's library stands there, dark blue eyes glaring at me, his jaw clenched and razor-sharp in the moonlight.

He grips me with one arm while the other clutches his side.

"Are you off your chump?" I shout. "Absconding me from my own home, manhandling me onto a boat?"

"I was told to escort you from your home at all costs, Miss Ford," he growls. "And time was of the essence—"

"Ah. Right then. Next time shove me down the steps, might be quicker—"

"William? Is that you?" A voice like silver bells rings out. "Oh, Father, Lord Tembroke! Leona! They're here! William and Miss Ford have arrived!"

I glance behind me, toward the voice, to find a lithe, shadowed figure in a huge mink stole bouncing down the long train of marble steps of an estate.

I blink, eyes adjusting to the blistering glamour. The stately white mansion behind the woman is easily as large as my entire Queen's College dormitory, with two-story columns that frame a pair of cherry-stained doors. The marble steps unfurl to a perfectly manicured lawn that shimmers like jade in the moonlight. We're docked at a private wharf off the lawn.

I spin around, dazed, peering across the rippling black water at sprawling nighttime Manhattan; in the distance, the sparkle of the Great White Way. We must be on the southern end of the Hudson River Valley.

William calls out, "Yes, sister, we've arrived safe—er, mostly safe and sound!"

The woman, William's sister apparently, laughs and bends

down to remove her slippers, then casts them onto the lawn. She starts giddily skipping toward us.

I shake my head. "Am I dreaming?"

William steps toward me, blocking my view. "So short were we on time, in fact, that, ah, I was robbed of the chance to formally pose the question," he says tightly. "But I've been assured that our union will make my father, you, your grandmother, everyone happy. A short engagement, with the wedding overseas—"

"Wedding?" I repeat.

The disparate pieces of the past hour begin swirling into one tempestuous storm. What is happening? No, what has just happened? This helter-skelter kidnapping . . . that was a proposal?

Oh my gods. Lila will murder me.

If Grandmama doesn't do it first.

I bite my lip, nerves electric now. "And instead of asking the lady, you smuggled her out of her house?"

"You wholly monopolized our conversation, Miss Ford, despite your insisted preference for tête-à-têting with walls. I had no time to explain. Consider the question implied—"

"How romantic."

"William!" His sister swishes between us, embracing him. She pulls back, giggling again, and fixes her radiant smile on me.

She's older than William, likely in her midtwenties. Auburn curls, ivory skin, bright green eyes. Beautiful and gloriously fancy. Underneath her stole is a white satin gown adorned in tinted irises and brilliants. She looks like she's been lifted straight from the *Delineator*, that brainless fashion magazine the girls in my hall treat like the Holy Writ, the one I sometimes flip through in secret after they dispose of it.

"Miss Ford, may I present my sister, Mrs. Davies."

"Oh no, please call me Annie." Annie grabs my hand,

squeezing. "And you must be the incomparable Miss Lila Ford. Oh, William, your bride-to-be is simply gorgeous."

I can't help but blush at *gorgeous*, though there are so very many misassumptions in that statement. Have I actually managed to ruin Lila's debutante ball *and* subsequent engagement, all in one fell swoop? Gad's sake. High time to figure this out, set the record straight.

"Mrs. Davies, there's been a grave misunderstanding. You both obviously think—I mean, I'm not—"

"Comfortable doing away with formalities? Please, Lila, we're going to be sisters." Annie gently embraces me.

"Instrument of chaos," Lila called me. She really wasn't so far off the mark.

"Ah, right. Annie, then. But please, I—"

"And welcome to my home, which you must treat as your own until we leave tomorrow." Annie steps behind me, deftly fixing my hair as she goes on, instantly transforming the tangled cloud with two brisk twists and one of her own barrettes. "An engagement on the high seas, a wedding in Paris! Lila, are you excited? My mother's beyond thrilled with this match, as is your grandmama. We do so wish there wasn't a dark cloud hanging over the affair, but we promise to keep you safe from your father's entanglements. Hence the precaution of taking you abroad."

Safe. Wait, that's right, William kept insisting that I, that Lila, was in danger. And this peril relates to Dad? Odd, given that he didn't even bother making an appearance tonight. Besides, last I heard, things were going swimmingly with his tomb KV55 excavation, and how would the Hendricks family even know about my father's dealings?

Maybe Grandmama is spinning lies about him. I wouldn't put it past her, if it assured a speedy proposal.

"You probably know more about the nuptials than I do,

sister." William interrupts my train of thought as he sets a brisk pace toward the manse. "Tell me, has Father also chosen our honeymoon locale? Our marriage home? The first names of our children?"

"You would do well to play nice tonight," Annie chides. "Everyone's already inside waiting for you, champagne in hand. The earl and Lady Leona have come all the way from Devonshire, and the Avondales—"

"Please, William, Mrs.—Annie, could we slow down and—"

But the front doors sweep open as soon as we reach the gallery. Two footmen in matching gold-buttoned uniforms stand on either side, beaming like wax votives.

I'm ushered into a grand hall three times the size of our home's parlor. Marble archways, gleaming chandeliers, a sprawling staircase iced in red velvet. An astonishing number of glass surreys line the hall's perimeter, filled with ancient relics from all over the world: A trio of oblong Egyptian oil lamps that I recognize from the Roman period. Large Etruscan antefixes. Countless amulets carved from lapis, carnelian, gold. So then, is Annie interested in archaeology? One spot of luck. Perhaps I can use our shared passion to smooth over this colossus of misunderstandings.

"Welcome!"

"Congratulations!"

"Bravo, William! And look at the lovely Miss Ford!"

Startling, I grasp the sleeve of Annie's stole.

In the center of her parlor stand two dozen people, all raising their glasses to us in toast. Warm faces, cheery tones. All their eyes fixed on me.

"This is your moment," Annie whispers. She squeezes William's shoulder, then pats my hand and drifts away.

On second glance, I notice that the sea of faces oddly mirrors my panic. The revelers' stances are stiff, those champagne flutes grasped a bit too tight.

But the crowd shifts, breaking into loose groups to socialize, before I can sort it.

"My moment," William murmurs. "Come. Let's get the necessary introductions over with."

Before I can protest, he whisks me toward a stout, bearded man in an expensive suit, champagne flute in hand. The man stands in the center of a coterie of middle-aged chaps, holding court, laughing too loudly.

"Father," William says. "Allow me to present my fiancée, Miss Lila Ford. Miss Ford, this is my father, James Hendricks."

I open my mouth to set him straight at last but stop when I see that Mr. Hendricks is glowering at me, a look of resigned disdain on his face.

He and William resemble each other undoubtedly. Mr. Hendricks's thinning hair is the same dark color as his son's. Impeccable dress. Similar deep blue eyes. Though while William's are reminiscent of the surface of a lagoon, Mr. Hendricks's are beady as lapis.

With a forced smile, Mr. Hendricks steps forward, taking my hand.

"Miss Ford," he harrumphs through his fog of self-importance. "The heralded lady of the hour. The genius, come to save us all."

Well, that's an odd choice of greeting.

I falter for a response when he adds a dismissive, "I suppose congratulations are in order."

One of his acquaintances steps forward. I recognize his face from the papers, as he's featured quite often, is infamous, really: the tycoon behind Avondale Rails, known for paying his employees peanuts in addition to working them to the bone.

"Ty Avondale," the man introduces himself, flashing William

a leering wink. "Well done, young man. Easy on the eyes, isn't she? Though hardly the point. Let's put her to good use before the world has another damned revolution on its hands."

I keep my polite smile affixed, though now I'm furiously perplexed.

"The peons may uprise, but worthier minds shall always prevail," Mr. Hendricks intones.

He promptly lights his pipe, its cloying smoke choking my lungs.

"William, I really must speak with you," I say, coughing, once he and I politely break away. "Explain myself. And I've got myriad questions—"

"After we've made the rounds," William says crisply. "And perhaps you can save those questions for your insects?"

I shiver at his chilly tone.

"Mr. Hendricks." I grab his arm, my eyes narrowing. "Am I right in having the distinct impression that you do not want to marry Lila?"

He barks an incredulous laugh. "So you speak in the third person too. A woman of many talents." William leans closer, eyes icy. "Forgive my tempered excitement, Miss Ford. But wedding myself to you and your eccentricities is just the latest in a lifetime of unexplained and often onerous responsibilities. Complying with demand after demand. Sculpting myself into an heir worthy of an inheritance I haven't even the slightest interest—"

He must clock my outrage because he stops himself. Clears his throat. Rearranges himself into the image of a perfect Knickerbocker.

"Apologies. I'm sure we'll make the perfect pair," William says, tone still frigid. "I am thrilled, needless to say. *Elated.*"

Not waiting for my thoughts on the matter, he takes my hand and ushers me across the room, past a few more magnate types in crisp tuxedos who have broken off, clutching their cocktail glasses, whispering to one another. Did I just overhear someone mutter, "Slapping down the masses"?

"Our wedding will be quite the affair," William continues, seemingly unheeding. "No expense spared, just as they weren't for Annie. You'd never suspect from this grand home, but Theo came from nothing; he's self-made, insatiably ambitious. And your family will attend, naturally. My mother will travel with your grandmother to Paris a few weeks from now, once they've smoothed any ruffled society feathers, given your flight from your own ball. And your sister—Tess, is it?—she's given her full blessing as well, if that's what you're concerned about. She'll join us directly from London for the wedding."

I stutter-step but otherwise don't react to this blatant lie.

Furtively I study William's face, searching for a sign, a tell—as Dad once taught me during his swift tutorial on poker at Oxford years ago—but William's expression remains placid. Bored, even. He firmly believes what he's selling.

So then, who is lying to him?

"As for your father," he goes on, "mine often makes a point to keep me in the dark on particulars, but I understand Warren Ford has fallen in with some bad men as of late. Not to fret, though. That's why we're taking you abroad, to ensure your safety."

"William Hendricks, you old thing!" a voice booms. "You haven't introduced me to your burgeoning rose."

I look up to find an extremely tall man, dressed in an ostentatiously gilded British military uniform, beckoning us over.

As we cross the room, William announces, "The Earl of Tembroke."

I nod, but my mind is now spinning faster than a Senet piece. Jackasses, villains, liars. Is this really the future my sister has to look forward to?

"The eldest daughter of the dashing Warren Ford. Brains *and* beauty, I see." The reedy gentleman finishes the last of his flute, then brushes his thick gray mustache across my hand. "Pity about your father getting mixed up, eh? But hurrah, you are here, on the right side of history. And where is that enchanting new wife of mine to introduce? The Lady Leona. Devonshire's own Cleopatra. A welcome companion for you, to be sure."

The earl sways as he scans the room, like a tree wavering in the wind.

He tips his empty flute in the air, signaling for an unseen waiter to bring another. "And a fellow countrywoman! Boston and New York are around the corner, if I'm not mistaken . . ."

As William turns away to greet another engagement party guest, I seize the chance to goad more from this tippled fellow. "So nice to meet you, Lord Tembroke. And yes, a pity about my father."

I summon my nerve, leaning in. "May I inquire, do you know what type of trouble he's mixed up in? I only heard something about 'dangerous men.' Are they poaching his latest excavation? After the talatats, perhaps. Looking for the Serpent's Crown?"

The earl's eyes cloud over. "Eh, oh dear. We seem to have wandered off script."

What a discomfiting answer. "And what, pray tell, *is* on the script, Lord Tembroke?"

"Merriment!" Lord Tembroke raises his glass, letting out a guffaw. "Leave it to the Hendrickses to turn this all into a party. What a grand idea. A wedding!" Another champagne flute arrives on a serving platter. The earl slings it back. "Truth be told, given our time constraints, I'd have thought you'd be hard at work by now."

I falter, addled again, but my interrogation window has closed. A butler comes into the parlor, announcing dinner will be served.

"Excuse us, Lord Tembroke." William takes my arm per-functorily, leading me toward the train of people meandering into dinner. Annie joins us as we step inside her luxurious, Renaissance-styled dining room, complete with a tiered chande-lier and two fireplaces, rich aromas wafting in from an unseen kitchen.

"Not the evening you expected, I know," Annie says with a conspiratorial wink. "My family decided it best to present our engagement plan to your grandmother tonight, despite the com-plications it created. We couldn't risk attracting the attention of the men who are after your father."

She edges me away from William, and together we pass her long table adorned with candelabras, towering floral arrange-ments, gilded chinaware, decadent place cards. I notice each ornate setting card is embossed with the same insignia. Not ini-tials or a family coat of arms, as one might imagine, but a tangle of silver snakes.

"I do hope the food and company tonight will go some way toward tempering your disappointment," Annie adds with a rue-ful smile. "I'm sure it would have been a lovely ball."

As we find our seats, she whispers, "And not to worry, Miss Lila. We will look out for each other, always."

I swallow. If ever there was a moment to come clean about my own mix-up, it would be now, and certainly to Annie, by far the most approachable of the Hendricks set.

And yet, I find myself at a loss for words. I'm very sadly aware that I barely know my sister anymore, but the Lila I once held dear would never, ever wish to join high society on the premise of lies, or start a future with a man who so clearly doesn't wish to be engaged. Besides, I'm fairly positive she wouldn't be able to stomach William any more than I can.

Yes, I know that she and Grandmama are desperate; and our

current financial situation is perhaps more dire than I realized, if last week's tense conversation with my school bursar over late tuition payments was any indication.

But surely there must be another solution. The prospect of my sister being trapped among this cadre for the rest of her life might be more than I can bear.

Lost in thought, I slink into the chair between Annie and William, near the empty head of the table. I watch as William's father, Mr. Hendricks, plops down at the other end, red-faced and smug. He lights his pipe anew, a cloud of smoke encircling him.

Mr. Avondale and his elegant wife take seats to Mr. Hendricks's left, while Lord Tembroke stumbles into the seat on his right. A pretty young woman, the earl's wife, Leona, I gather, rolls her eyes and settles beside him, moaning, "I do not understand why I must be here for this, Bertie. I am missing Carrie Astor Wilson at *Manon Lescaut!*"

He chortles into his glass. "Try to enjoy yourself, dear. We're in the midst of our own satire performance."

He's drowned out, though, as more guests filter into the dining space, and then more, the expansive room now as loud and hectic as the gallery.

Then all the noise cuts, a needle lifted from a phonograph.

I follow everyone's gaze to the gallery's entrance. A man loiters in the doorway. Middle-aged, barrel-chested, in a near-blinding white suit.

"Don't stop carousing on my account." The man strides into the silent room. Taking his time. All eyes on him.

Mr. Hendricks conspicuously scowls at him.

This latest addition to our unsettling menagerie slides into the empty seat next to Annie, who dotingly takes his hand. Annie's husband, then. The host of Lila's engagement party. He's older than I expected, though clearly well-off, if this treasure-loaded castle is any indication. Handsome, with chiseled features and wide amber eyes, a determined set to his jaw. He looks familiar. My mind's never been able to hold a candle to Lila's when it comes to maths or languages, but I never forget a picture or a face.

Maybe he's an athlete. A player for the Brooklyn Trolley Dodgers.

I realize that as I've been studying him not one person has said a word.

Mr. Hendricks breaks the silence, raising his glass across the mile-long table. "So you finally deigned to join us."

His fury is barely suppressed, his tone stiff with sarcasm.

Annie's husband doesn't look up as he snaps open his napkin. "My apologies, James. I'm rather unaccustomed to interrupting my work for the cocktail hour—"

"Please excuse your future brother-in-law's tardiness." Mr. Hendricks cuts him off. He's speaking to me, I see now. His smile, all bristly beard and teeth. "A stellar work ethic is something to commend, wouldn't you agree, Miss Ford? But there is a time when celebration must take precedence."

"Of course." Annie's husband clears his throat and picks up his glass of champagne. "No more work tonight. We're here to honor a prosperous union—"

Mr. Hendricks drowns him out. "And the triumph of the worthy!"

My stomach churns while a rowdy "Hear, hear!" roars through the room, and guests around the table overzealously clink their flutes.

The first course of soup is served. I manage to take performative sips, but my appetite has been dashed. As dinner conversation falls to a tolerable clip, I can't help sneaking another glance at Annie's husband.

I surely know this man. The way he stares down his champagne flute, as if scheming how to murder it. His salt-and-pepper hair, distinct features. Those keen, wolfish eyes.

"Are you not hungry, Theo?" Annie murmurs, studying his untouched bowl.

I let out a low breath, leaning back in my chair. There it is.

Theo. Davies. *Theodore Davies*. That's it. I knew I recognized him from newspaper clippings. Egyptology enthusiast. Lawyer turned archaeology sponsor. Self-made millionaire. "New money," as Grandmama would so tactfully put it.

Davies is Dad's sole funder for his latest expedition to the Valley of the Kings, the unearthing of Akhenaten's long-lost burial site, tomb KV55. Dad, myself, and the rest of the Egyptology world also hoped the tomb would in turn be the resting place of the Five Ladies and, by association, the location of the legendary Serpent's Crown.

Alas, it was not. Still, the site is an historical treasure, more than three millennia old. A window into the New Kingdom, a priceless trove from the past. I've been saving all my pocket money and gambling winnings, in fact, to patch together a trip to visit Dad's site during this spring recess, as it's been three agonizing months since I've last been on Egyptian sand. But I've yet to join the dig and thus have never met Davies personally. At least before tonight.

But why would Dad's funder be involved in Lila's engagement?

I look up to find William beside me, hand extended. "Miss Ford, if you'll permit me one more introduction."

I shrug, mind still elsewhere, and he yanks me to standing.

"Theo, you look well-rested after all this traveling," William says once we reach Davies. He flashes his sister, Annie, a quick yet indiscernible look. "Please allow me to introduce you to Miss Lila Ford."

Davies takes his time studying me, just as I studied him. Surveying me, like a potential find. He finally extends his hand.

"Miss Ford," Davies says curtly, his amber eyes boring into mine. "You come with quite a reputation. Let's hope you earn your keep."

For a moment I'm too stunned to speak.

Perhaps I did not, in fact, ruin things for Lila tonight with my silly antics. Perhaps I'm in the process of saving her from a life of lies, an insufferable partner, a cadre of deplorable wisenheimers. If I can just play along a little while longer, through dinner, bide my time, I can slip out tonight, unseen, dash this ill-fated engagement, and spare her a world of regret.

Hell, one day Lila might even thank me.

"Isn't Miss Ford a doll?" Annie croons to Theo Davies. "She's really everything we dreamed."

"Oh, please." I stand taller and force out my sister's airy laugh. "Do call me Lila."

CHAPTER 5

LILA

ﻬ

I AM SITTING CROSS-LEGGED BEHIND THE LAST ROW OF seats. Babyish for my age, but nobody's looking; the few women in the front row of the gallery are too busy gawking at Father to take any interest in me. Tess perches beside them, equally rapt, chin on fist, hardly blinking as she listens. I am in my starchiest white shirt, and I have my notebook, and I do intend to make notes on Daddy's lecture about the Hittites, but he forgot to pack me a pen today, so I grow restless and scribble in my thoughts instead, numbers, probabilities, averages, measurements of time.

How many minutes since Mother . . . My eyes begin to sting. No, no, stop it with that.

One hundred two people in the lecture hall below, 90 percent taking notes, ninety-two notebooks, eighty pages each, twenty-six lines to a page, eleven words per line makes two million one hundred four thousand nine hundred and—

I see a man. Up here. In the back row. The numbers blink

themselves out of my head. He looks like a grandfather. Both of our grandfathers died before we were born, but Tess and I have agreed on a Platonic ideal consisting of three elements: old, twinkly, eccentric. It's strange that he's in the gallery, where women and children sit; even stranger that, unlike the ladies in the front, he's only half paying attention to my father's lecture—in little fits of snorts and scowls, as if he's listening only out of spite. Mostly he sits murmuring to himself, scratching notes, referencing a separate bound book, back and forth, back and forth.

I sneak behind him, stealthy as a mouse, to peek. In place of words, the bound book is full of squiggles and curved shapes like fishhooks. How curious.

Time blurs and passes. My eyes go fuzzy, sharp, and I see the key, the way to arrange it, the order behind the muddled mix of symbols as if lit up in electric filament.

I straighten. The old man startles at the sight of me.

I whisper to him, "There's a pattern."

"What do you mean?" His question feels weighted.

I point to the page. "I play games like this when the house gets too quiet. I mix up words and solve them. Yours took a while, but I think I have it. It's the ones that look like Cs, with the fishhook underneath. That's the way to figure out the rest."

The man's small eyes grow more sparkly. He leans in, whispering, "Alors, mademoiselle. Show me."

I point to the hooked Cs, ever so slightly darker, like maybe they're the kings of the game, Very Important Symbols, and all the other funny squiggles are working for those names or working for the things that work for the names.

"It's like Fordish, you see," I say. "There's a root from which . . ."

My voice has grown deeper. I glance down in surprise. I'm taller, older, wearing a crushed silk ball gown.

A snake slithers from underneath the seats. It peers up at me as it coils around my ankle.

"Qu'est-ce que c'est que . . . Fordish?" the old Frenchman asks. Belot, that's his name. Dr. Belot.

"It's the language I wrote." I feel dizzy. "My sister speaks it too. What am I doing here?"

He doesn't look surprised to see the change in me, that I'm not eleven anymore, that I'm a young woman. "You keep coming back to this moment, my dear. Again and again."

I shake my head. "Why?"

"Because . . ." He pats my hand, then grips it, much too tight. "This is where you lock yourself away."

⌘

Whether it's the stench, the screaming, or a trickle of drool that wakes me, my eyes open from one nightmare into another.

I am in a narrow sort of chamber, with half walls serving as dividers. A cracked gas lantern flickers. My vision adjusts. The ceiling is stained, brown and gray, dripping at the corners, the outer walls seeping with damp. Somewhere beyond, a baby is crying, another child shouting, a shrill woman shrieking for both of them to sleep. Under me is a thin, bare mattress, the rusted coils of a brass bed frame, a cracked clapboard floor.

A cockroach scuttles into view beneath me. My body seizes with revulsion.

Limbs tight, corset bayonetting my ribs, I shift only enough to take in the rest of wherever I am. There's barely any furniture: this bed, two wooden chairs penning in a small round table with a half-drunk bottle of whiskey displayed in the middle like a proud centerpiece, next to a tiny window, a frayed armchair.

In it sits a man.

He's facing away, so I see him only in silhouette, but I know in a blink it's not Father. This fellow is taller, leaner, with thick curling hair and sloped shoulders. He is unnervingly still.

I mirror his stillness, my mind muting my body. I remember it all now: the wharf, my father's bloody knuckles, my sister. Kidnapped. *They've gotten me too.*

I scan for escape routes. The path to the room's sole door leads directly past this mysterious figure, but the table with the bottle is closer to me than to him. If I can remain stealthy . . .

The bed threatens to screech, so I move slowly as I rise from the mattress. One foot touches the floor, and I realize I am not wearing shoes. Only stockings between me and this putrid, unswept, vermin-infested— Never mind that. Bare feet are silent; this will help.

I glide soundlessly toward the table, eyes locked on the man's back. He hasn't budged. His head droops against the chipped window frame. Is he asleep? Could I be that lucky?

I calculate the distance: five steps to get to him and do what needs doing; or, less violently, eight to the door, four seconds to work the latch; more if it's locked.

I don't like those figures. I don't like any of this.

Sweat drips down my neck, my vision spotting with terror, but my fingers curl around the whiskey bottle. As a question of logic, I know what I must do.

Three slow, silent strides closer to the window, careful not to slosh whiskey, not to creak a floorboard, not to breathe. The man is unmoving apart from the slow rise and fall of his shoulders. Step four: I calculate the arc it will take to connect this bottle with the back of his head. Step five: I cock my arm in readiness, but heavens, the bottle is heavier than I expected—and my arm far weaker— and the liquid within renders its equilibrium unpredictable.

He turns, a blur, seizes my wrist, splashing whiskey down my dress. I shriek as he shoves me to the floor.

An instant before impact, my head connects with something soft.

It's his hand. He's cradled my fall. His other hand presses my wrist, pinning my arm down while my fingers slowly open and the bottle rolls out of reach. He hovers inches over me, the demon. My heart threatens to collapse this entire clapboard house around us, but I stare up, defiant.

Goodness. He is handsome.

Irrelevant, Lila! He's young, yes, likely too young to be a master criminal, too clean to be a hired goon, with dark wavy hair, wide brown eyes, warm bronze skin, and faint stubble on a strong jaw, smelling like toasted almonds and freshly sharpened pencils.

He blinks down at me as if taking his own inventory. Then he bursts out laughing. The heat of him rivets me to the floor.

"Lila Ford," he says, drawing out my name like the punch line to a joke. "Not at all what I expected."

He's an Englishman? This is very strange.

"Who are you?" I shout the question, hoping someone beyond these thin walls might come to my aid. "Why have you taken me?"

"Land's sake, I haven't taken you. I'm protecting you." He loosens his grip as he inches away. "The way your sister describes you, I pictured a paper doll. Were you really going to bludgeon me with that?" He glares at the whiskey bottle and then back at me with a mix of resentment and respect. "You're not thinking of doing it again, are you?"

"I certainly will, if you give me reason to."

"You Ford girls." He shakes his head. "Cut from the same damn cloth."

He offers me a hand. I ignore it, heaving myself upright as

elegantly as I can under the circumstances, my mind scrambling for purchase. I dust off my skirts, but it's no good; the dress is a ruin.

His eyes rove my figure more freely than a gentleman's should. I shoot him a lofty glare. "I shall ask once more, and this time I demand an answer: Who are you?"

"I take it back—you're exactly what I expected." Before I can decide how much offense to take, he clears his throat. "Alexandre Ibrahim d'Auteuil at your service, madam."

His accent changed to French when he said his name, but his second name is neither French nor English, and d'Auteuil . . . Why does that sound familiar?

"Pleasure to make your acquaintance," he goes on, sounding anything but pleased. "I assure you that this was not how I expected to pass the evening myself. Dr. Ford will return anon and—"

"Oh, you're Alex! The field assistant."

Sheepishness flashes briefly over his face. "Yes, apologies. I probably should have led with that. And stayed awake. Even so, how did you manage to sneak up on me like that?"

I feel giddy pride extinguish my shame over not having been able to adequately hoist that bottle. "Finishing school. We took lessons in elegant entrances. Among other things."

"Balancing books on your head. I can picture it perfectly."

"We also took lessons in astronomy, physics, French literature," I huff. "We Veltin girls contain multitudes, sir."

"Including Walt Whitman references." Alex raises his eyebrows. "Consider me chastened."

Enough of this. "Where is my father?"

"Booking us passage."

"Passage? Goodness, where?"

"I'm not sure yet. He was debating the question when he left."

48

This does not inspire confidence. "Where are we now?"

"Orchard Street."

"Oh, it's awful." I glance guiltily at the wall, as if the woman beyond with all the squalling children could have heard me. The poor soul might be inclined to agree.

Alex's face betrays nothing. "I've seen worse. But yes. It's a far cry from your world."

So small to be called a *world*, the discrete boundaries of New York high society extending from Washington Square to Madison Avenue to the stately, quiet, just-this-side-of-unfashionable Riverside manse where we live. But do I live there anymore? Did my ball end with an inquest? Does Grandmama know I'm safe? Am I safe?

I turn my questioning upon Alex. "Let's have it all out. Why was my sister taken? Why am I in danger? Why are we hiding in Orchard Street, of all places? Is there even an orchard here?"

"Why don't you sit down?" Alex offers.

"I'm perfectly fine. And I have a right to know why my life's been upended."

He opens his hands wide, a concession. "I'm trying to figure out how to describe the mess we're in delicately."

"I'm not a paper doll, or however you put it."

The room begins to sway the instant I say it.

"You did faint tonight." Alex's smugness drops away as he examines me. "And you're in danger of doing so again."

"I am not!" I am.

He pulls a wooden chair from the table and catches me in it. I sit, swaying. Like a paper doll.

"I'm confused," I say, burying my face in my hands. "I'm scared, disappointed, but the confusion. You have no idea how frustrating it is."

I hear the scrape of another chair being pulled up opposite

49

mine. "As a matter of fact, I spend my entire career in a vague, constant state of bewilderment. Your father is not an easy man to keep up with. But I do recognize that this is of another order."

I feel a glass bottle nudge my hand. I peek through my fingers to see the remains of one swig of whiskey.

Alex nods. "This might help."

I roll my teary eyes and slug it back. Disgusting.

As I fight to stifle a grimace, Alex carefully places the bottle on the exact spot on the table where I first saw it upon awakening. How strangely fastidious.

He stares at me. "The people who took your sister are looking for the Serpent's Crown."

A snort sneaks out of me.

The Serpent's Crown. Ah yes, the legendary object of power sought by everyone from Alexander the Great to Napoleon through time immemorial. "The serpent calls the worthy," as they say. Why not.

"This is hardly a time to be making jokes, Mr. . . . ." I've already forgotten his last name.

"I wish I were joking, believe me." He sighs. "For the past few years, we've been excavating at Karnak, in the Temple of Amun. Your father found a series of talatat stones there, which, in combination with several other artifacts, pointed to the fabled resting place of the Serpent's Crown. The Tomb . . . of the Five Ladies."

He pauses again, as if waiting for me to reel in wonder, but I haven't the faintest idea what he's talking about.

"As it happened, KV55 was not what the legends described. Davies was livid."

"Davies." My mind catches on the name, one solid fact amid a mire of nonsense.

It has a familiar ring to it. Isn't there a socialite with that name? There's a mental thread unspooling, but I'm too muddled to pull the seam taut.

"Theodore Davies, our funder. I never liked the man. No regard for preservation and documentation. He chipped the sarcophagus in his all-fired rush to open it. But it wasn't until a few weeks ago that it came to a head. Someone at camp left a note for Dr. Ford exposing the truth. The real funders of the expedition style themselves the Fraternitas de Nodum, the Brotherhood of the Knot, a highly resourced network with a decidedly authoritarian bent. Their true interests lie in neither the study nor the sale of antiquities but rather . . . world domination."

"What on earth does the Serpent's Crown have to do with geopolitics?" I huff.

"There are some who believe the Crown possesses actual supernatural power. That it allows its wearer to control minds." Alex squirms in his seat. "It's nonsense, of course. Absolute rubbish. But we learned that our lovely funders were fervent believers. And more pressingly, that they planned to kill us as soon as they saw no further use in us."

I cross my arms tighter to hide my shudder. "Not an ideal scenario."

"Far from it. And so we ran, by night, and laid low in Cairo, continuing our decryption work. Eight days ago we received a telegram from the same mysterious source." Alex peers out the window. "It said that Dr. Ford's daughter was in imminent danger of abduction. That it would take place at your ball. So to New York we came, as quickly as we could."

Not quickly enough. "This Davies person. You're certain he's involved in Tess's kidnapping?"

"Quite certain."

I gaze past Alex the field assistant, my mind gone quiet. The moon is shining into the room now, partly obscured by a line

51

of washing hanging outside. In the milky glow, I spot my shoes sitting on the floor, white silk stained with green grime from the docks.

With that, I blink alert. "Thank you for the bedtime story. And the name."

I snatch up my slippers, tug them on, grime and all, and start for the door.

Alex spins around. "Where are you going?"

"To get help."

I click three locks open and swing the door wide before he can reach me, emerging into a rickety, narrow stairway reeking of urine and sick. I keep my hands clasped tightly over my nose and trot down the uneven steps at a dizzying clip.

Alex is hot on my heels. "Your father said not to leave the room until—"

"My father forfeited the right to tell me what to do a long time ago. You stay. I'll carry on."

"'Carry on'?" He lets out an incredulous laugh.

"Doing what we should have done in the first place: alerting the authorities about this Theodore Davies." I stumble but right myself. "Someone has to be a rational adult in this family, and as usual, it's fallen to me."

At last, the exit appears. I draw in a lusty gulp of night air, so thick with coal smoke that I choke on it. I don't know what the hour is, but the street is busier than I expected. One short block down I see the lights of a rum-hole. Such a place wouldn't be safe for a young woman of any class, but it's still the most likely spot to find an officer of the law.

From nowhere, a saucer-eyed street urchin appears before me, tiny hands silently cupped.

"Oh," I murmur. "I'm so sorry, I don't have anything to give you."

His sooty face drops. Only after he darts away do I realize how I must look. Soiled or not, my gown is of the highest quality—Grandmama agreed to economize on servants and cutlery for the ball, but certainly not garments—and atop my frayed hair still sits that golden ornament. I couldn't possibly part with Mother's comb, not even for this unfortunate lad, nor will I disrobe, for heaven's sake, but I do feel a stab of frustration that I have nothing else to offer.

I'm not utterly powerless, however. I can at least help my sister. I quicken my pace.

Alex runs, hand raised, like I'm a streetcar he's trying to catch. "You cannot trust the police. You can't trust anyone."

"For heaven's sake." I growl with exasperation. "You and Father have been in the wilderness too long. We're not lone wolves. We live in a society."

Alex clenches and unclenches his fists. "But *whose* society, Lila? Listen to what I'm trying to tell you."

I turn back before he can spout any more folderol and see a figure emerge from the rum-hole wearing a blue, buttoned uniform, comforting in his ordinariness, helmet donned, nightstick twirling. I start toward him.

"I'm telling you, the people who took your sister are powerful," Alex harshly whispers behind me. "They're tied to everything and everyone—here in New York City, in London, in Paris, nearly every upper echelon you can think of, and they'll stop at nothing to get what they want."

"Such as abduction. Yes, I've noticed."

"Worse!" He breathes as if he's praying for patience. "Your father tasked me with one thing, Lila: keeping you safe, upstairs, until his return."

"The lofty assistant, bound by noblest duty." I narrow my eyes. "In which case, you should probably address me as Miss Ford."

I whirl back around in time to witness that sweet beggar boy approaching the police officer, cap in hand. I begin to wave, flagging the officer, when he raises his baton . . . and strikes the child with it. The boy drops to his knees, hands protecting his head, but the blows from the nightstick keep falling until the desperate waif manages to spirit himself between shanties and away while the policeman twirls his stick and laughs.

I cannot move. How could anyone behave that way, let alone an officer of the law, sworn to protect the weak, to provide justice for all? Is this the way of things here?

If he did that to a child, what might he do to a young woman, unprotected?

A hand lands warm on my trembling wrist.

"Miss. Ford." A vein is pumping in Alex's neck. "Please. Come back with me. Let me pretend to protect you for the next twenty minutes, and after that, I promise to relinquish you to your own devices."

"All right," I say, accepting Alex's arm. "Yes, fine."

When we return to the tenement, Father is back, treading the floorboards. The relief on his face as we tromp through the door is swiftly eclipsed by annoyance.

"Funny. I could have sworn I told you not to let her leave."

Alex motions to me like a showman as he walks past. "Your daughter is not as placid as I was led to believe."

The barest hint of pride flashes across Father's face, and my silly heart surges, but just as fast he's pacing again, refusing to look at me, and my heart shrinks back to its usual dimensions. "There's a lot at play right now, princess. I need to know that you're in line."

I cross my arms. "Tell me precisely what line we're treading, in which direction, and why, and I'll be happy to comply."

Father walks briskly across the room to reach into a leather traveler's case I hadn't noticed sitting there. My body stills in readiness, but for what exactly? Eschewing rationality, part of me expects him to stand up brandishing an ancient Egyptian head-dress shaped like a snake, crackling with lightning or whatever magical relics are meant to do, but from the glimpse I manage to catch inside the case, all looks humdrum—a folded map, a large bit of leather bound in twine, a sextant—before Father dumps what he's holding into my arms.

Clothing. Male clothing. *Used* clothing.

"If they're after you, too, they'll be looking for a deb," Father explains. "And the way we're traveling, it's safer if you're a boy."

I feel all the blood in my body rush to my face. "This isn't some Shakespearean comedy. No one will believe me as a man."

"It's worth a damn try." Father grips the back of one of the chairs so hard that it looks fit to splinter. "Tess got nabbed. I've gotta live with that, but for once in your life, would you listen to me so the same thing doesn't happen to you?"

"Why have they even taken her?" I demand as he paces away. "Is it for leverage or . . ."

My eye catches on the strap crossing his chest. He's been carrying another thin satchel this whole time, I realize, hidden under one flap of his jacket.

I nod to it. "What have you got in there?"

"Nothing you need to worry about." He glances down at it, a self-satisfied smile creeping over his face. "Just a keepsake. Something that'll put a wrench in their gears."

"So that's why they took Tess. To get their keepsake back." I could strangle the man.

"They don't know I've got it," he tosses back. "That it even exists in the first—"

"Do you know where this Davies lives? Nearby, I presume. Couldn't you go there, give it to him, whatever it is he wants?"

"It's me they want. My skill, my brain, my expertise. They want to wring every bit of use out of me they can and then toss me in a canal somewhere for vultures to peck at the rest. They want the Serpent's Crown, they want Egypt, and I'm not giving it to them. No, I'm going to use this brain of mine to get your sister back. That's what I'm gonna do."

I close my mouth tightly, unsure what will come out should I open it. What does he mean, *they want Egypt*?

Father pinches at the bridge of his nose, breathing slowly. After a long moment, he smiles tightly at me. "Just put the clothes on, Lila. They'll keep you safe."

"Right," I say, masking my nerves with brisk imperiousness. "Fine. I'll need some privacy to change."

Change everything, my entire life. But was my life ever what it appeared to be? Father is a brute, Alex far from the tweedy academic I'd pictured, and the upper echelon, as he put it, a pack of crazed treasure raiders. I know far less about the world than I'm comfortable with. That needs to change, and if I need to walk this serpentine line to learn, so be it.

It's a blessed relief to take off my corset, but my eyes flood when I remove the stuffing for my bosom and my hips and reveal the real me, far from a Gibson Girl, a reedy, skinny nothing. I tear a strip of cloth from my petticoat and wind it round my breasts, though I hardly need bother. I pull the comb from my hair, stare at it for a long moment, and then secure it decisively against the strip, hidden above my heart.

If I were indeed a modern Viola donning the guise of Cesario to survive on unfamiliar shores, one might expect this moment of transformation to carry exhilaration, the breath of freedom and self-determination, but the crunchy sweat stains inside the armpits of this shirt go a long way toward spoiling the effect. The trousers chafe in the seams, drag in the hem.

I catch a glimpse of myself in the one remaining pane of glass in the window. Another costume. A boy one this time. Bah. I strangle my loose hair into a braided knot, tie it in place with a few pins, and stick the cap Father gave me over it. It smells like sweat. I try not to think about it.

I open the door and Alex, waiting in the hall, averts his eyes as if I might still be naked.

"In line, ready for duty," I announce glumly. "We're leaving New York, I take it."

Father evaluates my getup with a stifled chuckle. Then he nods, smirk dropping away.

"Where are we heading?" I ask.

"Cairo," he says, and though it's the answer I half expected, I still reel.

Egypt. Land of pyramids, ancient tombs, civilization upon civilization piled one atop the other, as different from the Upper East Side as you can get. Long before Tess set eyes on it, she made up stories of the city so vivid I swore I could see the souks and silks and camels painted on our bedroom ceiling. The first time Father allowed Tess to accompany him to Egypt during a school break, she wrote to me in raptures, and though I'd never dream of admitting it, I longed to join them, to laugh with my sister, bask in my father's glow. I was too jealous to even write her back. I'd been ignoring most of her letters anyway, since she'd left me for London. But I foolishly kept hope alive that Father might extend to me a similar invitation. He never did.

Until now.

"I know this is a big ask, princess," Father says more gently. He seems to mistake my excitement for misgivings. "But this is where they'll be headed with your sister. They don't know I got tipped off; they think I'm still in Egypt. So that's where they'll go, bringing Tess to me as leverage for a swap. And we'll be there, all right. But one step ahead of them."

"Grandmama," I blurt, remembering. "She'll call the police, declare me missing."

"That's a risk we'll to have to run." Father at least looks regretful. "I know she'll be worried, but if we send her a message, odds are it'll get snapped up and used against us. We're on our own for now, Lila."

Alex's eyes meet mine, warm with sympathy, before he leads the way down the steps.

I turn to shut the door before following them and catch a glimpse of my discarded dress lying on the dirty tenement floor, my blue confection, my dream.

It kept its shape somehow. It looks like a corpse.

CHAPTER 6

TESS

❧

Cunard Pier 54, Lower Manhattan

I ADJUST MY NEW BURGUNDY EMBROIDERED JACKET, one of the many pieces the Hendrickses had custom-ordered for Lila, as William and I walk with the rest of their party through the noontime bustle of Pier 54 and toward the RMS *Lucania*. This costume is far finer than anything I own and yet it cloaks me with dread, the ensemble a blatant reminder of what a vexing situation I've gotten myself into, and how foolish I was to even pretend I could fill my sister's shoes.

I recall, of all things, the last spring I spent at home, before I left for Queen's College, when I was ten and Lila was eleven. Grandmama had always had a preference for my sister, even before Mother's passing. But that spring, her hatred for me had turned pointed, as sharp as a katana blade.

Grandmama had planned an April garden party in our old

Madison Avenue courtyard: a big affair, inviting her most important friends so she could introduce her little granddaughters to
the right type of people now that her adventuring son-in-law
had accepted a position at Oxford and taken himself out of the
picture. In a rare, thoughtful gesture—likely to feign the appearance of equality—she custom-ordered Lila and me matching lace
frocks with gold ribbons and little sparkling slippers with heels.

"We look like twins," Lila had said that morning as we studied ourselves in our standing mirror.

With those words, our house felt like a home again. It had
more resembled purgatory, honestly, ever since Dad had left.
It wasn't as if our father sought out my company, but he used
to allow me to tag along on his research trips to the New York
Society Library or the Metropolitan Museum, so long as I
remained self-sufficient. I'd even taken to studying his history
books and scholarship each night, as my sister no longer seemed
to care for my company. I wanted to be ready to ask Dad the right
questions so he'd know I was invested: *Why did Akhenaten worship only the sun god, Aten? Where did the Serpent's Crown come
from? How many daughters and wives did he have?* I got the sense
that it delighted him, having a rapt, perpetual audience. And I
missed delight—the laughter, the full sounds of our house.

But he was gone now. And Lila was essentially a shadow of
her former self: she barely spoke to me in English or in Fordish.
She spent all her time with Grandmama, conversing in hushed
whispers over tea, the two of them recounting memories of
Mother, along with subjects I obviously wasn't trustworthy or
mature enough to handle.

And yet here Lila and I were, together again, that April
morning. Shoulder to shoulder.

The Fearless Fords once more.

"Allow me to introduce the Royal Highness of Perfection,

60

Miss. Lila. Ford!" I angled my back, cocked my chin, and placed one hand on my hip dramatically, like the cover girls on those variety store magazines.

Lila giggled and broke into a showy version of my happy dance. "And I'm the Honorable Tess. Imperial Queen of the Mess."

"Such a pleasure to meet you, Queen Tess." I framed my face like a Grecian goddess.

Lila hiked her skirts like a swashbuckler and bowed. "The pleasure's all yours."

We devolved into laughter and danced our made-up quadrille in front of the mirror, stepping on each other's toes, twirling until our tittering reached fever pitch.

"What are you two doing?" Grandmama barreled into our nursery.

I watched my sister shrink into her shell. "Only a bit of fun, Grandmama."

Lila's meek answer turned me defiant. "Because there's never fun in this house! We don't have Mother, and now Dad's left, and you're taking away Lila too. We were just pretending to be each other. We look like twins, after all."

"Twins." Grandmama started fussing with Lila's ribbons. "Twins. Are you delusional? Look at Lila's posture. Look at her hair and that tangle of yours. Your dreadful hem, for goodness' sake."

She yanked at my dress.

"Do you think I planned to tend to a pair of young girls at my age? I should be in the parlor right now, gathering myself, and yet here I am, corralling you two because your father is selfish, self-absorbed, incapable."

She peered at me with beady eyes.

"And you're just like him, aren't you, whining on about fun. Do you want to shame this family too? Do you want to tarnish your mother's good name even more? Because mark my words, young lady, she would be appalled."

Tears streamed down my cheeks.

Grandmama straightened. "Guests will be here in less than an hour. Where on earth is Margaret?" She spun, retreating in a huff.

I saw then that Lila had vanished too. In the mirror, her eyes were vacant, her color drained. "She's right, you know. There are rules. We need to follow them."

Then she scurried out of the room. And didn't utter another word to me that entire day.

In one sense, we've never moved past that April morning. Later that year, after a summer of screaming matches with Grandmama, I was accepted at Queen's College, London. Lila was just as furious as our grandmother about it—God only knows why. My sister largely ignored my letters, and my trips home became civil at best. I started throwing myself fully into the pursuit of archaeology, mythology, and the study of the past. Every chance I got, I visited Dad at his Oxford flat and attended his lectures, taking solace that at least one person in the living world didn't actively resent having me around. I thought I had left behind the world of modistes and high tea. And yet look at me now.

Perhaps I am indeed an instrument of chaos. And perhaps I no longer know my sister. But I am determined to make at least one thing right between us and set Lila's future on a brighter course.

Our fine procession of ladies in chic travel suits and men in their Sunday best now bottlenecks at the ship gangway. Here is my moment: the time to take advantage, slip away, jaunt across the pier—but the crowd keeps moving, and I'm jostled straight into William.

"Pardon," William says gruffly, motioning me forward. "After you."

I narrow my eyes. "If I linger, will you summon a servant to manhandle me?"

"Quite the opposite." He smirks. "I assumed if I didn't let you pass, you'd deck me."

I shrug and step ahead of him, onto the thin, narrow gangway connecting the pier to the towering ship. Directly ahead is Lord Tembroke, overdressed in a gold-crested sailor's suit, still bemoaning his hangover; his pettish wife, Lady Leona, walks prettily beside him.

"You're quite sure Madame Aurand made all my gown arrangements with the House of Worth?" I can almost hear her pout. "I don't like leaving such important details to a foreign maid."

"I've been assured she is capable, dear." Lord Tembroke chuckles. "You shall glow like Theia—no, Amaterasu—at the Louvre."

The rest of the Hendricks party, including Annie and Theo Davies and the ever-grumbling Mr. Hendricks, trail behind us. I'll cause too much commotion if I try to run now. My only real option is to sneak off the ship once we're all on board.

Thankfully, I know the RMS *Lucania* well from my recent journey home with Miss Nutter. The ship's first-class accommodations may be unfamiliar, but I remember the main cabin, along with the timetable. We docked at port for two hours at Southampton, so the same is likely true in New York, which means there are two hours to discreetly slip out before I'm trapped, headed to Paris for "Lila's" wedding. I'd obviously hoped to get away much sooner and leave the Davieses' manse last night, but there was a guard standing at attention outside my guest room door all night.

"Where did you learn fisticuffs, anyway?" William says as we reach the gangway end. We step into the grand first-class hall, lavish in the style of the French Renaissance.

"Our father thought it wise to teach us self-defense," I say.

Not exactly true, as all the fighting moves I learned from Dad I picked up only by witnessing a few of his scuffles. But I like the way William's eyes bulge before he can recover.

"He really is a nonconformist, isn't he?" William muses as we glide down the hall. "Though your father was able to carve his own path. No footsteps to follow for a man like him. No one with any expectations of him."

I roll my eyes. "Indeed, no one expects much from *any* of us Fords. Thank goodness for cantankerous Prince Charmings to save us from our own inferiority."

"Are you always so disagreeable?"

"Only when provoked."

"And commentary is provocation?"

"I told you I preferred speaking to walls."

He sighs and catches up with me. "I meant only that a man like Warren Ford is able to pursue his own passions. It's a rare thing, believe me, in my world."

"The past should be everyone's passion, Mr. Hendricks," I say absently.

We follow the crowd into the first-class dining saloon, three decks high and bathed in sun, given the room's expansive skylight. The coffered ceiling surrounding it glimmers gold. The mahogany walls are adorned with actual pillars, as if the ship devoured a temple for lunch. I nearly laugh. Is this how the Hendrickses always travel?

Goodness. No wonder Grandmama didn't bother vetting the boy.

Their entourage—Mr. Hendricks, the Davieses, the Tembrokes,

the Avondales—gather around the long, gleaming dining table in the center of the saloon, where the captain waits to meet them.

I wait for William to follow suit, affording me a chance to break away. Instead, though, he lingers.

"And how do you mean?" He sounds genuinely curious. "About the past?"

"Oh. Take our current circumstances, for example," I say, feigning brightness. "You called marrying me an . . . What was it again? An 'unexplained and often onerous' responsibility?"

He balks, cheeks reddening slightly. "Not sure that's an exact quotation."

"You view marriage as one more chess piece, a perpetual game your father plays with your future. But your grandfather might have done the same meddling—and his father before him."

"Go on."

"And their actions, responses, to millions of other choices, obligations, responsibilities. Decision after decision, running like a current through time, shaping the tides of custom, beliefs, morality. Of what is considered done or proper or even right."

William swallows as I step closer.

"You see, we need to uncover the past, Mr. Hendricks. Down to the pottery, the shards, the bones. To understand why we do what we do, what we believe. How we are all connected. The past, simply, is everything."

William, for once looking chastened, breaks our gaze first. He gives a little laugh. "Passion, indeed."

I sober. *Good gods, Tess, now is* not *the time to spout heartfelt soliloquies about archaeology.* I must get out of here, end this affair for good.

The captain, thankfully, saves me from myself, booming down the table, "What a fine day to set sail!"

Everyone, William included, turns and cheers. The crowd clusters nearer to the saloon table, eager for the welcome speech.

Now's my chance.

As the captain begins describing the weather, the route, his credentials, I inch back toward the exit to the corridor. I survey the group to see if anyone's noticed, but no, there's just a uniform sea of smiling faces. I watch them warily as I retreat: Lord Tembroke, still pitifully holding his head; Lady Leona, standing with Annie Davies. Annie's father, Mr. Hendricks, is dangerously close to the door; he's scowling at the captain, but even he appears engrossed.

Fifteen more steps until this wretched affair is over. Ten now. Goodness, nearly on my way. Five—

"Going somewhere?"

I startle, spinning around inside the corridor to find Theo Davies mere inches away. Only when I blink do I realize his hand is firmly gripping my shoulder. I shiver, trying to gently shake him off, as the crowd behind him breaks into applause.

"I'm actually feeling a bit seasick," I tell him. "Just a short trip to the powder room, won't be but a moment."

Behind Davies, Annie catches my eye. She makes her excuses to Leona and hurries toward us, her expression opaque.

"The cabins are ready," Davies says coolly. "Annie and I can escort you. You can recover there while we have a word. In private."

Around us, the other guests are dispersing, clamoring up the steps toward the decks. Readying for departure, to bid adieu to the pier when the horn blares and the ship leaves port. The very last moment for me to break away.

Blazes, should I just come clean about my identity? I obviously cannot sail across the seas and travel on to Paris as my sister! Grandmama will be mortified when she hears of my ruse, but I'll explain, impress upon Lila that I had only her interests at heart. It will be a mess, but not as colossal as the one I'm in now.

"I actually want a word as well," I confess.

Theo Davies gestures toward a gangly porter waiting in the corner. "Then after you."

The three of us follow the porter into another interior corridor, toward the first-class cabins.

"Room one-twenty-four, good sir, madams," the porter says. "As specified."

The porter opens the cabin door, bowing his head.

"I hope you find it to your liking." Annie slides into the room. "We've had it outfitted especially for you. A special room for the bride-to-be."

"Er, right, that's what I was hoping to discuss." I slide into the suite, nerves on end, antsy to be rid of my lie now that I've settled on disclosing it. I notice this cabin is more than twice the size of the second-class room I shared with Miss Nutter days ago. Velvet curtains, brocaded upholstery, a private washbasin, and a perfect circle of powder-blue sky. An ornate writing desk is tucked into the opposite corner. Under different circumstances, I might be thrilled to call it mine.

"Wedding plans will have to wait," Davies says, walking past brusquely, waving for me to follow.

It's then that I see the large leather pouch on the desktop. Stitched onto the pouch's flap is the same strange insignia I spotted on the place cards at the Davieses' dinner.

That chilling knot of tangled, sinister cobras.

Davies unties the pouch. Inside, of all things, I see three carefully rolled papyrus scrolls.

Despite everything else, I gasp in wonder.

"As we journey across the seas—for your wedding—there's

something we need your help with, Miss Ford. Something absolutely crucial."

I lean closer. The scrolls are certainly Egyptian, and ancient; the fibers are worn thin and to a brown.

"It's a task that all of us, your new family, are counting on you to perform."

Davies carefully unfurls the nearest scroll.

My eyes dizzyingly scan the ornate dashes of ink. Hieroglyphics. Right to left, top to bottom and back again. The delicate scroll, a true relic, perhaps a funerary text or a book of spells from the New Kingdom.

"Do you remember the games you used to play with Dr. Belot while waiting for your father to finish his lectures?"

I stare at him. Out of the million things Theo Davies could have said, this might shock me most.

I mean, yes, Lila and I attended Dad's lectures together as children, once upon a time. But Lila rarely sat still, never seemed invested in the stories, and declared the whole pursuit "unladylike" nearly a decade ago. I'd since found her nose buried in an obscure logic game or crossword at home in the library, but when in the blazes did she ever play decryption games with Dad's rival?

I give a small nod, uncertain of what else to do.

"Well, Dr. Belot requires your help once again. These scrolls are an ancient puzzle, a series of texts written in an unknown language, a sequence that builds from scroll to scroll. A riddle, if you will. A riddle that will open a tomb."

A tomb? Is he referring to Dad's dig site, tomb KV55? But that's already been excavated. Another?

The *real* Tomb of the Five Ladies?

"A riddle," I repeat, dubious.

"Indeed. One of the world's most confounding, per Dr. Belot."

Davies leans on the desk, blocking out his wife, the window's light, reality, until all I can see are his unsettling amber eyes.

"And in order to decipher this riddle, you'll need to crack the first papyrus, what we call the *Ren* scroll." He points to the symbol at the top of the scroll. "We believe this scroll may be the key to a series of very important doors. Naturally the scroll sequence will take time to solve. But we have five days on the ship, plus more time in Paris as you prepare for the wedding, should you need it. And we'll be staying with Dr. Belot, who is quite eager to resume your collaboration."

My heart's beating louder than a sistrum. Not only am I being abducted, but I'm charged with a decryption riddle? Me, Tess Ford, passing maths at Queen's College by the skin of my teeth. Not to mention the only language I've ever managed to master—besides English and French, as one needs to survive in our circles—is Fordish. *Lila's* Fordish!

"This appears . . . quite a complicated sequence," I whisper. While I was always more drawn to the stories and history aspects of Dad's profession, I've seen enough hieroglyphs, hieratic script, and demotic in my day to understand that Dr. Belot is correct. On first blush, I doubt my father could manage this entire sequence. So why on earth does Belot think that Lila can?

"Which is why I cannot overstress how important it is that you give this your full attention while we are at sea." Davies's eyes sear into mine. "Rest assured, dear girl, if you prove as extraordinary as Dr. Belot insists you are, you'll make your future family very, very pleased."

He pulls away, straightening the garish watch chain on his vest.

"I'll send the porter by with dinner in a few hours," he adds. "I suspect you'll want the evening to fully dig in. Champollion is in the top drawer for assistance. Better leave you to it, Miss Ford."

He stalks out the door and closes it. Annie remains by my desk, though I still can't read her expression.

The truth tumbles out: "I can't! I know I should have told you earlier, but I tried to tell William, and then he was so horrid, I decided I should just keep my mouth shut and flee—"

"Lila." Annie's face contorts, confused. She raises her hands. "It's all right. Please, slow down."

"I'm not Lila!"

Annie's lips press into a thin line. "What?"

"I have no idea why Dr. Belot thinks my sister can crack an ancient puzzle, but her little sister most certainly can*not*—"

"Little sister?"

"I was having a lark with your brother, pretending to be Lila, as she'd been so awful to me last night. But then William seemed far too awful even for her, and I've been trying to slip away, scupper the engagement for her, but there hasn't been a chance, and I'm sorry, but I really need to go home. I cannot go to Par—"

Annie crosses the room in two graceful bounds. She grabs

my hands with one of hers and with the other covers my mouth. Tightly.

My eyes go wide.

"Listen very carefully," she whispers, close to my ear. "My father, my husband, this cohort is dangerous. Ruthless. They call themselves the Fraternitas de Nodum, and they will stop at nothing until that puzzle is solved and the Crown is found. They will kill you if they find out you aren't Lila."

"Whhht?"

"Quiet," she commands. "They'd planned to kill your sister anyway, once she was finished with the translation, stage an accident. There's never going to be any wedding. My mother's in on it, but they've kept my brother in the dark. They plan to leave him in Paris for appearances, the mourning fiancé, while they take the decryptions on to Egypt." She swallows. "Dash it, I thought I had more time!"

"Hmh mcchh tmmm?"

"You must stall, understand?" Annie's eyes are twin green moons. "Your father mentioned you attend his lectures; you know enough about the legends and the Crown. Fudge the translations until I find a way to sneak you out of here."

She releases me, spinning away.

"Wait, Annie, please, I—"

But before I can follow her, she rounds the door and thrusts it closed.

"I cannot actually be Lila!"

I hurry toward it as I hear a screeching, dragging sound, like metal across a tiled floor.

Lunging, I push, pull, shake the door. Flailing to pry it open. Did Annie wedge a chair under the knob? It won't budge. I attempt its hinges. Useless, useless!

Rushing back to the desk, I desperately scour the drawers

for a key, a comb, a pick, something to break me out of this nightmare.

Then I stop cold when I hear the sound thrum through the walls.

A long, deep, primal wail.

A sob of defeat.

The ship horn blast.

CHAPTER 7

LILA

❧

N 34°15'51.0", W 40°46'07.0" (The SS Stoat*)*

THE FOGHORN BELLOWS FOR THE THIRTY-SEVENTH TIME today, and for at least the thirty-eighth, I pine for dear old Orchard Street.

At least that vermin-ridden tenement floor was dry and steady, free from lurches, swells, and endless, torturous rocking; the stench, in reflection, comparatively mild; and that lovely, sparse room, so blessedly, beautifully bereft of other humans.

If one can even classify these men as human.

I have now endured three days of self-petrification between bouts of retching in a bucket, watching twenty-seven sweat-drenched bodies game and drink and brawl in waves so regular one might time them with a clock. I'd do it myself if I had a pocket watch, except that these ruffians would pinch it off me the second they caught a glimpse of something shiny.

I trace the golden object stashed against my breast, reassuring myself that Mother's comb is still there, and survey the men. Oh, but they're a ragged, jumbled bunch, one I'd never expected to share sleeping quarters with in my life, workers with scribbled contracts for their bulbous arms and the guns they cradle like dollies at night. Alex assures me they're not mercenaries but laborers, blacklegs brought in by the British. Still, I peg them all as adventurers in the worst sense.

Not that I'd give him the satisfaction of hearing me admit it, but Father was probably right to dress me as a boy. This is no place for a woman or a gentleman. Even with our financial difficulties, surely we could have afforded third class on a passenger liner. So why the SS *Stoat*, this hollowed cork, where no one of standing would . . .

No one of standing would think to find us.

This realization does not bode well for the rest of our journey.

I lie on my top bunk in the corner of the room, tucked away tight, and breathe slowly to quell my nausea. At least I managed to secure the one upper berth with no one beneath. Small blessings. Father sits on the bottom bunk across the aisle, elbows on his knees, staring at the unidentified liquid sloshing from bow to stern and back again. It's not seasickness afflicting him. His stomach seems forged of steel. He's wrestling with some angel in his mind.

Perhaps it's worry for Tess, his protégée, his shadow. He's hardly said her name in the past few days, as if his guilt won't allow him to face the thought of her.

My own mind keeps returning to the last conversation Tess and I had, every hateful thought I threw at her. If Father is indeed rending himself to bits for not being there in time to protect my sister, reason actually dictates that I'm the one to blame. If she'd walked out of the parlor with her usual presence of mind, sharp wits intact, she might not have been caught. We'd still be on the run, perhaps, but together.

Father sighs, stands, stretches. I could clock his movements, too, time brooding, time planning, time pacing the decks above, letting salty spray batter him like some form of Catholic penance. Sure enough, he glances at the narrow steps and disappears up them in two bounds.

He takes that slim satchel of his with him. His keepsake.

Alex lies supine on the bunk above Father's, looking for all the world as if this were a relaxing seaside vacation. He's inscribing notes on one tiny corner of a map. I see a winding crook of river and the words *Abydos* and *Deir el-Medina* before my eyes drift up to the spectacles he wears when he works.

I almost mourn the image of Alex I once held—of a scrawny, pale, freckled youth, that brainy Etonian following Father around like a lamb. All those years Tess has worked alongside him and never once thought to mention he looked like this?

He's caught me staring, bother it all. He peers over his spectacles at me. "Do you need the bucket?"

I shake my head. Oh, how I would love to issue a smart reply, but I might actually vomit again if I attempt one. The truth is, I'm desperate for the bathroom, but I'd rather die than ask him, once again, to escort me. He already sees me as a burden, the dainty lady with her hygienic needs. I tighten the cap on my head and swing my legs down to the floor, stifling a sob as my flat-soled boy boots connect with slosh.

Thirty-two steps to the closeted corner they call a "head." I've done it twelve times now with Alex. This time I'll make it on my own.

I mentally recite my half-baked ruse as I walk. *I'm a young lad, name is Jim, down on my luck, looking for an honest day's work, traveling to Suez to seek employment doing canal-type labor on the canal. Yep, that's me, Jim the Canal Worker, they calls me.*

Dice players form a writhing circle between the rows of bunks, blocking my way. I time my pace so that I can stride through between rolls. I've nearly made it when a shout rises from the clutch and all the men stand, two with knives drawn.

"Three sixes in a row? What are the damned odds?"

One in two hundred sixteen, I calculate, heart thudding, stepping sideways over someone's leg. Not common, not impossible.

"You calling me a cheater?"

Oh dear. Before I can so much as flinch, I'm in the midst of a melee, arms flying around me in incalculable directions. I let out a squeak as I duck low, my fists pressed to my face for protection. A knee rises, grazing my head, so I scramble downward and onward, fingers and knees covered in viscous liquid as the tide rolls back. I'm so consumed with disgust that I don't realize my cap's been knocked loose.

The crowd behind me goes completely still.

I feel my long, loosening braid tickle my neck as I turn.

As one, the men burst into snarling, crashing, uproarious hilarity, quarrel forgotten, so there's that at least.

I snatch up my cap, as if it can do any good now. They watch me rise and the skin on my back prickles, like a rabbit among hounds.

"A bit of jam on a cargo liner! Never in my life." One of the knife-wielders, whom I've decided is most definitely guilty of cheating, cranes his head. His grin is like a gash across his face. "What you running from, angel? Come and whisper it to me. I swear I won't tell."

He makes an exaggerated kissing face and the others whoop. Another man with a livid bruise on his forehead steps forward, eager, but the cheater pushes him back.

"I'm not running from anything." I try to force bravado into my voice, but it still comes out quivering. "Now, if you'll excuse me."

"Aw, join our game, sugar." The man twirls his knife. "I can make a place for you right here on my lap."

He thrusts his hips toward me. I squeak in horror.

"Step. Away," Alex snarls behind me. I hadn't even sensed him walk up.

The boat lurches, and I fall backward against him. Heavens, he's solid.

"So she's yours?" The man laughs. "How much you want for her?"

My hands fly to my mouth. Is he suggesting I'm a lady of . . . of . . . I refuse to articulate the word for what he's suggesting I am!

In one neat move, Alex sidesteps me so that I'm behind him, cocks his fist, and lands it square on the man's stubbly jaw. The ruffian staggers back, his knife soaring far out of reach. I'm on the brink of applause when the villain changes direction, a charging bull, flared nostrils and all, and connects with Alex's midsection.

Alex lets out a sickly grunt, grappling with the man while the others cheer. Are they placing bets? I prove worse than useless, backing away to avoid getting hit. If only I could find some kind of bludgeon. That whiskey bottle plan back on Orchard Street wasn't so bad, wrong as I was about Alex, and perhaps I could—

A shot rings out.

Everyone but me drops to the deck, hands on their heads, like they've rehearsed this. I'm too befuddled to do anything so sensible. I turn slowly, muscles locked tight, nose wrinkling from the acrid smell wafting past.

Father stands at the end of the cabin, a revolver in his hand, smoke curling out of its barrel.

"Now that you've met my daughter," he shouts, "we're gonna have some new rules around here. No brawling. No theft, petty or otherwise. We're gonna keep the gambling *civil*."

I hear a few wary chuckles behind me. Alex heaves himself upright, catching his breath.

"And . . ." Father strides forward, smirking, pointing his gun at each man in turn. "If any one of you touches her, even by accident, even if you just bump into her, you can expect the offending body part to be removed by my next bullet. Got it?"

A chorus of "ayes" resounds, Father slides the revolver into the back of his belt, and life resumes at a more mannerly pitch.

He ushers me up the aisle. "I'll keep a better watch on you from here on out, princess."

"*We* will," Alex adds quietly.

Father shakes his head, grumbling, "We should have cut off your damn hair."

I wriggle free from his arm, grateful for his exquisitely timed rescue but affronted nonetheless. I'm not cargo to be guarded, snipped and shipped from one port to the next, like whatever he's stowed in that satchel of his. I'm a person, one he hardly knows, a daughter he cast aside years ago, back when it mattered.

"You shot the ship," Alex murmurs as he lifts himself back onto his bunk, staring at a small splintered hole in the ceiling, murky daylight seeping through from the deck above.

Father kicks his feet up, hands behind his head. "They know I'm good for it."

His casual drawl makes me suspect this isn't the first time something like this has happened. What kind of life does this man have? And how is he "good for it," exactly? Will he pass the captain cash to patch up the damage—cash that could have been sent home to Grandmama to settle some of our considerable debts? If so, it will still fall to one of the deckhands to make the repairs, and by golly, it's lucky one of them wasn't struck by the shot he fired, now that I think of it. Does he consider these things? Or are the lives of the people around him no more than incidental stage dressing?

"Just a few more days to go, Lila." Father pulls at the bridge of his nose. "You don't have to talk to anybody but us."

I may as well talk to my boot. He's barely looked at me since we left Orchard Street, and our total words directly exchanged on board this ship has yet to top one hundred.

"Perhaps if there were something for me to read." I sigh. "To pass the time?"

Days ago I managed to find a daily newspaper tucked into the slats of the empty bunk below me. The only interesting stories in it were about Puerto Rico's vote in favor of self-government and a frankly infuriating editorial entitled "Lace Waist Suffragism." Hardly enough to warrant a reread. Father must've brought books, but he's hoarding his belongings like a dog with a cache of bones.

"Fresh out of fashion monthlies, I'm afraid." He's slid his hat over his face, retiring for the evening, but I still climb into my bunk so he can't see my cheeks redden.

I can scarcely expect my father to understand me. All he knows of his elder daughter must come from perfunctory updates from Grandmama, and the portrait she likely paints is that of a well-bred young lady untainted by her father's unsavory influence. It isn't an incorrect likeness, only incomplete, so what offends is not his hasty characterization of me but his lamentable lack of curiosity. If nothing else, I'd have expected the man to be perceptive.

I curl against my tiny, lumpy mattress, my body taking on the shape of a scowl.

I peek down. Father's chest starts to rise and sink more heavily. Land's sake, he falls asleep quickly.

My fingers move to my collarbone, tracing the curving line of my comb's inlay. I can feel bits of myself being washed away with every wave that distances us from New York, but that comb is still there, proof, at least, that Lila Ford once existed. And her mother did too.

I glance across the aisle to find Alex watching me. He blanches when we lock eyes. Perhaps he's seasick too.

"I, er, sorry. I just noticed you . . ." He blinks meaningfully in the direction of what would otherwise have been my décolleté. His voice drops lower. "You haven't got something secreted away, have you?"

"Not that it's any of your business." I glance around. Satisfied no one is watching, I pull out the comb, cup it within my palm, and pass it across the aisle to him.

Alex's eyes threaten to evacuate his skull. He leans way over to shove it back into my hand, hissing, "You mean to tell me you've had that thing on your person this entire time?"

"This *thing*," I whisper back, indignant, "is midcentury twenty-four-carat gold, inlaid with mother-of-pearl."

"Whyever did you bring it?"

Anger flares beneath my skin as I tuck the comb away. "Because I wanted to. I wanted to hold on to one thing that was mine. After all, I've let go of my coming-out ball, my home, my wardrobe, my safety, the limits of my sanity, but how frivolous of me, I know, not to sacrifice absolutely everything."

"You know that's not what I meant." His eyebrows lower over his spectacles. "If any of these men see it . . ."

"They won't." I recline. "Unless you keep jabbering on. And you might consider not staring."

I wait for Alex's eyes to rise from my bosom, rewarded by a rapid flood of color in his cheeks.

He flops onto his mattress, defeated. "I sense that you are dangerous when bored."

"Lucky for you, I pride myself on rarely becoming bored. Under normal circumstances I can always find something of interest to occupy my time. But this place . . ." I draw a woozy breath, taking stock once more—curved, dripping walls, an underdeck of a ceiling spotted with mold, lanterns waving back and forth and back again. "It is proving challenging."

Alex looks at me askance, as if he's wrestling with mental arithmetic.

"I might have some reading material for you," he says at last. "I'll warn you, it isn't your typical penny serial."

"I don't care for fashion monthlies or penny serials," I reply pertly. "Although I suspect the legend of the Serpent's Crown rivals anything you'd consider women's entertainment."

His dark eyebrows rise, sending his spectacles slipping. "Well, that would depend upon what version you've heard."

I feign a yawn. "Tess spent one obsessive summer talking of nothing but the Serpent's Crown, but that was almost a decade ago. Powerful hat, lost to time, sought by kings."

Alex's jaw twitches. He's dying to correct me.

"Go on then." I smile, indulgent, lolling onto my side. "Tell me the bedtime story."

"I suppose it might be useful for you to have a more academic grounding." Alex perches on his side. "It all begins with Isis, as most Egyptian myths do. She molded the serpent out of sun and dust for her husband, Osiris, to wear as first ruler of Egypt."

LEE KELLY AND JENNIFER THORNE

"An actual serpent?" I interrupt. "I was envisioning a . . ."

I draw a circle around my head.

"Hat. Right. No." Alex looks smug. "Most scholars agree that the physical relic referred to is a uraeus. A small ornamental snake that sits on the headdress of the pharaoh."

"And Osiris was the first pharaoh."

"Precisely. But when he was murdered by Set—"

"Murdered?" I do remember some of this now, but I like the way Alex's eyes ignite in the telling, so I pretend ignorance. "Egads."

"His body was, ah, dismembered." He winces apologetically. "Scattered across the kingdom, along with the Serpent's Crown he wore. Isis scoured the earth, managing to find and reassemble his body parts, most of them, anyway, but the Crown itself was lost."

"'Most of them'?"

"According to Plutarch, there, ah, was one rather key, er, section of Osiris's body that was never"—red creeps up his neck—"discovered."

"Goodness." I lean forward. "Which?"

"The anatomical part specific to gentlemen."

He can't even look at me, poor soul. I could drag this out further, but I bend to mercy. "So the Crown was never found?"

"Well, eventually it was," he whispers. "A lesser sun god known as the Aten, whilst languishing in the dark waters of Chaos, found the serpent and offered it to a devotee, a young pharaoh, Akhenaten. They struck a deal: the pharaoh would get the Serpent's Crown and all the unfathomable power and control that came with it, and in return, Egypt would henceforth worship only one god: the Aten."

"I'm sure that all went swimmingly."

"Only if by *swimmingly* you mean temples torn down; priests executed; capital cities razed, then rebuilt in Amarna by terrified slaves; an entire culture invaded and bastardized, if not replaced wholesale; uprisings quelled by a mysterious, absolute supernatural force."

"Supernatural force. Goodness. Someone should write a penny serial about this."

"I see you're one for serious scholarship only." He affects a solemn frown, teasing me.

"You said you had reading material?" I remind him with a glare.

A mischievous spark lights behind Alex's spectacles. "I do."

He reaches into his rucksack and hands across a thick, leather-bound notebook I've never seen before.

I reach over, but he pulls it away again, brow furrowed.

"Careful. It may not be much, but it is mine, and in time I hope it will amount to enough independent scholarship to warrant . . ." He trails off.

I sit up. "What?"

"To benefit your father's work."

That wasn't what he'd intended to say, I'm certain. Now I'm even more intrigued. I nod and take it carefully, so Alex knows I respect whatever power this book holds, but as he settles back to watch me, there is an almost prankish glint lighting his eyes.

I open to the first page and squint. I rotate it forty degrees, back again, trying to make heads or tails of it, seeing curving cursive at the top; small, orderly pictures in the middle; back to cursive script at the bottom. At the top of the page, beside a hieroglyphic image of a seated man, Alex has written the word *Ren*.

"Sorry." Alex chuckles. "Couldn't resist. Not what you expected?"

"No," I admit, the spokes of my memory slowly creaking back into a spin. "Is this called *hieratic*? With hieroglyphic symbols? Is it common for them to be mixed?"

Alex blinks.

I flush. "I used the terms wrong. Maybe this is demotic. I haven't looked at script like this for years. Tess is the budding Egyptologist. I'm just . . ." I sink, unable to complete the thought. What am I, anyway?

But the image in the notebook hooks my eye again, my mind reeled in by it.

"I was joking, Lila," Alex says. "I was going to give you an Arabic phrase book I hand out to greenhorns."

"Oh, I'll take that too. Thank you."

I idly take the little phrase book from his outstretched hand and put it to the side, returning to Alex's notebook. On the very last page, I find a neatly sketched chamber map labeled *KV55*. It takes me a few blinks to connect these letters and numbers to the news clipping hanging on our wall on Riverside, and from there to the story Alex told me back at Orchard Street.

KV55 was the tomb Father discovered this winter: the Tomb of the Five Ladies.

But the chart shows one sarcophagus, not five. I scan the rest: rubble, a fallen ceiling panel, something called a *magic brick*, for goodness' sake.

My finger traces a recess in the southern wall. "Canopic jars?"

"Every burial site has them," Alex says. "They typically hold the mummy's remains: stomach, entrails, lungs, liver. The body's vital organs kept safe for the afterlife, per tradition. That wasn't the case here. There were also five jars, rather than the typical four, another curiosity . . ."

I flip eagerly back to the first page of hieroglyphs and hieratic, those ancient characters lined up neatly, a puzzle to solve. The perfect tonic for a troubled heart, I've found.

"And there are markings on the jars that align with the five elements of the soul, per Egyptian mythology," Alex goes on. "*Ren, Ba, Ib, Sheut,* and *Ka* . . ."

"Did you write this?" I ask, cutting short his lecture.

"I transcribed it," Alex says like he's addressing a toddler. "Copied it."

"I gathered that." I glance up, annoyed. "From what?"

"A papyrus fragment. A scroll, to be specific."

"Found within the jar marked *Ren,* presumably?" I prompt but don't bother waiting for confirmation. "You don't happen to have any sort of decryption reference, do you?" I squint at the page. "I may be able to figure out the hieroglyphs myself, but it'd be faster if somebody's done it before me."

Alex's lips quirk. "Somebody has. His name is Champollion. He cracked the Rosetta Stone."

"How careless of him." I roll my eyes before Alex's mouth can open any wider. "That was a joke. Calm down."

"Lila Ford punning. What wonders I see before me." He reaches back into his satchel. "You're in luck. I never travel without Champollion's *Lettre à Monsieur Dacier.*"

I flip carefully and halfway through find glorious columns of Coptic letters next to their demotic and hieroglyphic counterparts. I have the vague, exhilarating sense that I've looked at this exact page before, copied from it, even, back when I was fascinated by these things. It's not a direct key for this specific puzzle. Demotic was everyday Egyptian shorthand, if I remember correctly, whereas the hieratic Alex copied into his notebook is a more formal script, used by ancient Egyptian religious types. And Coptic is connected to the Greek alphabet, with similar links to

A		
B		
Γ		
Δ		
Ε		
Ζ		
Η		
Θ		
Ι		
Κ		
Λ		
Μ		
Ν		
Ξ		
Ο		
Π		
Ρ		
Σ		
Τ		
Υ		
Φ		
Ψ		
Χ		
ΤΟ		

the letters we use today. It must have sprung from the demotic, now that I'm looking at it. There are so many similarities.

This should be inscrutable, and yet I can already see an avenue toward inferring connections. The shape of this hieratic character here aligning with that hitched demotic character there.

Another document drops into my lap, a small blue book, its edges frayed gray. I pick it up, delighted. "Another phrase book. You're spoiling me."

Alex shushes me, pointing down at Father, who's still quietly snoring. "It's not comprehensive, but it's useful for New Kingdom, which is what we think this is. That's everything I've got. Have at it." He winces. "But have at it carefully, if you don't mind. The pages are rather brittle in some of these books, and I'd really rather my own work didn't get marred either."

"I will treasure every page as you do." I blink up at him. "I honestly will."

He continues to stare.

I huff a sigh. "You're not planning to watch me work, are you? I solemnly promise not to dog-ear, rip, or smudge, and this will take a few hours, at least."

"I should think so." He laughs, befuddled. "Have you attempted translations before?"

"A few times."

I'm ashamed to admit how long it's been. Seven years. I do try not to think about those days at Columbia University, except that I dream about them so often, the memory repeating nightly in my brain like a spinning zoetrope, sitting cross-legged behind the back row of gallery seats in Father's lecture hall, loose papers strewn about me, marking notations here and there, connecting them in the middle, while Father's colleague, Dr. Belot, gave me puzzles to solve, demotic script at first, then hieroglyphs. Yes, he was the one who first showed me this Champollion chart, wasn't

he? It all culminated with an entirely different sort of riddle, that novel cuneiform I'd first spotted in his notebook.

"What a mind," he used to say. *"You're a marvel."*

I'd started to imagine a future for myself back then, a life of the mind. Father used to parade us through the library, telling anyone who would listen, "These are my girls. Chips off the old block." I hadn't realized he only really meant it about Tess until the afternoon he saw me working with the kindly old Frenchman in his tiny office and pulled me out so forcefully my shoulder twisted. A slammed door, a carriage ride home, Father staring at the windows so hard I swore the isinglass would shatter. That was it. I never set foot on Columbia's campus again. The only reason Father would give was, "You girls need to spend more time with your grandmother."

I remember crying. Hating myself for it. "It's dull at home. You said we could be anything we wanted to be!"

He didn't answer, and that was answer enough.

For me, at least. After Father left for Oxford, Tess was permitted to go to Queen's College, assist him in the field. I knew better than to ask for those things. I already knew the truth. Tess was different. She was like him. And as Grandmama was absolutely determined that one of us should be like her, it fell to me. As the years went on, I could devote little of myself to pursuits that served no immediate practical purpose, intellectual exercises included.

And yet, by some miracle, I still remember how to do this. I feel it swarming back, waking my mind, causing my heart to race, fading the boat and all its unruly inhabitants to vague nothings.

Alex alone stands out. He reclines across the way, pretending not to monitor me, his pencil tracing the same parallel on his map over and over again.

"You haven't by chance got anything to write with?" I ask, all innocence. It's not as if he's making good use of it.

He mutely passes me the pencil. Bit blunt. It'll do.

I flip back and forth to an empty page in the notebook and feel myself sinking deeper into these strange characters as the ship batters itself against ocean swells, the men gamble more peaceably, Father sleeps, my stomach quiets, hours pass, and words, beautiful words, words that make sense at last begin to reveal themselves, magic conjured out of plain air.

"Seek you the snake, small, lowly man. First . . ."

CHAPTER 8

TESS

❧

11h55 Train, Cherbourg to Paris

"THE SCROLL FORETELLS OF A PROMISED LEGACY," I TELL Annie as I carefully trail my fingertip along the fibers of the first papyrus, underscoring a line of bold, jagged hieroglyphs.

We're alone in my train car, huddled in front of Lila's dresser trunk, en route from the port town of Cherbourg to Paris. Before us, spread out like a collage of fever dreams, are the trio of scrolls, Davies's tattered copy of Champollion, and the notebook I've filled with threads of remembered legends, tangents, decryption false starts. My notebook is open to the final page, which features eight words I've written in large, dark print:

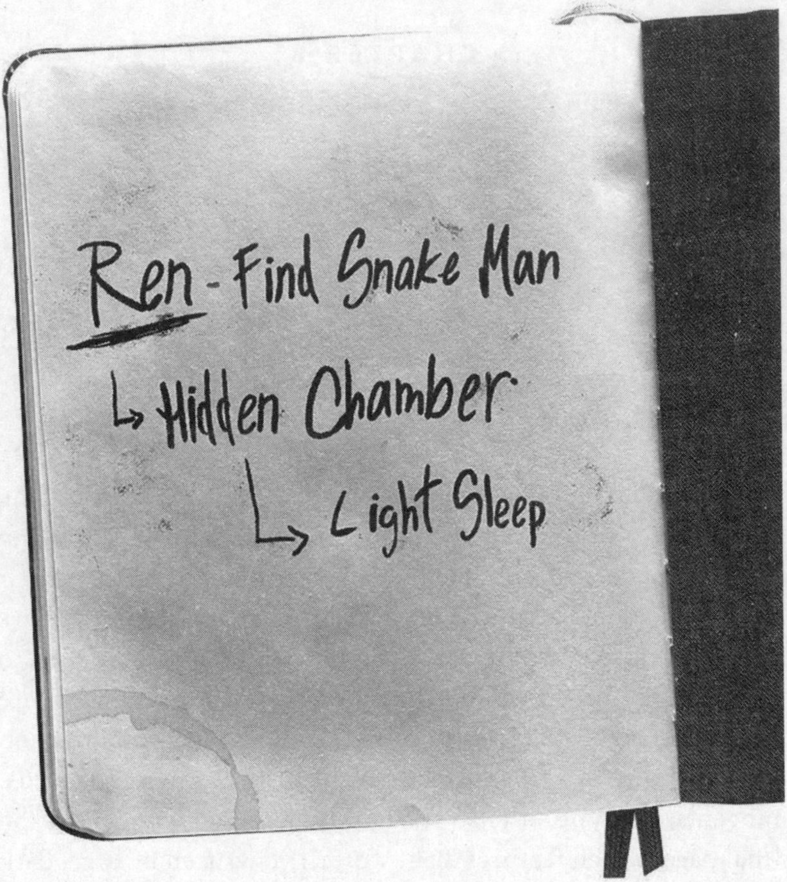
Ren - Find Snake Man
↳ Hidden Chamber
↳ Light Sleep

"'A worthy warrior is called to find a hidden chamber in a tomb, wherein he will discover a sleeping serpent lying in wait.'" I point to the little cobra hieroglyph. "'A treasure from the sun god, the one god, the Aten, which will grant the serpent's wearer infinite sovereignty. The power to control smaller men.'"

Annie arches an eyebrow. "You crafted all of that from a mere eight words?"

I shrug. "I've always been a decent bluff."

My sham decryption has done little to allay her concerns, however. I learned to read Annie's mood during the five days at sea, when we met under the pretense of tea and wedding planning to discuss what she's diplomatically taken to calling "our predicament."

She's frowning now, biting the skin around her nails.

"It's a bit on the nose, admittedly," I hasten to add. "A straight recounting of the Five Ladies legends. But I was caught off guard when Theo and your father cornered me about my progress after the captain's farewell dinner. They bought it, though, I'm certain—hook, line, and sinker."

"And *I'm* certain they believed you'd have cracked the lot of them by now." A worry line furrows her brow. "Though the moment you finish the work, of course, they'll . . . dispense with you. If only we could achieve some middle ground."

The train begins to slow with a low, chiding whistle.

Suddenly the train car feels too tight. The walls too close. The papyrus before me a dizzying, golden eddy.

"The next scroll, the *Ib* scroll, is impossible." I stand, pacing. "I'll never be able to make heads or tails of it. There are hieroglyphics, hieratic, and if I'm not wholly mad, a damn cipher overlaid atop of the puzzle."

"So make it up again." She follows me, plum skirts swishing

around the trunk. "A key insight, not the full translation, as we need more time to sort you a safe escape—"

"And where am I gleaning this *insight* from? The text must support my lie, Annie, else Dr. Belot might catch me in it."

I turn toward the train window, glaring at the last of the French countryside now slowly rolling past, the citrus-hued pastures and distant thatched cottages. Longing to run, though Annie assured me any such hasty attempt to flee on foot would fail, given that the Fraternitas has bribed most of the local police.

The Parisian skyline is taking shape: its hazy labyrinth of narrow streets; the Eiffel Tower, a small, proud parabola on the skyline.

I wonder where and how the Fraternitas plans to dispose of me in this city.

With a lurch, the train begins to slow, and a series of sharp raps sounds outside our door. On the other side, the train conductor begins calling, *"Paris! Dernier arrêt Gare Saint-Lazare!"*

I hurry to collect the scrolls for departure.

"We cannot dally any longer," Annie says decisively. "We must clue my brother in to what's really going on, ask for his aid, if we hope for your clean escape."

"Forgive me if I still don't trust a man who kidnapped me."

"He was afraid of failing our father," she insists. "But I assure you, William is not, nor will he ever be, one of them. He's wholly in the dark about the Fraternitas de Nodum and its aims."

"Even assuming that's true, he has too much to lose by helping us. The grand fortune, the keys to Hendricks Industries—"

"Which he'd gladly give up, given the chance." Her green eyes are clear, emphatic. "Once William hears of the risks I've taken, alerting your father and revealing their plans, he'll be fully aware of the danger I'm in."

"And he'll imperil his own life for yours?" I ask, dubious.

Annie straightens. "He is my only true ally in the world, Miss Ford. There is no one I trust more." She sighs. "I'm sure you understand that bond. Look at what you've gotten yourself into, trying to protect your sister. She's lucky to have you."

I doubt Lila agrees, as our own sibling alliance died years ago, and she's barely acknowledged my existence since. Though I don't bother correcting Annie, given that I'm suddenly choked with envy.

The brakes screech, and the train stops with a sigh, the bustle of our platform and the surrounding Gare Saint-Lazare station now on full display out the window.

Mr. Hendricks barrels through our door.

"Ah. Annie," he says as a porter slips past him to assist with our trunks. "Your husband was wondering where you ran off to."

His eyes narrow as they meet mine, his thinly veiled contempt at having to pander to someone clearly so inferior now unmissable.

"And, Miss Ford. Was the train ride productive?"

"Indeed," Annie answers for me. "Lila was just catching me up on her latest progress."

I flash her a wary look as we follow Mr. Hendricks into the vestibule. Good gods, here's hoping I'm afforded a moment of respite before having to share such "progress."

Our party exits the train. The late-afternoon sun dapples the lively 8th Arrondissement, polishing the city's white marble to a high sheen; the azure sky above, almost haughty in its irradiance.

"There you are," William murmurs.

His dark hair is most disheveled, his cheeks uncharacteristically flushed. He looks younger somehow. More vulnerable.

I clear my throat to squelch a laugh. "Did you happen to catch a nap on the train?"

He stretches with a groan, his muscular frame on full display. "Not necessarily fair, I know, as you work so tirelessly. But I was reading and dozed off."

"You'll have to share the title. Sounds riveting."

He laughs. "Truth be told, I'd been hoping to hear more about the Five Ladies on the ride. Theo informed me you're still helping with his scholarship, so I didn't want to bother you. Besides, I thought perhaps you had grown tired of story time."

Despite my argument with Annie, I'll admit that William has become slightly more palatable company since we left New York—though I'm still loath to trust him with my life. My impassioned speech about the past's allure seemed to crack something open in him. He's been asking questions about Pharaoh Akhenaten and the Crown every moment we have alone at dinner, and on the ship, during the group's nightly promenades around the passenger decks. It's been a welcome diversion, honestly, sharing these tales I know so well.

I can't remember the last time I told stories. Lila long ago stopped listening to them.

"What I don't understand," William says as he offers his arm and we join the slow parade toward the motorcars waiting curbside, "is how the Five Ladies didn't fall under the sway of the Crown—if it was so powerful, that is."

"Because Akhenaten never bothered to use it on them," I say. "His mother, Queen Tiye, his two wives, Nefertiti and Kiya, and his two daughters, Meritaten and Ankhesenpaaten—they were five *ladies*, after all. Mere women, in his eyes."

William arches a brow. "He underestimated them."

"As men so often do," I sigh, "which in this case was a crucial mistake. They banded together, drugged Akhenaten with an opiate, and stole the Serpent's Crown straight out from under him."

I risk a glance at William. His eyes are wide, transfixed, his mouth curled into a contemplative smile.

"Afterward, the people rose up, defeated Akhenaten, tore him from the throne, but by then the Crown was hidden again and eventually lost to time. Cleverly lost. The Five Ladies had taken the Crown's secret, perhaps even the object itself, to their graves. Which is why they say that, even now, the Ladies guard the Crown." I sneak another look. "Much as I like to hear myself go on, why, pray tell, are you so interested in this?"

Ahead, the Fraternitas party filters onto the road, a score of porters at their heels, jostling luggage toward the motorcars.

William shrugs. "General research."

This is so far afield from what I expect him to say that I must swallow a laugh. "What do you mean, 'research'?"

He glances at the crowd, then gently pulls me back. "Well, if you really must know particulars, I've, er, long been contemplating writing a . . . novel."

"How exciting."

"You're mocking me."

"Me? Never." I can't resist a wink. "Honestly, it sounds quite romantic. Heir to Hendricks Industries by day, dashing novelist by night."

He steps closer. "Much as I welcome the dashing, it's just a fantasy I entertain, one that will never come to pass."

"And why not?" I press. "Intellectually, at least, I'd think you up to the task—you know, attending *Yale* and all."

He smothers a smile. "As I mentioned, Lila, expectations are complicated. Unfortunately, not everyone has boundless support to pursue whatever passion they please."

I bristle. "Of course. I just—"

"In fact, do forget that I mentioned it. Erase it from your mind." He turns.

"Wait, no, I—" I grab his arm. "I like that you're interesting. Er, interested. In the stories. Really, should you need any more historical inspiration, I'd be glad to offer help."

He stands there studying me. Those deep blue eyes sparkling now.

"Well then. Consider me very much interested." He pauses. "In your expertise, of course." That little smile returns as he motions toward the car—though this time his grin steals my breath a bit. "After you, Miss Ford."

We leave Gare Saint-Lazare, Lord Tembroke situated in front beside the chauffeur, Lady Leona, William, and me in the second row. Leona begins prattling on about some gala we're all ostensibly attending, but the roar of the motor and the billowing open air soon render conversation fruitless. Instead, William's words about expectations, passion, and boundless support wind through my mind as we drive through the 8th Arrondissement.

My thoughts soon veer round to my own father.

Dad has certainly supported me in a way, allowing me to attend his lectures, to join a few of his research trips and expeditions. I was there at his revelatory dig in Karnak, after all, the winter of my fifteenth year. He'd been squarely in the midst of uncovering those mysterious limestone bricks, the tablets that proved the veracity of the Five Ladies tomb. I'd been keeping up with his expeditions via the papers, but after his latest talatats discovery, his dig was haunting my dreams. I had to be on the ground myself.

As with all things involving Dad, my telegram request to join him was met with a "Sure, kid." No help with money, or advice on travel, or suggested dates for the visit.

By the time my winter recess rolled around, however, I was ready. I left Queen's College with a suitcase and the money I'd cobbled together from playing knucklebones against girls in my hall and poker with some of Dad's students. I spent a full week on second-class liners, overnight trains, and rickety barges that would have given Lila cold sweats, subsisting on a small cache of cream crackers and Cadbury chocolate, fortifying myself instead with dreams of exploring the desert, touring testaments to history, wandering the corridors of the two-hundred-acre Temple of Amun. By the time I arrived at Dad's site, I was giddy.

Too giddy. That night, around the fire, I blabbered on about the Serpent's Crown legends—sharing my thoughts on the tomb's location and my theories for why the limestone bricks had been hidden in the Temple of Amun. But no one, including Dad, cared to listen. After a hard day of digging in the sun, he and his students wanted to relax, joke, and drink until their voices grew soft and loose, without any interruption.

I tried to engage with his team during the day, but funnily enough, nobody fancied a fifteen-year-old's take on Petrie's methods. By my third day on-site, some of Dad's students started groaning and laughing when I came around, calling me "Pest Ford."

It took Dad until lunch that day to even notice I was gone. He found me in the shadows of the Great Hypostyle Hall, battling tears.

I sniffed, wiping my face. "You don't want me here."

Dad leaned against one of the Hall's towering columns. "That's not true."

"It is. No one wants me. Not Grandmama, not Lila. I traveled halfway around the world to go to school nearby, and I barely see you."

He dusted off the column's carvings, then crossed the Hall and bent down beside me, sighing. "And what do you want, pea? For me to thank you for coming? Give you an award for managing to get here?"

He stared down the Hall's long central corridor, the towers of sandstone climbing into the sun-shocked sky.

"This is just the beginning of the sacrifices, kid. This business is tough. Ruthless. And if you're going to make it, you need to want it more than anything, understand? You need to be ready to give up everything else."

I cried myself to sleep that night, not just because I knew he was telling the truth, but because I missed home, my sister, and my long-gone mother so much that I physically ached.

The next morning, though, I picked up a shovel without a word. I trailed Alex d'Auteuil, my favorite of Dad's assistants, into the vestibule that he and some of the Oxford students were excavating, and dug until I had blisters. When the blisters broke and Alex suggested I rest, I shook him off, telling him that "glory was worth the pain" or some similar nonsense, and then I dug some more. At camp that night, I stayed quiet, resigning myself to listening, secretly assuring myself that one day I would lead a dig like this.

That I would make it. On my own. Just like Dad.

A few days later, Dad unearthed another life-changing find: a third talatat that all but confirmed the location of the Five Ladies tomb. And he kept on the hunt, fixated for years, even as Grandmama "nagged" him about expenses, even as I barely saw or heard from him unless I took it upon myself to show up on his doorstep, even as his visits back to New York dwindled to never—until his impassioned, singular pursuit was rewarded, and the talatats led him to KV55.

And led me here.

I bite my lip, still consumed by the memories, as we turn onto a manicured, hedge-lined road.

Our motorcar veers around to a private, landscaped courtyard lush with topiaries and foxglove and rosebushes, reeking of mulch. The other cars in our entourage have already parked around the gurgling center fountain.

Several footmen hurry to unload the luggage from Mr. Hendricks's car, as well as the Davieses' and the Avondales'. The Earl of Tembroke steps out from our own motorcar, stretching his gangly limbs and letting out a yawn.

"A little help, please?" he calls in the vague direction of the butler. "It's been such a long journey. I'm as tired as Odysseus returning to Thebes."

William quirks an eyebrow at that muddled reference. We both manage not to snort as he offers me his hand.

"*Mes chers amis!*" a French voice echoes over the cobblestones. "It is about time you have all arrived."

An old man with mottled pink skin and scant wisps of snow-white hair saunters onto the mansion's front stoop. He throws his stubby arms wide like a Vaudevillian.

Heart hammering now, I step down from the motorcar.

Dr. Belot crosses his courtyard, making the rounds, greeting the members of the Fraternitas like true brothers, doting on their wives. Belot has greatly aged since I saw him last. Chin weaker, hair thinner, blue eyes one shade closer to dishwater. A shrunken form of the man from my memories of Columbia. And yet, as he draws closer, his simper becomes youthful. Almost predatory.

"And the happy couple." He bows ceremoniously. "Young monsieur William, I have heard much about you from your brother-in-law."

As Belot finally turns to me, his wide smile transforms his blemished face into a ravaged minefield.

"And my marvel, at long last. Mademoiselle Lila."

"Dr. Belot." I clear my throat. "You look ever so well."

"As do you. Sacrebleu, my budding flower is now a stunning

rose. I cannot believe it has been seven years since you were a little girl solving puzzles with me in the halls of Columbia."

I shake my head, still struggling with the same notion. And yet there's probably a volume somewhere, thick as *War and Peace*, of all the things I don't know about my sister. "I can hardly believe it either."

"The good old days." Belot gives a deep laugh. "Before I left to conquer the Sorbonne."

He turns eagerly to Davies. "Tell me, was the ship crossing everything we hoped? Were the five days a success?"

Davies cuts a searing look in my direction. "That would depend on your definition of *success*."

Belot drops my hands. "I see." He spins to address the crowd. "I am sure you all must be exhausted from travel, *non*? We shall get you situated." He snaps at his staff, in French, "Show our esteemed guests to their rooms."

The servants hurry to bring the luggage inside. Davies, meanwhile, lags behind, leaning against his motorcar's trunk, arguing with a footman. On second look, the source of the debate is a massive wooden crate, at least three feet long and three feet wide.

"Help me—hold it underneath," Davies scolds the footman. "Gently now. It's priceless."

"*Bien sûr*, Monsieur Davies," the footman grunts, and they lift the crate in tandem.

The rest of us follow Belot, who leads the way into his resplendent manor—an expansive black-and-white tiled foyer, a mammoth Regency chandelier, curving marble steps that lead to a balustraded balcony. At the bottom of the stairwell awaits a hawkish-looking woman in a uniform, her long neck jutted out, her dark eyebrows nearly stitched together.

She steps forward as we approach her.

"Madame Aurand, take Monsieur Davies and Monsieur Hendricks to my study," Belot tells her, once Davies and the footman lug the crate inside. "I will join momentarily."

My body wilts in relief. I'm exhausted myself, eager for time away from the blasted scrolls.

But Dr. Belot grabs my wrist before I can follow the other guests upstairs. "*Avec moi*, mademoiselle."

He leads me down a corridor, the same hall where Davies and Mr. Hendricks have just disappeared.

"It is clear to me that my esteemed colleagues have not yet seen what you are capable of, but they will," Belot whispers to me. "I remember our successes, Mademoiselle Lila. Now *you* must remember as well. Do not be selfish. Do not be lazy. Your efforts are for the betterment of the world."

He licks his lips, and I have to dig my fingernails into my hands to keep from recoiling.

"Our games were ruined, weren't they?" he adds hastily. "Not fair or wise of Warren to waste such a marvel of a mind—"

"Dr. Belot." Davies pokes out his head through the last door along the hall. "Time's wasting."

"Perhaps I can situate Lila in the library?"

Dr. Belot and I turn simultaneously. Annie, once again, to my rescue.

She raises one brow, eyes twinkling. "I know my husband is eager to compare notes, Dr. Belot."

Belot releases me to kiss Annie's hand. "*Merci*, Madame Davies. *Charmante comme toujours.*"

As soon as he slips into the study, Annie's winsome smile drops.

"Come with me." Silently she pulls me into the small, dark powder room adjacent to Belot's study and closes the door. "Can you hear anything?"

I edge closer to the wall, shaking my head—the men's voices are too muffled—until I notice a thin ribbon of light beside the ivory sink.

"Look," I whisper, "a pocket door."

We press ourselves close to its frame, me crouching on the floor, Annie hovering over me. She takes a fortifying breath, then slides the door open just a crack. A sliver of an inch.

"See the display case?" I breathe out. "The mirrored interior? You can see the whole of the study through the reflection."

She nods. We watch through the case as Dr. Belot and Mr. Hendricks crowd around Davies, now tearing through the crate's mound of corrugated paper.

Davies stops, carefully dislodging a small piece of pottery.

I swallow a gasp as I register what he's holding. A canopic jar. The type of container used for storing viscera inside a tomb.

Davies lifts another jar from the crate and then three more, five jars now clustered on Belot's center table. Strangely, though, each container is sculpted in the shape of a woman's head. Not the typical canopic motifs of the sons of Horus, a jackal or a hawk . . .

I draw in a shocked breath. "Five jars," I whisper. "Five *Ladies*."

"And the texts?" Belot asks the men as he inspects the jars. "They were found inside?"

Davies nods. "Three contained scrolls. One was empty." He lifts the lid of the final jar. "But the fifth holds what we believe to be the remains of a fourth scroll."

My heart starts beating faster, mind reeling. *A fourth scroll?*

Belot peers inside. Frowns. The room is silent but for the fluttering of paper from a nearby open window.

"It has been reduced to dust. No one on earth is capable of such reconstruction work." Belot pulls back, crossing his stubby arms. "But the girl will come through, despite this complication. She is capable of *vrais miracles*—"

"Not anymore, Edwin," Davies says coolly. "She hasn't even surpassed your efforts."

"And there's a damn narrowing window!" Mr. Hendricks snaps, pacing. "Cromer's our point of entry into Egypt. We must have the Crown in hand before he's pushed out or there will be no taking Egypt. There will be no taking anything!" He kicks the empty crate, sending it slamming into a chair.

I look up, stunned and sickened, finding Annie's wide eyes in the dark.

This is why they want the Crown? To seize upon political unrest, take over all of Egypt?

Davies straightens the crate, then walks to the window to slide it shut. He flicks at the latch, peevish.

"Don't bother," Belot drones over his shoulder. "It doesn't work."

"Appears to be a theme," Davies says, walking away.

"I need ideas," Hendricks snaps. "Now. Tonight."

"There is, perhaps, someone else," Belot says, wincing deeply. "But I do not trust him."

"Who?" Hendricks barks. "Where?"

Belot sighs. "The Musée du Louvre, in an advisory capacity, but—"

"Fine, Monday then, at the ball. Introduce us, set a meeting," Hendricks says. "It's time to pursue alternatives."

Annie's hand snakes through mine. "We should go, before they discover us."

Together we hurry out, into the hall and then the library, whereupon Annie shuts the door.

"The Louvre," she says breathlessly. "The Gala Bienfaiteur, this coming Monday. I cannot believe I didn't think of it sooner; it's the perfect time."

"Wait, I don't understand—"

"They'll be distracted, meeting your decryption replacement."

"Must you be so confident I'm being replaced?"

"Don't you see, Tess, we will all be in attendance, you and William included, your first and only society appearance after the engagement. No one will be suspicious if your besotted fiancé whisks you off to tour the museum. Meanwhile, I know someone there. A trusted contact. He's helped me before; he can help us now, arrange to hide you with a shipment perhaps, an overseas consignment. We can sneak you out before they conclude their meeting. Before anyone notices you're gone."

Her proposed scheme washes over me in a swell.

It could work. It just might work. Still, I shiver. "But what of their plan, Annie? Conquering Egypt? They're truly so mad as to take over the world, one country at a time?"

"Indeed, we must think of a means of thwarting them." She frowns, biting the skin around her nails. "I've become quite adept at espionage, if I may say so myself. Perhaps there's a way to steal the scrolls too."

I give a wary laugh, but she waves my concerns aside, sweeping forward to place her hands on my shoulders. "I will speak to my brother tomorrow, yes? Tell him of our plan?"

I swallow. The Gala Bienfaiteur. My escape. In two days' time.

Nodding, I turn away. A wordless assent, though my heart is still hammering.

William Hendricks—at a ball, quite specifically—pulled me into this whole mess.

Now I can only pray he will get me out.

CHAPTER 9

LILA

❧

Port of Alexandria, Egypt

I SAY A SILENT PRAYER, GRIPPING THE SHIP'S RAILING, until the moment we hit the dock with a muffled *thud*. Then relief courses through me like fine wine. At last, arrival!

While dockhands catch the lines, I catch my bearings. It's warm here, everything within view a muted pastel. I spy a beach in the near distance, tall, spindly palm trees, a seaside hotel midway through construction, great cargo ships, sailing vessels bobbing everywhere, paved roads, fountains in the European style. Apart from the huge stone fortification we passed on our way into port, it's all so very modern.

Where is the lighthouse—the Pharos of Alexandria? The Great Library? Yes, yes, every schoolchild knows they were destroyed by the Romans, but there still remains a mad glimmer of hope that I might spot them rising in the distance, ghosts of a forgotten age. It's how Tess would feel if she were here with us.

For a moment I afford myself the pleasure of denial and smile at the specter of my sister, imagining her safe beside me for one blissful moment.

When I have smiled in the past few days, it has been for an altogether different reason, one grounded in reality—treacherous fits of glee as pieces of text start to reveal themselves, as my mind spins back to life after how many years asleep? As stirring as the sight of this shoreline is, my heart races most at the thought of getting back to work, uncovering yet more. The next scroll Alex transcribed into his notebook is labeled *Ib*. It whispers to me even now, along with a singular, terrifying question.

What will Father say when I show him what I've achieved?

The gangplank goes down, and with my long braid now loose over one shoulder, the deckhands are gallant as knights. Three step back while another offers me a hand onto the docks, and Father and Alex linger close enough to dissuade anyone from making smart comments about me until I'm out of range. They can say what they like. I am on dry land, *new* land. Egypt!

A spiced smell wafts down from a nearby balcony, its doors flung wide to let in the balmy breeze. The scent is unfamiliar, dizzyingly delicious, especially after days upon days of hardtack and tinned beans. I clench my mouth to keep from groaning in hunger.

Alex falls into step beside me. "How are your legs?"

I squint at my feet.

"No." He stifles a laugh. "I mean, are you dizzy? The ground always feels unsteady for a day or so when I travel that long by ship."

"I'm perfectly fine." On cue, the earth starts rocking beneath me. I shoot Alex a scowl, suspecting he triggered it, then nod over my shoulder. "What's keeping him? I thought we were in an all-fired hurry."

Despite his entreaties this morning for me to be first to disembark so we can hotfoot it to goodness knows where, Father is still lingering at the docks, hat pulled low, passing what looks like a wad of cash to one of the deckhands from the *Stoat*.

I seethe, mentally listing everything I've sold in the past year to stave off our creditors. "Paying for the damage?"

"Among other things."

I tap my foot until Alex glances my way again with a beleaguered sigh.

"If you must know," he leans in to murmur, "he's making sure that if anyone comes sniffing, the crew will swear that no one fitting our descriptions was ever aboard."

"Bribery. Fine start to the day, all very normal."

"Have you . . ." Alex is looking at me strangely again.

"Have I what?"

He leans in once again. "Have you still got your comb?"

I notice how strenuously he's working not to peek down my chemise and can't help but smirk as I casually answer, "*Bi-tabieat il-hal.*"

He laughs, astonished. "You did study the Arabic book. I'd wondered."

"Only as a respite from Champollion." I find myself blushing under his open admiration.

As Alex opens his mouth to retort, Father walks up. "You two talking shop? Or is Champollion also the name of a women's weekly?"

He's teasing again. I try not to show my irritation.

"Perhaps a little shoptalk." My fingers fumble nervously in my jacket pocket, finding the edge of a torn-out piece of notebook paper. I was careful not to disturb Alex's work, as promised back on the boat, but this is my translation. By rights I should get to keep it. "You see—"

Before I can so much as tug the paper from my pocket, Father steps past us briskly, and, oh, fine, we appear to be off. He leads, we follow, across the seaside promenade and into what's clearly a fine or at least on-the-up section of town. Smartly outfitted carriages roll along the wide avenue, while farther up the way, workmen lay tracks for what looks to become a streetcar line.

A phaeton stops street side and two finely dressed women with parasols step out to take the seaside air along the promenade. They're wives or daughters of European officials, I'd guess. Perhaps relations of Lord Cromer himself. They call the British who operate here "the Agency," which sounds a far sight snappier than, say, the Bureau of Foreign Financial and Political Overreach. As critical as I may feel about their dubious presence, I can't help but admire the cut of these women's light tweed jackets.

As if reading my thoughts, the two ladies turn and each give us the once-over. Father doffs his hat politely, waiting for them to pass, and Alex bows. Still, the younger woman's eyes widen at the sight of us, while the older and more elegant of the two looks positively appalled. Heavens, do we appear that ragged? It's me, isn't it? This filthy braid, this boy's getup.

Father clears his throat and steers us away. Without so much as an "*allons-y*," he strides across the avenue, still expecting us to follow. Which, of course, I do. I positively scamper, pathetic creature that I am, calling ahead, "Father, as a matter of fact, I have been meaning to tell you something."

"Rooftops," he replies.

"What?" I look back to see Alex glance furtively at the upper levels of the buildings lining the narrow street ahead.

"Clear for now," Alex murmurs.

"Keep sharp. Cromer's on their payroll. He'll have eyes everywhere."

Does he mean *Lord* Cromer? Consul general of Egypt?

"What do you need, princess?"

"Right." My heart starts thudding the second Father's eyes lock on mine. "I don't *need* anything. It's something I might be able to offer, by way of assistance. On the ship, I do hope you don't mind, but I took it upon myself to attempt—"

"Kid." Father makes a furtive hand gesture. "Step lively."

At Father's words, Alex picks up his pace, flanking me on the left, one hand resting on my elbow. The feel of Alex's fingertips sends static jolts up my arm.

"Yeah, we're being trailed," Father says, and land's sake, so we are, now that I look behind us. We're being followed by half the dirty passengers who just got off the SS *Stoat*, and the quality of the neighborhood we've stepped into has assumed a steep decline. The streets are narrower here, piles of horse filth left steaming on the sides of the track. My shoulders tighten with dread.

"It might be easier to talk once we've stopped. Where are we headed next, exactly?" I hope against hope that the next stop is somewhere we can eat; even a café in this dubious quarter would be a welcome respite. "Are you trying to get in touch with your secret contact?"

Father glances around, his eyes landing hard on mine. "Keep your voice down."

I'm stung speechless, so he gets his wish—and anyway, here's my answer.

We have arrived. At a saloon.

The mercenaries knock past me and through the skinny doorway, threatening to dislocate my shoulder in their haste to get their first proper drink in days. Judging by what I can view of the establishment's interior through the long array of small amber-colored windows that line one wall and twist around the other, there are no women inside, only one slight man sitting at a corner table, reading a newspaper. If I tuck my braid into my collar, I might look adequately boyish, and there is the scant possibility that this saloon has a kitchen, so I square my shoulders and step inside with as much swagger as I can muster.

Father spins me around and marches me back out.

"You two stay out of this." He talks past me to Alex. "This could get messy, but it won't take long. Meet me between the kettles and the rugs. I'll be right behind you, and if I'm not, you know where to go without me."

I peer up at Alex. Did any of that make sense to him? Apparently it did. He nods sharply, motions for me to follow, and starts away, while Father saunters into the saloon.

Curiosity ignites in my veins. I stare through the first warped window, watching Father stroll through the crowd of passengers straight to the long oak bar. Window two: he slides into the small space between two remarkably burly men. One is the scarred gambler I remember from the ship. How lovely. Window three: Father seems to be smirking. Saying something to the fellow that makes the back of the man's thick neck turn red.

The bruiser is cocking his fist!

I can only watch what comes next through the cracks between my fingers. But wait. Father is gone. Not at the bar. Has he ducked? He has!

And, oh no, Alex is also gone.

I scurry after him around the corner of the saloon.

"Ah, Alex?" I point to the next cracked window as we approach it. The two burly men are now throwing punches . . . at each other? And so is everyone else. It's pandemonium! "Was this the plan?"

Alex glances back with a chuckle. "This is generally what your father refers to when he uses the word *messy*."

I goggle through the amber glass in sick fascination. Where is Father now?

"Careful," Alex says, his smirk dropping as he yanks me back—milliseconds before a flying tankard shatters the window behind me.

Through the next window I spy Father's hat bobbing in and out of view among the crowd. He's sliding out a back entrance. The man with the newspaper rises to follow.

"What on God's green earth is he doing?"

"Establishing contact."

"I know that, but with whom? Who is this friend of yours? Just because you two trade in codes doesn't mean you need to constantly talk in them."

I'm lapsing into petulance, but Alex merely laughs. "You're no slouch with codes. Those KV55 scrolls are devilish—"

"You're changing the subject."

He smiles, ignoring me. "But I saw how much you managed to decrypt whilst your father slept, in fits and starts."

He didn't see just how much; he himself had been lightly snoring throughout my last decryption session. Still, it's oddly thrilling to hear him compliment me, even if he did drop his voice a few decibels, as if worried Father might somehow over-hear us from whatever back alley he's disappeared into. No matter, Father will know soon enough what I've been up to.

A complete translation of the first scroll, *Ren*.

"Come on," Alex says, scratching his floppy brown hair. "There's always the chance we're actually being followed."

I peer up the narrow street, turning the word *Ren* over in my mind, along with its symbol, the fanned staff, still wonder-ing how the title of the scroll relates to its contents, only to be arrested by the sight of a woman standing outside a shop stacked wall-to-wall with bags of colorful spices. She's pouring tea from a kettle with a parabolic spout, steam rising around her in an undulating line. Every inch of her body is covered in draping fabric, apart from a strip revealing her animated eyes. I will not gawk like some tourist—I smile politely and glance away—but I'm struck by how much more at ease she looks than those two smartly dressed European women. Perhaps the dark dye absorbs heat from the body. I suspect no part of her is corseted or contorted or squeezed, and with her face hidden, she can go about her day without concern for prying eyes, react how she wants to react, think her own thoughts without bothering to maintain a perfectly practiced placid expression.

A great latticed gate rises ahead of us, its many arched doorways leading into a bustling space beyond. It looks like something out of a dream.

"Is this a souk?" My bad temper is gone, replaced by wonder at the colors, smells, and shapes surrounding us. This market is nothing like I imagined it, which is to say exactly as I dreamed it would be. Entirely new.

"*Shay?*" An old man with a long gray mustache waves to us from an arched doorway. "*Fanajin ash-shay laziz?*"

I turn, mind whirring, and glance up at Alex. "Cup of tasty . . . Oh, if only we had time. I'm desperate for a cup of tea."

Alex pulls me gently from the doorway. "He's not selling tea. He's trying to get you to buy a lantern."

"A lantern?" I look back. The man is still waving. "That sounds like a good thing to have. Should we look?"

"Why would we need a lantern?"

"For light when it gets dark."

"I take it you do a lot of shopping back in New York?" He's got that detached look back.

"It's not about shopping. I want to conduct a transaction. What's the currency here?"

"The pound. Egyptian pound." There's a hint of diffident pride in his voice.

I glance over my shoulder, seeing two local ladies walking arm in arm, their veiled heads touching as they chat; a tiny boy putting out a cobalt-blue bowl for a waiting cat, his head cocked at the *clip-clop* sound of approaching horses.

"Should I be veiled?" I muse aloud. "Is it rude not to wear the niqab?"

A queer look passes over Alex's face. I must have mispronounced the word.

"Not rude," he says curtly. "Not every woman wears it, and there are plenty of Europeans here. More and more every day."

The hoofbeats behind us grow louder. I turn to see British officers astride fine gray coursers, all three of them stiff-backed in their light brown uniforms, mustaches waxed to a high sheen. As they approach from the side street, the two women and young boy rush for the buildings flanking us, watching from the shadows. Only the cat remains, staring defiantly up at them until forced to move by the horses' steady progress.

The air is thick with tension. I catch it, too, feeling it settle leadenly over my shoulders. Are these Cromer's men? The ones Father warned us of?

"You'll want to step back, Lila," Alex murmurs, drawing me to the side with effort.

My feet feel rooted to the road. I nod to the soldiers the way I do when New York officers pass, but these ones don't tap their hats and nod back respectfully. One of them spits on the ground by my feet, and I jump back with a squeak.

It's the way I'm dressed. They don't see a lady. I have little doubt they would have treated me entirely differently if I'd been one of those parasol-laden women on the promenade. This getup grants me uncommon powers, it seems. The ability to summon forth truth. Not to mention that if they were looking for Warren Ford's eldest daughter, they were thwarted from spotting her. I cannot believe it, but I'm intensely glad to be dressed so shabbily. Still, I relax only once Cromer's soldiers have passed into the next alley and out of view.

"They don't do much to dissuade one from seeing them as invaders, do they?"

Alex takes a moment to reply. "I agree that the optics are less than ideal."

I watch a wave of emotion cross Alex's face, murky and bitter, before he covers it up again, and wonder where his allegiances lie. He was educated in Britain, and yet it occurs to me that's the only thing I know about him.

"Surely it's more than optics." I force myself to whisper. Smug *Times* editorials be darned, I know where my allegiances lie. "They're marching in, taking over, running the government, the money."

"As did the French before them. The Turks before the French, the Romans before the Turks, the Macedonians before the Romans."

I think back to my history lessons at Veltin: Cleopatra, the Ptolemies, that line of Macedonian imports playacting at being pharaohs, generations of outsiders seeking to grasp power here. History strikes me as a sine wave, ever-shifting but repeating, over and over.

"The Egyptian culture isn't a monolith," Alex goes on, his eyes darting cautiously about us. "It's a layering."

"Like a palimpsest. A layering through blotting out. A smothering."

Alex watches me for a few silent steps. "You talk like a nationalist."

I watch him back. "Is that a bad thing?"

"No, Lila. Not at all. Only surprising." His gaze lingers, warm. "Even so, I'd caution you not to voice such sympathies too loudly. Nationalist sentiments are dangerous things, even when it's a lovely Westerner who espouses them."

I sink, feeling distanced from Alex by the word *Westerner*. He's European himself, but he sees me as something apart. Something lovely, but even so.

"Not voicing my true opinion happens to be a particular skill of mine," I say brightly. "But in the interest of parity, what views do you hold, Mr. d'Auteuil?"

"Much the same as yours." His voice is barely above a whisper. "But with a deeper level of involvement. I support how I can, when I can. It is a subtle and secret endeavor, with many differing factions jousting to be heard, from workers to clergymen to the khedive."

Alex swallows hard and smiles ruefully, as if he's said too much.

I'm surprised to hear Alex mention the Ottoman khedive as one of the figures who supports Egyptian nationalism, but I can tell he's not of a mind to elaborate at the moment. I search gamely for a subject change, when something connects: Alex's academic specialty, his perfect Arabic, his full name.

"Are *you* Egyptian, Alex?"

"I'm not sure how to answer that." An old woman smiles at us from a silk stall, and Alex nods courteously back. "It's a complex question. I spent my early childhood here, but my mother was a French aristocrat turned academic, an archaeologist of some renown."

His last name connects now too. I recall a Marguerite

d'Auteuil, one of the pioneering lady archaeologists Tess would prattle on about in the middle of the night.

"Tess mentioned you have a home in Gizeh," I offer, remembering one of her few letters I did read in full.

He brightens at that. "I do. The house where I grew up. Your sister's been there, as a matter of fact. We stopped over on the way down to the Valley."

I ignore the stab of jealousy that little tidbit gives me. "So your father was Egyptian?"

"Yes, but I never knew him. My mother told me that he was *baladi*, from this country. I never worked up the nerve to ask more. And before I knew it, she was past asking."

"Oh, Alex." I nearly reach for him. "How old were you?"

"Eight when it started. Nine when . . ." He squints. "It was a slow cancer, but it did feel rather quick at the end."

"I was ten when my mother passed," I murmur. "Cancer as well, I believe, though they called it a wasting illness. Eventually her heart stopped. I misheard the doctor at the time and thought she'd died of a broken heart. Isn't that silly?"

He steps closer. "No. Not silly."

I press my fingers to his. He hesitates for a heartbeat, then his hand closes around mine, soft, and I forget to breathe.

Then I glance over his shoulder. "Kettles and rugs. The meeting place!"

"Ah. Yes." Alex lets me go and whirls around, motioning to a narrow alley between brightly draped stalls. "This way."

We emerge from the souk lane into a small, shaded intersection. Father is leaning against the dusty wall, hat pulled low. However did he get here ahead of us? In the distance I can just make out the man with the newspaper disappearing around the corner.

"Sorry we're late." Alex looks more flustered than I've ever seen him. Which is something. "All went as planned?"

"We're set." Father winks at me and pushes off from the wall. "He'll send word ahead to Samy."

"'Samy'?" I ask Alex. "And that's code for—"

"Let's make tracks," Father interrupts, motioning for us to follow. "That was a close shave back there, thus the diversion. Cromer's guys walked in right after I cut you two loose, so odds are they're wise to our arrival, and the old duck and roll won't work twice in one day."

I blink at Father's back as he jogs toward the sunny street ahead. "Did you start that bar fight deliberately?"

Father smirks over his shoulder, giddy as a schoolboy. "And didn't get hit once."

A woman steps around the street corner, blocking Father's way. Just as my mind latches on to her as one of the handsomely dressed women from the promenade, she cocks her arm and lands a neat slap to my father's jaw, the blow so hard that his head twists like a weather vane, lip split and bleeding.

With a tear-streaked huff, she spins on her heels, back into her glossy carriage and away.

Father dabs at his wound and then, to my continued amazement, lets out a rueful laugh. "Lady Winthrop. I had that coming."

My jaw practically unhinges. Bar fights? Rooftop spies? Wronged women? What next?

He adjusts his workman's hat and points down the avenue toward a gleaming body of water that must be the Old Port, to the west. "Better go. We've got a boat to catch."

I stop walking. "You must be joking."

Alex walks backward to grin at me. "Different boat. A felucca. Trust me, you'll like this one better."

Father leads us up the road to another dock, not far, where a line of traditional wooden boats bob, one twin-masted, its sails unfurled and filling in the Mediterranean breeze. He waves to the two wiry sailors, then extends a hand to help me aboard.

"We'll get you some smart new clothes in Cairo, princess. Things should settle down once we get there."

I don't want them to settle down, I nearly shout. *I want to find Tess!*

It strikes me afresh that he still hasn't mentioned her name. Not once today, amid all this frantic scheming. Not since we left New York. What is his plan for rescuing my sister? Does he even have one? Or is this merely the next in a long line of misadventures to him?

The sails fill, the long felucca rises and falls, the sail snaps in a new direction, and the slim vessel lists starboard, drawing a dotted line behind us and the harbor. I grip the boat's solid railing and squint into the sun, letting the truth settle around me, finding its own balance.

Do I trust my father? Have I *ever* trusted him?

I did. Once. Right before he ripped my hopes out from under me.

"What was it you wanted to talk to me about?" Father eases himself onto the deck with a groan. "Got plenty of time between here and Cairo."

Finally, the man wants to talk. Choirs of angels should be singing at the sudden miracle, and yet . . .

I reach inside my pocket again, my fingernails tracing the edge of that folded bit of notebook paper. My *Ren* translation. My remarkable achievement.

I can decrypt all three of the scrolls, given adequate time and resources. I know I can; I feel it. If I can solve them all, I'll have them as leverage. I can use them to save my sister.

What would Father use them for? I don't know. And that terrifies me.

I extend my hand.

He squints down at the phrase book I'm holding. "Arabic, huh?"

"Do you think you could help me with some of the pronunciations?"

He shrugs, turning away. "Why don't you ask Alex, kiddo? He's practically a native."

I've lost my father's interest. Again. While my heart aches like I used to imagine Mother's did right before the end, the greater part of me is relieved.

He's forgotten what I'm capable of.

And I'm not entirely certain he deserves to remember.

CHAPTER 10

TESS

❧

35 L'avenue du Bois de Boulogne, Paris

"BREATHTAKING," ANNIE SAYS. "YOU ARE A TRUE VISION, Miss Ford."

She stands behind me in her own stunning emerald gown, surveying me through the cheval mirror as Belot's maid secures my hair with a few final pins.

A vision, indeed. I barely recognize myself, though my glamorous reflection provides an odd kind of comfort, perhaps because no one would suspect this high-society girl of scheming to flee tonight. I'm set to stun in my extravagant silk cream gown, my skirt's gilded roses sparkling like mica glitter. My chestnut hair swept up in lustrous Marcel Waves; neckline dripping with dazzling ice.

"Madame Aurand," Annie says, "would you be so kind as to give us a moment?"

Madame Aurand's eyes narrow. *"Tres bien,"* she finally concedes and slips out the door.

Annie turns. "Are you ready?"

I let out a juddering breath. "As I shall ever be."

"William and I spoke last night. He's in an understandable state of consternation about it all—my father's and Theo's involvement with the Fraternitas, their endless lies—but he's agreed to help, just as I knew he would."

I bow my head, nodding—humbled, elated. "Quite brave of him. Of both of you."

"René Cellier, too, is ready at the Louvre. I spoke with him yesterday. He's to stow you with a consignment headed for the Egyptian Museum and plans to alert Dr. Ford through safe museum channels." Annie gestures toward my neckline. "And you'll have those diamonds on hand to sell, should you need them."

She sweeps forward, taking my hands. "Oh, Tess, everything is falling into place."

"Indeed," I breathe out, blinking away my sudden tears. "Annie, I . . . I owe you my life. How can I ever repay you?"

"Don't be silly; it's the right thing to do." She holds my gaze. "Besides, I know you stand with me. That you and your father will help ensure the Fraternitas never gets the Crown."

She bends to smooth one of my dress's silk roses.

"Very lucky you and your sister are the same size, by the by. This gown fits like it was made for you."

I startle at her comment, looking anew at the mirror, my reflection; understanding now the true source of its solace. The illusion of Lila is so exact, in fact, it feels as if I can reach out and hold her hand through the glass.

Nodding tightly, I look away. How I pray tonight is a success, that I might see Lila incarnate in a matter of days, tell her how I've missed her.

Together, Annie and I float down the corridor, past Belot's tall casement windows, a parade of eerie portals to the deep blue evening sky. I get the strangest sensation of walking down a lushly carpeted gangplank as Belot's staff watches, cowering, from their various posts along the hall.

We sweep around the balustrade, the mammoth Regency chandelier casting brilliant specters across the foyer. My pulse quickens when I spot the rest of Belot's guests below, waiting to depart.

Annie and I join the ladies clustered near the stairs, who are gossiping as to who shall be in attendance tonight, tittering about the latest social scandals. Lady Leona looks predictably gorgeous in her sleek black-and-white evening dress, while Mrs. Avondale has chosen a pink gown of Liberty silk. Beyond them, huddled closer to the door, are the men. Mr. Hendricks holds court as always, his face flushed, hands waving maniacally as he airs one grievance or another. Theo Davies looks on coolly beside him, like the watchdog he is, I suppose. Dr. Belot, pasty in his white tuxedo. Lord Tembroke, in a Victorian tailcoat and topper, already slinging an amber-colored cocktail.

The large crowd shifts and parts.

And there is William, leaning against the vestibule entry.

My stomach flips at the sight of him. He's staring at me, his gaze searing, though I can't quite place the emotion behind it. Regret, perhaps. Or grief. His old concerns about a life without passion—of running Hendricks Industries—pale in comparison to the newly revealed depths of his father's depravity.

Or perhaps he's on edge. Terrified about tonight's risks, like I am.

William crosses the room. He looks just as dashing, magnetic, as he did the first night I met him. Well-cut tuxedo, inky-blue eyes shining, black hair slicked back like a stage star.

He slides beside me, gaze roaming over me. "Miss Ford. You're . . . perfect."

I can't help but blush.

"Perfect, am I?" I force a laugh, bucking my nerves. "And here I thought men of literature were prone to flowery, overlong descriptions."

His eyes, smoldering now, fix upon mine. "Why use a dozen words when there's only one that truly fits?"

My breath catches. For once, I have no retort.

Glancing around, he clears his throat. "Tell me, Miss Ford, were you aware that tonight's gala is being held in the Louvre's antiquities wing?"

His change in topic and tone is so abrupt, it hits like a slap. "Ah, no. How lovely."

"I remember one story you told me about the . . . *Wilbour Papyrus*, wasn't it?" William says. "The Egyptian spell book, if I recall, for snakebites and other such ghastly afflictions. I've heard it's on loan at the Louvre. I should very much like to see it."

I study his face again, my mind's wheels churning. Because this is our script, isn't it? Our cover story for tonight, Annie's plan. William and I sneaking away, under pretenses of touring the museum. He must be laying the groundwork. A smart plan after all, as we're surrounded by Fraternitas ears.

I hasten to play my part. "I've heard the Louvre's collection is extensive. Palettes from Nekhen, Middle Kingdom jewelry, the *Seated Scribe*."

"Then it sounds like we must find time to slip away."

I take his arm, trying to ignore the warmth that ignites under my skin where our arms lock, where his body presses into mine.

Forcing myself to focus on the plan. Because this is truly happening. I am leaving, escaping Davies, Hendricks, the rest of these blackguards, tonight.

I have to bite back a battle cry of elation.

The crowd filters out to the courtyard, where three horse-drawn coaches wait in front of Belot's fountain, glowing under the courtyard's lampposts like liquid moonlight. William and I join the Davies party in the second coach. And then we are off, trotting through the 16th Arrondissement, the cool, brisk evening air whispering "freedom." I feel breathless with hope as we turn onto the bustling Avenue du Bois de Boulogne, the Arc de Triomphe shining silver as we pass.

As our carriage *clip-clops* along the River Seine, Davies breaks our silence. "I'm so glad you're feeling better, dear Annie. Tonight's gala wouldn't have been the same had you been unable to attend."

His amber eyes are piercing, even in the dark of the carriage, as he considers her.

Annie gives a little startle. "Pardon, Theo?"

"Our late luncheon. Yesterday. I'd intended to include you, but your lady's maid claimed you weren't feeling well."

"Right," Annie says breezily. "Much better, thank you, just a passing spell."

"And yet Madame Aurand informed me you weren't in your room when she delivered the meal."

A new tension coils around the coach. Annie had sneaked out yesterday to meet René Cellier at the Louvre and discuss tonight. Good gods.

William leans forward hastily. "That must have been when you'd taken the air, Annie. I'd wanted your thoughts on honeymoon plans, remember, and came looking for you."

"Yes, Belot's Blue Room, I must admit, is sweltering." Annie laughs dismissively, covering well. "Took a short jaunt toward the Tower. The fresh air did me good." She throws Davies a dazzling smile. "I'm sorry to have worried you, Theo."

Davies snakes his hand around hers. "Feels as if I've barely seen you since we departed New York."

"Well, you've been working so hard these days," she says brightly, gesturing to William and me. "And these two have been keeping me busy, with ever so much to plan for the wedding."

Davies gives an absent nod, staring out the coach as we turn into the Cour Carrée du Louvre. Apparently satisfied, as he doesn't say another word.

We join the museum's long procession, dozens of carriages curving in one long, glimmering line in front of the Louvre. The courtyard is bustling with hundreds of attendees filtering toward the museum. Ladies in embroidered jewel-toned silk tea gowns, dramatic headpieces. Men in black tailcoats and toppers. So much excitement, energy, welcome chaos.

I take a centering breath as we follow the throngs toward the vaulted entry. As soon as we're inside, William gently steers me toward the outskirts of the crowd.

"A little late in the game," he says, tone raspy, as we pass between the corridor's lofty marble columns, "but perhaps a proper introduction is in order. *Tess*, is it? I'm William."

Our eyes meet.

"I was hoping to call you my knight in shining armor," I breathe out. "But maybe it's a bit premature for that."

We continue toward the ballroom, past collections unfurling like labyrinths on either side.

William's laugh is hard. "I'd like to pretend Annie's revelations were shocking, but I really should have known. '*Use any means to secure Miss Ford*,' my father told me the night of your sister's debutante ball. No particulars about Paris, the wedding, the future—only clipped orders, per usual." He shakes his head. "What a perfect pawn I am."

"You cannot blame yourself for this, William."

"Nor can I keep my head buried in the sand." He sighs, looking behind us, surveying the crowd. "I will make this right, for your sake and my sister's. Theo's obviously on his guard; Annie's taken far too many risks herself."

He leans closer, dropping his voice another octave as a couple sweeps past us. "All we need to do is keep up appearances, at least until my father and his cronies break away for their meeting. Then we can do the same while they're gone."

"Do you know who they're meeting?" I say, studying him again, his new role of ally undeniably alluring.

"Annie said another archaeologist. Hans Adalard Schafer, I believe."

I shudder at the name, recalling the rumors swirling about Schafer in archaeology circles. "He's a peach—resorts to bribery, extortion, violence to achieve his finds. He'll fit right in." I furrow my brow. "Though what do you mean, 'keep up appearances'?"

"The papers will be taking photographs," William murmurs. "There are guests we must greet. We can't give anyone a reason to suspect. When the window comes for you to flee, it must be entirely without fanfare."

I nod, though my nerves are galloping now. "Lead the way, Mr. Hendricks."

He whisks me into the grandest ballroom I've ever seen, the Louvre's antiquities wing transformed. Porcelain vases of roses sit atop tables draped in cloth of gold. The glow of thousands of candles animates the collection's trove of inscriptions. Towering columns, glass surreys, countless relics on display. And in front of it all, couples whirl across a marble dance floor like a living kaleidoscope, not one corner or pillar without partygoers—drinking, laughing, merriment. A dream and a nightmare in one.

"Come," William says. "There's Carl Randolph, an old friend of my father's."

"The sugar tycoon?"

William stops short, sighing. "He's another member of this sinister cadre, isn't he?"

I nod. "As are likely most of the wealthy, self-important men in your father's inner circle."

William shakes his head with an incredulous laugh. "I really have so very much to work through."

We meet the domineering Mr. Randolph and his wife, then weave around crowds of French guests to greet Edward Fane, the King of Coal, and another "family friend" of the Hendrickses. And then a few of William's mother's acquaintances, here on holiday. As we break away from the group, a trio of reporters stops us with questions, asking for pictures.

After the last of their flashes, we sink in simultaneous relief—only to find Lord Tembroke, in his ostentatious white tailcoat, jaunting toward us.

"William, good boy!" Tembroke shouts, raising his glass.

"Keep that smile up," William reminds me through gritted teeth. "He's probably tippled by now. He'll move on quickly . . ."

William trails off as Lady Leona swishes past us, glaring. She keeps on the move toward Annie, who's been cornered by several society matrons a few tables down.

"Another drink will do you good, dear," Lord Tembroke calls after Leona. "Do forgive the countess," he says, turning to us, downing the rest of his drink. "She's just upset, you see, having found out that some of the gentlemen and I went slumming without her last night."

Slumming. These men are truly intolerable.

130

"Ah yes, heard all about the sordid adventure at breakfast." William flashes the earl a forced smile. "Tell me, would Lady Leona have also appreciated the scuffle that ensued over cabaret seats last night?"

"Oh no, no, let's keep that detail to ourselves, good chap."

The earl, glancing at me, pulls his topper farther down on his forehead. Only then do I notice he's concealing a small purple lump near his temple.

"The riffraff has such gall these days. Unchecked entitlement," he adds with a harrumph. "James is right; we must find the Crown before the world falls apart."

My heart races at the mention of the Crown and their turpitude. But the earl is in his own world, snapping his fingers at a nearby waiter, his face breaking into rapture when a glass of champagne arrives in seconds.

"I tell you, dear boy, it is high time that worthy men seized back the control that is theirs by right—"

"Lord Tembroke," Davies interrupts. "We need to speak with you." He throws a loaded glance in William's and my direction. "Alone."

"Ah!" The earl promptly finishes his glass. "Time to meet Schafer, is it?"

"Exquisite timing, Theo," William says smoothly. "I was just about to ask Miss Ford to honor me with a dance."

As Lord Tembroke and Davies break away, William and I head toward the dance floor. The early, yearning notes of "The Blue Danube" fill the room. William offers his hand, placing his other around my back.

He begins to slowly spin me, both of us watching as Davies and Lord Tembroke cut across the ballroom, the pair stopping when they find Mr. Hendricks near a cluster of tables. Mr. Hendricks nods, checks his fancy pocket watch.

William leans in as we continue to twirl, whispering over the vibrant tune, "I do believe freedom is moments away." His lips quirk. "And hopefully not just for you."

I arch a brow as we waltz past another couple. "You aren't implying that you're coming with me, are you, Mr. Hendricks?"

At that, his smile turns unfettered.

He clears his throat, looking away. "Annie. The next step is getting her out of here, though I'm at a loss as to how. She has this mad plan to steal the scrolls and sabotage our father. She's going to get herself killed."

"Not so mad," I whisper as we twirl. "You heard the Fraternitas' plans, did you not?"

"You mean the earl's modest declaration that he deserves the world on a platter?"

"I'm serious. Many Egyptologists, including me, believe the Crown holds *actual* power. If the Fraternitas was to find it, why, it could bring about war, chaos, the very destruction of Egypt—"

"I know." William fixes his inky eyes on me. "I've been torturing myself over it. If I'd only . . . I don't know, woken up, I might have thwarted them back at your Riverside home. Somehow ruined their plan, right at the start."

His words sink in as we spin across the floor.

"Well"—I break our gaze, edging closer as he leads me—"if this is a final confession of sorts, take comfort that you weren't the only one living in denial." I swallow. "My father was obviously mixed up in this too."

"Don't, Tess," he says, but his tone is kind. "Annie told me Dr. Ford took off as soon as he discovered Theo's true intentions."

"Maybe so." I pause. "But for as long as I've known him, my father has resorted to any means and methods necessary to pursue his quest. He doesn't ask questions he doesn't want answers to, and he's never let anything as inconvenient as scruples factor into his plans."

William gives my hand a little squeeze as the music rises.

I lean my head against his shoulder, thinking about the countless times I've made excuses for Dad. Covered for him. Ignored how his dogged pursuits have hurt my family, his assistants, colleagues, rivals. Goodness, the many countries he's pillaged in his hunt. And through it all, I've cast Lila as the enemy, the rain on Dad's and my jaunty parade.

"Sometimes I worry I'm becoming just like him," I whisper.

"You? Unscrupulous? No questions asked?" William reels back, feigning shock. "I rather think of you as a little Spanish inquisitor. Unearthing my true passions with swift efficiency. Cross-examining a room, er, its walls rather, with tenacity."

"Which is my point." I stifle a groan as we smoothly glide between two couples. "That night I met you, there I was, sabotaging Lila's purported future. Acting out like a child after she was short with me."

"If it's any consolation, I've never met anyone so wholly memorable, regardless of who you were pretending to be."

My breath hitches. He brushes a stray lock from my temple.

"What a pair we are." William places his hand on my back again, forcing a laugh. "I was so furious with my father that evening and so positive we'd be disastrous together. But perhaps we might have made a fine match after all."

My heart beats faster than the jumpy tune. "You and I in real life. Ha, can you imagine?"

"Is it really so hard to conceive of?" he murmurs, smirking, before pulling me close again. "Insect dissections in the morning. Duking it out over lunch. Kidnappings—"

"We'd save that for special occasions, William."

"Naturally. For anniversaries. And our children, all enamored by history, mythology, thanks to you."

"Though it's fairly clear *you're* becoming the true storyteller between us."

"On the contrary. I'm only captivated by recent . . . inspiration." He stops, pulling back, searching my face. His eyes, molten now.

The waltz promptly stops. The room cascades into soft, tempered applause that rattles like thunder. All the while, William stares at me, that look in his eyes obliterating the room. In a wonderful panic, I think he might lean in, sweep me into a kiss, right here, despite everything.

He breaks our gaze, sobering. "They're gone. My father and his men." A forlorn smile plays on his lips. "Suppose it's time to say goodbye."

Flustered, I step back as well. "Indeed."

He offers his hand. "Perhaps we might take a look at the *Wilbour Papyrus.*"

We leave the dance floor, snaking through the throngs of lingering couples. Smiling, nodding, as the notes of "The Skater's Waltz" wind through the room. My heart unbridled, now that we've begun our escape. Slipping between tables, past displays of inscriptions, Middle Kingdom jewelry, and pottery under glass.

Steps away from the shadowed interior corridors of the Louvre.

William's arm tightens around mine. "Nearly there."

"Putain!"

We both startle at the profanity, stop, turn, but don't see anyone.

Hurried footsteps boom down the darkened hall.

The voice, louder now. "I told them he cannot be trusted. I cannot work with such an *imbécile!*"

"It's Dr. Belot," I whisper to William, heart plunging like a stone. "Come, we must run for it—"

"Mademoiselle?" Dr. Belot calls. "Is that you?"

The footsteps quicken.

"I must speak with you *immédiatement!*"

I spin, game to run, but William grabs my wrist. "Tess, stop, he's seen us."

Belot's ghoulish, labored breath echoes through the vaulted corridor. "Mademoiselle!"

"Ah, Dr. Belot." William sweeps forward hastily. "How lovely to find you walking the halls. We were just about to view—"

"Leave us, William." Belot steps around him, grabbing me, dragging me back into the ballroom.

I glance back as Belot roughly ushers me toward an empty table, desperation clawing up my throat, a scream teasing, William's somber silhouette frozen in the corridor.

Belot huffs me into a seat, sliding into the one across from mine. "Mademoiselle, this *will not do.*"

He leans forward until all I see are his milky-blue eyes.

"Unlike your father, I live and die by my partnerships, by the people I choose. Sir Petrie, when we were newer to the field. My assistants. Now, Monsieur Davies, Monsieur Hendricks." Belot steals a breath. "I know my weaknesses as well as my strengths, and I am an impeccable judge of capability. Because I must be. Because without *la symbiose*, I am nothing."

My head spins like a macabre carousel. "Dr. Belot—"

"And in all my years of fieldwork, teaching, scholarship," he barks at me, "I have never encountered a mind such as yours. Such limitless potential. I believed that you and I, together, could open doors, move mountains, change the world." He narrows his eyes. "But you should have solved it by now."

"The next scroll?"

"The entire puzzle!"

"You, ah, must understand the past week has been a whirlwind, Professor. I'm planning my wedding, after all, and life has been spent in very different pursuits lately—"

Belot waves away the Fraternitas' flimsy pretext.

"There is a first time for everything," he seethes. "Yes, I believe I've miscalculated. Overestimated. Pity, when you had so much to gain by proving yourself. When so many were counting on us both."

"You can count on me, I assure you. It's all returning . . . slowly."

But I see it in his beady eyes, hear it in his tone. This conversation is a last resort, a final chance, somehow, for both of us.

I scan the revelrous ballroom in a fever, the laughing couples looking sinister now, the looming marble columns inching in.

"I can't understand it," I whisper, blinking back tears, as I do not want to give Belot the satisfaction of seeing them. "I'm missing something. I can't do it, can't . . ."

And then an image floats up from the depths of my mind.

Belot's study. The five jars on his center table. One empty. And one . . . with the remnants of a fourth scroll.

Perhaps that scroll belongs in the middle of the sequence, and that's the very reason Belot cannot solve it, the reason Dad struggled himself.

The sequence I'm working with could be incomplete!

I meet his eyes again.

"We have three scrolls in hand: *Ren*, *Ib*, and *Sheut*. But *Ib* has been impossible to decipher, as you yourself must have found, and I believe that is because there's a gap in the sequence. I had been working on the *Ib* scroll with the assumption that it was the second in the set, but now I believe it to be the third." I square my shoulders, feigning confidence. "I wonder, scholar to scholar, whether a missing piece was lost to time. Destroyed?" I say, selling the lie. "Or perhaps enemies or vandals stole it?"

"Enemies." Belot begins to perk up, visibly intrigued now.

"I assume this *Ib* scroll builds upon a missing second installment. But alas, without the actual second text in hand, I can't be certain." I straighten. "Not to worry, Dr. Belot. I will keep on, best as I can, with the limited resources available."

When I look up, I expect to find Belot in deep contemplation, or even registering some measure of remorse. And yet his face is frozen in rapture. Eyes wide, as if delighted.

"The empty jar," he muses quietly. "One of the scrolls could have been stolen . . ."

He lurches forward with a sickening, worrisome smile. I have to keep from recoiling.

"Mademoiselle Ford. You may well have cracked this riddle after all. *S'il vous plaît.*"

My hand shakes as I reluctantly take the one he offers, imagining now those columns around us roaring, raining down, crashing in a commiserative, furious torrent of stone.

"A dance, perhaps, with an old friend?" he coos.

I nod indiscernibly, unable to speak, barely able to even think as Belot escorts me toward the museum's ballroom floor.

As his clammy hand clasps mine, I spot the Fraternitas filtering back into the ballroom. Davies and Mr. Hendricks lead the charge, followed by the earl, Avondale, and Fane, all of them with self-satisfied smiles plastered across their faces.

The meeting has concluded. Annie's plan has been ruined; my window to flee has slammed closed.

Those tears finally fall as Belot, oblivious, waltzes me across the dance floor.

CHAPTER 11

LILA

❧

The Egyptian Museum, Cairo

"AND WHO IS THIS FELLOW?" MY VOICE ECHOES ALONG the columned hall, though I have tried to keep myself muted.

"Khafre," Alex whispers, nodding to an impressive stone figure seated upon an elevated throne. "Old Kingdom, Fourth Dynasty. It was during his reign that the Great Sphinx was constructed at Gizeh."

My heart leaps at the prospect of seeing the Sphinx, but I don't show it. I'm awed enough by the sculpture before us now. It is an incredible depiction, preserved so perfectly it looks like it was carved last week. The Egyptian Museum's collection as a whole is staggering, many statues so lifelike they startle me into saying "Pardon me" as we pass, small figurines and busts staring out from inside their glass boxes, thousands upon thousands of artifacts.

I'm surprised to suspect I could stay here for days and not

grow bored. But I'm too irritated to admit it. "How long is Father going to keep us?"

Alex tears himself away from the aproned figure he's examining. "Not long, I expect. He'll want to get to Samy's rather sharpish."

"And what or who is Samy?" I cross my arms.

"General Samy Pasha. Old friend of your father's. He's graciously offered to accommodate us during our stay in Cairo."

I stroll into the next gallery, a display of fragmented papyri under glass. Under other circumstances I would be eager to examine them, but today I feel only the strain of playing tourist while Father discusses my sister's fate with a stranger.

The museum director. Gaston Maspero. Another old friend, apparently.

"So we have a place to stay." I breathe, quelling a wave of dizziness. "Until when? Until what?"

Alex reaches from behind me to clasp my hand.

I glance at him, startled, before realizing the gesture wasn't tender. He's keeping me from being trampled by a stream of large sculptures carried by sweating workmen.

A pink-faced man suddenly shoulders past us, shouting at the workers, "Damn it, two of you on the Nofret!" He points to a sculpture precariously balanced on the shoulders of a tiny man who looks about to buckle under its weight. "If you break that, so help me . . ."

"Another friend of Father's?" I grumble.

Alex smirks, shaking his head. "Howard Carter. Foul-tempered on a good day. I'd say you get used to him, but . . ." He grimaces. "Best we stay out of his way."

We slink discreetly around the corner, into a corridor with a lower ceiling, affording space for offices above, no doubt.

"How's the *Ren* decipherment going?" Alex asks, an attempt to small-talk me out of my sulk.

"The first scroll? Finished it ages ago."

I amble past him, gazing out the windows at the city beyond. When we arrived this morning after two days' journey via felucca, my first impression of Cairo was of its shape—flat and sprawling—and its surprising modernity. The view through the museum window now showcases hotels built in the Beaux Arts style and a bridge over the Nile that swings open with impressive engineering, nothing of antiquity discernible, except vaguely, at a distance . . . statues of lions? Are those ancient or new construction?

Once again, I am abashed. How provincial of me to imagine Egypt as an ancient site preserved under glass. Cairo is a modern city. Egyptians live here, people of the current age, more alike to me than different by virtually every measure.

I turn back to find Alex gawking in my direction.

"Show me," he blurts, then clears his throat. "Your translation. May I see it?"

I must admit I'm pleased by his professional interest. *Is this what it's like to work at a university?* I wonder as I pull from my jacket pocket my neatly folded translation.

Alex takes it from me as gently as an original papyrus.

"This is good work," he murmurs. His eyebrows dart up and I peek over, wondering what's surprised him. "And quick. It took Warren a good ten days, but to be fair, his work was bifurcated by our flight from camp and hasty trip to New York, and the first scroll *is* by far the most straightforward."

"Yes, the next scroll. *Ib*, the second—"

"Third," Alex corrects.

"I've been trying to work it, but the phonetic markers come out garbled. And the scroll after that is even more fragmented."

First scroll ~ REN

Seek you the snake, small lowly man.

First ride you in Hennu into night, where the Aten,
he who drivest away death, keepeth his rest. The
glorious rays of the One God bury themselves from
human sight, and in that place remains only dust,
the end of man and the beginning. Find you then
the chamber that is hidden, make offering to the light
and the light will shine upon the tomb where sleeps
the snake of the gods. Then let fear quicken in your
loins, for the unworthy will perish in their quest,
burned in the serpent's gaze.

"That's how we arranged them, in order of coherence." Alex sounds sheepish, suggesting this is not the most academically rigorous way of doing things.

But I reach for him in my excitement. "I think that's exactly right."

His bicep contracts beneath my fingertips. I pull away, blushing.

"There's a logic lurking in the background," I say, holding my hands safely behind my back as we stroll. "A progressive cipher, I'd wager. But there seems to be something missing. An intermediary key between the first scroll, *Ren*, and the second, *Ib*."

"Third," Alex corrects again, and this time I listen. "We believe *Ib* to be the third scroll of the four. *Ren*, *Ba*, *Ib*, followed by *Sheut*. The last, reduced to dust, is presumably *Ka*."

He watches, smirking slightly as my eyes widen.

"There are four scrolls?" I breathe. "And the remnants of what may be a fifth? But there are only three texts transcribed in your notebook. Where is the missing intact one? The second in the sequence. *Ba*?"

Alex parts his lips, clearly grappling with whether to answer, but no need. I have it.

"The satchel," I say, triumphant. Too triumphant—my voice echoes again. I drop it to a whisper again. "That's the keepsake Father took from the site. They can't solve the scrolls without it."

I turn away, muffling myself. Something is tickling my senses, the suggestion of sound vibrations behind us, along the wall.

"They don't know it's missing." Alex sniffs, adjusting his spectacles. "I was the one to inventory the site and they were too busy treasure-hunting to take note of such mundane relics as canopic—"

"Shh!" I hold up a hand.

He blinks in apparent offense, but I motion for him to join

me deeper into the gallery. Once I've found the spot, I point upward, toward an iron vent in the corner of the plaster ceiling, so he can hear what I do: Father's voice, clear now.

"Listen, old buddy, it's simple economics. Right now the Met's the highest bidder."

There's a quirk to the acoustics; if we stand just so, we can make it out as if we were standing upstairs, right beside him— exactly where he insisted we not be.

With a grimace of capitulation, Alex joins me in the corner of the gallery. Together, we tilt our heads in the correct orientation, breath held.

Someone else is speaking now. French-accented. "But surely in exchange for our assistance with your daughter's rescue from the Louvre—"

I blink at Alex, heart pounding.

Father interrupts. "That's a separate matter. A personal favor."

"A dangerous favor," the Frenchman grumbles. "Why not have her sent to the Metropolitan Museum? Closer to home, *non?*"

"It's not my call," Father grumbles back.

"Yes, yes, your man on the inside. Better by far for you to get the Crown than them. But listen to me, Warren. If it is real . . ." Father lets out a low laugh, but the man cuts him off.

"Then this is its home, and I will ensure it remains here through diplomatic means."

Father's next laugh is sharper. "'Diplomatic'? As in the Agency."

The Frenchman grows huffy. "Can you not understand that it is an Egyptian—"

"All I understand is I've got bills to pay. Hell, Gaston, I'd love nothing more than to live in a world where scholarship was funded entirely on good intentions. But you and I both know that ain't this world."

There follows a long, long silence, in which I can hear only my own heart. My eyes dance to the dip in Alex's throat, watching it pulse. He's listening, hard. And he's not happy with what he's hearing either.

"*D'accord*," Gaston says at last. "We will outbid New York, London, anywhere else. Only keep me informed."

"Good man." A creak sounds. They've both stood.

"And where will your next expedition take you?" Gaston asks in a much more collegial tone.

"You know me. I've got a couple leads. Cyprus. Nepal. Nothing Egyptian." Wryness creeps into Father's tone.

Gaston chuckles. "That is music to my ears."

Their footfalls suggest movement onward, and their voices are lost to us.

Alex pushes off the wall, stalks away.

"Was that the museum director?" I whisper as I follow after him.

He nods, curt, avoiding my eyes.

"I cannot believe, with Tess kidnapped, Father's up there trying to sell the Crown. Business as usual." My words sputter out of me like flames. "And it does belong here, you know. Not in New York, certainly not England."

Alex glances nervously at the door, waiting for Father to stride through.

A wild impulse strikes me.

I rush to Alex, clutch at his elbow, and whisper, "What would you do with the Serpent's Crown? If you were to find it, instead of him?"

Alex answers calmly, readily. "I'd make my name with it. Establish myself. Use my position to do as much good for this nation as I can."

"An Egyptian Egyptologist. First among peers. I can see it."

144

"And I would never in a million years sell the Crown off to a Western museum." He shakes his head, bitter. "There's no sense in dwelling on daydreams. No one but Dr. Ford can solve these scrolls."

"I can." I peer up at him, unblinking. "I just need the one in the satchel."

The echoing booms of rapid footfalls announce Father's arrival, but I keep my eyes locked on Alex, watching him take in what I'm asking him to do.

"Good news," Father calls out, startling both of us into turning. He's waving a letter in the air as if trying to kill a mosquito. "Your sister's getting out. My man on the inside came up trumps. He'll smuggle her from the Louvre and bring her here."

"Tess is in Paris?" I blink, struggling to fall into step beside him as he passes. "But . . . when is this happening? How?"

"It's all in here, straight from my contact. She'll be with us in a matter of days."

"I don't understand." I squint, trying to make out the words in the letter he's clutching. "What's the exact plan? Is there a backup contingency or—"

"Don't worry your pretty little head about that." Father gives my braid a tug.

I find myself utterly speechless with indignation.

As we step out into the museum's courtyard, baked dry by Cairo heat, he has the further gall to turn to me and chuck me on the cheek.

"I've got it all handled. Only thing you need to worry about is smartening up. Because tonight . . ." He strides out before us with arms extended, blotting out the view. And then, to cap it all, he shoots me that rascal's grin. "You'll be dining with a legend."

CHAPTER 12

TESS

❦

35 L'avenue du Bois de Boulogne, Paris

"TERRIBLE LUCK, THAT'S ALL," WILLIAM SAYS, VOICE soft with feigned assurance as Annie paces fitfully among Belot's library shelves. He looks between us earnestly. "But we will find another way, another window of time."

"And yet time is running out." Annie shakes her head. "What was Belot even doing, wandering the halls at the gala? He was supposed to be in the meeting with Schafer!"

"Schafer is clearly a rival, not a collaborator," I say glumly. "Belot was palpably worried about getting cut out, which was why he must have stormed out of the meeting and came looking to berate me in the first place."

I shudder, recalling Belot's grotesque, gobsmacked smile at the gala after I'd realized there was indeed a gap, a missing scroll in the decryption sequence.

William must misinterpret my trembling because he gently

takes my wrist, inspecting for damage. "Belot could have been a sight more gentlemanly with his supposed protégée."

I try very hard to ignore the sparks erupting at every point he touches. "I've been in worse scuffles."

William stifles a smile. "Oh, of that I am sure."

"I'm positive Theo's onto me," Annie mutters as I quietly pull away. "I tried to sneak out yesterday to see René Cellier, explain what happened, ask what can be done, but Theo has refused to leave my side since the gala. At least he's gone off again to the Louvre tonight. I can hardly stand being near him anymore."

"Sister," William says, placing a hand on her shoulder, gently halting her pacing.

She looks up at him, pure terror etched across her face, her ivory skin now bone white. And though I'm only in this mess because of their family, the danger I've yanked her and William into pummels me with guilt.

"William's right," I say, glancing at him. "We'll find a way. There must be some other means, another moment. And, Annie, any such arrangements must include you coming with me."

Annie's laugh is hollow. "Theo would track me to the ends of the earth for my betrayal. I'd only be placing you in jeopardy by leaving with you."

"Maybe my father can help," I press. "He must. We are in your debt. René can smuggle us all away, out of France, somewhere no one would ever think to look for us. It's easier than you might think, to disappear."

"My mind keeps running in circles." Annie groans, rubbing her temples. "Trying to see a way through. A way we might emerge from this unscathed."

She looks up, sobering, shakes her head. "We should join the others. They must have gathered for drinks by now." She smooths her blue silk evening dress. "Come. All we can do now is work to temper suspicion."

We leave our clandestine sanctuary and find the rest of our party in the parlor, cocktail hour already in full swing.

William takes his leave to join the men clustered near Belot's cut-glass windows, where Lord Tembroke animatedly regales his cronies with a lively story. Edward Fane and Carl Randolph have also joined for dinner tonight. William's father and Dr. Belot, though, are nowhere to be seen. Perhaps they accompanied Davies to the Louvre. That would be one silver lining amid tonight's gloom.

"Ah, Annie," Lady Leona coos as we join her and Mrs. Avondale, the two lounging on the rounded-arm chenille sofa and high-back chairs near the fireplace. "We were just bemoaning how uneventful the gala was. Don't you agree?"

"Oh, I don't know," Annie says breezily as she accepts a glass of champagne from the butler. "I found it quite full of surprises."

"Excitement follows you everywhere, doesn't it?" Lady Leona strokes her blonde high pompadour, then fixes her haughty gaze on me. "And what about you, Miss Ford?" She throws Mrs. Avondale a conspicuous wink. "Were reporters hounding you and William, eager to hear all about your *engagement?*"

Beside her, Mrs. Avondale smirks as she sips her glass.

So they know. These two are Fraternitas women through and through. They're waiting for me to be killed, as if my predicament is some perverse kind of theater.

For a moment my mind goes blank. What vultures they are, goading me, delighting in my purported ignorance.

"We were just discussing wedding details, in fact," Annie answers for me. "Lila's been so busy, you see, helping my husband—"

148

"Yes, yes, this scholarship everyone's always droning on about. They're off again, aren't they, at the museum?" Leona's full lips pull into a mock frown. "Poor Annie. Theo leaves you often." She taps Annie's hand resolutely. "Not to worry. My dear Bertie will safeguard you tonight."

Before either of us can respond to the vicious gleam in Leona's eye, Belot's footman sweeps in, announcing dinner.

"You might want to prepare yourself," William whispers, joining my side as the guests filter out from the parlor. "The last time Lord Tembroke hosted a dinner, he ended up in his fountain. He was just boasting about ordering up a dozen bottles from Belot's cellar, so safe to assume tonight's getting out of hand."

"After these past couple of weeks, I'd prefer something stiffer than wine."

William throws me an amused smirk. "Brandy?"

"Whiskey is actually my spirit of choice."

"Mine as well." He fixes his inky eyes on mine. "Let's hope one day we might have those whiskeys, far, far away; this whole affair a distant dream."

A twist of longing coils around my abdomen at the notion—of not just living to see a future but one so rosy I'm toasting whiskey with William Hendricks in it.

We turn into the dining room, which is resplendently set with gold linens, glimmering china. Sumptuous candelabras and exotically arranged bouquets of green, blue, and red blooms.

We find our seats together down the table, William on my one side and, alas, Lady Leona on my other. Annie is seated across, sandwiched between the visibly tipsy Lord Tembroke and Mr. Avondale.

Dinner, per usual at Belot's, is a parade of extravagance, a first course of champagne and oysters, a second of soup and sherry. The sherry, as William anticipated, soon gives way to glass upon glass of Château d'Yquem, and with it, polite tête-à-tête surrenders to raucousness. The earl has appointed himself the group's default grandee, given Mr. Hendricks's absence, monopolizing the conversation with boasts of the men's recent exploits through the city; their prior adventures abroad; even how he and Leona came to tie the knot. Lady South Slope of Boston sounds far more strategic than I'd realized. I make a mental note to remember that. All the while, Belot's sommelier fills our glasses.

"And I must propose a toast," Lord Tembroke practically shouts as he waves his glass, his thick gray mustache wriggling over his grand smile. "To the beginning of a new era. One of reason, balance, and proper order. An era where the world is finally made right again!"

At this, all the men around the table—Mr. Avondale, Fane, Randolph—raise their glasses with rambunctious, animalistic hurrahs.

I catch Annie's gaze. She only dips her head, disgusted.

"Excellent selection, Lord Tembroke," Carl Randolph muses, swirling his ruby-red glass. "As were the selections before, I must say. You've got a keen eye for pedigree."

Lord Tembroke finishes his glass with a satisfied cluck. "Far easier when your host has a limitless trove, I assure you. Monsieur Belot's collection spans the cellar stairs to the catacombs."

I nearly drop my fork. Did I just hear him correctly? *Catacombs?*

Glancing across the table, I find Annie staring, wide-eyed, clearly also processing this revelation. I lean back in my seat, heart thrumming.

If Belot's manse has an entrance to Paris's hidden cemeteries, it could very well change everything. The legendary labyrinths, once used to bury the dead, sprawl across the city's various arrondissements. If I—if *we*—could somehow sneak into the cellar, we'd have a fighting chance of truly escaping, hiding, fleeing the city limits unseen!

"His collection even rivals Maxim's, I'd say," the earl continues as he stabs at his haricots. "Though the cellar reminds me a bit of Cabaret du Néant, truth be told. Tad Gothic. You gentlemen will see for yourself tomorrow."

"Lord Tembroke." Mr. Avondale laughs uneasily. "Need I remind you, we are in mixed company."

"Quite right. Apologies." The earl waggles his bushy eyebrows. "Can't divulge all our sordid secrets to these proper ladies."

A footman clears my plate as yet another crystal goblet is slid beside my place setting.

The conversation begins to roam—to the best vineyards, recent trips to Provence—but my gaze stays firmly fixed on Annie, who is pointing discreetly at the dining room entry.

Beside me, William lets out a low breath, murmuring, "Annie wants to meet. In the parlor. Follow my lead."

He stands abruptly, commenting in a louder tone, "Bit too much to drink too fast, I agree, Lila." He dramatically offers his hand.

I look around, wary. But no one is paying attention to us. The men's faces are ruddy, eyes loose, full wineglasses waved around like little red flags of surrender. Even the women are visibly inebriated. Beside me, Lady Leona slurs, with ridiculous fervor, that Mrs. Avondale "hasn't lived" until she's attended a séance, while Mrs. Avondale herself appears seconds away from plunging face-first into her vegetables.

William adds, "Respite in the parlor may do us good."

And then we are off, whisking through the dining room, past the footman, into the parlor. Annie joins us in minutes. She shuts the door behind her.

"I cannot believe it," she says breathlessly. "The Parisian catacombs have been under our feet this entire time." She paces in front of the parlor's marble fireplace. "A more dangerous plan than the Louvre, but we've reached the point of desperation. And with the cats away—"

"The mouse might run away," William offers.

Annie clasps her hands. "Precisely!"

"Is there any chance Lord Tembroke was lying?" I say, unable to believe this swift turn in luck. "Attempting to lure us into a trap?"

"You give him too much credit," William says. "He's out of his mind right now."

"And yet Tess makes a good point." Annie stops pacing. "We must confirm before hinging her life on the earl's pontifications."

William gives a curt nod, striding for the door. "I'll check the cellar."

"I'll come with you," I add quickly.

Annie blocks us. "Far too suspicious, the two of you roaming around again."

"And less so if you do?" William asks incredulously.

But Annie will not be swayed. Indeed, she has that manic, self-assured fervor about her that I've borne witness to before, when she was trying to sell herself on her own ideas.

"I've been a guest in this maze of a mansion before, remember?" Annie says. "And have a better chance of remaining undiscovered than either of you. I won't be but a moment."

William sighs. "Annie—"

"Should anyone catch you in here, you and your fiancée

are . . . sharing a stolen moment together." She sweeps past us with a wink. "Wish me luck."

Then she slips round the door and closes it.

"Well then," William says grimly. His eyes fall upon Belot's serving trolley. "Perhaps it's time for that stiffer drink?"

Letting out a resigned sigh, I nod, following him, watching as he pours from an amber-colored decanter into two glasses.

"She's always doing this," he mutters. "If I'm guilty of burying my head in the sand, Annie simply rushes into the tides, throws herself at the sea gods, without another thought."

"Siblings can be wholly infuriating."

He takes a gulp. "An understatement."

"Though she means only to protect you," I say. "Lila does the same, her 'help' sometimes enough to send me screaming."

That sobers him. "I'm sorry. Raging on when, here you are, without your sister." He squeezes my hand. "This situation has just rendered me so helpless, so twisted up . . ."

His eyes fall upon something just over my shoulder. He glances at me with a new touch of recklessness. "Perhaps true respite is in order."

Before I can ask what he's implying, he briskly sets past me, stopping at the phonograph near the fireplace.

I scoff. "Are you suggesting we dance right now?"

"Good a reason as any for being in the parlor," he mumbles after finishing his glass. He bends, his muscular physique flexed in his fitted vest and pleated shirt as he hastily fishes through the device's lower cabinet. "If someone comes looking, wonders why we've dallied, at least we have a believable ruse."

He places a record on the turntable. In seconds, "The Blue Danube" gently hums through the room.

William turns, features softened now.

Our eyes meet.

The waltz from the gala. Our dance together, the one I found myself troublesomely thinking about, aching about, as I lay alone at night.

"Oh, a ruse, is it?" I say, unable to quell the flutter in my voice.

He shrugs, though his gaze is searing. "You, in that gown, made quite a lasting impression."

I take his hand. The air in the room is now so charged it could carry an electric current. We slowly spin, without another word.

I try to close my mind, quell my heart, ignore it altogether. Because right now I want nothing more than to return to the gala, that lost moment when I'd bet my hand William was going to kiss me.

"What are you thinking right now?" he whispers.

"Likely best if you don't know."

"I'll come clean if you do."

"What I always think about," I whisper back. "My insect collection."

He stifles a snort. "So it's to be more stories, then?" he says, slowly twirling me. "Have you heard the one about the poor chap who stood to inherit Hendricks Industries . . . until he abducted his perfect match?"

My heart jumps—soars—at that, fear and delight coiling through me like the staff of Hermes.

"Perfect match, am I?" I manage. "I'd say that's awfully inconvenient, seeing as your father's men stand to kill me."

"Truly torturous situation."

"Tortured, are you? Poor baby."

"Ever since the first moment I met you, I've been plagued."

"Oh." I laugh. "You made it abundantly clear that you loathed me that night."

"*Loathed* is a strong word. Besides, despite all your asserted eccentricities, I still begrudged you as the most stunning woman I'd ever seen."

My cheeks are scorching now. "I . . . *may* have found you appealing as well. Physically, at least. You were awfully pompous that night, weren't you. And frantic."

"I wonder why." William's hand trails teasingly down to the small of my back before pulling reluctantly away to change records on the Victrola.

Another song, this one a rag, fills the room.

"Do you remember, Miss Ford," he says slowly, "when you teased about whether I intended to run away with you at the gala?"

"I remember everything about that dance."

He pulls me closer. "What you said to Annie tonight, about how she can't stay here." He swallows. "I keep imagining a different future, for both of us, out from under our father. Free to pursue the lives we choose." He's so close now I can feel his pulse racing under my own skin. "The people we choose."

"Is this another fiction you're spinning, William?" I whisper. "Another fantasy that will never come to pass?"

"If that's what you want," he concedes. "If you tell me that you don't feel this too."

I swallow around my thrashing heart, drowning in all the lies, desperate to come up for air.

I shake my head. "I can't do that."

The dinner party must have noticed we're gone by now. Annie might return disappointed, with news that we've reached the end of the line. And yet I cling tight to the fantasy of this room, the crinkling of the record, the feel of his body against mine. I ache to grab him, pull him into me.

His searing gaze drifts from my eyes to my lips. He lifts my chin, curling his body closer. "I think about you constantly."

I lean closer, daring him. "William . . ."

"There's so much in play. I want to be honorable." He takes a deep breath. "It's just taking every ounce of my self-con—"

I press into him. The kiss, soft at first, but then a mounting hunger slinks around us both. A rush of heat, now roaring through my core.

William's hands slip from my shoulders, press against my back, urging me closer, urging me to lose myself in him.

We shouldn't be doing this. This is madness, true masochism, leaping into any kind of entanglement with him, a tightrope act without a net.

And yet.

What if this is *not* the end? What if we truly escape, all of us, William and Annie with me? Tonight, even, we run, find my family, figure a way to stop his father, end this nightmare for good—

"Where is she?"

We both flinch. The voice is jarring, booming, familiar. Right outside the parlor room door.

"They're looking for me!" My pulse hammers as I pull away from William.

Another roar from the hall: "Answer me, damn it!"

"My father's back," William whispers.

Footsteps charge past the parlor door.

William and I promptly dash from the room, race into the corridor.

A door slams from somewhere deep in the manse, followed by the sound of shattered glass.

A distinctly female scream.

"That's Annie," William sputters, looking wildly at me.

We hurry past the dining room, empty now, the guests having filtered into the drawing room. Inside, I hear the ladies tittering, the speculative whispers.

William and I reach the foyer, spotting Mr. Hendricks barreling down the opposite wing. He slams Belot's study door behind him, but we still hear him bellowing, "You traitorous wench!"

Frantic, we run for the study door.

"Do you not understand? I have eyes everywhere! I own everyone! You stupid, selfish girl!"

William twists and yanks at the knob, but it won't budge.

I hear Davies tsk-tsk. "Quite disappointing, sweetheart."

"And your antics have done nothing," Hendricks keeps roaring. "All you've done is set the trap for us!"

"Father!" William shouts. "Father, stop this!" He cuts off when the door swings open.

Mr. Hendricks's face is sweating, red as a demon. "Oh, we need to talk, too, dear boy." He grabs William by the collar, waving his other hand in my direction. "Edwin, get her out of here."

"No, wait!" I shout, resisting Belot, who has stepped around Hendricks. "William, Annie!"

"It is an *affaire de famille*," Belot seethes, dragging me back toward his entry. "Where are your manners?"

Madame Aurand joins from some unseen, watchful corner and takes my other arm. Together, they haul me up the stairs.

"Dr. Belot, please, wait. *Stop!*"

They throw me into my room.

"Sleep, mademoiselle."

The bedroom door slams behind me. I turn, lunging, mauling at the knob, even though I know with certainty it's locked.

I spin, sinking to the ground, a sob escaping.

Because I know just as unequivocally that all fantasies about running, a second chance with William and Annie, a happy ending . . . are gone.

CHAPTER 13

LILA

Bayt al-Raziya

A GUST OF EVENING WIND BLOWS MY BRAID AGAINST MY shoulder, like a ghost tapping for attention. I look back, shivering, seeing no one, as we step down the lantern-lit pathway to the entrance of a towering mansion.

Perhaps there are ghosts here. The general's home must have been built hundreds of years ago, unlike the colonialist monstrosities I've seen dotting the cityscape throughout the whirlwind course of today, imitations of houses in Paris, London, or New York plunked down with barely a nod to the culture surrounding them. No, the facade of General Samy Pasha's home is a study in contrast—stark, high, flat white walls bordered by balconies and trellises ornately carved from rich mahogany. Walking to this castle feels like stepping closer to the true Cairo, the spirit that yet abides beneath what Alex diplomatically called a *layering*.

The breeze may be rattling my nerves, but the abrupt drop

in temperature comes as a relief. When earlier today the rickety one-horse phaeton we hired in haste outside the museum deposited us in what looked to be the center of a maze of buildings, the temperature was midsummer Manhattan blazing with an added layer of open-oven scorch, and my worn jacket felt thicker than a wool cloak.

Above the discomfort, though, I felt wonder. There were spires and minarets in every direction, in every geometrical combination, mathematical dreams come to architectural life. Between streets, I could catch a glimpse of the old citadel rising above the city like a watchman, the stoic past promising swift consequence should the rowdy present get out of hand. Motorcars sputtered down grand boulevards, narrowly avoiding ramshackle carts and couriers and actual camels. I hardly expected reproductions, but there was something about the nearness of them, the smell, their snuffly noises, that made me realize how far from home we actually are.

And now, I take it, we have come to meet a legend.

Alex filled in a few details about our host on the way over. General Samy Pasha: highly placed in the Egyptian government, adept at collaborating with the British, "preternaturally well-connected" and "completely corrupt."

"And yet we trust him?" I'd asked.

To which Father put in, "That's why we trust him."

Lantern light draws an undulating line along the pathways of a rectangular garden as we're welcomed inside the gates by bowing servants. Father speaks to them in surprisingly fluent Arabic, patting one on the arm. They seem to know him and Alex both.

As we step past, Alex leans in to whisper explanations. "There are two sections of the house, with two different entrances. The *selamlik* is for entertaining, and over there is the *haramlik*, where the family lives."

He nods past an intricately embossed iron door. My gaze travels up and around, soothed by shapes, lines, math everywhere, until I spy a tall woman step out from a doorway just beyond the lantern light and straighten my posture in readiness.

As the servants clang the gates shut behind us, a substantial man of around forty steps into the courtyard, arms stretched wide to showcase his crisp blue jacket, shining green sash, five gleaming medals, glossy black mustache, and a stately tarboosh atop his head. All in all, the effect is formidable, but for all his military bearing, he wears what might be the most unfettered grin I've ever seen.

"Welcome, friends, welcome! We are delighted you are back again so soon."

Father strides forward. "General."

He extends a hand to shake but they embrace instead, clapping each other on the back like brothers as servants hurry to carry off our luggage, meager as it is.

Next the general greets Alex warmly, but upon turning to me, his expression is so taken aback that a flush rises over my cheeks. I glance at the tall woman, his wife, no doubt, with her lilac veil in place, and me here, bare-faced, filthy in my boy clothes.

But the general lets out a booming laugh. "Forgive me, forgive, but I was not expecting a young lady in men's costume. What do you make of this, Nura?"

The veiled woman, Nura, I presume, replies by simply stepping out, hands outstretched to clasp mine. "*Is-salaam alaykum.*"

At her warm greeting, I don't feel so ridiculous after all.

"*Wa-alaykum salaam,*" I answer, grateful.

"And she's got some Arabic." The general motions to me, delighted.

I catch Alex smiling down at his shoes.

"Only a bit," I say. "*'Alilan . . . bas?*"

Nura's gaze brightens like a hearth. "Very good. Just watch, we'll have you fluent in days."

As the general leads the way inside his home, I trail the throng, but Nura motions for me to instead follow her farther into the gardens. We reach a lantern-lit archway set deep in the ancient stone wall. As Nura opens the door, I see henna markings ornamenting her outstretched hand, as intricate as the lattice-work on the house. At the top of a set of interior stairs, a servant waits to take our shoes and replace them with silken slippers.

As strange as it feels to break from Father and Alex, my constant companions for the past twelve days, I do find myself eager to spend time with Nura here in the *haramlik*. We emerge first into an airy sitting room with hanging tapestries and cushions on the floor elegantly distributed beneath a colorfully painted ceiling, a far cry from the dull rigidity of our parlors in Manhattan. There is something about this house that reminds me, strangely, of my old nursery back on Madison. The air is permeated with a strong feeling of home.

Nura removes her veil. She's older than me by a decade or more and has the kind of face I like best, sharp with shrewdness, faint lines etched around her mouth that look like they've come from laughing. I imagine Tess might look a bit like this when she's older.

If she gets to be older.

My stomach seizes. *Stop it, Lila. She's coming home. There's a plan. Only a matter of days.*

"We've prepared the hammam," Nura says slyly. "I had a feeling you would prefer to wash up before catching up."

I'm too grateful to take offense, so I simply nod as Nura thanks a servant bustling past, her arms laden with embroidered towels.

"You speak English so beautifully," I comment as Nura leads

me down the corridor, deeper into the living quarters. "I'm afraid you'll find me an awkward student in comparison."

"English is my third language, so not my strongest." But Nura sounds pleased by the compliment. "I speak Arabic and French. Some German. A little Coptic, although that I did not learn at university."

"You went to university?" I ask, eager as a child.

"Not officially." Her hazel eyes flash with unexpected mischief. "I was educated at home, as is customary, but my father noticed that I was racing ahead of my tutors, teaching them more than they were teaching me. And so he did something that was *not* customary. He allowed me to go to France with my brother, Qadim, who had been invited to study at the Université de Montpellier. Do you know it?"

I nod, rapt. We round another corner.

"I sat in the back of the lecture halls and didn't make a peep, and if anybody asked, Qadim said, '*C'est ma soeur,*' and no one knew how to respond. They thought, *Oh yes, yes, Egyptians bring their sisters with them wherever they go, everyone knows that,* and so I was able to stay and learn as much as Qadim. History, philosophy, law. And all the languages they spoke as well."

"What a father you have." I picture my own practically dragging me from that back row of the Columbia lecture hall by my braid.

"Had," Nura corrects, looking upward. "Yes, he was very special. *Allah yirhamhu.*"

I share a smile with her in sympathy before I ask, "Does it bother you that you didn't get a degree alongside your brother?"

"It's only a piece of paper." Nura shrugs, then she laughs. "But yes, it does bother me. There are those of us making plans for a new university here in Cairo, which will admit women as well as men."

"How incredible." I imagine myself staying here, attending this new university of theirs, perhaps with Nura as my professor. After all that's happened to divorce me from the life I expected to lead—the canceled ball, kidnapping, removal to another continent entirely—it doesn't actually feel that far-fetched.

Nura stops outside an open doorway, through which ribbons of steam escape. There's a light of caution in her eyes.

"Our plans are not common knowledge. The British government does not support higher education in Egypt. Lord Cromer seems to believe it will spur a nationalist revolution, no matter how much he is assured otherwise, and so all donations have been made in secret."

"Have there been many?"

"We have the land, enough funding to at least begin. There have been a few disagreements among some of our esteemed intellectuals . . ." The twinkle in Nura's eyes suggests these intellectuals are of the male persuasion. "But we move forward with hope. The winds of change may yet blow in our favor. And in the meantime, we are careful in whom we trust."

"I won't say a word," I hurriedly promise. Not that I have anyone to talk to anyway.

Except perhaps . . .

"Alex knows," she says, smiling. "He's one of our principal donors, in fact."

A donor? Alex? Heavens. I remember his mother was born into an aristocratic family but hardly assumed any wealth would have been passed along to him. He certainly doesn't act like a man of means. I suppose that's one reason I like him so very much.

"We have not," Nura goes on, almost apologetically, "shared this with your father."

My mind changes tracks. "Is it an issue of . . . of trust? I know you've known him for quite some time."

"It is sometimes hard to know where Dr. Ford's alliances lie," Nura says carefully. "And when one isn't sure, it can be helpful for me to maintain the image of what all our esteemed foreign guests believe an Egyptian wife to be. Quiet. Polite. Rigid with tradition."

"I'm embarrassed to say I carried that assumption myself."

She motions me toward the steam bath with a wink. "Well, you've been here for, what? A few days? I think you can be forgiven. And the truth is, some in my own family are all of those things, so the idea is not wrong, exactly, only lazy. We are women, all of us different. You understand."

I think of Tess again, describing me that way: rigid with tradition. I wish she were here now to see the change in me.

More than that, I pray I won't find her terribly altered by whatever she's facing now.

Nura leaves me to wash privately in the hammam, without instruction, and it proves a diverting challenge to suss out the sequence required for bathing. There are several rooms, the first of which is dry and cool. Through the steam of the second room, I make out mosaic tile and dark wood, eyelets cut from the ceiling to allow in light, but no tub. I find bowls laid out with mittens for scrubbing, fragrant soaps, perfumes, and funny little clogs that I slip onto my feet. Multiple seats have been cut into the walls, suggesting this is at times a social space.

I scrub, then lather, then wash away the past twelve days in a fountain of blessedly warm water.

Upon returning to the first room, wrapped in one of those gorgeous towels, I find two delights: a cool wind blowing from the north and clothing laid out. For a woman. All in the Western style—clean and pressed and near enough to my size. No corset, thank goodness, only practical wear: crisp linen blouse, tweed skirt to midcalf, light jacket to match, and a little straw boater that'll look quite smart pinned just so once my hair has dried.

Fresh and dressed, Mother's comb tucked into the pocket of my jacket, I emerge happily from the hammam and bumble my way back to Nura's sitting room.

She rises from her cushion. "What a transformation!"

"A welcome one." I laugh. "Thank you so much."

With a "shall we?" smile, she extends an arm toward the far archway of the room, opening into an outdoor colonnade. As I follow Nura through it, I smell something savory and spiced and have to close my eyes for a moment in silent prayer that whatever's cooking is intended for us.

A giggle echoes along the tiles. In the evening lantern light, I see two small, grinning faces poking out from a darkened doorway. Nura scolds them, but it's playful, and they clearly take it as such, not budging an inch, peering at me like I'm a giraffe that's been invited inside.

"*Ahlan,*" I greet them, and that sends them fleeing, giggling all the while.

Nura shoots me an apologetic grin. "I had better see them back to bed. I'll only be a moment."

As I wait for my hostess, my eyes graze the stone shelves set deep into the corridor's thick walls. A collection of objects lines the way, whether antiquities or new acquisitions, I can't tell. One sculpture, a green imp figure, reminds me of the Bes figurine Father keeps in his study at home. Beside it, pressed copper in the shape of a hand, worked into dizzyingly detailed patterns. Farther along, a simple carved horn with a rawhide strap attached, then an ink-blue figure of a hawk with a crack running down the center.

"I broke that one," Nura says, emerging from the children's

room. She points to the hawk. "Threw it off the roof of my house when I was six. I was convinced I could get it to fly."

"Did your family have an interest in archaeology?"

"Not really; these are just family heirlooms, passed down through the years. This once sat in the window of my grandmother's bedroom." She picks up a glass jar, green with streaks of yellow. "The light would shine through it and paint the floor while she sat combing my hair."

Placing it back on the shelf, Nura turns away toward the outer stairway and pins her veil into place.

Our footsteps echo softly as we step down into the high-ceilinged space where, I see, the men have already gathered for dinner.

"Is this a *qa'a*?" I ask Nura, motioning to the sitting area. "Am I pronouncing that right?"

Her eyes crinkle. "Very nearly."

Father laughs outright at the sight of me. "There's my girl. I'd almost forgotten what you really look like."

It takes real effort to swallow back the obvious retort to that comment. *Perhaps if you hadn't abandoned me.*

I slide my gaze away to find Alex staring at me and then, just as intently, at his feet.

"*Kushari!*" the general announces as servants pass bowls to each of us. "Your first trip to Egypt, Miss Ford. This is what you absolutely must eat."

I straighten on my settee. "Thank you, General Pasha."

Alex leans forward, stifling a smirk. "*Pasha* is a title, not a name."

"It means I'm a great man," the general says, mock-grave. "It is an honor. I am grateful, but please call me Samy."

Nura takes a large bowl from a servant and ladles out portions. When I rise to help her, she shoos me away kindly. The meal is indeed what I'd smelled and unlike anything I've eaten before, a mix of rice, pasta, lentils, and chickpeas. I manage to restrain myself from licking the bowl as the men dine more slowly, discussing politics.

"How much longer do you think Cromer will hold out?" Father asks.

There's that name again. Lord Cromer, apparent friend to the Fraternitas de Nodum, British-appointed consul general of Egypt, embroiled in controversy thanks to a nasty business in one of the provinces. I read about it in the *Times* last year but can't remember the details.

I glance at Nura, wondering what she thinks of all this, how it relates to her university plans, but she's serving Father another helping, playing at not listening.

"They want him gone there; they want him gone here." The general shrugs. "I hear weeks. He is writing and rewriting his letter. The crates are being packed for him at the Agency."

Tonight, I find, I cannot hold my tongue. "What's happened to drive him out?"

"The oldest story, my dear," Samy says. "Power grows, tips over the edge, and the people fight back."

"That's one angle on it." Father snorts.

I'm not sure whether I've imagined Alex's flinch.

Samy, for his part, looks even more amused. "And what would you call it, old friend?"

Father groans, waving away the question. "Nah, not falling for that trap. You know me. I don't get involved in any of it."

"Some might say that to be alive is to be involved," Samy says. "And to be alive in one's own country is the fullest life there is. I am not one of these Turks, you see; I am *baladi*. I know Egypt through and through, its moods down to its *makhbas*."

I hate to interrupt Samy's speech, but after I hand my empty bowl off to the waiting servant with a shy "*Shukran*," I put in, "What are *makhbas*?"

"Secret chambers," Samy answers eagerly. "All old houses have them."

"How old is this house, exactly?" I glance around, thrilling afresh at the hanging lanterns, inlaid mosaic patterns, latticed woodwork, iron, stone.

"More ancient than the Sphinx." The general's voice goes even more storyteller deep, echoing over the stone floors. "These walls were built a mere—*pfff*—four hundred years ago, but the ground itself is far older. This land was once a mountain, you know, worn down by time."

I roll my eyes with a smile. He is definitely teasing me now.

"But it's true! The very mountain where an important boat came to rest. How do you Yankees tell it? All the animals, two by two?"

A laugh flies out of me. "Noah's ark? It landed here, did it?"

"We have wonders you would not believe, child, right here on these grounds." Samy turns to point behind him. "We have a well."

"A well." I frown around my laugh. "An ancient one."

"Not just ancient. Magical. This is not to boast; magic wells pepper the landscape here. Ask your friend Alexandre; he will tell you."

"I've only ever seen ordinary wells," Alex answers drily, "but I admit, water does feel rather magical after a ride through the desert."

I let out another laugh, and Alex grins back at me, appreciative of my reaction.

But the general's expression is graver than ever. "When you look into this well, it will reveal to you your true love's face.

What do you say, young man? You know where it is. Fancy an after-dinner stroll with Miss Ford?"

I stare at my lap, cheeks flushing hot yet again, wishing I'd worn a veil after all.

Nura says something in Arabic now. The general's laugh dwarfs my own.

"I agree—leave the kids alone, Samy." Despite the lazy humor in his voice, a line has dug its way between Father's brows.

Samy relents. "Let me tell you one more tale, about a relic sought for thousands of years. They say the Crown holds great power, that it corrupts even the one who possesses it. I say it corrupts everyone who seeks it out. Akhenaten, Rameses, Napoleon." Samy fixes Father with a stern look. "Et cetera."

Father's hand twitches against his knee even as he maintains his smirk.

"What is its great power, exactly?" I cannot resist asking.

"If you were a leader, a reformer, or a colonizer . . ." Samy says the last word politely, with a tap on his tarboosh. "If the people were growing angry, if you felt the priests were a threat to your authority, or to use a modern example, if nationalist voices were rising, demanding the self-determination of Egypt, the expulsion of the British, and the people were eagerly listening, if everyone was shouting at you in a language you did not speak, what power would you wish for?"

"I would wish to understand them."

The general cocks his head. "Would you? Or would you want them to understand *you*? To think like you, to do as you would want them to do?"

My mind darts to Tess, the night of my ball, how I wished I could force her to fall in line. The memory hurts. I push it away.

"Is this how they intend to use it?" I ask. "The Fraternitas."

"Most certainly." Samy's jollity drops away. "Before Cromer leaves, before the board shifts, they will use it to assume control. And furthermore, I believe we're only a proving ground for a larger conquest."

"'Larger conquest.'" I stare around at the group. "But that presumes the Crown has actual power. Do you truly believe it does?"

He spreads his hands wide. "In my official capacity as *fariq*, lieutenant general of the Sultanate of Egypt, I must answer no. It is a mere myth."

Alex squints, thoughtful. "Its status as a myth doesn't negate its historicity."

"True, very true." The general reaches for the silver teapot the servant laid out. "Or its significance as a symbol of control over Egypt. I will confess that I went looking for it myself, in my youth. The Serpent's Crown. I thought I could be the one to find it, do good with it."

He hands me a steaming cup of tea. I take it, rapt. "What happened?"

"I gave it up," he says. "'The serpent calls the worthy'; you've heard this expression? In my heart, I knew I wasn't worthy. You see, every time it evaded me, I wanted it more. It shook me, realizing that I was becoming like all the poor, weak souls who came before me. So I gave up the hunt and turned my mind to more important pursuits."

Nura's eyes slide away. I presume she was the object of that last pursuit, with a much more favorable outcome.

"To be worthy is to know oneself unworthy." Samy turns to face Father. "The Serpent's Crown should not be found. By anyone. It simply isn't safe."

Weighty silence descends.

Father breaks it with a growl of a yawn. "Samy. My friend.

Thank you as ever for your lively hospitality. I think I'd better get my daughter off to bed before she drops off right here."

I take Father's offered hand and stand, scowling at the implication. Me. A child with a bedtime.

But then I think of the children upstairs, those sweet, sleepy faces peering into the hall, and turn back to Nura. "We're not putting you at risk, are we, by staying here?"

"Kind girl," Samy says, glancing dotingly at his wife. "I'll tell you a secret: I am invincible. This nation is a powder keg, you see. Any harm to an Egyptian man in my position would set it all ablaze. They are reckless with greed, these brothers of the knot. But not yet *that* reckless."

"We'll be safe here," Father puts in. "You can finally get a good night's sleep."

There's a gruff sort of tenderness in his voice that surprises me into acquiescing.

I bid the group good night, catching Alex's lingering glance last of all, then allow Nura to lead me upstairs to a gloriously cozy bedroom with an inlaid wooden screen overlooking a garden. As I change into a starchy linen shift, I breathe in the scent of the night-flowering plants below.

The house settles into silence around me, and though I am indeed exhausted and the bed extremely comfortable, I find my body too restless, my mind too anxious, to succumb to sleep.

I've rolled onto my side for the tenth time when I hear something strike the window screen. I sit up, and there it is again. Not an insect. A pebble?

Rising from bed, I sneak to the screen and look below to find a man with wildly messy hair standing in the garden, peering up, lantern in hand.

Alex bends for another pebble, but I hiss a "Shh!" and he freezes like a stag.

"Be right down," I whisper.

It's no small feat navigating this maze of a house in the dark, into the tucked-away northwest garden, and from there around towering plants to where Alex's lantern light hovers.

He's standing beside a well, his arms crossed. Nervous.

My own heart begins to drum. Has he invited me here to gaze into the water together?

Then, silently, he passes me something. A sheet of paper.

"I had to rush, as he was washing," Alex whispers. "But it's an accurate copy."

I hold my breath, recognizing the text by the fact that I cannot read it. Not yet, anyway.

"Oh, Alex," I breathe. "You're a dream!"

The second scroll. Dad's stolen keepsake. *Ba*.

CHAPTER 14

TESS

⁓

35 L'avenue du Bois de Boulogne, Paris

I SHOOT UP IN A PANIC, TEARING MYSELF OUT OF A nightmare . . . only to remember that I'm squarely in the midst of another. A real one.

Belot's guest room. Morning. The bright light from the courtyard slices through my curtains like a shard. I must have finally drifted off after pacing and fretting into the wee hours of the night.

Thrusting my covers off quickly, I hasten to change into a simple blouse and skirt, then try my guest room door again.

Still locked.

"You cannot keep me in here forever!" I shout, rattling the knob.

The door finally swings open. Madame Aurand stands primly in the hallway. "Do you need something?"

"Annie. I must see her."

But Belot's maid squares her shoulders, blocking my path. "She is no longer here."

"And just what is that supposed to mean?"

Madame Aurand's eyes turn steely. "*Le chariot* arrived for her at dawn, bound for Charenton asylum."

My stomach plunges to the cellar. "What? As in the sanitarium?"

"*Je comprends* she has not been feeling herself as of late."

I push past her, queasy, into the hall.

More lies, I assure myself. Mr. Hendricks cannot be such a monster as to commit his own daughter. Davies would not commit his own wife!

Belot's housekeeper hurries after me. "Mademoiselle Ford, stop *cet instant*!"

I halt when I reach Annie's propped-open door, gawking as I survey the interior. Her entire room is being ransacked by Belot's staff. A young housemaid sits cross-legged on the floor, upending the bureau's drawers. Another maid yanks dress after dress from Annie's closet with manic fervor, while a third woman scouts under the canopy bed.

"Mademoiselle," Madame Aurand hisses.

Exploiting my fleeting moment of freedom, I hurry onward, past the staircase, to William's room along the manse's other wing, not even wasting time with a knock when I reach his door.

He's inside, one small mercy, across the room, seated on a settee before the fireplace. He peers up at me, wrecked. Eyes molten from crying. Face mottled with grief.

"William," I whisper, throat closing. "Oh, William, I—"

"What are you doing here?" Mr. Hendricks says from inside the room. He steps into the doorway and blocks my path.

I attempt to move past him, to find William's gaze once more, but it is useless.

175

"Mr. Hendricks, yes, I . . ." I swallow, gathering myself. "There's been a terrible injustice committed, which must be made right if you ever expect me to progress on the scrolls—"

The door slams inches from my face.

Madame Aurand catches up to me, huffing. "I have orders, mademoiselle. You are not to leave your room."

"It's all right, Madame Aurand. I've got her."

I turn.

Theo Davies stands, smirking, in the center of the hall. The morning light through Belot's casement windows transforms his eyes into liquid gold.

Madame Aurand gives a curt nod, flying off.

"I assume you heard about my wife." Davies steps forward, letting out a theatrical sigh. "Such a pity, isn't it?"

"You cannot do this," I growl. "Have mercy. She will rot in a place like Charenton and did nothing to deserve such a fate!"

"I beg to differ, Tess."

I let out a telling gasp, startled momentarily by the sound of my true name.

Davies crosses his arms and laughs. "Oh yes. I found all her hidden correspondence. The letters she's been writing to your father. The 'secret escape plan' she tried to enact with René Cellier at the Louvre." Davies steps forward. "The trouble is, Tess, René could be bought, same as anyone else."

I search his face, pulse roaring now. "You must have loved her once. Surely you understand you're sentencing her to torture, a slow death—"

"She made her bed; now she must lie in it," he muses.

I croak out, "Do what you must to me, fine, but don't be monstrous. Spare her!"

"Though the traitor did help us discover your true value." Davies swiftly takes my arm, escorting me back the way I came.

"Your sister clearly got the smarts, didn't she? But everyone's good for something." He slings me into my room with surprising finesse. "Dear old Dad, I'm sure, won't resist saving his little protégée."

"Wait, my father?" I scramble to my feet, turning. "What do you—"

But before I can get another word out, the outside lock has snapped.

❦

All day they keep me in this room, alone, with scant portions of breakfast and dinner delivered to my door. Time passes in a frantic whir of pacing, fretting, regret. I don't even have access to the confounding scrolls anymore to distract from my tormenting thoughts. Annie, my ally, confidante, friend, sentenced to a life of imprisonment, agony, *torture*, because of me. And what of William's fate?

I picture him in his room, his heartbroken face, his father roaring at the door.

What, too, will become of me?

When the sun finally sinks from my window, two young maids come by with buckets of water for a bath. I think about starting a scrap, besting both of them, running down the hall and into the night—and yet how far would I get? The entry? Would I even make it down the stairs?

Quivering, I settle into the frigid bath. Perhaps they're planning to kill me tonight. Really, what use do they have now for me?

My stomach begins churning at the thought. Maybe they poisoned my dinner. Or maybe the Fraternitas have instructed Madame Aurand to murder me in my sleep.

Davies's taunts, though, still prickle.

"Dear old Dad, I'm sure, won't resist saving his little protégée."

I bite the skin around my nails, which makes me think of Annie again. I stop. Do the Fraternitas hope for some kind of exchange: to trade me for the real Lila? They cannot be so deluded, can they? Are they planning to abduct Dad instead?

I sit up, shivering, sudden surety chilling my bones.

I cannot let my father or anyone else fall prey to these fiends.

Dressing quickly in a simple blouse and skirt, I grab my decryption notebook from the bureau, flipping past my manic scribblings and deranged doodles until I get to a clean page, possessed now with the certainty that I must get out of here, tonight. No matter what it costs or what it takes.

I rip out the page and begin hastily sketching possible escape routes. My room door is locked, obviously, and Annie warned there are extra eyes on the house. Not to mention scores of bribed French police, should I make it past the grounds and into the city. But if I can be stealthy, slip outside my window, scale the exterior of the house unseen . . .

I stop my drawing for a moment, conjuring Belot's study in my mind.

That afternoon Annie and I spied on Mr. Hendricks, Davies, and Belot, he mentioned a window latch that wasn't working. Amid all this flurry around the scrolls in the past few days, would he have had time to have it repaired?

Assuming the window's lock is still broken, I could sneak back into his study from the exterior and steal the scrolls, as Annie had planned to do herself. From there, I could dash down into the cellar, navigate the catacombs, and escape the city.

I press my eyes closed, attempting to calm myself, quell my shaking over this precarious plan, and immediately William's face appears in my mind's eye. I can almost hear his voice, too, feel his lips on mine, a bone-shaking pang of regret reverberating through me as I allow myself, painfully, to imagine what could have been, what *should* have been, if only we were given the chance.

Could I somehow get to his room, find him tonight? Could the two of us run away together?

I fold up my hasty map, tasting bile, the bitter tang of inevitability.

I cannot let fantasies be the death of me.

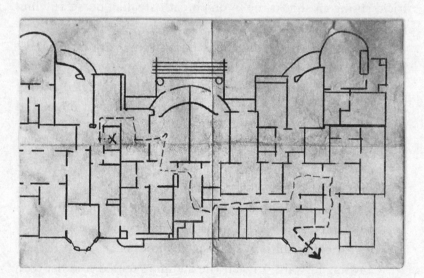

I wait until the clock on my wall turns to midnight, until I can no longer hear any sound outside my door. Then I gather some of my wardrobe's clothes and stuff them under the coverlet in the vague shape of a body in case Madame Aurand checks on me. I decide on the alligator purse from my closet as my getaway bag, which has plenty of room inside to house the scrolls.

Nerves electric, I set toward my front window.

From this vantage, I can see into the cobblestone courtyard

below. All looks humdrum: the sleepy gardens, the fountain, the lampposts, now off. But I know Belot's butler, Georges, is likely standing guard at the door.

I press my forehead against the glass, willing my pulse to slow. This won't be easy. And yet tonight, this way, is my only chance.

I release the window's latch, quietly easing the glass upward.

Gathering my skirt, purse over my shoulder, I heave myself through and then twist to balance on the outside sill. The fresh, frigid spring air shocks me in one breath-stealing burst, ruffling my hem, snaking up my back.

Unsteady, I grip the outside window frame with both hands. Then with my boot heel, I slowly slide the window fully closed.

Shivering, I glance both ways. The first-floor shingled awning of Belot's side entrance can't be more than five feet down and away to the right.

"Let this work." I breathe deep. "Just a hop, skip, and a . . ."

Before losing my nerve, I push off the ledge, leap, and land on the awning with a limb-splattered *thud*.

"Blast," I hiss, scrambling for purchase on the shingles. I need to secure myself or I'm going to slip! I pull myself upward, muscles shrieking, until I've managed a foothold.

Crawling forward, I reach the awning's tented middle, then slowly scoot down around its other side. Halting for a moment when my boots reach the gutters, I scan the back gardens, looking for any of Belot's staff patrolling the grounds.

After deeming the coast clear, I survey the house's exterior, calculating. The closest first-floor window is six feet away, seven tops. I'll have to jump, no question. But if I correctly angle my leap, I can grab the window's top frame and cushion my landing on the sill.

Inhaling, I leap, arms wide, for the frame—but my angle is

off, because my hands slip and feet crash loudly into the window's bottom ledge.

My ankle throbs from impact.

"*Qui est là?*" a voice rings out across the yard.

Wincing, I thrust my hands against the window's sides, pinning myself flat to the outside glass. Holding my breath, I glare through the window.

I've reached Belot's study; I can see it inside. The mirrored display case, the round oak table. The tabletop still holds the five jars that Davies brought over on our voyage. And on the desk opposite: the satchel of scrolls. Its snake insignia glimmers in the moonlight.

"Monsieur Belot?" the watchman calls again, though I don't hear any footsteps this time. He can't see me like this, can he, pressed flat against the house?

I count to ten, twenty, fifty for good measure, enough time for the watchman to well and truly leave. Then I step down carefully onto the grass, scurry over to the study's far window, and test it.

It easily slides ajar.

Pushing the glass upward, I climb inside, onto the study's carpeted floor, and shut the window behind me. Next stop, Belot's desk. I carefully place each papyrus inside the purse's cradle.

Only once I'm out the study door, into the hall, do I find myself stopping, panting, peering into Belot's foyer.

A creak of footsteps sounds from above.

Hurried now. Heavier.

Another watchman. Madame Aurand? Davies?

You cannot risk dallying. Go, Tess!

Through the cellar door, down the pitch-dark stairs—I can't afford to carry a lantern—and onto the basement's cold tile floor.

I blink, waiting for my eyes to adjust, and look around.

Lord Tembroke wasn't exaggerating about Belot's collection. There must be thousands of wine bottles extending like a long procession down the narrow hall.

Dank air wraps around me as I inch forward, the buzzy allure of freedom mounting in my veins.

The collection eventually gives way to an austere, windowless room with a few chairs clustered around an oval table. A lone lantern sits atop it, with some type of red velvet garment draped across a table chair. Beyond the table, I see a mottled wooden door embedded into an expansive stone wall.

I cover my mouth to keep from roaring with relief. This must be the door to the catacombs, Belot's secret entrance to the underground sprawl!

I crack the door open, revealing a windy, shadowed tunnel. The air inside is frigid and rank. Textured, rippling rock surrounds on all sides: floor, curved walls, ceiling.

The Paris mines, I understand, are subterranean cemeteries, an ancient system of tunnels unfurling like a spindly web beneath the city. Countless entry points, exit points, and while it's going to be difficult navigating my way around and out, I am finally leaving Belot's, that much is clear. I'm so elated I start racing, the cumbersome purse beating against my side mercilessly, but I hardly care. Lila, Dad, hell, even Grandmama, *I am coming home* . . .

A sound stops me cold.

I look around.

There it is again.

A groan.

Horror washes over me, an immediate, irrational certainty that there are demons crawling just out of sight, slithering toward me, inches away from the kill.

I reach out a hand to steady myself and nearly screech when

I realize these sinuous cavern corridors are not rippling walls of rock but of bones. Skulls. Femurs. Ribs. Tibiae. Skeletal remains stacked on top of one another as precariously as children's building blocks, teetering, as if one wrong move could send an army of skeletons hurtling toward—

Dad's voice, of all things, sounds through my mind.

Come on, kid. These ain't so different from mummies. Don't be a milksop.

I set myself to rights, absorbing his as-always bristling advice.

Skittering away from the wall, I somehow continue on, hands affixed to my sides now, deeper into the tunnels. But with every step, the groaning grows louder.

Small comfort, but it's definitely human. Speech.

Chanting. Not English, not French.

I look ahead in a panic, and yet see nothing but thick, stale darkness. I spin around. There's no other path to take unless I want to crawl back to Belot's in defeat. No, in order to escape, I must go this way, past the underworld's vampires, through their labyrinth of bones, and into the light.

I follow the bends slowly until the thick darkness transforms into a hazy azure. There truly is light up ahead.

"Éna myaló gia na apofanthei."

Who's down here? The voice is clearer, but the language . . . Gods, do I wish, for the two hundred seventieth time, that Lila and I were together. My best guess is Greek, which I've just started studying this year. The chanting crescendos again, same words, clearer this time: *"Éna myaló gia na apofanthei."* One . . . mind . . . one mind rule?

I take another step. Another. The source of flickering light becomes visible: there's a cluster of lanterns up ahead.

As I duck behind a curve in the wall, the chanting grows ever louder, more certain. "One mind to rule . . . one mind to rule . . ."

Inside a small stone alcove up ahead, forms begin to take shape. A dozen figures, robed in red velvet.

I press my shaking fingers to my lips. They're hooded; I can't make out their faces.

They stand around a thick slab of stone roughly ten feet long, bordered with a collection of mismatched chalices: some gilded and narrow, like vases; others silver and squat; other various styles glittering with jewels.

Cold numbness washes over me, the distinct sense that I've stumbled upon something both ancient and terrifying. Not a monster in the literal sense but something potentially just as monstrous.

Rapt with terror, I survey the alcove's arched ceiling, where a wrought-iron cage dangles above the table. I blink, unsure whether I'm seeing things. Three live lambs have been stuffed inside the cage, their fluffy white frames toppling into one another like dominoes, their collective bleats a staccato to the chanters' chorus.

As I adjust to see better, my shoulder skids against a bone jutting out from the wall, almost sending it tumbling.

I pull back, shaking.

The chanting is insistent, louder now. The robed man on the table's far side turns and steps away.

I stifle a shriek when he returns with a snake, lifted in sinister offering. Writhing, hissing, bending, twisting seductively around the man's forearms, glittering under the low light like jade. As the man lifts the python higher, his hood falls from his face.

"*Eláte brostá o ánthropos!*" James Hendricks bellows. "*Kai metaschimatízete se kápoion pou eínai áxios!*" Step . . . man . . . become . . . worthy?

Mr. Hendricks beckons to another robed figure—Davies, I see plainly—who steps forward into the main fray. Mr. Hendricks lifts the snake. Theo Davies disrobes and—

Oh my gosh, he's stark naked!

I shield my eyes, desperate to keep his full frontal from cementing in my mind.

When I peek again, he's lying faceup on the slab underneath the cage. The collection of chalices surrounds his body in a gilded border.

I must go, *now*, before they finish this grotesque ceremony and head this way to return to Belot's. Still, I find myself unable to move, sickly riveted to the spot.

Davies's face remains still as the stone beneath him, but I can see his chest rising and falling; he's panicked now, breathing tight, as he stares up at the cage. His icy demeanor, for once, shows cracks.

Mr. Hendricks floats toward him like a crimson ghost, python in hand, lifting the snake toward the lambs. The serpent moves in swift coils, hissing, its bulbous body slithering between slats of the iron cage. The lambs' bleats reach fever pitch, the men's chants thundering now across the stone.

"*Éna myaló gia na apofanthei; ena myaló gia na apofanthei; ena myaló gia na . . .*"

The python coils around the nearest lamb. The poor animal screeches, its thin legs buckling as the snake winds around its body and snuffs out its soul.

My limbs strain from crouching, hiding. I'm desperate to stop this, but I can't. If I make a sound, I'm done for; there must be almost a dozen of them versus me.

In a flash, Mr. Hendricks brandishes a knife from his robe and stabs the lambs, finishing them. Blood spills forth in a grotesque

LEE KELLY AND JENNIFER THORNE

fountain, cascading into the cage, overflowing the curves of the iron, trickling like nightmarish fingers onto Davies's bare chest and into the chalices. The men's chanting turns ravished, ecstatic, as the blood pours onto the Fraternitas' newest initiate. That's what this must be, mustn't it? Some unhinged induction, an unholy swearing in?

The robed crowd grabs the chalices, their garments slipping as they hold their glasses toward the cage, eager for more. My stomach turns as I recognize every one of them. Dr. Belot. Ty Avondale. Carl Randolph. Even Lord Tembroke, taking blood to his lips.

Mr. Hendricks rattles the cage of the fallen lambs with a manic grin. "To the triumph of the worthy!"

The men let out a raucous cheer, and then they gulp the blood like they're desperate for it. It trickles around their mouths, chins, curling in red ribbons. My stomach heaves. I need to run; I need to go. I swallow a gag, lunge instinctively for the wall to keep from getting woozy, my fingers scraping bone.

The skull beneath my hand wobbles under my grasp, sending loose stones rolling, dropping, clattering onto the ground.

I freeze. The men do too.

"What was that?" Mr. Hendricks says.

I slide against the wall, flinching, breath ragged. *Please let the darkness swallow me. Dismiss it; it was nothing.*

I close my eyes.

"Did you hear me?" Mr. Hendricks shouts at the others. "Go. Check."

The footsteps come quickly.

Turning, I sprint, mad now, a bat out of hell. The footsteps behind me multiply, cascade, as I dash down the passageway, my pounding cadence beating through the tunnel like a giant's heart. I reach the mottled door to Belot's cellar and yank it open, stumbling past the corridor of wine, snatching a bottle from a shelf and flinging it over my shoulder in defense. The sound of glass breaking, a shocked wail from Dr. Belot as I flail toward the staircase. They're hot on my heels, a red wave surging forward as I careen up the steps.

As soon as I reach the upstairs corridor, Madame Aurand appears like a conjured ghost. "Tsk-tsk, Mademoiselle Ford."

I halt, spinning around, but no, the army of titans is right behind me, advancing.

I rush into the study, slam its door closed, racing for the windows. I shove the glass upward, but before I can crawl through, they're on me, a dozen hands pulling me back, tearing away my purse, pushing me to the ground.

"Get off me!" I lash out, scrambling for purchase.

The circle of faces closes in, blocking out all light, liberty, hope.

Dr. Belot's pockmarked mug floats above mine.

I compel myself to plead, sob, beg—my only hope of salvation now—but my mouth goes dry when Belot grimly lifts a stolen scroll out of my bag.

"*Imbécile*," Belot hisses as Davies muses coldly, "We can't very well go losing you, little lamb."

Davies yanks me past the other men into the study's corner. I writhe to get away, but his grip stays tight. "Let me go!"

"Best to preserve such a crucial key to this puzzle."

I look past him, growling at the others, "I'll shriek bloody murder, wake all your precious wives, I swear it!"

"They won't hear you." Davies kicks forward the large wooden crate that once held the canopic jars. "Nor would they care."

I shake my head viciously, now realizing his intention. "No."

But they've already lifted me, thrashing and kicking, inside.
"*No!*"
The lid comes down with a thunderous *thud*.
I know it won't help.
I scream anyway.

CHAPTER 15

LILA

❦

Bayt al-Raziya

NO ONE IN THE HOUSE CAN HEAR US, BUT WE STILL KEEP to whispers. We sit close together behind the raised bed of fragrant herbs, obscured from the windows above. In the darkness, the scent of night-blooming jasmine ribbons around us.

For five days and nights, this has been our routine at Samy and Nura's home while we wait for Tess's arrival. After retiring to our bedrooms, Alex and I both listen for the plaintive sounds of the Sufi *dhikr* circles echoing across the city before stealing away into the gardens together, staying up until dawn's early light seeps over the garden walls. I wake in the late morning and get right back to decrypting, often in Nura's sitting room while she smiles, offers tea and small round cakes, and dotingly keeps our secret. Throughout my stay here, I've felt feverish with newness, curiosity, thirst for this work.

And other mounting sensations that have little to do with

scholarship. Every day I long for nightfall. For time alone with Alex.

He sits so near me now that I feel the warmth of him, stronger than the glow from the lantern we share. When he peers at my notebook page, his brow furrows with frustration. I itch to reach out and smooth it.

"And you're sure there's no cipher?" he asks for the third time.

"For *Ba*? No. For *Ib* and *Sheut*, most likely, but not for the *Ba* scroll. I knew you and Father had already attempted the *Ba* decryption, and since you're both, well, who you are, I surmised there must have been some obstacle to solving it beyond a straightforward cipher."

"I appreciate your faith in us." He sighs. "All our efforts have indeed been focused upon various iterations of potential ciphers. I'm embarrassed to admit that neither of us contemplated for a moment a different sort of key."

"Perhaps it took an outsider to see it." I shrug. "Or perhaps I was just lucky, but before I even began in earnest, I spotted this."

I point at my notes. The first hieroglyph of the *Ba* scroll, after the title, depicts a man crouched beside a box.

"*Jmn.*" Alex interprets the symbol. "Meaning 'to hide, conceal.' As a matter of fact, this was the only part we've been able to translate, despite the odd syntax: 'To hide the cobra.'" He slides his finger along the first few hieroglyphs. "It's inscrutable after that."

"You've fallen for a trick." I rise onto my knees to show him. "It's not the cobra that's hidden; it's the characters that form the *word* for cobra. Or the cobra goddess, I suppose, Wadjet. You notice those characters never reappear in the remainder of the text?"

I quickly sketch it out for him on the top of my notes: a quail chick, a snake, a semicircle.

"So it's a question of finding where these characters are meant to go and putting them in." I point to a few spots where I've done that very thing, spaced out the existing characters and placed the new ones in to form actual words and phrases.

His eyes widen as he stares at the paper. "How the devil did you—"

"It's a puzzle," I whisper. "I love puzzles."

"As do I, though I'm clearly not so skilled. What sort of puzzle games have you played?"

"Lewis Carroll." I shrug, somewhat embarrassed. "And those silly Wehman's books. Have you ever read them?"

"I can't say I have." Alex laughs quietly. "But my mother used to write out codes for me to solve so she could get on with her work." He shakes his head. "I haven't thought about those for years."

"You don't talk about your mother much," I say carefully. "But then, I suppose I don't talk about mine either."

"What was yours like?" he asks. A skillful deflection, I must say.

"She was . . . lively. Charming. Everything around her was bright and beautiful. She insisted on it. Not luxury, really, just lightness. Fun. Tess and I would do little performances for her, songs and melodramas, and she'd applaud like mad, no matter how bad we were. I think she must have been awfully lonely, with Father gone for such long stretches. Her life wasn't what she'd expected it to be, but she made the best of it . . . until she couldn't anymore."

"Tying oneself to an archaeologist is not the easiest path."

Alex watches me sidelong, as if for my reaction.

I find myself flushing and opt for my own deflection. "Your mother was a pioneer in her own right. She tied herself to no one. Tess used to talk of nothing but the achievements of the great Marguerite d'Auteuil. Someone who insisted on ignoring the naysayers telling her she didn't belong."

Admiration rings in my voice. Perhaps she's a hero to me as well.

"That wasn't an easy path either." Alex gazes up at the star-strewn sky. "Still isn't."

"What do you mean?"

"Well, let's see." Alex chuckles mirthlessly. "In Gizeh, I was the son of *il-khawagaia*, 'that foreign woman.' When she died, before my grandfather sent for me, the neighbors left gifts, food, notes of condolence, but only furtively, on the doorstep. Afraid of catching ill, I'd thought at the time, but now I wonder. And then off I went to France, to Grand-père, he of few words in any language. I spent more time with the gamekeepers and stablehands than with anyone of my own supposedly exalted bloodline."

His voice drips with disdain.

"Didn't you attend Eton?" I ask.

"Yes, Eton." He lets out a rueful laugh. "Where my class-mates had a keen eye for lapses in pedigree. They let me know I was an outsider. Daily. Creatively."

"Goodness, Alex, that's wretched. And, might I add, foolish."

I recall afresh his display of fisticuffs on the *Stoat*. "Who would bully you?"

Alex winks. "I wasn't always this tall."

He is rather tall. If I had the nerve to nestle closer, I could fit right into the crook of his shoulder.

"I began to feel most myself after your father plucked me from the throng at Oxford, remembering my mother, and hired me to join him out here. I've found a passion for my work. For this place, this nation, this cause. And soon I'll forge my own path, strike out on my own expeditions."

"I don't suppose you'd consider a female field assistant." I nudge his shoulder with mine. "For any of your endeavors."

"Are you putting yourself forward, Lila?" He peers at me appraisingly over his eyeglasses. "You'd need a bit of training up. Carrying water and gear, saddling horses and camels, erecting tents."

I hoist my chin, grinning. "I'm a quick study."

"Aren't you just." His eyes linger on mine. "I'm afraid I'll need to know where I'm heading before I can take on staff."

"Well then." I swat him on the arm like a school chum. "We'd better get back to work."

As we try to refocus, my body thrums with restless energy. I feel myself drawn to both the document and the man beside me, competing gravity fields. It's wrenching, intoxicating, and when the garden begins to sparkle with the early notes of the dawn chorus, we stow away our notebooks, pick ourselves up off the garden ground, and start back inside together. I have to fight to keep my pinkie from stretching out to clasp his.

At the doorway to the *haramlik*, Alex turns to me, his elegant throat bobbing. "I know you have young men lining up for you in New York," he blurts. "And this ramshackle life is not what you imagined. But you seem so at ease here, with me . . ."

My heart begins to hammer.

"I'm bungling this," he mutters, dragging his fingers through his messy hair.

"Bungling what?" My voice comes out tiny.

He gathers himself together before he turns to me. "I'd like to call on you, Lila."

I try not to laugh, but the formality in his voice in this context throws me entirely. "Call on me where? New York? Here?"

"Wherever you are."

And I believe it. He'd follow me to Manhattan and court me, but there'd be no need. I'd elope with him tomorrow if he asked me.

"Here, then," I say teasingly. Not in any practiced way. Everything with Alex is easy. "We can start with lunch."

Elation lights up his face. He takes my hand and kisses my fingers and lightning shoots through me. "Until tomorrow, Miss Ford."

"*Adieu*, Monsieur d'Auteuil."

Goodness, it will be hard to sleep, but I must. Tomorrow holds so much promise. The scrolls, tantalizingly close to being cracked wide open. Alex as an actual suitor.

And Tess.

I settle into my soft mattress, anticipation beating bright in my heart.

Tess will be returned to us tomorrow.

❧

Lunch is not exactly romantic, held as it is with our hosts, their family, and Father to boot. We chat about everything but tonight, Father's crucial errand—his rendezvous at dusk, the inside man delivering Tess safely as promised to the Egyptian Museum. I've tried and failed to wrest even the barest of details out of Father, perhaps because he doesn't know them, which leaves me to imagine my poor sister packed into a crate, filthy and cramped and sneezing from the sawdust. But free.

Whatever she's suffered, we can soothe, if only we have her with us.

These are the thoughts filling my head when Alex finds me out in the courtyard later.

"What are you playing with?" he asks from over my shoulder.

"A cipher disk." I'd forgotten I was even spinning it. I offer it to him. "Don't tell me you've never seen one?"

"Not with hieroglyphs!" He rotates the central wheel. "The order is . . ."

"The order of characters in the first scroll, *Ren*, minus repetitions, and with the three Wadjet characters restored as they were in *Ba*. I knew there was a cipher somewhere in the sequence and suspected there was a carryover from one scroll to the next, and . . . so . . ."

Alex's eyes blaze with astonishment.

"Of course," I sputter, "the hard bit was figuring out the inner disk, determining which characters aligned with which in the *Ib* scroll."

"'Was'?" He sits beside me, his eyes landing on my bare feet. I'd taken off my shoes to splash with the children in the fountain. It really does relieve the heat to cool one's ankles. "Don't tell me you've solved it in a morning."

"Not the whole sequence," I protest, blinking. "I've still got *Sheut* to go, and that means a brand-new inner wheel."

Alex sighs, gazing at the rooftop. "I'm not sure what I bring to this partnership."

My heart thuds, impulse striking, and before I can second-guess myself, I kiss him on the cheek.

At his rather delighted expression, I shrug away my blush. "I like the sound of partnership. Anyway, would you like to see it?"

He shakes his head, recovering himself, before he manages to stammer, "Y-your *Ib* decryption? Yes, show me!"

I watch him while he reads, my face growing hot again. "Is it what you expected? The text? It makes no real sense to me, but then, I don't know the first thing about ancient Egypt."

He blinks back up at me, startled. "I keep forgetting."

"Forgetting what?"

"That you're not my linguistics professor."

"Hmm. I'm imagining this professor. Male? Elderly? Tufts of white hair sprouting from his ears?"

"Precisely." Alex grins, motioning to me. "The resemblance is uncanny."

I squawk a laugh, feigning offense, but his hand rises to my cheek and slowly tucks away a loose lock of my hair, and I find myself overcome by an entirely different emotion.

"Uncle Warren!" little Safiya shouts in her lovely lilting English, giving Alex and me time to both inch away and stow the evidence of our decipherments safely in his satchel before Father strides up.

Father swoops Safiya and Ali up, one on each hip, with a jocular growl. A memory comes back—the very same move, the same sound. Tess called him Daddy Bear. He'd growl and stomp with us to our nursery before tucking us both in. It didn't happen often, but when it did, it was heaven.

Tears spring to my eyes. Father sets the children down and turns to me, frowning. "Don't worry, princess," he says, crouching to pat my knee. "I've got this handled. It's as simple as running an errand. Back with your sister before you know it. Enjoy the quiet in the meantime."

He tries to wink, but it looks more like a flinch. Then he stands, offering Alex a handshake.

"Good luck, Dr. Ford," Alex says.

I rise. "You're not going now, are you?"

In answer, he flips his watch and slides it back into his pocket. I fleetingly make out the edge of a gun holster beneath his satchel strap. You'd think he'd leave the *Ba* scroll home for once. Perhaps he insists on wearing it now out of habit.

Samy fills the doorway to the house, arms crossed. "I do wish you would allow me to send along some reserves."

"It's a quick trip. A pickup. I'll be back before you know it." Father's tone brooks no argument. "And besides, you're too caught up in this mess as it is."

Samy doesn't exactly look like he disagrees.

"Besides, I've got a bit of business to handle with Gaston in private," Father shouts over his shoulder.

Business. He means money. Haggling for the Crown. The man never stops!

I try not to let my expression sour as I see him off.

I watch from the front of the house until he disappears through the iron gates and into the city. Then I let out a slow breath and return inside, back to the only thing that quiets the panic in my veins. The fourth and last intact scroll. *Sheut*.

It feels like barely a blink when I hear voices out in the courtyard and peer up from my scribbled page to see shadows stretching long through my bedroom screen onto the tiled floor. I shove the notebook under my pillow and hasten downstairs.

Father. He's back with her! It seems a little early, but then, he did leave with plenty of time, and this must mean it all went to plan.

But when I scrabble downstairs into the front courtyard, it

isn't Father's voice I hear but another familiar one, fraught with panic, speaking French.

"It may be too late," the man says. He's bald. White-bearded.

"Slow down, Gaston," Samy answers in French, calming his guest with one hand while motioning behind him with the other.

Gaston Maspero. The museum director.

"I barely got away," Gaston gasps. "They have guns. The British battalion turned their heads and allowed them to invade my museum. It is an outrage!"

Alex emerges from the house and steps up beside me. I grab his arm, my heart pounding, watching the iron gate open, through which half a dozen Egyptian men gather together at Samy's gesture and fall into line.

The general motions for them to stop, his eyes locked on Gaston. "Who, my friend? Who has invaded?"

"What do they call themselves? Some silly name."

"The Fraternitas," Samy mutters. "Warren's walked into a trap."

"Was there a woman with them?" As if from far away, I hear myself call out, "A girl who looks like me?"

Gaston Maspero turns to me. "As a matter of fact—"

CHAPTER 16

TESS

❧

The Egyptian Museum, Cairo

"GASTON, BUDDY?" THE WARM, FAMILIAR VOICE SOUNDS as though it's coming from the bottom of a well. "Hello? Got lots to discuss!"

My father's voice still lingers, I suppose, from a consoling dream. I shake the last of sleep's grip on me, trying to lift my head, and my neck spasms in pain.

"Blast," I croak out between parched lips. I move to rub out the kinks in my neck . . .

Before remembering that my hands are tied to a chair.

I peer around the room where the Fraternitas have bound and stored me like a relic after hauling me across the Mediterranean and into Egypt. Four days of being stuffed into steamer trunks, locked in windowless cabins, crammed in motorcars. This latest prison is a converted office; my best guess, a room on the first floor of the Egyptian Museum. I can see the shipment tags on the large crates and parcels stored in the far corner; hear the Maghrib prayers from nearby mosques. Smell the fumes, too, from fresh coats of paint.

Though perhaps I should doubt my current acuity, given that I'm imagining voices.

"You hiding somewhere?" And then a laugh—undoubtedly my father's—echoes up from the courtyard outside the window.

Giddy hope consumes me.

"Dad?" I struggle to stand, fighting against my ropes.

Dad, oblivious, laughs again down below, muttering, "Little dramatic, gotta say, closing the museum down . . ." His voice trails off.

For a moment, the silence below is deafening.

"What the hell are you doing here?" he growls.

How quickly my hope is devoured by dread. Who's out there? What's happening?

I revolt against my rickety chair, using all my remaining resolve and then some to fight against my binds and get to the window.

A cold laugh sounds from below. Then, "Waiting for you."

I close my eyes.

It's Davies.

"Dad," I breathe out. "Dad, you need to get out of here."

A crescendo of heavy footsteps sounds from the courtyard.

I let out a stricken whimper. So then it's not just Davies; it's Mr. Hendricks's entire cadre, the Fraternitas. Do they have Dad surrounded?

Desperate to reach the window, I rock my chair wildly, side to side. The rock becomes a frantic pendulum as I propel myself back and forth, attempting to gain a foothold. Back and forth and back again—and then, gods above, somehow I am on my feet.

I hobble, the chair still affixed to my back, toward the window.

Leaning against its pane, I huff, breathless, able now to see the sky painted in violets and dwindling orange, the courtyard cloaked in mounting shadows below. I can spot the back of Davies's head, as well as those of the men gathered around him. Mr. Hendricks on one side, Belot on his other. The rest of the Fraternitas, hands in their pockets, standing smug, plus no shortage of hired goons.

My father stands opposite, hands raised in surrender. His face, despite everything, is arranged into a sheepish smirk. He's hiding it well, but I can tell he's thrown. He hadn't expected to greet the Fraternitas.

"Now, come on, gentlemen," Dad says, throwing his head back, a forced laugh. "We can work this—"

He stops because we've locked eyes. Because I'm waving, frantic, wide-eyed, through the window at him, sweat-crusted hair in my eyes, tears streaming down my cheeks. I don't dare call out again, but he sees me, I'm sure of it. The smirk slides off his face.

"All right," Dad says, low and ragged. He takes a gallant step forward. "You want my help." He gestures to my museum window. "Well, I'm only coming with you if I see you let her go, send her running," he says, voice ringing with surety. "After Tess is free, I'll write the translations down for you. I solved them, obviously." He taps his head. "Got 'em all stored right in here."

"Is that so?" Davies sounds almost amused.

"You are *délirant*." Belot seethes at Dad, lurching toward him. "The only *académique* capable of such decryptions is *la fille* Lila!"

Dad startles as Belot's words sink in. I hear him process the surprise with a growl of rage, though I don't understand. Did Dad think they had intended to kidnap *me*? His ripple of alarmed anger, though, is quickly subsumed by feigned nonchalance, like a fish in dark water.

"Enough chatter," Mr. Hendricks snaps, waving his hand at Davies. "Take care of it!"

The air of the courtyard shifts.

"Dad, please," I mutter through gritted teeth, helplessly watching. "No. *Run!*"

"Edwin's right, Warren," Davies says. "We never wanted you."

He steps forward in a rush, grabbing my father.

When Dad resists, frantically fishing for his holster, two more Fraternitas goons step forward and restrain my father's arms.

Davies reaches across Dad's chest and grabs my father's revolver. "Where is the missing scroll?" Davies says evenly.

"Go to hell, Davies," Dad growls, resisting, but it's futile.

Davies knocks him across the jaw with the revolver.

"Dad!"

Again, Davies pummels my father's face with the weapon, blood spraying from his lips.

Dad roars, attempting to shrug off the goons, fight back, but they have him firmly. All the while Davies searches Dad's person with fervor. Digging through his jacket, his pockets, his satchel, his—

Davies stops.

And pulls a golden papyrus from Dad's satchel.

My breath catches.

The fourth scroll.

Stolen.

Davies backs away, smirking in triumph. "In fact," he purrs, "now you're merely in the way."

He raises his arm in one fluid motion. Cocks my father's revolver.

And fires a bullet into Dad's chest.

A scream rips from my throat. "Dad!"

I flail against my ropes. Desperate to free myself, to run to him. Dad topples down, hitting the courtyard in a torrent of dust, blood blooming across the dirt like a grotesque rose.

My stomach heaves, bile flooding the back of my throat. "Oh. No, no, no, no!"

I sob, slamming the glass of the window. My father. There in the dirt. Alone. Gone. *No*. Memories pummel, all at once, an ambush. Dad in the Temple of Amun; behind his lectern at Columbia; in his office at Oxford; in our grand foyer, his arm slung around my mother.

I blink through sweaty tears.

"Get up," I cry at the window, though I know it's for naught. "Get up, Dad, *please.*"

Mr. Hendricks looks up, spotting me. He narrows his eyes. "Take care of her too."

Davies turns, striding across the courtyard.

I stumble away from the window.

No. I attempt to dislodge my shoulders, shake my hands free.

But it's useless. Turning, I slam my back against the wall, attempting to break the chair. Again and again. Until the chair seat cracks against the plaster with a groan and at last splinters down the middle into broken limbs.

The ropes around my wrists immediately slacken. I stumble away from what's left of the chair. My hands are shaking uncontrollably; still, I manage to untie the rope round my feet.

Footsteps echo below, the *click-clack* sound of expensive soles across marble. Davies, already in the atrium. Davies, my father's *murderer*; the cause of Annie's incarceration. Davies, my cold viper of a warden; the reason I'll never see William again.

With a muffled, furious cry, I attack the remains of my chair, stepping on its splintered seat for purchase. I tear at one of the legs until it surrenders, fracturing off. Now I hold twenty inches of solid wood.

Hurrying across the room, I tear through the crates, the shipments, until I spot a box labeled *Middle Kingdom, Miscellaneous*. Quickly digging through the shipment paper, my hands find a flat, cold slab. With a heaving breath, I dislodge it from the box.

A game board. Hounds and Jackals.

My heart aches over using even a durable object like this on Davies. Whispering a plea for forgiveness, I swiftly begin affixing the slab to my plank, covering and tying it off with the shipment's corrugated paper.

Once my hastily fashioned weapon is complete, I skitter behind the storage room door.

Impressive, kid. Chip off the old block, aren't ya?

I pinch my eyes closed, Dad's voice nearly shattering me.

Tears streaming down my face, I picture him again, falling, that red, his body splayed in the courtyard.

But I cannot crumble now.

Because this is the end. Davies is on the hunt for me—the Fraternitas' sinister plan, my "tragic accident," finally coming to fruition.

I settle in the shadows, waiting.

Let the bastard try.

CHAPTER 17

LILA

❧

THE ADHAN SOUNDS AROUND US, CALLING ALL MUSLIMS
to prayer, while we ride through Cairo, chasing the sun between
streets as it drops over the horizon. I hold tight to Alex's back,
my hair flying loose behind me, my bare heels clinging to our
horse's flank. There wasn't time to put on shoes; Samy's men
would have left without me if I'd hesitated for even a blink.

As it is, the four riders ahead of us pull in their reins when
we reach the Nile, motioning for me and Alex to stop. We circle
beside a bridge with great bronze lions. Alex jumps off easily,
extending a hand to help me down. I slide, my bare feet cramp-
ing, and pace to shake the pain.

"Why are we stopping?" I ask, staring at the huge neoclas-
sical building to the north, shining gold in the dusk light. They
are in that building—my father, my sister—or lost already. Lost
forever.

In answer, a mule-drawn wagon draws up beside us with canvas stretching over its cargo bed. Of all people, General Samy

Pasha himself is at the reins, though he wears no tarboosh now, only a dun desert headdress disguising his strong features.

He dismounts from the buckboard and holds me by the shoulders to peer into my eyes. "We don't know what's waiting for us there. Stay with Alexandre."

Alex nods, taking my numb hand in his. Together, we watch Samy's battalion hurry silently north on foot, the wagon rolling close behind.

I begin to shiver, teeth chattering with panic. Alex, concerned, moves to draw me in, warm me, but I shake my head and walk away.

"I don't deserve comfort," I say, bitter. "This is my fault."

Alex frowns. "What do you—"

"I picked a fight with Tess the night of my ball. Accused her of trying to spoil all my ridiculous plans. I really thought I could control our future. Control her. If she'd been herself, with her wits about her, she never would've been taken. Dad never would have walked into this."

"And we never would've met," Alex says quietly. "Though I know that's small consolation."

"Not small." I shake my head. "I've been so alive with you these past weeks. So myself. It's been a long time since I've known who I am."

Now I let him draw me in, my cheek resting on his warm chest. My shoulders drop, my breath keeping time with his heartbeat, which has grown rather rapid.

A blast rings out from the north. I step away. "What was that?"

Alex swallows. "Try not to leap to conclusions, Lila."

He offers his hand again, but I turn away, pulling at my hair in anguish.

"We can't, Alex. I can't! How can I be happy when she's in

206

trouble? I should be in there with her, facing the same danger. It isn't fair."

I've just about determined to set off barefoot up the road when I spy Samy's mule cart coming around the side of the museum, two of the guards hanging off the side.

Samy slows the cart only enough for me to see the panic in his eyes. "Get in the back, Lila, but careful. Alex, on horseback, in the rear. We have to get to a doctor."

"Tess?" Alex asks before the word can form on my own lips.

Samy shakes his head, hands Alex a pistol. "I have men inside. They'll find her."

I scarcely have time to breathe, let alone ask for more information, before Samy whips the mules into a faster clip, forcing me to chase down the cart and heave myself up onto the cargo bed and under the canvas.

My hands touch something warm and viscous before my eyes adjust to take in the figure lying slack next to me.

"Father?" I grope for him, his cold hand, his lifeless face. The bullet wound in his chest.

And then I touch his clammy neck . . . and feel a pulse.

A weak one.

One of Samy's guards, younger than me by several years, climbs inside and presses a compress to Father's chest, murmuring a prayer.

I clasp my father's hand in both of mine, close my eyes, and offer up my own as we bump away from the bridge, the river.

Away from Tess.

CHAPTER 18

TESS

❦

"WHERE THE HELL IS SHE?" MR. HENDRICKS ROARS.

My pulse is pounding so loud, I fret that he and his men may well hear it and discover me, hidden as I am downstairs behind the massive statue of Pharaoh Khafre on his throne. Surrounded by crates, boxes. Lying flat on the ground with a tarp thrown over me, my game board weapon lying by my side. Thank gods this gallery is a mess.

A crescendo of footsteps clacks through the museum atrium. I pinch my eyes closed, willing my heart to slow.

Please do not see me, do not hear me—

"It's bleeding again." Davies, closer now, huffs a growl. "Little bitch got me good."

"I'll do worse than that to you if she gets away." Mr. Hendricks is so near I can hear his labored breath.

"Need I remind you I've been initiated," Davies says evenly. "I am no longer your dog to be kicked around."

"Do not kid yourself." Mr. Hendricks's tone is slaying. "Your worth lies only in your proximity to Warren and your ability to heel, so get it done."

The footsteps retreat, Mr. Hendricks shouting at the other men to spread out, to "search every room on the damned ground floor!"

I wait one moment, another, and then risk peeking out from the tarp. Across the atrium, I see the first floor's arched windows, the slate sky beyond. Nighttime. In the dark, at least, I might manage to slip out of here.

I perch beside the cold backside of the statue, listening. The men have gone for now. This is my chance; I might never get another.

Nerves screaming, I carefully slip out from the tarp, weapon in hand, and then scurry, frenzied, a few feet over, ducking behind a Nofret sculpture.

From my new vantage point, I can see into the next exhibit hall, off the atrium, which, if I've mentally mapped correctly, should lead straight toward the museum's courtyard.

I dash, breakneck now, for the atrium, though stop on a dime when I hear *pitter-patter.*

My breath catches. Definitely footsteps. And whispers. Arabic?

Abruptly I change course, darting instead into the next room along the hall, dark but for the gleam of the myriad glass display surreys. Keeping tight to the wall, ears straining for notes of my pursuers.

Finally, I reach the room's opposite entry, which in turn leads into a long, narrow interior corridor.

I crane my neck into the hall. Halfway down is a puddle of soft light. I am preparing to take off in the opposite direction when I hear muttering coming from the source of illumination. Growls. Harsh, staccato shouts of frustration.

"Die schriftrollen sind unmöglich! Impossible, *unmöglich!"*

Schafer.

I look both ways down the hall. Still clear.

I affix my gaze on the pool of light once more. Schafer undoubtedly has the scrolls in that room, just a few paces away. The keys that will unlock the reign of terror the Fraternitas plan to usher into the world.

Blinking, I lean my head against the smooth marble wall. Imagining Annie, during one of the last times I saw her, when she so dauntlessly assured me of my own commitment to right-eousness, that Dad and I would never allow the Crown to fall into avaricious hands.

How can I let her down after everything that has happened? Indeed, what has all this suffering been for, the sacrifices, if I save only my own hide in the end? If I didn't manage to thwart them at all?

Resolved, I slip along the corridor, the source of light becoming brighter, warmer, as I skirt forward.

I peek inside the room.

A squat, middle-aged blond man sits at a desk, against the adjacent wall of an exhibit space teeming with stacked crates. The trove of glistening papyri is spread out like an unfinished jigsaw on his desktop, gleaming copper under his lantern light.

Schafer mutters another curse in German, reaching forward wildly as if to crumple the ancient papers, then lets out a long, weighty sigh instead.

Stealing a quivering breath of my own, I scan every inch of his makeshift office, but indeed, he is alone, at least for now. Beside him, lined up on a gilt carved table like a tribunal, rest the five canopic jars from KV55.

The Five Ladies of stone.

Schafer rubs his neck, hovering over his notebook and the

four scrolls before him. His eyes are wide now, glassy with concentration, and of all things, I'm reminded of my sister, years ago, when I'd find Lila buried in a book of Wehman's riddles in our library, so engrossed she couldn't, or wouldn't, hear me.

Here's hoping Schafer's the same.

I move before I can doubt myself, crossing the room behind him without a sound, tiptoeing across the space, my weapon held tight to my chest all the while. Inching up behind him, I lift the game board slab, mouthing another apology or prayer, I'm not sure.

And then with two hands, I bring the slab crashing upon his head.

Schafer goes down hard against the desk.

I grab the canvas satchel beside his feet and swiftly roll up the four scrolls, placing all of them, plus his notebook, inside—though before bolting, I remember the jar whose contents had been *"reduced to dust,"* as Belot described it. Impossible to reconstruct, he'd said. Could that jar possibly house the remains of a fifth scroll? Or does it relate in another way to this puzzle? Regardless, it must be important, and it's prudent not to leave any piece behind.

With frantic hands I lift the jars' lids, peering inside each container until I locate the one containing the dust. After stowing the jar in the satchel, I heave the heavy bag over my shoulder.

And run.

Down the corridor.

Out into the brisk, star-dappled night, the wind smelling of earth and blood.

The dirt courtyard behind the museum is eerily quiet. I scan the flat terrain, heart thrumming, aching to see my father one last time, to fall by his side—but his body isn't here.

Where is he?

Racing across the courtyard, I search the bushes surrounding the yard, but the only sign of him is a large spot marring the dirt—dark crimson and thick like tar in the moonlight.

"Then search the perimeter," Mr. Hendricks's voice rings out. "No loose ends! She cannot have gotten far!"

I flail into the bushes, scrambling behind the shrubs. Hurriedly following the line as it curves around toward the front of the museum. Scanning the horizon frantically for my pursuers . . .

And then I spot it, wavy onyx in the moonlight.

The Nile. Glimmering in all its glory, gift of the gods, giver of life!

As I scurry toward the museum front, a long bridge over the water comes fully into view, two regal bronze lions standing like sentinels at its entry. I race as fast as I can toward them, the heavy satchel slamming against my side, my legs stiff and clumsy from being bound so long. Dad's voice, of all things, whispering in my ear, *Faster, pea. Go. RUN.*

The pounding sorrow and fear do not relent, will never relent, but they are transcended by the moon, the rumble of the Nile below, the sweet allure of survival.

I hobble onto the bridge, tearing past the lions, faster, *faster*—

Until an unknown beast roars behind me.

Shrieking, I nearly drop the satchel.

Behind me, a motorcar turns onto the bridge, its headlights two haunting beams slaying the dark.

Mr. Hendricks? Davies?

I wildly look around for cover, but there's nowhere to hide. Glancing at the Nile angrily churning below, I madly debate jumping.

The engine's roar becomes unbearable, a demon's breath on my neck. My legs buckle, though still, I flail onward. Skittering, wincing, bracing for the impact of the motorcar.

But the engine doesn't grow louder. It stops.

"Wait!" The car door opens and slams shut. "Land's sake . . ."

I blink away the voice. My fantasies are taking over. Or perhaps I've been hit, died upon impact, and this is the afterlife.

"Tess, wait! It's William!"

I spin around.

And there he is, silhouette framed by the headlights' celestial glow. His dark hair on end, deep circles around his eyes.

He begins running toward me, and I do the same, stopping only when I've collapsed into him fully and he lets out a mirthful little *oof!*

He holds me tight as I sob, my words a torrent. "They killed him, William, my father. I saw them. I saw it all."

"Oh, my dear Tess." He strokes my tangled hair, rubs the back of my ripped, mangled dress, whispering, "I'm so sorry. So very sorry . . ."

"So I took everything from them!" I shake the satchel as evidence. "For Dad, for Annie, I—"

"Come." William takes my hand, hurrying me toward the motorcar. "You're not safe here."

He helps me into the front seat, and within seconds we are off, roaring across the bridge, away from Cairo. My teeth, only now, begin to chatter with shock.

"I cannot believe I found you," he shouts over the engine. "I've been agonizing over losing you. Ever since that night they took Annie, my father's barely spoken to me. No one will tell me anything. I had no idea if you, if they . . ."

"So you've heard nothing of Annie?" I say softly.

William shakes his head tightly, eyes pinching. "My father's holed me up at Shepheard's Hotel with the Tembrokes. Plans to ship me back to school. I suppose two children in a sanitarium is too much even for him." He shudders. "Tembroke hit the bottle hard tonight, started going on about some switcheroo at the Egyptian Museum. I put two and two together, stole his car, hoping I wasn't too late, and came looking for you."

"My knight in shining armor after all."

He grabs my hand, kissing it. "Tess, back at Belot's . . . I meant what I said. I cannot live with lies any longer. You and I . . ." He glances fervently at me. "We can run, have another chance, away from all of this."

I close my eyes, pain now wrapping around my limbs, my temples, as adrenaline retreats.

"But your sister was right. Don't you see? We must help her. And you and I will never have a real chance unless we stop their madness first."

"What are you suggesting?"

"That we beat them to it."

"The Crown?"

I lift the flap of the satchel. "I finally have all the scrolls—along with Schafer's notes; I stole them too. And whatever scrolls he hasn't cracked, maybe I can glean insights myself, same as I did with the first."

His grip tightens around the steering wheel. "Tess—"

"There's a hidden chamber, I figured out that much, and once we're at the tomb we can attempt to find it. I know nearly every-thing about Akhenaten's reign, after all; that has to count for something—"

A groan escapes him. "This is . . . No, Tess. We can't. It's far too dangerous—"

"Plus, my father's assistant can help us. Wherever Dad goes, he's never far behind. This isn't about fortune and glory anymore, William; it's about people, so many who've already fallen at their hands."

"This is the exact type of thinking that led Annie to where she is."

My lips tremble. "You know I can't do this, won't do this, without you. Because I want all of it, same as you do, our sparring luncheons, anniversary kidnappings. But that will never come to pass unless we put an end to this for good!"

He stares at the dark ahead, his jaw set into a hard line.

"Are you with me?" I blurt. "Because I am with you."

He finally looks at me, in that searing way of his. "Always."

Everything I've been holding in crests and crashes into one huge wave of relief, of surrender. I lean against the leather seat of the car, exhaustion finally winning.

"Tembroke's car," I manage to say. "It's far too conspicuous, unfortunately. The Fraternitas will piece together what happened, come looking for you, for it, soon enough. We should leave it across the bridge, go on foot."

"And what then?" William says.

"We can go to ground," I say. "There's a safe place nearby. A first stop. We'll regroup there."

"Then lead the way."

He slips his hand through mine as we leave the Nile behind, winding into Gizeh.

CHAPTER 19

LILA

❦

Old Cairo

I SIT IN THE DIRT, COVERED IN BLOOD, WATCHING through the sickly predawn light as Samy's men smoke and pace and lean on balcony railings across the narrow road, guarding every street corner. If I look away from them, turn toward the building behind us, I might see Father lying on that pallet, pale as death. I cannot face him. I can only sit here and breathe and remind myself that my father has a chance.

This is a local hospital with effendi doctors, educated in Europe, returned home now to help their own. When they carried Father inside, Samy's boys whispered, "Not British," as if to reassure me that we were safe here, sheltered from those who may hunt us still, and I shuddered more deeply, realizing how far that vile network's roots extend. The Fraternitas de Nodum, brotherhood of the knot. I long to shove said knot down their horrible throats.

This building looks more souk than hospital, archways and alcoves leading to an open yard triangulated by cloths tied for shade, where patients lie on thick bedrolls and pallets. Few are here tonight.

I hear a shout and turn to see a cluster of activity in a corner of the peristyle, where Father's boot pokes out from a dark blue blanket.

Alex's fingers curl around mine. "We've done what we can. Let's let them work."

I stare at Father, at the doctors. *"Allah yisallimak."*

Alex nods behind him and repeats it. *God protect you.*

I stare numbly again at the men across the street. Everyone in this neighborhood is loyal to Samy. I remember now what Father said about the general being corrupt: *"That's why we trust him."* Now I do, too, more than ever.

As if summoned, General Samy Pasha strides out of the hospital with the quick gait of a soldier. I hurry to my feet, but he's already shushing me, taking my hands in his. "He is stable. He rests now. The bullet passed through him, and the bleeding has stopped."

Long-restrained tears spill from my eyes.

"The worst is over," Samy says.

"Thank you," I sputter while Alex grips my shoulder. "Any sign of Tess?"

Samy's face is grave. "There were indications that she had been brought to the museum. But she was not inside."

I try not to crumple entirely. I suspected as much, in the absence of good news throughout the night.

"We will protect him, *amira*," Samy says. "And find your sister. *Wallahi.*"

I shake my head, drowning in questions. "Can I see him, Samy?"

He presses his hands together. "Of course. Go."

I reach for Alex to join me, but he shakes his head. "I'll wait for you."

There's such warm solidity in the way he speaks those words that my trembling subsides by the time I step into the hospital.

Father is awake, but any words of greeting dry up in my mouth as I approach. His eyes are thick-lidded, sweat beading beneath his graying-brown hair. There are cloth bandages wound around his stocky torso. I touch the edge of one gingerly, praying it's clean, that these physicians are as skillful as Samy promised. Since they've gotten him this far, I can only be grateful and trust in the rest. I reach up to touch Dad's forehead. It's reassuringly cool.

"Well." He smiles, with effort. It drops with his sigh. "I'm an idiot."

I crouch beside him. "What do you mean?"

He manages to raise an eyebrow. "Marching up to that museum, all on my own."

"It was probably not the smartest choice you've ever made."

He gazes past me, the lines of his face deepening. "She was right there. Waving at me from the window. My little girl. And I couldn't get her."

"You're not all-powerful, Dad."

He smiles at that. I'm not sure why until he squeezes my hand. "*Dad*. It's been a while since you've called me that. Not since Columbia."

I'm too shocked by him bringing up Columbia to muster any reply.

"He was there, you know, your old friend from Columbia." He grunts. "Part of the welcoming committee that shot me."

"Who?"

"Professor Belot." Dad raises his eyebrows. "He mentioned you."

"What? Your colleague?" I shake my head. "Why?"

"Who knows. To rile me up. Gain the advantage. Or . . ."

I think for a moment that Father's fatigue has caught up with him, rendering him silent. Then he blinks, and I realize he was merely thinking.

"I'm not a *total* idiot, you know. I've noticed you scribbling in that notebook of yours, back and forth with Alex's phrase book. Not Arabic. Hieroglyphs."

I blink in momentary surprise, then hesitate with an answer. How to explain why I've hidden my work from him without voicing reproach for all the years I could have been doing this alongside him, if he hadn't taken me away from it all and then run off himself?

"You've solved the scrolls, haven't you, princess?" he asks softly.

I look him in the eye. No rancor. Only the truth. "I'm still working on the last one, the *Sheut*. But I'm close."

"I was afraid of that." He doesn't look afraid. For one breath, he's incandescent. "I tried, you know, despite Samy's best attempts to distract me, dissuade me. I was determined to crack the whole set, solve the riddle, find the Crown, sell it off, move on. For all of us. For our debts, for your future."

"You were going to pay our debts?" I can't hide the surprise in my voice.

"Of course I was. I am. I'm your father. That's my job." He sounds so defeated it makes tears pool in my eyes. "The Crown would have done it, and then some. But it's not just about the money, if I'm honest. The past fifteen years of my life, my scholarship, have all led up to this. It's not so easy to let go. But working those scrolls and making no headway, I started to realize I was going to have to. I thought, *There's not one soul alive who can make sense out of these.* I forgot about you, Lila. How could I have forgotten about you?"

He reaches for me and holds my hand, too tight. I don't complain.

"I remember you sitting in the sunroom of the old house on Madison." His voice goes hazy. "You had on this blue frock and your skirts were fanned over the carpet like a fire balloon, and you were holding this notebook I'd brought home from the university. I looked at what you were working on, thinking it was probably a drawing—flowers, butterflies, our family. But it was a diagram for a language you'd invented—root words with lines to suffixes, prefixes, linguistic variants. You were six years old."

I stare at the floor. "Fordish. It was a game I played with Tess."

"She's always been something else, too, don't get me wrong. She had an intensity about her, a doggedness for discovery. That's why I allowed you two to tag along to the university with me in those days after your mother passed. Get you out of the house, out of your grief, get your minds active. Your grandmother never liked it, which made me want to do it even more."

He chuckles, but his energy is giving out. I long with all my heart to know more, but not at the risk of enervating him. He's just been shot, for goodness' sake, so I gently peck him on the cheek, ready to slip away, when he reaches for me again.

"I've got to know, Lila." He stares at me, unblinking. "Did Belot hurt you?"

I frown, confused. "What?"

"Did he ever do anything that made you uncomfortable or . . ."

"No!" The word booms out of me, a clap of thunder followed

220

by a shocked laugh. "No, never. It was just the cuneiform. He'd been studying this script and he asked me to unravel it."

In hindsight, it does appear to be an inappropriate arrangement, asking a child to do academic work for you, but not in the way Father's suggesting. He thought it, though, didn't he, back at Columbia? This is why he pulled me away.

Father looks vastly relieved. "I saw you in his office, and the responsibility your mother left me with came crashing down. I felt I'd failed you. Fathers protect their daughters, and I . . ." He shakes his head. "After I saw what happened with Belot, your gifts terrified me. They'd always scared me a little, if I'm being honest. If you'd been a boy . . ."

I suck in a sharp breath. He winces at my reaction but keeps going.

"If you'd been a son, I probably would have pushed you. I wouldn't have worried. But a girl with genius? It made you vulnerable. And I didn't know what to do with that. It seemed to me your place was with your grandmother and my place was in Europe, at Oxford, doing what I know how to do. I'm not saying I was right. I'm only telling you why I did what I did."

"So you did leave us. On purpose." I feel hot tears streaming down my cheeks.

"That's about the size of it." His face is grim, but before I have time to follow my impulse to move away, he pulls me into a hug, and with that, I'm small and he's 'Dad,' and I close my eyes as he says fiercely, "Believe me. I will never do it again."

I wipe my nose, sheepish, as he lets me go. "What about Tess?"

"She's the one who changed my mind about it all, through sheer bullheadedness. Wouldn't let it go until I said fine, sure, come along on a dig. I reckoned you'd do the same, but you never—"

"I meant," I interrupt gently, "what do we do about Tess? What's our contingency plan?"

"You mean the plan I should have put in place when we arrived," Father says wryly. "I don't know."

It looks like it costs him something to admit that.

He can't quite bring himself to meet my eyes as he adds, "Maybe you can help me figure it out."

And just as my heart starts to float, he says, "Not now, though. Now we've got to get you hidden away."

I rock backward. "What?"

"Samy's place for now, but we might need to find someplace more secure. Alex has that house in Gizeh." He's muttering to himself, I realize, not to me. "If they can't crack it, even with all the scrolls, they're going to get more desperate. And Belot sure thinks—" Father's eyes suddenly dart to mine, wide. "This cuneiform. What did it look like?"

"Oh." I draw a breath, steadying myself. "It was sort of squiggles? Fishhooks?"

"'Fishhooks,'" Father repeats with a feeble grin. "Son of a bitch. Belot published your work, you know. Won awards. My professor back in Chicago once told me you're not a true academic until somebody plagiarizes you." He reaches out a hand for me to shake, firmly, as if I were a peer. "Welcome to the club."

I laugh, delighted despite myself by those four magical words, but his smile is fading, his eyelids staying closed longer and longer with every blink. I press my hand gently to his forehead and force myself to go.

I slip back through the open arches into a far-from-certain future. Despite his pride, Father still sees me as a treasure. A scroll to be slipped into a satchel, hauled around and hidden.

Alex waits on the street with our borrowed horse.

"He's sleeping now," I say.

"Good," Alex says. "I'd like to get you into bed too."

A laugh lodges in my throat as I watch him process what he's just said.

"So you can sleep," he blurts. "You need your rest."

As he offers me a hand into the saddle, I realize that rest is the very last thing I want right now.

An idea strikes. I place my hand on Alex's shoulder, stopping him. "Father was worried I wouldn't be safe at Samy's. He wants us to go to your house in Gizeh."

Alex pushes his spectacles up. "Just the two of us?"

"Less conspicuous."

❧

As Alex mounts in front of me, Samy steps alongside us, checking the horse's bit. "Not a bad plan. Your father's still got his wits about him, I see. I'll send someone out to check on you tomorrow, but for now, may I offer an escort?"

Around us, I notice others falling into line, five more horses, two riders to each mount.

"Don't worry about them," the general says. "They know what to do."

With that, he smacks the rump of our horse and we're off at a gallop. I cling to Alex's back, finding my balance anew.

We careen down alley after alley and erupt from the narrow streets onto a wide boulevard. Heads turn as we thunder past; even in the early-morning gloom, the streets are more active than I would like. I see a blonde woman being escorted out of a carriage by a man in British military garb—back from a ball?—and bury my face in Alex's back. We must make quite the sight, six glossy Arabian stallions charging through the city like we're off to war. However will this retinue disguise our destination?

Just as I think it, the horses around us break formation. One veers northward, along the river, while another rears around and canters back the way we came. We continue onward, a smaller cavalry now. Two more riders peel off and one more draws in the reins just before a newly constructed bridge—which doesn't even appear to be officially opened—and they wave for us to cross.

Now it's only me and Alexandre d'Auteuil, crossing the Nile.

When we reach the edge of the Gizeh district, Alex quiets our horse to a slow trot, then pulls her up around the far side of a *sabil*, an ornate stone building housing a public fountain and trough. I would imagine it's usually bustling with residents filling jugs, but at this hour, no one's here apart from us.

Us and them. Because there they are, rising out of the day's first light. Ancient, watchful, eternal, line upon perfect line, dizzying in their dimensions.

The Great Pyramids.

As I gaze out to the horizon, tracing their impossible silhouettes, Alex slides off the saddle. I feel a shock of aloneness without the warmth of him against me.

"What do you think?" He offers me a hand down, nodding to the view. "Do they meet your expectations?"

"They eviscerate them. They render void everything I've once deemed permanent or consequential."

"Not everything, I hope." There's a languid edge to his voice, a heat, and my entire body goes warm in turn. "How long did Dr. Ford suggest we wait here on our own?"

His question is cautious. Loaded.

As I fumble for an answer, he laughs. "This wasn't his plan, was it?"

He turns away toward the *sabil*, his head bowed as he dips a hanging ladle into the flow of the fountain.

"It was *a* plan," I argue. "One that wouldn't require saying goodbye to you."

"I'd have stayed with you at Samy and Nura's." He pivots back with the full ladle, offering me a drink. "It wouldn't have been goodbye."

"Oh, but it would. Every night, goodbye until the morning."

As his eyes meet mine and see the intent in them, his hand falls slowly slack, water spilling onto the sand.

I step forward, powerless. "I can't bear the thought of being apart from you for even a moment."

And at long last, Alex leaps.

His mouth finds mine. It's soft and warm and opening and, oh, wonders. His arms rope around me and my fingers dig through his hair and we're tangled up, one heart, one body, lighting up the whole desert, more glorious than the rising sun.

When the horse snorts, impatient, Alex pulls away. His spectacles are askew. I laugh and slide them back onto his nose, touching his cheekbones, his eyebrows, marveling at each beautiful detail.

"Let's get home." Alex's voice is husky with need.

I feel myself shiver, less scandalized by my own reaction than electrified.

"We are, ah, rather exposed here," he says.

I intend to become even more exposed, but for now, I straighten my blouse and smooth down my skirt as Alex leads the horse gently along the road with us.

The home we stop at is one of a long row of tiny clay-baked cottages, windows cut out like gingerbread houses. It's charming inside, modest but clean, one tiny bed in the main living area, a writing desk, a simple kitchen.

The bedroom is certainly on the dusty side but has an austere femininity to it. I wonder afresh about Alex's mother, the esteemed French archaeologist. How strange it must have been for her here, so far from her own world, with a young child in tow. She could have continued her studies in France, after all, resumed her university post, returned to Egypt for expeditions like other Europeans in her field. So what compelled her to live here? To stay?

Perhaps it was love.

I feel tingles spread across my shoulders and turn to see Alex standing in the doorway, watching me.

I laugh, breathless, and that's it. My decision is made. He draws me close and kisses me again, my forehead, my cheeks, my mouth, and goodness, now we cannot stop. Well, *I* can't.

Alex pulls himself away, hands in his hair. "We mustn't. I mustn't."

"Why not?" My voice is plaintive, but I stop myself from reaching for him.

"I cannot take your honor."

"Of course you can't." I huff. "My honor isn't to be found in chastity but in the purity of my intentions and actions."

Alex flinches. "I didn't mean to suggest—"

I draw him back. "The purest thing I can think of right now is this. Alex, my father's been shot, my sister is missing, I have no idea where my future lies, but I know I want you. I don't want a perfectly planned and executed life; I want a beautiful mess of one, now. Nothing else is guaranteed to us."

His hands stretch wide across the small of my back.

My lips graze his neck as I murmur, "Please come to bed with me."

And his voice is low, gravelly, utterly powerless, as he answers, "All right then."

It is strange and wonderful to undress, to see him fully and he me, to feel his fingers explore my contours even more lovingly than he traces the lines of his sketches and maps. I am his world now and he is mine.

It is stranger yet when we lie down together and join, uncomfortably at first, I must admit. Questions form in me as we move; first a simple, *What is this thing that lovers do?* and then another question, yet more mysterious, sharp and ineffable, and growing in intensity. I grip his shoulders and wonder, closer and closer to an answer, until it arrives, and it is not something I can describe with any language I know, except to say to myself, *Yes. This. Alex is mine and I'm his and this is right. This, for now, is home.*

Afterward, we lie warm and lax together, feeling each other's heartbeats, listening to Gizeh wake up around us.

"I do intend to marry you," Alex says.

I laugh, perching to glare. "I do believe you need to ask the lady first."

"Where are my manners?" He smirks. Oh, help me, but arrogance does look good on him. "Lila Ford. Would you do me the great honor of allowing me to be your husband?"

I pretend to consider, only for a breath, but as I grin and move to kiss him, Alex freezes. He sits up abruptly, finger to his lips in warning, and then I hear it too.

There is someone in the house.

My heart flails with panic. I reach for Alex, to forestall him, but too late; he's already sliding from the bed with the sheets wrapped around his waist, bending to retrieve an iron doorstop and passing through the bedroom door like a shadow.

A shriek sounds from the entryway. Frantic, I reach for the quilt that's fallen on the floor and tug it around me as I sprint out behind him.

A young dark-haired man, a stranger, leans against the fireplace with a dizzy expression. Alex stands frozen in the middle of the room.

227

A gasp resounds against the low ceiling, and I don't know how, but I recognize that particular intake of breath.

She shuts the front door behind her, staring at me in complete astonishment, my face a mirror of hers, I'm sure, and I can't do anything but hold the quilt in place with one hand and extend the other and wait for her to race to me.

It takes her no more than a moment. I draw her in with the full intention of never letting her go.

She is warm and trembling and alarmingly pungent.

"I never thought I'd see you again!" I cry.

Tess presses her hands to my cheeks. *"Na ru li tippa kemper!"* *Oh ye of little faith!*

Then, "Wait."

She steps back, eyes wide as planets.

"Where are your clothes?"

CHAPTER 20

TESS

❧

THE SHEER INCONGRUITY OF FINDING MY SISTER HALF
naked with my father's assistant, in an Egyptian safe house,
halfway round the world from where I last saw her, utterly
silences me.

I laugh.

Lila laughs.

"Dad," I finally manage. Shock, fury, grief, bubbling and boiling over. "Lila, I . . . I don't know how to tell you this, but our
father is . . . Well, it slays me to say that I saw him—"

"Alive," she blurts, taking my hands. "Oh, Tess, he's recovering; shot, yes, but they all say he's going to make it."

I tremble with cautious hope. "But I saw it happen, saw
him fall."

"The Fraternitas might have tried to kill him, but they
failed. I assure you he's resting, with Samy Pasha's own doctors
attending."

"Your father's an alley cat, you know that," Alex says kindly, placing a hand on my shoulder. "He's got a few more lives left in him. Four, I'd say. Possibly five."

"I . . . Oh gods, Lila, that is— Well, this is . . ."

I burst into tears.

"Tess," Lila and William say in unison.

William steps forward to comfort me.

"I'm fine," I croak, wiping my eyes. "Just unbelievably relieved. This is William, by the way."

"Who apologizes for intruding." William extends his hand to Alex, flashing me a smirk. "Though it's a particular talent of mine. William Hendricks."

Alex, flummoxed, shakes his hand. "Alexandre d'Auteuil."

"My father's assistant," I explain. "Soon to complete his own doctorate."

William nods. "And a pleasure to finally meet the real Lila Ford."

"William *Hendricks*, did you say?" Lila mumbles, a small line forming between her brows. "The same William Hendricks who, ah, was due to attend my ball?"

"Who did indeed attend your ball," I say breathlessly. "He was the errand boy tasked with whisking you away on this sinister escapade."

"'Errand boy'?" William pretends to be affronted before I wink and chuck him sportively.

My sister murmurs, "I am wholly confused."

"Oh, right, of course you are." With a fortifying huff, I set my shoulders, then explain how Mr. and Mrs. Hendricks staged a hasty wedding engagement, looping Grandmama in at the final hour, as reason to take Lila and set her to task on the scrolls.

"But then . . ." Lila shakes her head. "Why did they take *you*?"

William answers before I can. "Case of mistaken identity." He shrugs jovially. "It happens."

When Lila and Alex exchange a dubious glance, I forge on swiftly. "Anyway, all this time, during my travels and in Paris, William and his sister, Annie, were my clandestine allies. The Fraternitas planned to kill you regardless, Lila, down the road, but they surely would have disposed of me immediately had they known my true identity. William and Annie even helped me attempt an escape—"

I stop suddenly, wincing now, remembering afresh Annie's screams that night, the sound of broken glass.

"And your sister?" Lila asks William.

William's jaw clenches. "Was not as fortunate as we were to flee."

Lila gives a tight nod, her eyes brimming. "Tess, that last night we saw each other . . . I just kept thinking, a thousand times, I wished . . ."

I watch as a mix of emotions seems to overwhelm her.

She pulls back, remembering herself, pulling her quilt higher, toward her collarbone. "Goodness, my decency. I'll get clothes on. Then I can sort everything, where we go from here, and how—"

"I already have a plan," I blurt gamely.

Lila halts, queenlike in that quilt gown.

I break our gaze, picking up the satchel I've placed on the ground, showcasing its contents: the scrolls, Schafer's notebook, the woman-shaped canopic jar.

"And you cannot talk me out of it, Lila, so please don't bother. There are four preserved scrolls, as you probably know, Alex, since Dad was hiding the *Ba* scroll. Davies took it from him, but as you can see, I've got them all now, plus this jar of dust. Not sure we've got any use for a destroyed scroll incapable of reconstruction, but I still thought it best to leave nothing behind." I grab Schafer's note-book and begin flipping through it in demonstration. "They're working with Hans Adalard Schafer, if you can believe it, but I've also managed to steal all his transcriptions, translations, and notes, which means William and I are well ahead of them—"

"We probably don't need the notes," Alex interrupts gently. "Lila is already close to cracking the *Sheut* scroll."

The rest of my explanation scatters, sand in the wind.

I blink, disbelieving.

My father, Dr. Belot, Professor Schafer, even *me* on the case—and my sister, who spent the better part of the past few years balancing books on her head—is the only one able to crack this ancient, confounding puzzle?

I let out a wild laugh. Not because I refuse to believe Lila capable of what Alex has claimed. No, that somehow makes sense, reflecting back on her years spent poring over logic games and riddles.

I laugh because, inexplicably, her accomplishment feels like a betrayal. All this time she's kept so much of herself hidden from me, hasn't she?

Thankfully, William breaks the silence with his own chuckle, eyes glittering in my direction. "No wonder Belot was so insistent on 'your' genius."

"Quite amazing." I force a smile. "Which means we're even further ahead of the Fraternitas. Schafer will be back at it soon, however, with the limited resources he's got." I close the satchel flap. "And we should leave as soon as possible, given what the Fraternitas is planning."

"Namely, world domination," William mutters.

"They want history to repeat itself," I agree. "They want to pull all of Egypt under their sway—and maybe more than Egypt."

Alex says, "Which is why they're so desperate to find the

relic before Cromer's pushed out. With Cromer granting them access, they could begin by controlling the khedive, and thereafter meet with the opposition parties in apparent good faith, only to exert control over their minds as well. In a short time there would be no one left to stand against them."

"Hence why we must get it first." I stop. "Alex, what would it take to end this? To end them, their hold over Egypt?"

"A change in order," he supposes. "A wholesale dismantling of the current government."

Lila steps forward. "Say we were to get to the Crown first. If we were to give it to Samy, Alex, what do you think he would do with it?"

"It's a hugely powerful symbol for the country." Alex crosses his arms, pacing a bit, thinking. "I suspect he would use it to rally Egypt's disparate nationalist movements into one unified force. Place the country's destiny in her own hands again."

"Would Egypt then expel the Fraternitas from their shores?" I ask.

"Oh, more than that." Alex laughs. "They've racked up plenty of crimes here to warrant imprisonment. They'd be tried, arrested—"

"In which case, we could save Annie too." I look at William eagerly.

Though he's still unconvinced. I can tell by the way he's staring into Alex's fireplace, avoiding my eyes.

"You're making several large assumptions," William says finally. "One, that you can actually beat my father. He's not the type of man who takes well to being bested, Tess. After your stunt at the museum, he will hunt you until he finds you. And if we have the Crown by then, he will take it from us and destroy us." He looks at me, eyes haunted. "They will not stop until they get what they want."

LEE KELLY AND JENNIFER THORNE

I cross the room, taking his hands in mine. "But, William, once the Crown is in the right hands, the Fraternitas are finished. This will be over. We won't have to spend our lives running, in perpetual danger, wholly at their mercy."

Though a sudden thought strikes me.

"And yet." I glance at Lila and Alex. "If the Crown's power is real, as I've always believed, is it too dangerous, unearthing the relic at all? Should it be placed in anyone's hands?"

Lila bites her lip. "Samy said the very same thing."

Frowning, Alex remains silent for a moment. Then he looks up. "Given everything at play, perhaps it's a risk we'll have to run. Besides, if anyone can handle the responsibility, it's Samy."

I exhale a weighty sigh, nodding, still a bit incredulous over the enormity of what we're agreeing to do. "So then, it sounds like we're heading down to the Valley? All of us? Together?"

William shakes his head. "As the person who's spent a lifetime bearing witness to my father's callous resourcefulness, I really feel I must impress: this is going to be far from easy. The Fraternitas will have eyes everywhere. Tomb guards deep in my father's pocket. Lookouts, I'm sure, in every outpost from here to the Valley."

Alex presses his spectacles against his nose, conceding, "And it will be a long journey at that. At least a week, and that's without any hiccups."

"Then I suppose we shouldn't dally," Lila says.

I smile as she finds my eyes. In this moment, it's as if the past few years have been erased and we see each other plainly.

"We'll need to send word to Father," she tells me. "We wouldn't want to worry him."

"No, not with all he's been through," I agree.

"Though if we admit what we're attempting, he's likely to spring from his cot and come chasing after us," Lila adds.

Alex considers this. "Definitely can't have the man risking more bodily injury."

I stare again at the two of them, wheels churning now.

"Then what about a lie?" I suggest. "A fake engagement—er, unless there's a real engagement. Not to pressure you, Alex. We tell Dad that you and Alex ran off together, and since we happened to be reunited, I came with you to join the wedding party as your dutiful sister. That should buy us some time, yes?"

William crosses his arms, a little smile on his lips at last. "That cover story sounds familiar."

"It's not bad," Lila says, contemplating. She crosses the room, grabbing a pen from the desk tucked into the corner of Alex's living space. "Do you mind, Alex?"

He smiles slowly. "You never did answer my question."

"Oh. Yes!" She turns to me, eyes bright. "We're engaged!" And promptly begins scrawling a note.

I shake my head in bewilderment. "My sincerest congratulations."

"We should get dressed," Alex says. "Get ready quickly and gather provisions: food, water, securing travel. I've got a bit of cash on hand, but not much."

"Happy to help there," William offers. "Though I'm short as well. Wasn't contemplating desert travel when I dashed out of Shepheard's."

From the desk, Lila calls out, "I'll sell the comb."

Alex balks. "Your one thing? You can't."

"Wait, what comb?" I then remember the golden heirloom Lila grandly paraded the night of her debutante. "Wait, are you meaning to say *Mother's* comb? Don't you think you should first ask my opinion on the matter?"

"Perhaps you two could talk it through whilst arranging a *babur*?" Alex suggests gently. "I'll handle the provisions."

William sighs, picking up the letter Lila's just written, newly folded on the table, and wags it in my direction. "Guess that leaves me to find a lad to deliver this."

I peck him on the cheek, whispering, "Told you. Couldn't do this without you."

The four of us spring into action. Alex uses his local connections to hastily procure water, a tent, wooly coats, blankets, simple foodstuffs. William sets out to deliver our story to our father, while Lila accompanies me down to the water to arrange transport and purchase clothing.

Thirty minutes later, we're reconvened and ready.

Once Alex scours the streets for onlookers and declares the coast clear, we filter out of his old home, striding in silence toward the river. The pyramids, our beacons, gleaming golden under the midday sun.

CHAPTER 21

LILA

Sahara Desert

THE SETTING SUN CASTS A CITRINE BLANKET OVER OUR camp, a new color to add to my palette of memories: the wavy gold of the desert, the pure, lush green fed by the Nile. We'll keep following that green south until we reach the Valley of the Kings, but for now, we rest here, inside the continual unknown.

I must say, everyone seems to know this unknown a far sight better than I do.

It's been nearly three days since we first sailed out of Gizeh. William Hendricks has been sailing our *babur* by day and has proved a skilled yachtsman, while Alex makes a fine first mate. Even Tess somehow knows her way around the ropes, giving the boys a chance to take breaks, and I . . . Well, I managed not to be sick. Honestly, I can't think of a single thing I've done to contribute toward our journey since bartering Mother's comb for a boat and two sets of boys' clothing for me and Tess.

Oh yes, I'm in trousers again, wide brown ones in the rural style of the *felaheen*—far more comfortable than what Father stuck me in back on Orchard Street—covered completely by a long, light garment called a *gallabiyya*, which I was delighted to find has pockets in the sleeves. Tess and I wrapped up our hair in scarves called *kufiyya*, the match of Alex's, and there we were, to all casual glances three desert guides escorting a rich Western explorer, William.

Once we set off down, no, upriver—I have a hard time keeping that straight—I found myself slipping into the bewildering sensation of being a passenger, as if I'd been the one to engage the three of them to ferry me to the Valley of the Kings. The first day I didn't dare risk my notes to the wind and river water, and so while we sailed, there was nothing practical for me to do except listen as Alex pointed out landmarks along the way in a soft whisper, none of the so-called sights close enough to see properly. At one point I spotted a party of German-speaking tourists along with local guides and started to wave a polite hello, when Tess and Alex grabbed my arms in unison and sat me down like a stroppy child.

"We'd do better to stay incognito," Alex said very sweetly.

"Any other time we could make a party of it, I think." Tess's voice was upbeat.

I may not know my sister as I once did, but I know enough to recognize the look she and Alex exchanged, clearly their default for any green archaeology dabbler, and now, hurrah, it's me.

Thus far, we've eschewed the modest outposts where travelers before us tend to stop for the night, tying our *babur* in the tall reeds instead and disguising it with river detritus, as if it's been washed ashore, broken.

At first, I offered my assistance in setting up camp. Today I haven't bothered. They always decline, citing prior experience, so now, while Alex stokes the fire and Tess and William laugh conspiratorially, taking turns fastening tent pins into the sand while the fabric flaps about their heads, I study a blank page of my notebook, pretending to make marks, pathetic soul that I am, trying to restore a bit of my self-possession by going through the motions again.

The first two nights they made excuses, likely trying to preserve my dignity. *"Lila needs to work." "Lila's close to finishing the* Sheut *scroll."* But now I've done it. All of it. Three layers of cipher on that last one—progressive, yes, each building from the prior one, but still. I should feel more triumphant than I do. Instead, I am bereft.

The thing of it is, for all the words I've deciphered, they still feel like a tiny piece of a larger puzzle, a mere eroteme at the end of a blotted-out question. Perhaps it's because of that last jar—the final scroll, *Ka*, that was destroyed. This may be an impossible puzzle to fully solve, due to the ravages of time.

The other members of my party, however, are buoyant with hope.

I scratch my forehead with the pencil and my gaze floats upward to watch them, these shining people: William with his linen sleeves rolled up, so gallant, capable, disarming despite having been born into enemy ranks; Alex, glowing like a god under the setting desert sun, wiping his spectacles with a handkerchief every time a cinder from the fire he's stoking hits him in the face; and Tess.

Look at her, hands on hips, kufiyya off, dark hair blowing loose in the desert wind, glittering eyes and eager laugh, every muscle relaxed, each move purposeful. She looks like she can conquer any challenge, exempli gratia: infiltrating a secret society, sussing out their aims, escaping from the tightening vise of death, stealing scrolls and a canopic jar right out from under them. In a word, she's *worthy*.

If this journey had been an interview for the position of field assistant, Tess would have swiped it right out from under me.

Whatever I can offer, I've already done. My worth is in the past. Which makes me an artifact to be toted about after all.

I gaze behind me at the river and breathe in the sharp air with its mineral scent. In the distance, fishermen pull in great wide nets, making the river ripple with sunset light. Mothers wash clothes while their children play in the shallows. I'm struck with sudden surety that someone living thousands of years ago gazed upon this exact scene without alteration, and for a moment, I feel all of me open wide to the world.

Alex walks over with a blanket. "Come to the fire. It gets cold quickly out here."

"I wouldn't want to be in the way."

He crouches, eyes sympathetic, hand extended to draw me close—no, to wipe off my forehead with his thumb. "Have you run out of paper and started writing on yourself?"

"Oh." I sigh down at my charcoal pencil. "I don't know what I've run out of."

He wraps the blanket around me and kisses the top of my head.

"Well, I, for one, have run out of cleverness." He shoots me a cheeky wince. "Would you give me a hint?"

I press my lips together to keep from grinning as he pulls out my cipher wheel, set for *Sheut*. I'm not certain whether he really needs help, or if he's pretending so to bolster my spirits, but as I watch him spin the wheel, forehead scrunched like a child learning to read, I suspect the former.

He is far too adorable. I have to look away.

He glances up before I manage it.

"Ah." He smiles slowly, and my cheeks flush from the effort

it takes not to throw myself at him. "So. Inside the cartouche, I have 'follow.' Could that be the key this time? It couldn't be that simple."

"Not quite." I smile. "But nearly. If you pass the characters through the last scroll's cipher disk . . ."

"You identify the actual missing characters for this one." He swears softly to himself.

"And the transposition of the rest."

"So I need to reset the disk—"

"For *Ib*. And then you may as well use my *Sheut* disk. No need to reinvent the wheel."

I grin, waiting.

His eyes crinkle appreciatively. "Lila Ford and her puns," he says, leaning in.

Just as my fiancé's lips hover above mine, I hear a sniff behind him.

"Are you talking him through the decryptions, Lila?" Tess asks, rocking back and forth onto her heels, oblivious to what she's interrupted. "I'd love to hear your logic myself, if only to fill the time."

"I'm not sure I have any energy left tonight." I sigh. "Perhaps during tomorrow's travels."

She looks let down, but then, so do I, watching Alex retreat to the fire to join William in conversation.

Tess sits close beside me. Her elbow feels awkward against mine, like we're playacting at being sisters.

"It's so strange seeing you here," she says.

I stiffen. "Why?"

"It's like collage, like you're a paper doll I've taped into a photo of Egypt." She says it so brightly, simply. She can't know how plainly she's just voiced all my insecurities.

As I turn my charcoal pencil to dig it into my palm, she leans closer.

"And yet you're so much more yourself here, Lila. You've changed, and you haven't. It's like you've taken off a costume."

She's right. And I'm pleased to hear her say it. But at her choice of words, the memory of my state of undress at our reunion, I forcefully clear my throat, and she snorts.

"I wasn't actually referring to that—but it's a big change, isn't it? You are nothing but surprises these days, Lila. And then . . . there's this." Her eyes flick back to the book. "Can I look, at least?"

I shrug, nonchalant, then watch with mounting pride as she flips back a page, seeing the translations, and another, another, shaking her head.

"You've really done it. I heard Belot ranting about your genius ad nauseum, and I know Alex said the same, but to see it with my own eyes . . . You managed this." She cocks her head to stare at me. "Belot's mad as a hatter, but damn if he wasn't right about you."

I pull my blanket tighter. "I'm still unnerved that he's working with the Fraternitas."

"Who isn't? It's simply *the* club to be in if you're rich, powerful, and completely off your rocker."

"And William is different?" I have to ask.

Tess shrugs, smiling. "He's crackers, no doubt. But in a different way."

As if sensing her gaze, William looks over, his whole body reacting. When Alex passes him a whiskey bottle, still chatting away, he tears his eyes away from Tess with obvious reluctance. He's in love with her. And judging by the way she watches him—still, expectant, like a doe in a glade—she returns those feelings.

How bizarre to think that this is the very same man I was hoping would court me, marry me, save us all. It makes sense now, his mother's eagerness to pair us—not the wishes of a solicitous matriarch hoping her son would settle down but the machinations of an accessory to kidnapping. And Grandmama and I were all too willing to fall for the ruse.

That feels like another lifetime. It was mere weeks ago.

"Have you been doing this kind of work . . . decryptions, all these years, without telling me?" There's hurt in her voice under a porcelain layer of cheer.

"No." Defensiveness rises in me. "I haven't. I couldn't. Not since Father dragged us out of Columbia."

She shakes her head, confused. "You could have gone back to academia, Lila. All I had to do was ask—"

"It was hardly that simple for me." I stare at the dancing fire in the distance rather than at her. "We couldn't both pursue our passions."

Tess glances away from me, at William, an odd look in her eye.

"Someone had to set things to right." I intend this last word as a conversation capper.

But Tess grumbles, "And keep Grandmama in her silks and furs."

I know how appallingly Grandmama treated Tess throughout

the years, taking out all her grief and regret on a mere child—and I'm about to say as much, when Tess goes on. "Wait till she hears about Alex. She'd die of apoplexy if you told her you were marrying a field assistant, so do make sure you lead with his inheritance."

I am too appalled to even voice a squawk. Is she implying my attachment to Alex stems from an instinct for fortune hunting? My hand forms a tight fist in my lap, and lest I use it, I start to rise.

But Tess grabs my wrist, keeping me down. "There's something else I've been wanting to ask you."

I'm still too miffed to do anything but offer a stiff shrug.

"Why did you invite me to your ball?" Tess looks down, embarrassed, and it takes me a few blinks to grasp what she's asking. "There was no practical reason for me to be there. In fact, since I wasn't officially out in society, I was wondering whether I really should have been invited in the first place. But you were so insistent."

I look at her eager face, the sight I've yearned to see for far longer than these weeks that she's been missing.

Because I love you dearly. Because I was scared and I needed you.

"I thought it might persuade you to change course," I say tightly. "Join society. Take the pressure off me a little."

I can't quite look at her now, but I feel her sink beside me, even as she shrugs. "You should have seen me in Paris."

The dark has gathered with ever-increasing velocity, the heat sloughing away as quickly as Alex promised. With no sun to warm us, Tess and I shiver in tandem.

She stands and offers a firm hand, lifting me, blanket and all, so we can position ourselves next to the boys.

"And what are you two plotting?" Tess puts her hands on her hips, fixing Alex and William with a playful glare.

"Not plotting," William says with an easy smile. "Speculating."

"One can't help but wonder what the Fraternitas is doing now," Alex chimes in.

"They'll be heading to the tomb, same as us," William says darkly. "No question about that. It's only a matter of when."

I glance behind us, suddenly even more chilled.

"They can't realize we're ahead of them," Tess says. "For all they know, we're cowering at Samy's."

I think of Samy and Nura's home, those thick walls and gates, those posted guards, warm beds, and fragrant teas, and try my best not to feel I've made the wrong decision.

"They won't dally," William says. "I'm sure they're decrypting as they can, during the journey, as Lila did, wasting no time."

"Oh, but they had to have dallied some." Tess smiles like the cat who ate the canary. "They wouldn't leave without Schafer, their last best hope of solving the scrolls, and he needed at least a little time to recover."

We all stare at her as she passes the whiskey to William.

She shrugs. "There was a bit of a scuffle when I collected the scrolls upon my escape."

We continue to stare.

She laughs, hands in the air. "I hit him with a game board. He likely still has a headache, if not a concussion."

"Goodness, Tess," I say breathily, but I must admit, I'm impressed.

"Even so, we must keep up our guard," Alex says, pushing up his spectacles. "If any of their contacts catch sight of us, our expedition is as good as over."

William squirms a little on his perch. Uncomfortable, no

doubt, about his unwitting role in all their schemes. But then he looks up at me with a wide, relaxed grin. "So?"

"So . . ." I blink. "What?"

Alex hands me the whiskey. I wince as I take a sip and pass it to Tess.

"Tell us, already." William laughs. "What do the scrolls say? You're the only person on the planet who knows."

Tess bounces in her eagerness, but I hesitate. Am I truly ready to present this? The sequence feels incomplete, yes, but there's something else tugging at me, something insistent, a pebble in my boot. A flaw in my work. It's there. I just haven't found it yet.

Nevertheless, I pull out my notes. "The first scroll was nothing, obviously, a direct decipherment."

"'Nothing'!" Tess throws up her hands, raging at the heavens.

I squint at her, bemused. "I'm talking about the easy one, with no trick or cipher, the *Ren* scroll. I still don't fully understand what those terms mean. Alex, you said they're parts of the soul?"

"Yes, to the Egyptians, it took all five elements to make a person complete." Alex's voice takes on that dreamy quality it had when he first told me about the Crown's legend. "*Ren* is your name, your legacy. *Ba* is your individuality, your motivation and drive."

William wraps his arm around Tess. She nestles in.

"*Ib*, the heart, both, ah, literally . . ." Alex taps his chest. "And figuratively. Your conscience, empathy. *Sheut* is your shadow. Your actual shadow and the part of yourself that you hide."

I think of the dream that's haunted me for years, Belot telling me that I hide myself away in Father's lecture hall. The firelight seems to shine on me now, the real me, casting no shadows at all.

"Which leaves *Ka*." Alex nods behind him, toward the jar of dust. "The spark of life."

"Shame we can't translate that one," William says, echoing what we're all thinking.

But Tess brightens, nodding to me. "Go on, then. Tell us about *Ba*. I'm assuming that was the next one in the sequence."

It's time to show my sister who I've become. Who I could have been all along, if things had been different.

"It was indeed," I say. "In *Ba*, I identified a key to a simple cipher, and from there it was a question of discerning the additional layers of decryption as the cipher progressed from one scroll to the next."

Tess peers up at William. "Told you she was amazing."

All five elements of my soul glow at my sister's words.

"Honestly, the suspense. I can't take it." Tess leans forward. "What does it say?"

I take a moment to revel in the dry desert air, the sand beneath us stretching endlessly, the glittering stars above, timeless and watching, and then I begin to read.

"'On following with faith as Aten lowereth his face: the worthy knows not and fears not that which he does not know . . .'"

CHAPTER 22

TESS

En route to the Valley of the Kings

THE EXPANSE OF SAND BEFORE US SIMMERS WITH A molten orange glow, the midmorning rays searing my back like furious flames. Three days we've been trekking through the desert, and each day the Sahara sun grows more relentless than the last.

I keep one hand on my camel's reins, using the other to spread my gallabiyya across my forearms to better protect my freckling skin, and glance behind me at Lila in her own desert-guide disguise, her face wrapped to protect her fine features from the wind. My sister, the prim debutante, on camelback, plodding across the Sahara's sherbet dunes.

Almighty. If Grandmama saw her right now.

I still haven't fully absorbed the changes in her since I saw her last. A world traveler. A bona fide decryption *marvel*. Belot was certainly right about that. She's read the scrolls aloud every night around the campfire since we've relinquished our *babur* and taken to the sands, hoping to further elucidate their meanings, and has made it quite clear she wants none of my proffered legends or conjecture on the matter.

She may be more like Dad than she realizes. At least in that respect.

Uncomfortable with our long stretch of silence, I shout over the wind, "How's the ride? Have you tamed that beast at last?"

Over her camel's head, Lila's grim eyes find mine. "We've settled into a shaky truce."

I force a laugh. "Remind me of that saying from your finishing-school circles. You can take the girl out of Veltin, but—"

"Tess, if you don't mind, balancing on this camel's back is proving an arduous feat. Small talk might well be the proverbial last straw."

I bristle, turning away, though a bit pleased now by her riding struggles. Lila already fell off her camel once, back at the merchant near the Nile's banks, when our three-day journey upriver came to an end and we first took to the desert. Attempting to mount, she'd leaned forward when the beast stood up, and toppled straight over. She almost fell again when Alex spotted al-Qurn, the golden peak that towers over the Valley, and we tried to pick up speed.

I'd invited her to ride with me, but Lila refused the offer, as she's done with all my offers.

Somehow it never ceases to sting.

Alex gives his camel a nudge and sidles up beside my sister, repositioning his rucksack. Our most valuable possession, the bulky bag is bound tightly across his chest, secured snugly in front of him. All the scrolls, Lila's decryptions, and the canopic jar are stored inside.

"You see the wadi ahead?" Alex calls out to me. Everything

is covered but his eyes. They're heavy-lidded, exhausted; he's exhausted, we're all exhausted, and yet his tone makes me thrill with anticipation.

I turn and squint at the horizon as William trots up on my other side. I'm not used to navigating the desert. Every time I'd visited Dad in Egypt, he led the way, never bothering to explain the route or share his maps, and my previous trip to the Valley last summer went about the same. So at first I'm not even sure what I'm looking for exactly, growing anxious when all I see is a shifting wall of glitter, a hazy mirage of dusty wind and sparkling sand. But then there, in the distance, below the peak of al-Qurn, the sprawl begins to take shape. Carved paths and ancient walls wind through the hills, like sandstone impressions of colossal snakes.

My pulse quickens the same way it did the first time I saw the Valley.

"Should we stop at the gates?" I call back to Alex. That's what we did with my father last summer. Tomb KV20 is generally considered the gateway to the Valley. The place was excavated years ago, so it's a tourist magnet, always crowded, which makes the site an easy spot to blend in, regroup, and set up camp.

"Too much foot traffic, I think." Alex frowns and looks over his shoulder, as if the Fraternitas could be right on our heels, following us and the scrolls, step for step, across this never-ending breadth.

Despite the brutal heat, I shiver. I'd be lying if I said I've fully escaped. Every night in my dreams I hear Annie screaming, see those winding catacombs of bone, the goblets overflowing with red. A blood-soaked Davies capturing me. I told Lila and the boys all about the Fraternitas' grotesque initiation ritual the other night, when I was good and tipsy from William's whiskey and the whole ordeal felt more like a recollected nightmare; it oddly made for the perfect campfire story. Though sharing the horror did little to unburden me.

"He's right," William murmurs beside me as I force my dark thoughts to scatter. "We should assume the Valley will be crawling with spies. Given what we've learned of the Fraternitas, it's safest to assume their payroll extends to every corner of the country."

I slow my camel and pull out the Valley map we procured, then stretch it wide across the animal's coarse hump for the rest of them to see.

"So then it looks like we go north at the fork," I say.

Alex nods. "And we'll come at KV55 from the other side."

We ride in silence until the desert dunes settle into a stone-bordered road that winds up and into the hills. I want to stop, savor our crossing through the Valley gates. I experienced the same sensation the first time I was here: this sense of rapture, belonging, even; ebbing and flowing with the tides of time, sinking into the past.

And yet we don't have the luxury of dawdling and can't risk drawing a second glance.

So we plod right past KV20's entrance, beyond the scores of genteel men with their rented camels, the ladies with their broad-brimmed hats and parasols. Past a large group on holiday closest to the ingress, haggling with the local guards and angling for a peek at "Egyptian glamour."

We continue on, farther north through the Valley, up a steep incline, and around a series of peaks. All along the route are long, dark entrances to sacred pharaonic tombs, one after another, like a series of transporting portals. Each site a doorway into another New Kingdom dynasty, a moment in time preserved underground.

When we reach Rameses' resting place, which Alex confirms

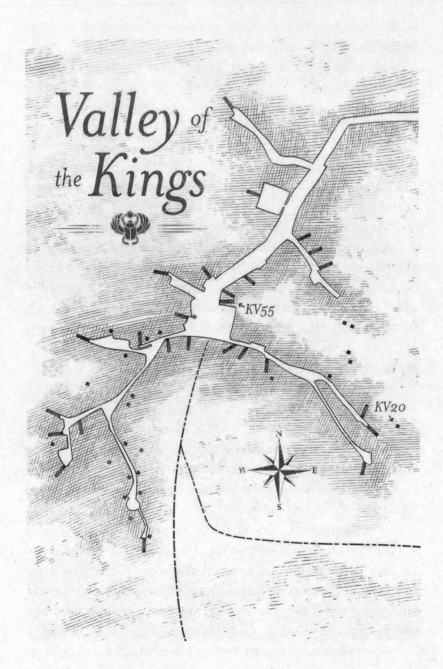

is only a few sites down from KV55, William and I break off to scout the area for any suspicious guards or familiar faces. Because Rameses' site is such a mess, a low-lying site destroyed by vandalism and flash floods, the tomb has sadly been relegated to storage space for other active excavations. I heard Dad once call it *"Egyptology's dumping ground,"* which made Alex visibly flare, and seeing the wreck again now, the site of such exploitation and careless rearranging, I can't help but become enraged myself. Still, the picked-over tomb is a blessing today, as it's currently deserted, our best bet for camping and remaining invisible.

By the time we've set up, the packs and supplies unloaded, the camels tied, it's late afternoon. Lila and Alex sit helping each other readjust their kufiyya. I can't help but smile, watching them. The sheer unlikelihood of the two of them getting married. All the more ironic given Lila's appreciation for mathematical improbabilities.

William plops down beside me, arching his back and groaning from the uncomfortable ride. As soon as his gaze finds mine, he winks, tucking a stray lock of my hair into my kufiyya. "I can hardly believe we made it."

His face might be speckled with dust, his garment positively filthy, but still, he's candescent, those deep blue eyes of his glimmering like sapphires. He loves this place, doesn't he? Same as I do.

"Is the Valley all you imagined it would be?" I ask. "From the stories?"

"It's beyond humbling, to be strolling past hundreds of years with each step, entire civilizations." He beams back at me. "You were right. About the past."

"And you might've been right about a thing or two. Something about a perfect match, was it?"

He smirks, stealing a kiss along my neck, our disguises not-withstanding. Fire ignites at his touch, heat waves rippling down my spine.

Blast it, I've become one of those wide-eyed ingenues I used to mock, swooning over some suitor, dreaming and waking and breathing for "true love." And I don't even care.

I wonder. Does Lila see the changes in me?

That would require her to acknowledge me, or even look at me instead of at Alex's satchel, which she's been staring down since we've stopped. While the rest of us sit stuffing our faces, Lila hasn't touched her lunch. No, as always, she's too "hungry for answers." One summer in Saratoga, I remember, she stayed awake for almost three days successfully solving every syllogism in Lewis Carroll's *Game of Logic*, plus all his diagrams to boot.

I want to be proud of her.

But watching her now, more closed off to me than ever—and here in the Valley, no less, where I've long imagined the two of us together—well, all I feel is hurt.

"Still thinking about the *Sheut* scroll, are you?" I say hastily. "I've been meaning to talk to you about the one before, *Ib*. When you read it aloud last night, the bit about 'readiness of heart,' something connected. Have you heard the ancient myth of the Hall of Maat?"

"Funny how one can't think while someone else is talking." Lila must see me flinch because she relents. "Actually, I'm still debating the meaning of the first one, the *Ren* scroll," she admits. "I know the most elementary translation points to a hidden chamber, but . . ." She lets out a loud sigh. "I'm not sure. The *jmn* symbol. 'Hidden.' It feels too facile."

Before I can get a word out, Lila cuts me off. "Yes, yes, Occam's razor, but still."

"I was only going to remind you that a hieroglyph can

represent a full panoply of meanings. So instead of 'hidden,' *jmn* might actually mean 'buried' or 'translucent.'"

Alex leans between us with a smile, pressing a finger to his lips.

"Right." Lila drops into a whisper. "Thank you, Tess, for the unsolicited decryption advice."

"Regardless, 'hidden' is clearly the symbol's meaning here," I whisper back, bristling now. "I was able to parse the first scroll, after all." At least a few words of it, but she hardly needs to know that. "Alex, you and Dad were searching for a concealed chamber in the tomb, were you not? I think that's where most Egyptologists assume the Crown would have been hidden."

"And yet Lila makes an excellent point," Alex whispers. "Dr. Ford's and my extensive searches revealed nothing of the sort. The entire time we were here with Davies last month, we were as meticulous as Sir Petrie himself, I assure you. There is no hidden chamber."

"It's beyond perplexing." Lila bites her lip. "And speaking of perplexing."

She gestures to the satchel, its loose fabric doing little to hide the shape of the canopic jar tucked inside.

"Is it possible that we do have the full puzzle?" William murmurs. "Perhaps those aren't remnants of a fifth scroll. Maybe the Five Ladies were kind enough to provide a cheat sheet, to help those with mere mortal intelligence to achieve what Lila has."

"I don't claim superior intelligence," Lila says.

William, good sport that he is, ignores her chilly tone. "Because you don't need to." He nods toward the satchel. "Proof is in the pudding."

Lila barely affords him a smile.

My heart jumps into defensive mode before I recognize her countenance: that same glazed-over expression she used to wear when hunched over Wehman's riddles and *Game of Logic*. True to form, Lila lurches to free the notebook from the satchel.

Alex gently pulls his bag away. "May be best to pause this debate until we're in the tomb itself. Wouldn't want to attract any unwanted attention."

As if on cue, we hear something and all startle. Voices. Close ones.

I look across our camp to meet Alex's worried gaze.

"We could leave the camels here and wait out nightfall around the back of tomb KV55," he suggests quietly. "When the guards change, we'll figure a way to sneak inside and poke around for the secret room ourselves."

We finish eating quickly, grab our lantern, satchel, and canteens, and scale the low stone wall off the Valley's path, traversing the hundred yards across the sand to the back of tomb KV55. Alex was right; the high dunes out here will provide shade from the setting sun, as well as an excellent vantage point to keep lookout on the tomb's entrance and cover from prying eyes.

After waiting silently, stiffly, for what feels like hours, dusk drapes a thick indigo curtain across the sand. In the fading light, by and by, we see motion outside the tomb, guards greeting one another, changing shifts for the night's watch. What appear to be two local Egyptians surrender duty to a pair of fair-skinned blokes, sweating and flushed in their British khakis, even in the evening shade. The pair of soldiers immediately squat outside the tomb, lighting two cigarettes.

Alex and I exchange a glance. These cads, touting their smoke in the middle of a desert, flirting with setting fire to priceless artifacts. It's the very portrait of careless imperialism.

I return my gaze to the soldiers, all of us reduced to waiting until their break ends.

One of the guards eventually bids adieu to the other.

Only one left. One guard, we can handle.

"Do you recognize the fellow?" Alex whispers to William.

"Hard to say." William squints. "But he's European, bored-looking, and overdressed, so fair to assume he's in cahoots with my father." He begins to stand. "I suppose I could talk to him."

I grab his elbow. "'Talk to him'?"

"Spin a story." He winks. "Convince him that I'm here on my father and Theo's account."

Alex considers this. "I'll come with you."

"Might be more prudent if I go alone, in case he recognizes you," William says. "You and Dr. Ford were at this site for weeks, after all."

Lila throws me a worried glance. "And what if he doesn't believe you?"

"Then I'll convince him another way." William shrugs. "If I've learned one thing from my father, it's that money talks, and fortunately we have cash left over."

"All right." Alex looks wary. "Call for us, should you need anything."

"We should use a code word," Lila says, perking up. "I suggest *Pi nu pi*—it's Greek for SOS with one layer of cipher."

"Lila." Gad's sake, my sister. "William, just cry *help* should you need us."

We watch as William scales the dunes, running to keep ahead of the slipping slope. As he disappears around the dune's cobalt bend, Alex, Lila, and I scramble up to watch.

The guard stands as William approaches. Even from here, it's clear that William is the image of deference, all wide eyes and charm. He waves his hands, obviously spinning some elaborate tale as to how Mr. Hendricks's son happens to be here, alone, in the desert.

But the guard's jaw stays set. A grim, hard line.

My stomach bottoms out.

"This isn't working," Lila whispers.

"He'll figure something out," I whisper back.

William pulls a stack of dollars from his pocket, slipping the bills toward the guard's hand.

The guard visibly recoils. William raises his arms, nodding slowly.

I sink. "And he'll know when to walk aw—"

William spins, lightning fast, and delivers a blow to the guard's stomach.

The three of us gasp.

The guard reels back, but William doesn't give him time to recover, winding up with a floorer to his jaw. The man goes down.

Then all we hear is the hollow wind across the desert.

William looks back at us and tips an imaginary hat.

"Or," I sputter, laughing, "he'll do that."

Alex coughs a chuckle. "Not the smoothest encounter, but I have no objections."

He grabs our lantern and satchel and scurries over the dunes. Lila and I clamber up behind him. Next to the heap of a guard lies a glowing oil lantern, which William takes and uses to light Alex's.

"Money talks, does it?" I tease while William shakes the pain from his hand.

"Can't say I'm all that ashamed about being dreadful at bribery." He grins at me. "Any pointers on my fighting form, by the way?"

I playfully jab him.

"We should hurry," Alex says, "before the other guard comes back."

Lila clears her throat. "And, ah, perhaps dispose of the evidence?"

We look to the fallen guard.

"Quick, gents, you grab his arms," I say. "Lila and I will take his feet."

After some awkward finagling, we manage to carry the guard around to the far side of the tomb, though at some point midhaul, Lila insists she sees him move. Following Alex's clearly well-honed method of verifying the guard's state of unconsciousness—no doubt an upshot of traveling for years alongside my father—we conceal the chap's body behind a pile of rubble removed from the site and camouflage him with loose debris.

Without another word, we creep into the imposing stone entrance and through the long shadows of the tomb. Alex with the first lantern, followed by Lila, then me, William trailing behind with the second light source. Alex's light casts a white, eerie halo across the rippled stone, like a luminous portent.

A portent of what, I'm not entirely sure.

"Watch your step," Alex whispers.

And then, one by one, we descend into a darkness worthy of Chaos itself.

"This staircase is cast"—Lila lets out a whimper—"at quite a dizzying tilt."

As I let out a strangled laugh, the deep, musty scent of time fills my lungs. "A little like the entrance to Dante's Inferno."

"And yet the portal to hell would be practical, wouldn't it? This is nearly forty-four degr—" Lila's steps skitter in front of me, and I hear a smothered whimper.

"You all right?" I grab on to the wall, centering myself in the rank dark.

I've never been inside a tomb without Dad. His presence used to feel like invisible armor against the forces of a thousand years; the new gods, the old gods, the sacred ghosts that whisper inside ancient walls. And yet, despite the terror, there's something undeniably exhilarating about being here without him. Seeing the tomb, the Valley, Egypt, through my own eyes. This feels nothing like the excavations I used to imagine, where I'd dream of being in charge, on my own, a relentless pursuer of "glory," like my father.

Though glancing downward at the others now, I can't deny this reality tops those fantasies.

"We've reached bottom," Alex calls up.

I gingerly take the remaining stairs and find my footing on the ground next to Lila.

William jumps down on my other side. "What a mess."

Together we survey the long, narrow space. Under the soft light from our lanterns, it feels as though we've been plunged under the sea, trapped in the belly of a shipwreck. Broken relics, panels, ancient pottery lie strewn about, shelves bent and damaged.

"Vandalism around these parts is shocking," Alex says, dismayed.

"And the flash floods don't help," I add.

Lila looks at me, curious. "Floods? In the desert?"

I shrug. "Believe it or not, it's common in these parts."

"Davies didn't help either," Alex mutters. "The sarcophagus had a perfectly intact gilded facade until he stormed in here like a rampaging rhino—"

William takes a step into the rubble, met with an immediate *c-c-c-rack!* "Oh dear."

"Watch your step, everyone," Alex says. "There are panels here that are thousands of years old; absolutely priceless, if not in the monetary sense, certainly in the academic one."

Nodding, William carefully edges around the inner sarcophagus lid leaning against a corner wall. It does, indeed, appear badly chipped.

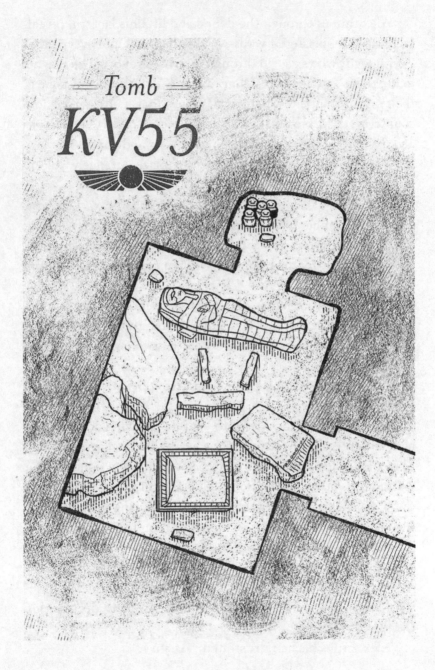

Alex tiptoes through the debris and lifts his lantern, revealing four bare, plastered walls—walls that Dad and every other Egyptologist who's passed through here have reported on, having found them downright puzzling. Tomb KV55 showcases none of the typically vibrant, artistic wall scenes that its New Kingdom counterparts do. No detailed visual shrines to departed pharaohs and queens, no elaborate renderings of gods and goddesses.

These walls of Akhenaten's resting place, strangely, tell no story.

"We should split up to find the hidden chamber," I suggest, "as we're down here on borrowed time. Lila, why don't you and I scour the alcove in the corner for a latch or door or any trick wall to a secret room. Alex and William can search the tomb's other side."

"You know your father has done this countless times before," Alex reminds me softly as he hands his lantern to Lila.

"But now we have all the information we need," I say, resolute. "What's one more try?"

Alex relents with his silence, and we split up, taking to our separate spaces.

As Lila crosses the alcove to examine its far side, I run my hand over the textured stone of the nearby wall, inspecting every corner for a clue to a hidden chamber. I search the floor, too, for a disguised pulley or trapdoor. All the while I try to summon the patience I've been forced to cultivate during my time with the Fraternitas. Sometimes the answers require looking again, a different perspective, digging deeper.

"Anything, Tess?" Alex calls out after a while.

"Nothing." I huff.

"I'm coming up short too," William adds from deep within the tomb.

Alex scrubs his hair, frustrated. "As am I."

It doesn't make sense. This tomb must hold the answer, and we cannot move forward until we find it. And so I run my hand over the wall again, retracing my steps, frantic now, over and over, nearly carving my own grooves into the floor.

That is, until I spot Lila absently running her hand over the alcove's curved wall as she reads to herself from the notebook.

"'Seek you the snake, small, lowly man . . . First ride you in Hennu into night.' Is *Hennu* some type of decorative cosmetic?"

I hurry across the alcove to discuss the decryption together, but she waves me off, distracted. "'And in that place remains only dust, the end of man and the beginning.'"

Thrusting her lantern upward, she studies the southern wall recess where the canopic jars, per Alex's site map, were originally found. Five little stone ladies.

One of which, I remember, still resides in Alex's satchel.

I carefully cross the space, stepping around a pile of rubble, until I reach Alex, warmly illuminated by his lantern's glow. He eyes me curiously as I open his bag's flap and carefully dislodge the canopic.

Returning to the alcove, I place the container on the recess. How awfully alone it looks now.

I glance once more at Lila, still pacing, debating the decryption with herself. She doesn't even see me, does she? Doesn't hear me, doesn't want to, never does, almost as if I'm wholly—

I let out a startled cry.

"Tess?" William says, starting toward me. "Tess, are you all right?"

I spin on my heels, my eyes finding Lila's.

"Invisible," I sputter. "The chamber is invisible!"

CHAPTER 23

LILA

TESS LUNGES FOR ME. I RECOIL IN ALARM.

"Let me see, would you?" she cries, motioning to my notebook.

I pass it over warily, watching her scan my text.

"Yes, this is it," she says as if in awe. "You were right, Lila, about being wrong. The word *hidden* is a mistranslation!"

Odd time to be criticizing my work, but just as I'm about to retort as much, it connects.

"*Jmn.* Not *hidden. Invisible.*"

I look up at her and she at me, and as one, we burst out laughing.

"Ah." William exchanges a bewildered look with Alex. "Care to fill us in on the joke?"

"It's right here," I say, pointing to the notebook. "'Seek you the snake, small, lowly man,' and we are seeking it!" I glance back at William. "I'm not calling you a 'small man.' It's in the text."

He raises his eyebrows. "I assumed as much."

"You're of perfectly average h—"

"'First ride you in Hennu into night,'" Tess reads on, then murmurs, for my benefit, "Hennu is a barge. In the underworld."

"Oh, that makes much more sense."

She goes on. "'Where the Aten, he who drivest away death, keepeth his rest.' A reference to the afterlife? What do you think, Alex?"

Alex steps gingerly over artifacts to steal a peek. He takes the lantern from my arm and holds it out so we can all see the notebook.

"'The glorious rays of the One God bury themselves from human sight'—meaning down here—'and in that place remains only dust, the end of man and the beginning.'"

She slams the notebook shut and beams at the men.

They look as blank as the walls of the tomb.

"Dust!" I say. "Don't you see? 'In that place remains only dust.'"

William stares at the bottom of his boot. "There's certainly no shortage."

Tess makes an exasperated noise and reads on. "'Find you then the chamber that is hidden, make offering to the light and the light will shine upon the tomb where sleeps the snake of the gods. Then let fear quicken in your loins.'"

I warm on the word *loins*. Alex is standing awfully close.

He shakes his head slowly. "I . . ."

"For heaven's sake." I spin to the recess and snatch up Tess's canopic. The jar feels cool in my hand, astonishingly smooth after all these millennia. Like the four others, apparently, its lid has been carved in the shape of a woman's head.

I stare at her and she stares back, placidly waiting.

"Do be careful, Lila," Alex blurts, his eyes flashing panic. "That's—"

"Valuable? But why?" I ask.

Tess walks over to me and lifts the little head like it's that of a doll's, peeking inside. "That's the same question I've been asking myself since I first laid eyes on this jar in Paris. There's not even any sections of papyrus scroll left, as we can all see."

I stitch the last few threads for them. "One might even more accurately call its contents . . ."

"Dust." William steps forward. "Great Scott!"

Alex marvels. "All this time, since the first scroll was solved, and no one made the connection."

Tess giddily wraps an arm around my waist, careful not to jostle what I'm holding. "What now?"

I point to the lantern in Alex's hand. "'Make offering to the light.'"

"Ah. Yes." Alex blinks down at the flickering flames, then at the jar. "This is where I ask whether you're joking."

"Not in the slightest." A wild giggle escapes me. "It's the jar marked *Ka*, isn't it? Meaning the 'spark' of life?"

Alex still looks wan. "If you're wrong, Lila . . ."

"We'll have destroyed some useless dust," William says.

"Nothing is useless," Alex mutters back.

I watch him, my darling fusspot. "What are your instincts saying?"

Alex's eyes meet mine, the tension in his body releasing. "To trust you."

Warmth ripples through me at those three simple words.

Tess opens the tiny glass door of the lantern, exposing the flame. No one moves or speaks. I lift the jar and carefully pour. A bit of the dust escapes onto the ancient floor, but the balance finds its way onto the fire. I stop, wait, watch, though for what, I'm not sure.

The lantern's fire flashes, sparks, a tiny Fourth of July, and soon begins to shine the oddest shade of blue, nearly green, like a turquoise pendant made of flame.

"That's it?" William leans closer.

Tess grabs his wrist with a gasp. "Put out your lantern."

William extinguishes his light. Our eyes adjust to the strangely tinted luminescence.

My mouth falls open.

The once-bare walls are glowing, not blue . . . but gold.

I pick my way across the chamber to the far wall, touching what was bare plaster a moment ago, now illuminated, images shining in every direction as if this entire tomb were thrumming with lines of energy, purest sunlight in arrow-straight strands and winding threads and hieroglyphs and enormous, glorious votive images, throngs of men and women bearing platters of fish and game, bulls and rams, dangling incense and sheaves of wheat, a feast for an honored guest.

"Incredible," William whispers.

Tess wanders with him, chin lifted to take it all in, eyes sparkling wild like when we were children playing fairies in Central Park. "My gods, how advanced must they have been to have achieved this. What do you suppose they used to do this, Alex? Some type of mineral alloy?"

"I couldn't begin to guess." Alex beams at the walls, as if *not* knowing were a treasure in itself.

I understand the sentiment. I'm wonderstruck, struck right in my heart, brain useless, all instinct now, and what a glorious sensation it is.

We've found the invisible tomb.

Hand outstretched, longing to absorb the gold into my skin, I follow the image of a cobra, a pharaoh crowned, the sun god this Akhenaten fellow worshipped hovering like a disk above him, its rays descending on hundreds of small kneeling figures, the river winding behind them, all the way back to the recessed altar where the canopic jars must have stood when Father first opened the tomb . . . the place where the Five Ladies rested for millennia.

I lift the turquoise lantern higher, revealing more of the images.

"Oh, Isis." Tess presses her hand to my back. "This is it."

"'The light will shine upon the tomb where sleeps the snake of the gods,'" Alex recites.

"So simple," William says. "Right here the entire time."

I'm too full of awe to feel any pride. My eyes travel up the golden, shimmering, waving line, tracing each curve and marking. I don't know which way marks north or south, up or down, but I know that the line must represent the Nile, and that the curved, ominous, beckoning golden snake coiled to the right of it marks a place on the map.

Alex lifts his hand, murmuring to himself as he marks landmarks and curves of the river from memory.

And now we know. The Serpent's Crown is not in KV55. It never was.

It's in the Eastern Desert.

"So now we know where it is," William says. "But then what are the other scrolls for?"

"Perhaps the journey will illuminate the rest," Alex says, frowning. "It may be that further trials await us once we get there."

My eyes meet Tess's. She shrugs.

"Let's worry about that bridge when we cross it." She turns to Alex, handing him the notebook. "Take a quick sketch. You're better than I am."

"Your skills are coming along," he says.

She snorts. "Since when do you bother sparing my feelings?"

I glance over my shoulder and find Alex looking at me with such intensity, like he wants to gather me up and kiss me on the spot. Swept up as I am by this setting, the beauty of all the gold, history, and magic surrounding us, the feeling is so very mutual.

"Ah." Tess smirks. "Since lovely Lila came along."

I kick her in the boot. "Don't spare her feelings on my account, Alex."

"In that case, you're dreadful at field sketches, Tess," he announces. "A barn cat with a pencil caught in its paw could draw with more accuracy."

"Ouch!" Tess clutches her heart.

"Watch yourself, d'Auteuil," William says, cocking an eyebrow. "Some of us do have a vested interest in this young lady's feelings."

Tess leans into him, more kitten than barn cat. Alex and I aren't the only ones feeling the romance of the moment.

I whirl, drinking it in again, as Alex sketches furiously. This chamber, invisible for thousands of years, has revealed its secrets to us, of all people.

"Who's down there?"

We freeze.

"That you, Tompkins? You know the boss don't like any pokin' around." Footsteps echo down the steps and then stop. "That's funny."

Heart clenched tight, I grab the lantern from Alex and blow it out in a *whoosh*, plunging the chamber into darkness. My hand darts out for him but touches something else, wooden, damp, flat. I hear the others scamper away, Tess letting out a near-silent curse, and my eyes adjust, a dim orange glow issuing from the entrance. It's enough to let me see William pull Tess behind a large panel resting against the far wall.

Alex slides swiftly behind a scrap of fallen roof. He's reaching for me, imploring, but it's not big enough for both of us, and the lantern light is growing nearer, along with the guard, muttering to himself, "Get a hold of yourself, Louie. Curses ain't real." The recess behind me provides no cover, and the thing I'm touching is a sarcophagus, bigger than me by a factor of four.

I open it, silent, climb inside, facedown, but it can't be helped. I lower myself carefully, carefully, so carefully until the sarcophagus surrounds me and I am hidden. I cannot see a thing in this position, but I can smell. Oh, help. And every whiff is raw horror.

I strain with everything in me to stifle a whimper. And all the while my nose is scraping something cold, hard, bumpy.

I am not alone in this coffin!

My heart begins to hammer so loudly I'm certain we'll all be discovered. Stars gather in the corners of my eyes. A gag rises, but I swallow it down. It's only a body under all that wrapping, semi-decayed biological matter, mere scraps of what once was human, possibly even a pharaoh. I'm lucky to have had this experience. How many American girls can boast that they got this close to Egyptian royalty? Akhenaten himself, the famous heretic! What a coup for a tourist like me.

Now it's a laugh that threatens to burst from my throat, my shoulders shaking so hard that I actually hear bones rattling beneath me, when two rough hands grip me tight and haul me out. My fists fly upward and start pummeling, but the second I connect with this particular hard jaw, I recognize its curve. Oh, that dear face. I hope I haven't damaged it.

I throw my arms around Alex.

"The guard's gone," he whispers. "Didn't stay but a minute. I think he was terrified."

"There's a mummy in there," I whisper back.

"I know, darling." He sounds apologetic.

"I touched it." I'm not sure whether I'm boasting or complaining, but Alex holds me tighter.

I hear Tess and William making their way to us, my vision all but useless until they huddle close.

"He's still up there." Tess sighs. "How are we going to get out?"

"I believe this is where I come in handy once again," William whispers.

I hear the scratch of cotton against skin. Is he rolling up his sleeves?

"You can't just go around punching everyone," Tess hisses.

"Am I hogging all the action?"

Tess begins to pace.

William pulls her in before she can get very far. "I do enjoy watching you fret over me, but I assure you, I can handle this. Hold tight."

We hold everything—thoughts, words, muscles—as we listen to him bolting up the ancient steps. The sound drops away and eternity descends. He could have been shot for all we know. Except that we'd have heard the blast.

Finally, a grunt echoes down the stairwell, followed by a sloppy sort of clamor and a decisive *thud*.

Footsteps resound once more, jaunty ones, taking the stairs two at a time. Within seconds, William's lantern lights up the room in plain old firelight, revealing bare walls all around.

We let out a collective exhalation.

"Another henchman bites the dust," William says, breathless. "Old Hendricks would be thrilled if he knew how I'm upholding the family motto."

"Do I dare ask?" Alex arches an eyebrow.

"*Semper callidus*." William slips his arm through Tess's.

"Ever resourceful," I interpret.

"Ever foolhardy," Tess huffs.

"Only for you." William kisses her cheek, then glances over his shoulder at the chamber one last time, regret plain on his face. "Shame it's the walls, really. This belongs in a museum."

Alex and I share a dubious smile at that declaration, in tacit agreement.

This marvel belongs precisely where it is.

In moments, we emerge from the musty stairs, tiptoe over the latest unfortunate guard, sprawled supine on the top few steps of the tomb, then scale the wall back to the Valley's path. I suck in desert air, stingingly dry, blessedly clean.

Which is much more than I can say for myself.

"Where to now?" William claps his hands as if we've just emerged from a music hall.

"Where else?" Tess holds up the notebook, open to Alex's hasty but excellent sketch, the river winding past an expanse of desert, a high ridge of hills, like a long spine, in the middle of it, and nestled into one crook, that tiny coiled, dangerous, priceless symbol. "Mustn't keep the serpent waiting."

CHAPTER 24

TESS

❧

Deir el-Medina, Egypt

WE RIDE ON CAMELBACK TO LUXOR, ALEX AND WILLIAM
setting the pace ahead, Lila and I trailing behind. No one has
really spoken since we left the tomb hours ago—the sheer
wonder of what we've just witnessed, had the privilege to
share, rendering any attempts to describe such magic wholly
inefficacious.

Still, as we leave the sprawling temples of Deir el-Medina
and the Colossi of Memnon take shape against the starry night, I
find myself increasingly restless to tête-à-tête with Lila. Itching,
specifically, for her to admit she did, after all, benefit from my
expertise. Same as we've so greatly gained from hers.

"We worked well in the tomb together, wouldn't you say?" I
ask softly. As our camels fall into a rhythmic clop, I nod toward
the two watchful statues puncturing the skyline. "We made quite
the pair."

Lila affords me a rare, unrestrained laugh. I'd forgotten how wonderful it once felt, drawing that reaction from her.

"Tonight was incredible," she agrees.

"You know, every time I've traveled with Dad to the Temple of Amun, and here in the Valley, I've always imagined what it would be like if we were here together," I admit.

Lila glances ahead, her profile turning stony.

"I know you said before that it wasn't so simple for you." The words tumble out, pebbles skittering off a cliff. "But if you'd only asked Dad to join, or asked for my help even, instead of being martyrish about it—"

"Pardon?"

"I only mean to say that things weren't so easy on my end either. Dad goes it alone and expects everyone else to do the same. All those letters I wrote, begging you to join me. You ignored every one."

"I suppose I was busy playing martyr." Her steely eyes latch upon mine. "Tess, do you have any idea what overseas travel costs?"

"Yes, in fact. Dad hardly helps with my—"

"Or how much his latest expedition set us back? His trips to Karnak? Boarding school in London, for that matter."

My cheeks sting as if she's slapped me again.

"In fact, it may be best if I start handling provisions once we get to Luxor." Lila shakes her head. "Wouldn't want your heedlessness to bankrupt us."

She fusses with her reins—an attempt to trot off with the last word, I suppose—but her camel gives a low groan, ignoring her.

I slow my own beast to a halt.

Rage consumes me for the rest of our journey, on our barge ride across the Nile, our tedious plod into Luxor's surrounds. All of my elation from the tomb is now extinguished.

By the time we reach the city center, it's nearly three in the morning, per Alex's pocket watch. But I am wide awake, indignity a kind of motor fuel, keeping me running.

"You have that look in your eye," William whispers, sidling beside me, "like you're about to clock someone."

I shake my head, lips quirking. "Oh, I would not rule it out."

We soon stop in front of a three-storied building at the road's end, adorned with arched windows and narrow balconies and framed by two thin palms, its signage reading *Pension Allemande*.

Alex dismounts, offering his hand to Lila, who, after some production swinging her legs around the camel, plops down beside him.

"Let's remember Cromer's men could be anywhere," Alex says. "We should keep to disguises in the washroom, the common areas. We're just a wealthy explorer and his desert guides, passing through."

After William and I hitch the camels, we join Lila and Alex inside and secure, via a quick exchange with the hollow-eyed bellman, three adjacent rooms on the third level. My sister and her new fiancé in one room—I suppose there's no use playing at chastity now, seeing as William and I found them half naked—while William and I will take single rooms. Despite my protests that we might save money by bunking together, which is the antithesis of heedless, I might add, William insisted he could not take my honor.

"After all of our fake plans for a wedding," he murmured with a wink while we were in the lobby, "let's make the real one worth waiting for."

We split off, settling in, though surprisingly, I don't see Lila when I take to the lavatory to freshen up. The Lila of Riverside spent more than two hours preparing for her ball. Maybe weeks of traveling with Dad throughout Egypt has rid her of such excessive primping rituals.

I can't help but linger in the showers myself, the blessed steam, the luxurious hot water.

Once dressed, though, I set down the hall, newly fortified for a second round in our spat.

Her earlier accusations must still haunt, because at the last minute I veer off and rashly knock on William's door instead.

"Well." He leans against his doorframe, his shirt half-buttoned, a delicious stretch of his pale skin exposed. "And how do you do—*oof!*"

I press him backward into his room, closing the door behind us. I hastily run my hands through his thick, wet hair as I kiss him, pressing my body into his.

"Tess—" He attempts to speak, but I shush him, kissing him angrily.

"Wait, Tess." He blurts out a laugh, kissing me back, the barest of pressure as he holds my shoulders. "Slow down a moment—"

"Why?" I say, my voice raspy, into his ear. "Doesn't count as taking my honor if I'm the one instigating."

"Tricky logic there."

"Please, I do not want to *talk* anymore tonight—"

"All well and good, if I didn't get the impression I'm the romantic equivalent of a punching bag. Not that I entirely mind."

He gestures to his folding bed, lips quirking. "Tell me what's really going on."

I huff as I sit on the cot.

"Sorry. It's my sister. As usual."

He slides down beside me. "And what has Mademoiselle Lila done now?"

"It's worse than her cutting me out. Now she's aggressively picking fights." I shake my head. "She's completely rewritten

277

history, casting me as this clueless, reckless little . . . little instrument of chaos!"

William appears amused but stays silent.

I shoot him a sidelong glare. "Fine, yes, I've made some questionable judgment calls in the past, but I have changed. Besides, this is my world; I'm letting *her* in. It shouldn't feel like the other way around."

"Well," he says slowly, taking my hand. "As a wise woman once told me, 'siblings can be wholly infuriating.'"

I pinch my eyes shut, remembering the moment I comforted him with those very words. Remembering where Annie lies locked away, even now.

"I know I should be grateful we're reunited. That I have her at all," I whisper. "And yet I don't really have her, don't you see? We are nothing like you and Annie; we haven't been close for ages. I was hoping this quest, these weeks together, set to task on the same goal, well, that it might fix everything."

William smiles sadly. "Might take a bit more than that."

I study our hands, entwined together. "Maybe so."

"Keep at it," he whispers, resolute. "First, because you are the most dogged person I have ever met and I worry for my own safety during your bouts of frustration, and second . . ." His eyes cloud over like an oncoming storm, even as he smiles. "Because fate can be cruel. As I know too intimately, one never knows when a moment together might be your last."

"You will see Annie again, William." I stroke his cheek. "We will save her, I know it, after all of this is done."

He squeezes my hand, nodding, though his eyes remain troubled.

I kiss him on the cheek and stand. "Best let you sleep. Tomorrow's another long, sweltering day—"

"Tess, wait."

I turn to find him standing too.

"These past few weeks have all but obliterated my world. My future, once laid out so carefully, is now up in flames. My father, the vicious cad, and Mother, always willing to play along with his machinations so long as she reigns supreme in society, are likely scheming how to get rid of me. And Annie."

He gently presses my wet hair away from my shoulders, taking my chin, angling it toward his.

"But I would not give up a moment of my time with you, not for anything. Promise you know that."

"I do." I place my hands on his cheeks and whisper, "In fact, Mr. Hendricks, I'm not sure how I once survived without you."

He kisses me again. Long and deep this time. So warm, so perfect, I want to crawl into this moment, live inside it, like a cocoon.

"Get some sleep, Tess," he whispers, smiling, and closes the door.

☙

The four of us attempt to sleep in a bit, given that today's ride into the Eastern Desert stands to be even more brutal than the last. By late morning, though, we're ready in disguises—a good thing, we find, as Agency men in their light brown uniforms skitter like cockroaches throughout Luxor's bazaar.

The city's open-air souks are a colorful parade of markets selling fresh pears, lemons, olives, *sheesha*. Coffee shops tucked into darkened alleys and copper wares pedaled below crumbling archways. The air smells of spice, leather, and smoke, and the sound of bright chatter resounds in every direction. Above the hectic sprawl looms the quiet magnificence of the Temple of Luxor.

"Let's divide and conquer," Alex says once we've convened near the market's fountain. "I'll secure excavation tools, as quite likely the tomb is covered by sand. William, why don't you handle water. Tess and Lila, food."

I cut a wary glance at my sister.

Alex pulls a notebook page from his garment pocket. "If the hidden map on the wall of KV55 is drawn to any sort of scale, which is, ah, a rather large assumption, we're looking at . . ."

He hovers his finger around the bottom-right corner of his hand-drawn map, takes out his pencil, and draws an X.

"Lila and I calculated these figures last night." He frowns. "But now that I'm reading them again . . ."

"Nineteen hours and twenty-eight minutes," Lila chirps from memory. "Given a steady pace, with four people on two camels, not including time resting or getting lost. Let's just agree not to get lost. So there and back, we need thirty-two rations for four people."

Alex squints at his scribbled notes, then looks at my sister with tender amazement. "To the letter."

"Should we meet back here in an hour?" I ask quickly.

Alex tucks our map into his pocket. "Sounds like a plan."

Before I can head off with Lila, William discreetly slips his hand around mine, giving me a little squeeze of support.

With a determined nod, I follow Lila across the square. Past the throngs of haggling tourists; the rows of fresh herbs, incense, spices. I take a breath, reveling in the promising bustle, the signal of a new journey, a fresh start. In many ways, hopefully.

"Let's get bread first," I say to Lila, steering us north. "There's a market Dad's used before, past the fruit stalls."

"After I buy some dates. Alex loves them."

"Staples are more important. Plus, you're going to need me with you to barter."

She appears affronted. "I most certainly will not."

I blurt a laugh. "Unless you've learned cursory Arabic since I last saw you, I beg to dif—"

My throat closes when I catch that self-satisfied smirk on Lila's face.

"So in addition to all your decryption work, you've picked up another language?"

"I'm hardly fluent."

"How industrious you are."

"I'd like to think so."

"Failing marks in correspondence, though, let's be honest."

She stops abruptly. Then makes a show of brusquely digging into her gallabiyya pocket.

"Let's split up, on second thought. You can get the bread yourself."

I block her way. "It's a valid point, Lila; years, without one letter."

She slaps a few pounds into my hand, hissing, "Now don't go squandering this."

"Says the woman dealing in golden combs. And while we're on the subject, I've been wondering, how much does a life-size Sargent portrait cost?"

"Tess." Lila grabs my arm so tightly it makes me gasp.

"Ow!"

"Just please, turn around. *Look!*"

Still smarting, I follow her gaze through the crowd, toward a stretch of stalls across the road.

And then I see it—him rather, William—across the market. Backing away from a tent, hands lifted in apparent surrender. His face, arrested with panic, eyes frantically scanning the bazaar. A man with pallid skin under a clumsily tied kufiyya inches toward him.

I blink again, looking closer, a startling flash of light reflecting off a silver blade.

A *knife*. A knife in the man's hand.

Lila snatches my shoulder before I can dart for William.

Alex, huffing wildly, appears at our sides. "They've found us!"

"No," I say quickly, "no, that's impossible. We've been so careful . . ."

But the words die on my lips as another man emerges swiftly from around a fresh-fruit stall across the street. Stocky build, gleaming white suit, chiseled features.

Davies himself.

I stutter-step backward.

Alex looks over my shoulder, cursing under his breath.

I whip around, following his gaze toward another bloke, armed and barreling through the crowd toward us.

"Oh heavens," Lila whispers. "What do we do? We need to go!"

Panic flaring through me now, I glance back to the place where William just stood, but he is gone.

Nowhere to be seen among the fruit stands, fish stands, *sheesha*, coffee shops, alleyways. He's not there; he's not anywhere. As if he were some apparition, conjured, disappeared.

"I can't find him!"

Alex and Lila, though, have already dashed away.

"Wait," I shout. "Stop, Lila, stop!"

Running after them, I hungrily scan the market, on the hunt for a flash of dark hair, a crisp white shirt. But I can't find him. Where is he?

I catch up to Lila and Alex at the fountain.

"Where are the camels?" Alex shouts.

"Over there," Lila gasps, "twenty-eight paces."

"Don't even think it," I say, blocking her path. "We cannot leave without—"

But Alex has already taken both of our hands, propelling us across the dirt road, toward the market's shaded far side where our camels sit, oblivious to our plight.

"Stop it, Alex, slow down. We're not going!"

"We do not have a choice." He clambers onto the back of his beast, thrusting his hand toward Lila. "Come on!"

Lila flashes me a sickened glance, then grips his shoulder. "Alex, she's right. This isn't right; we shouldn't just leave."

"Those men will kill for our sketch, you understand?" His face has gone waxy with terror.

The world tilts. I can't think, can't process.

Lila gives a helpless cry, then swings on behind him.

"He'll survive," Alex urges. "William's father and Davies will be furious, but they will spare him; he's legacy."

I grab the reins of their camel. "I told you what they are capable of!"

"Which is why we need to run," Alex says. "It's not just our safety on the line."

My ears ring, my eyes go glassy; still, I search the market.

"Get on the damn camel, Tess!" Alex sounds so much like my father that I could scream.

"We don't have enough water," Lila sputters behind him, "or food. We're down to a few loaves of bread."

"Unless you two have derringers hidden somewhere, we're better prepared for the desert than facing a small army." Alex pushes their camel forward.

I look down and find myself already hitched onto a second camel's back, hanging on while it stands, the jagged knife of fear, survival, resignation, propelling me forward.

And yet I'm floating outside myself. Less than myself. Torn open, mixed up, the world rearranged along with me.

As Alex waves us onward, tucking us into the tail of a

departing caravan, William's words from last night spear through my heart: fate, the cruelest of tyrants.

The market's compact dirt surrenders to rolling desert waves; the horizon, expansive before us. I buck against its unbearable blankness.

My once shimmering future with William, evanesced like a mirage.

Gone.

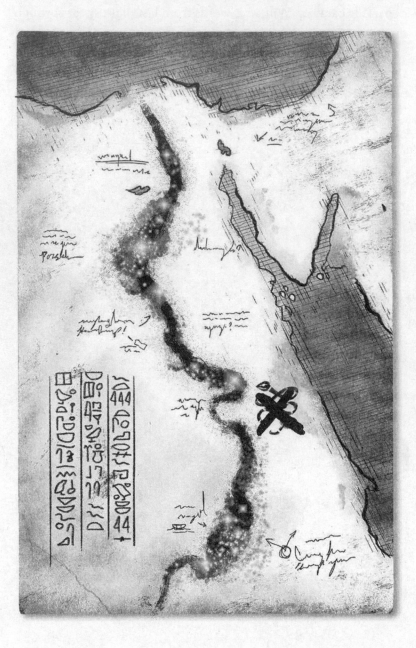

CHAPTER 25

LILA

᠀

Eastern Desert, coordinates unknown

"THE FEARLESS FORDS . . . WANDERING . . . THE BRUTAL desert in search of rarest treasure!"

My voice cracks as I force the words out of my rusty, dry throat. I grip the camel's reins tighter, yanking a tuft of the poor beast's hair in my efforts. He glances back, irate, but doesn't unseat me again. The poor dear is probably too fatigued to attempt it.

It is agony to talk, torture to move, but the pain immobilizing my sister's face is the most excruciating factor of all.

I persist. "We were bound to wind up here, Tess, don't you think? After our exploits in the Amazon basin, climbing Mount Kilimanjaro to escape that horde of wild gorillas, rescuing the kidnapped empress and returning her to the Forbidden City, what was . . . what was left, really?"

My memories of Tess's stories are flimsy, awkward, stilted.

They only serve to highlight how distant we've become in the years since the Fearless Fords quieted into strained silence, but these tales are all I've got, the one bit of bait I have left to put on my hook and draw Tess out.

I look over my shoulder at her again, brace myself, and smile. My bottom lip cracks.

Tess stares ahead at the dunes as if asleep, dreaming something unfathomable, just as she's done the past twenty hours, through fleeing the city, peeling off from the caravan, camping for the night, continuing on this morning, this midday, this . . . I don't know. Time no longer makes sense. There may be something to that. Time as a subjective relativist state, none of this real as we know it, matter itself mutable.

"We'll find it," I say firmly, startling myself alert. "I'm sure of it."

I've never been less sure of anything in my life.

"Tell me that story," Tess says, her voice parched of emotion.

I'm not sure what she means until she slowly turns her head to fix me with a stare, her eyes fathomless with grief.

"Tell me the story of everything working out," she says. "Tell me our happy ending."

"No endings," I say, leaning on my camel's hump, imagining it's comfortable. "Only beginnings."

I spin her another tale, and Alex too. We find our treasure, alongside a magical feast and the sweetest water we've ever tasted. Upon our return from the desert, we discover that Cromer has been driven from power. Egypt has seized control of its own fate and appointed Samy as president and Nura as the chancellor of an already-under-construction university. The members of the Fraternitas have all been captured, tried, and imprisoned for life while Annie and William return home safely, awaiting a joyful reunion with Tess.

That thread of the story causes Tess to sink lower on her camel, and so I unravel a new one.

"And it is only a few years from now that we all find ourselves at the top of the field of Egyptology. Tess is a hero to young women throughout the world and hosts scores of students on her own digs—her expedition that has discovered the . . . ah, the Golden Fleece!"

Tess snorts, but I can tell she's perking up a little.

"And Alex and I love nothing more than to join her when our scholarship aligns. We bring the children along, because they're never apart from us, and they do so love their auntie Tess . . ."

My voice is giving out. It feels like scraping a straight razor down my throat to utter another word, and so we ride for a while in silence until Tess asks, "Where will you and Alex have your wedding?"

If I had the water to cry, I would. There will be no wedding. No happy ending.

Alex, walking alongside me to spare the camel from overexertion, slides his sandpapery hand into mine.

"Egypt," I say.

Tess is quiet for a moment. And then: "I will expect to be maid of honor."

I laugh silently but get out, "Of course."

Alex lets go of me to cradle his rusted compass in one outstretched palm. He treats that tiny wavering needle like a talisman, and heavens above, if only it were such a charm. We require magic, and fast.

But even more than magic, we require water.

I am trying not to think about it. Thinking about water makes the craving sharper.

William was the one charged with gathering water for the journey. When he was taken, we fled east from the market with

LEE KELLY AND JENNIFER THORNE

only the stores we had in our canteens when we arrived in Luxor, and some of it had already evaporated. Yes, we're one unfortunate young man short of a full party; even so, we're running dry at an alarming rate. We allow ourselves the barest droplets at regular intervals. But with the arid climate and the exertion from our onward progress, I estimate we are losing one liter of sweat per hour.

We may survive one more day. Two if we stop walking, stop moving. Give up.

We were meant to have stopped already. Whether or not Alex will admit it, I know we may well have passed the spot on the map already, having surpassed my previous calculations, and if what we are looking for is real, an actual landmark, objective matter, something capable of being found, surely we'd have seen it; but we're walking and walking and never appear to get anywhere. The horizon is a constant. It's as if the desert is trying to trick us.

Perhaps the sands claimed the site thousands of years ago. That's the most likely thing to have happened. Why didn't we consider sooner that the tomb might be buried too deep for us to even see it, let alone uncover it? We probably plodded over it, none the wiser. It's not a thought that bears facing.

But if we reversed course now, we wouldn't make it back to Luxor. Besides, we're too turned around, too muddled to even find a clear shot line. We probably couldn't reach the Red Sea, and if we did, the water it contains isn't potable, so we'd have to expend yet more energy seeking out a settlement, an oasis, or a well. We've come too far into this waste and now all our hopes rest upon the sketch in Alex's notebook, the dodgy compass in his cracking hand, his assurances that this is the right bearing, that those are the right hills on the horizon. But the hills haven't drawn any closer since the sun rose, and Alex's assurances have since dwindled into nothing but silence, labored by the mounting realization that there may not be any water on the site, even if we were to find it.

Alex's ankle turns. He stumbles and stops, and I draw in a gasp even as he presses on his knees and soldiers on.

"Let me walk a bit, won't you?" I try for singsong but come out with a croak.

He shakes his head. "You can't keep up."

"Then I'll catch up."

He makes a sound like he's trying to laugh but his throat won't allow it. If Alex is weakening, if he cannot go on, we are well and truly lost.

"My legs need a rest and so do yours. Let's swap."

"Your logic is failing you, darling."

Logic isn't the only thing failing me. My eyes are going spotty. I knew to expect this; I was warned about those ubiquitous desert mirages, but it's jarring how much I keep imagining things: pyramids that turn out to be crested dunes; a wavering city wall to the north, clear as day, that turns into no more than a distant line of dust kicked up by something. The wind, probably.

Every time I see something, I shout it out, brimming with hope, and Alex corrects me gently and Tess doesn't say anything at all. She rides well, though, even slumped as she is, and as long as I can get her water, there will be time to comfort her, connect with her, build a bridge across all those lost years.

If I'm unable to do so, if there is no water, no Crown, no direction, no chance of survival, then this is all we have. We'll end it like this, closed to each other, full of regret. How pointless the past seven years were, and how foolhardy this adventure.

Thus will end my engagement as well. What a brief romance. Worth every blessed moment, but I want more time with Alex;

I'm greedy for it. I've already named those children. And he's here because of me. He'll die here, too, for nothing.

And Father—what would he say if he knew where we truly are? He wanted me safe. He's probably seeking news of our shocking elopement even now from his hospital bed, and how long will it be before he learns where we are, what really befell us? Will they even find our bodies, or will we remain missing forever? He'll look for us for the rest of his life, all other treasures forgotten. We will be his fool's quest, on and on without end.

What have we done?

Alex holds my camel's reins now, pretending to help guide it, but I know the beast is steadying him. I feel as if I'm standing outside myself, gazing at the three of us, painting a tableau: "Rootless Travelers' Endmost Breaths and Tragic Extirpation." Perhaps a bit overlong, that title. Ah, my mind keeps slipping. In an oil painting of the current style, we'd have hands clasped to our breasts, Alex's outstretched to the skies, pleading for help. To whom do we pray in this desert, the Egyptian pantheon or Aten, the one true god, according to our precious scrolls? Was he even real? Was Akhenaten's faith true, or was the sun god but a testament to his own ego, a way to obliterate veneration for anyone but the pharaoh himself?

Faith in oneself. It has a lovely ring to it, and the notion positively revved my engine back when I was solving scrolls, but in the past day, the sentiment has sputtered and died. I need more than that. I need a serpent to come calling, or whatever the expression is, to look at me and say, "You, yes, you, you're plenty worthy; you'll all be all right," leaving no room for doubt.

Tess coughs, a convulsive sound. I turn to her and extend my hand. She doesn't take it, but she does wince at me and nod, eyes locking with mine at last, acknowledgment that she's still here. She's with me.

Alex squints up at the sun and stops us with a gesture. He pulls out the last leather canteen, shaking it to confirm whether there's any water left. His face flinches, minute evidence of his dismay, but he holds it up to me nonetheless. I shake my head and point to Tess. It's too hard to talk now. He gives it to her and she draws a tiny sip, coughing on it. I motion for her to drink one more, but she won't. I pretend to sip, just enough to wet my lips, and hand it to Alex to finish it, and then that's it.

The water's gone.

He hands me his notebook, as he does each time we stop to rest. I stare up at the hills, as usual, marking the tawny peaks that match those in the sketch. I train my eyes on the blank spot nestled between them, the place where the snake should be coiled, and as usual, I see absolutely—

No.

I blink, hard, swipe my eyes with my kufiyya, succeeding only in rubbing more grit into them, but it's still there, gray among the gold, rectangles sharp against waving lines, and green.

Vivid green.

"*There!*" My shout rips my throat apart, but I don't care. I point, wild.

The notebook falls. Alex bends to collect it. "Lila, save your energy. It's a trick of the sand."

The sound of Tess's gasp may be the most beautiful thing I've ever heard.

"I see it," she says.

I turn to watch her sit straight up, awake, alive.

Alex has seen it now too. Color has returned to his face, spirit to his eyes. Even the camels are huffing with excitement. The long stretch of green in the distance is real, that gray smudge clarifying into a stone tower, a largish building at the center of a walled . . . Can it be a village? I don't even care if the Serpent's

Crown is inside. What's the point of a bit of useless gold, but if there's green, water, hope . . .

Even so, as we spur the camels into a quicker clip, Alex jogging frantically beside us, the village looming larger with every stride, a strange, queasy faith blooms in my heart again.

It may be delirium, but I feel the serpent watching. It's close. It doesn't want to be kept waiting.

CHAPTER 26

TESS

❧

I DIG INTO THE SIDES OF MY CAMEL WHILE ALEX BEGINS careening forward on foot. Lila barely hangs on as her beast bellows loud as a foghorn and staggers across the sand. We barrel forward together, a whirlwind of dust and grunts.

The sprawl of sand-toned buildings and curving spires ahead looms larger with every step, and soon we're galloping onto an actual road, paved on both sides with small, rectangular stones. A walled limestone castle, no, settlement, sprawling and real and more beautiful than every last one of my hallucinations. Do I spot a true church? And what looks like a mill, a bell tower in the distance?

My camel and I careen through the carved entrance in the surrounding wall first, which is mercifully open and—

"There's a well!" I cry out.

We canter gleefully into the settlement's dusty square. I yank my reins to stop, stumble off my beast, and dash straight toward the square's centerpiece—a well indeed, flanked by two columns of stone and crowned with a wheel and dangling jar. I yank the lever to lower the jar into the water . . .

"No."

"What is it?" Lila says, tying off the camels. "What's wrong?"

I heave out a dust-spackled sob, folding over the ledge, and close my eyes, unable to face the empty pit below me.

"Blast it all," I croak. "We're dying here. Curtains."

"'Curtains'?"

"Dry," I tell her. "Not even a pail."

"Wait, but . . . that cannot be," she sputters. "Not after all this. No! I refuse to believe it."

Alex calls our names from somewhere deeper within the fortressed settlement.

I whirl around but still don't see him.

"The gardens!" his voice shouts. "Come look!"

I stand, trailing Lila, both of us following his sound into a verdant lawn speckled with sunflowers and dandelions.

No, not just a lawn. Gardens. Luscious, rolling, green gardens.

Tended jasmine and sharp-angled eucalyptus border the expansive glen, along with manicured bushes, olive and pomegranate trees, planted rows of mint and dill. Sheep graze in gated pastures beyond. Horses too—fine Arabians from the looks of them—tied up at the mill bordering the square. And in the far distance, a narrow, serene blue stream.

I'm about to shred the last of my vocal cords by roaring in relief when Alex appears in my line of sight, walking toward us with a full, sloshing bucket—from another well, I see now, in the center of the glen.

Lila and I run to meet him, and the three of us collapse against the well's stone circumference and begin scooping, cupping, splashing the glorious liquid into our mouths. The water scorches on the way down as I gag, choking, laughing, crying. I find Lila's wide, wild eyes over the bucket as we take greedy, luxurious sips. Once we're satiated, we let the camels quench their thirst too.

We slink against the stone. My belly, so full and sloshing with water that it's uncomfortable. I tilt my pounding head back, closing my eyes.

An oasis.

This must be the place. I feel the certainty reverberate through my whole being.

The sacred resting place of the Five Ladies.

We made it.

Lila stands, twirling around now, soaking it all in. "What exactly is this place?"

Alex, still leaning against the well, runs his fingers through his stiff, sand-crusted hair. "A self-sustaining monastery of some kind. One tucked so far into the Eastern Desert that it's stayed secret, managing to evade all maps."

"It has to be Coptic Orthodox, don't you think?" I ask him, surveying the mill, the cistern, the church throwing long shadows across the square. "Likely from the fifth or sixth century, based on its architecture."

"The farm is obviously in working order," Alex says, peering around. "There must be people who can help us."

I shake my head. "Assuming they're not tasked with fighting off every traveler who rides through here."

Alex considers this. "Let's scout around. Discreetly. Starting with the church."

We take our most prized possession—Alex's satchel, containing the notebook and the scrolls—and leave the rest of our supplies with the camels before journeying back toward the square.

We soon reach the church, and with a grunt, Alex pulls open one of its commanding oak doors.

Inside is all soft darkness, punctuated by islands of light from the church's narrow stained glass windows. Shadowed, vaulted ceilings undulate over a long nave of ancient stone pews, the nave bordered on the far side by decorated alcoves.

We slip inside, one by one. As we do, I notice that one of the alcoves holds a large display of long, thin candles. Two of their wicks are lit, nearly burned down to the ends.

I tilt my chin toward the alcove, pointing out the signs of recent life to Lila and Alex. Given this, I'd wager monks, perhaps, are somewhere inside, gathered in silent prayer or service.

Unable to resist, I walk over to the little niche, take an unlit candle, bend it down to kiss one of the burning ones, and then place the newly lit taper beside its sisters. I glance behind me once more, at the stone benches and the marble altar at the end of the aisle.

My heart sinks. I've been trying not to torture myself, mooning over what's been lost, but I can't help but dwell on Lila's stories in the desert. Our triumph over evil. The Fraternitas imprisoned. My reunion with William and Annie. Perhaps William and I would have our own wedding, too, in a thousand-year-old church like this one. "The Blue Danube" playing, dancing together under the desert stars afterward.

I wipe my eyes briskly, aching to do something useful, so I light another candle, this time in prayer. How I hope Alex was right, that William's father will show him mercy, somehow forgive him. That I might actually stand a chance of seeing him again. And yet, look at Mr. Hendricks's "mercy" when it came to his own daughter. I imagine William now, alone in a dark, dank room, roaring against a straitjacket—and a sob escapes.

"Find anything?" Alex says behind me.

I turn around, my eyes glassy. "Just some more light."

He crosses the space between us and places a hand on my shoulder. "Well. That's something."

He rips one of his tattered shirtsleeves, wrapping the shred of material around his torch, using my candle to light it anew.

I muster a smile. "Always thinking, aren't you, d'Auteuil?"

He winks. "Best to be prepared."

We join Lila, and the three of us walk down the aisle together. With Alex's newly lit torch, the altar soon comes into better view.

We stop in front of it abruptly with a collective gasp.

"Oh my word," Lila whispers.

Sharp, angular hieroglyphs cover the altar, painting its archways, curving around its columns. Nestled among crosses and icons of Christ are ibises, wheat sheaves, ankhs. Thousands of cartouches mark the names of gods and pharaohs and other sacred beings. And snake symbols . . . they're *everywhere*.

The Egyptian cobra hieroglyph is watching us from every direction.

My footsteps make hollow echoes as I spin.

"I don't understand," Lila says. "I thought you said this was a Christian church."

"Churches of the Byzantine period incorporated Egyptian rituals into their practices," I whisper back. "It helped make the foreign religion more palatable to the people and their traditions. Not a conquest but a marriage." My voice cracks on the word *marriage*.

"A layering," Lila offers, and Alex smiles.

I clear my throat. "These churches are some of the only places left that still showcase ancient Egyptian culture, besides the tombs themselves."

"What about all the snakes?" Lila asks.

Alex and I exchange a glance before he answers. "The snakes are not typical."

We take the stairs to the cube-shaped altar, then pass the dozen stone pews facing the front. Beyond is an arched entrance into a dark, narrow corridor, beside which hangs an intricate mosaic of the Madonna, curled protectively around her newborn Savior. Hieroglyphs crawl up and around the image like a frame.

And yet, still no monks.

"Perhaps it's a sanctuary," Alex says, reading my mind.

As we head into the corridor, a scuffling sounds behind us.

"Greetings?" Lila's question echoes into the darkness. "You have some unexpected visitors. I hope we're not intruding!"

We wait a moment. Another.

The monks are clearly not here inside the church, although it still feels like we're being watched. As if someone else, or something else, is waiting for us. I nearly ask Lila and Alex if they feel it too. But I'm bone-tired of being the fanciful one.

When no one emerges, we exchange a nod and continue on. The corridor is pitch-black—thank gods for Alex's torch—and rather narrow. In the flickering light, the walls appear crude and unadorned, a jarring change from the ornate chapel we just left.

In a few more steps, the corridor tightens to such an extent that we're able to touch the rocky walls with both hands. By and by, the hallway twists and turns, releasing us into a wide, circular, windowless interior.

"Finally some breathing room." Lila grasps Alex's arm in relief. The gesture sinks Alex's torch an inch, and the floor flashes like it's crackling with hidden lightning.

I jolt, fixed to where I stand. "Alex," I hiss, "look at the ground."

Lila whimpers. "If there are insects, don't tell me."

I shake my head. "Shine the light down, Alex."

He pauses for a moment, then bends to illuminate the floor.

We gasp again in unison, watching as a thousand mosaic pieces of varying hues glitter underneath us like a colorful, billowing sea.

Alex turns, and his torchlight reveals a large cast-iron brazier a few steps away. He lowers his flame to light it. The base ignites, cocooning us in a tiny sphere of warm firelight.

Now we can see the full, sparkling mosaic underneath us— its gilded tiles extending from a center point, coiling outward like a spiral, widening into the head of a hissing snake. Two red shards for eyes, a thin trail of green for a tongue.

I don't dare hope . . . but, oh blast it, I *do*. We've found the Five Ladies tomb. It must be here, waiting, under this serpent.

Alex thrusts the torch in my direction. I take it with shaking hands so he can pull the notebook from his satchel. Hurriedly, he flips to his sketch.

Lila and I teeter over his shoulders, breathless with anticipation.

The snake on the floor. The one in the book. *They're identical.*

"The tomb," I cry, certainty seizing me. "It's underground, right in this spot!"

A huge grin cracks across Alex's face.

"Have we really found it?" Lila yelps. "We've found it!"

She grabs my hands and spins me, whooping as Alex leans closer to the floor. "Strange." He glances up. "Here, have a look at this."

Lila and I stop our twirl and bend beside him.

I scan the mosaic until I find what the devil he's even looking at. Then I see it: a nearly imperceptible fissure winding through the tiles. I trail my fingers across the mosaic, feeling the thin groove of the break, almost as if the floor has been cracked down the middle.

"Odd, isn't it?" Alex takes the torch from me. Keeping his hand firmly affixed to the fissure, he scoots forward, following the broken line.

A scream rips through me just as Lila jumps backward, shrieking. Alex, too, stands and scrambles away, but his retreating light can't erase what we've seen.

There's a body. Lying in a puddle of blood on the far side of the room.

A monk. Dead. Mouth hanging open, eyes frozen in eternal fear, his lush saffron robe stained crimson.

A hollow *click* echoes through the vaulted room. I reach for my sister.

"Ah." Alex breathes out. "Perhaps best if you two don't move."

We stiffen, slowly turning in tandem to find a gun barrel pressed to Alex's head.

A rather distinctive set of eyes glisten beside Alex. Eyes I know. Eyes that have stared back at me, simmering, searing, wanting, countless times.

"I don't understand," I say aloud. But in a subliminal sense, I must, because tears are streaming down my face.

Other forms are moving in the dark. So many. An army of specters taking shape, just beyond our torch's pool of light, the brazier. Advancing toward us. Closing in around those sorrowful deep blue eyes.

"No," I blurt angrily. "No, this can't be. I won't believe it!"

But William steps forward, dipping his gun. Reaching for me. "I'm so very sorry, Tess."

CHAPTER 27

LILA

AS WILLIAM TRIES TO DRAW TESS IN, SHE SLAPS HIM, hard. The sound of it startles me into reality.

He's here.

Which can only mean he's betrayed us.

William takes the blow stoically, with only a hard blink and a tightened jaw. But his gun, I see, remains trained on Alex's back. "Tess. I can explain."

A light sparks to our right. Another to our left.

Tess glances with me, inhaling sharply as figure after figure brightens, a circle of avenging demons.

They got here before us. Not just William, the entire cadre. Perhaps that line of dust I hallucinated back in the desert wasn't a mirage at all, not kicked up by wind, but the evidence of a trail of fast horses outpacing us to this very spot. Those Arabians grazing near the garden grounds . . . they must be theirs. While we drank from the well, as we laughed and hoped and searched, the brotherhood was watching us, lying in wait.

And William was with them.

He must have copied Alex's map somewhere along the way. How else could he have found this site before us?

The other members of the Fraternitas de Nodum are somewhat more past their prime than I'd imagined, if indeed they ever had a prime, but the sight of them circling us, lanterns held high to cloak their figures in shadows, makes my soul go cold.

There are so many men.

"Tess, please," William whispers desperately, "listen to me."

Tess turns away from him with a disgusted sob and grips my wrist in her clammy hand, as if to keep me from bolting. I follow her gaze as it moves around the chamber. Near the front of the pack of invaders is a man in a garish riding costume who looks rather like a walking stick with a mustache; one step ahead of him is a red-faced, bearded fellow bearing a slight resemblance to William. His father? There's something in his posture, and the way everyone moves when he does, that marks him as this group's general. A bit apart stands another gentleman in field gear. The lieutenant, maybe. In the back of the mob, I see the gleam of a bald head and wonder numbly whether it's the same accomplice Father roughed up back on the Hudson River docks.

But it's the lieutenant whose eyes catch mine, icy and hard. "On your knees."

I glance at Tess. She gives a small, nauseated nod. We sink downward.

"Tess, I promise this isn't as bad as it seems," William whispers again, gliding backward, pulling Alex. "It's our only true way out of this mess. I had no choice—"

"No *choice*." Tess blinks in fury. "No choice but to betray us."

"Land's sake, Tess, can't you see I'm ensuring your—"

"Enough chatter," the lieutenant snaps, and William's mouth clamps shut.

As he strides over to William to seize the revolver from his hands, my momentary relief at Alex being out of immediate danger gives way to shock. I recognize the gun, now that it's illuminated by the clustered torchlight. The last time I saw it out of its holster, it was shooting a hole in the deck of the SS *Stoat*.

The lieutenant looks ever so comfortable holding it. He turns it over in his hand, almost admiringly, and I know without question that he's the one who shot the monk. He must have shot Father as well. With his own gun.

Rage rises in my throat, but it's interrupted by another voice, this one familiar. French. *"Alors*, Mademoiselle Lila, *l'authentique*, at long, long last!"

He's older now, Professor Belot, but then, he'd always seemed ancient to me. As he steps from the shadows, that kindly glint still shines in his eyes. I see it for what it is now: calculation, wheels turning endlessly.

"You and your sister must think me a great fool. The switch you pulled. Brava."

There's menace in those words, even as he smiles dotingly. He is not a man who enjoys being made to look foolish.

"Oh goodness, I can't claim credit for the *switch*, as you call it." I tilt my chin to the ideal nine degrees, and then a little higher. "As an academic, you know how unscrupulous it would be to pass the work of others off as one's own."

His face goes from pink to red as he realizes that I know the truth. Those puzzles I played with him as a child back at Columbia were the very cuneiform decipherments that established his academic reputation. It's no wonder he sought me out to crack the scrolls, targeted me for kidnapping. He wouldn't have a name if it weren't for me. How extraordinarily pathetic.

"You have cracked them all now, young William confessed,"

Belot murmurs, recovering his pallor. "I am eager to see your work. Academic to academic."

I force a derisive laugh out of my throat, so sharp a sound that Belot startles backward.

It continues to echo through the anteroom as Tess chimes in. "None of you will see her work, I'm afraid. The notes are lost. We were forced to use them as kindling when we last made camp—"

"Don't, Tess," William hisses. "There's no use lying anymore."

His voice pinches to nothing as the lieutenant stalks toward us. I notice even Tess drawing inward at his approach.

"Theo," William says carefully. "They're unarmed. Harmless, as I assured you they would be."

Theo ignores William entirely, stooping instead to peer down at the snake mosaic, his eyes lit with religious rapture. So this must be the sinister Theo Davies, the funder who betrayed Father.

William's neck bobs with tension as he swallows. "I do believe it's time for us to go." He nods to Tess, to me, and even more apologetically, to Alex. "Wouldn't want to get in the way of your work."

"You've done it." Davies stares at the cobra mosaic, making me wonder whom he's addressing—William, the serpent, himself?

Then he peers up at William.

"You've kept up your end of the bargain," Davies says.

William exhales with apparent relief, a train emitting steam.

Davies goes on. "But understand this. As far as I am concerned, my wife is dead. She will retrieve not a single item from our house. Nor a single penny. You will collect her and take her out of my sight forever. After today, if I ever see either of you again, I will consider the terms of our agreement revoked."

William nods. "Understood."

Davies rises, striding away.

William turns slowly toward Tess, his face twisted, sallow under the brazier light. "He'll need to confer with Father. Then they'll let us go. They've got to."

Tess's eyes have narrowed to slits. "'Agreement'? What did he mean by that?"

"Annie." William breathes out the name. "Her release from Charenton. I couldn't let her rot in there, fall prey to some staged suicide. She is my *sister*. I know you know what that means."

I glance at Tess. She's gone silent, cheeks flushed furious crimson.

"In Gizeh, as you formulated all those desperate schemes," William continues in a rush, "I realized there was only one thing that would truly ensure Annie's safety, her freedom. A bargain. That's all they respect, Tess—commerce—and as the odds seemed so recklessly slim that day of succeeding on our own . . ."

"Gizeh." She blinks, eyes glittering with horror. "All this time."

He squints away, pained. "I sent them a letter before we set off, alerting them to our direction. Our plans. When they met me in Luxor—"

"*Met* you," Tess growls. "We'd thought you were abducted!"

But he pushes on, dogged. "I'd memorized the map, the dip between the hills. I didn't dare write anything down or record the coordinates, because then they'd have simply taken it from me. I made them order Annie's release, then and there, in the telegram office. And they did it. Sent it off while I watched. She's free even now, Tess. All I had to do in return was lead them here. I'd hoped you wouldn't venture out at all, that you'd stay in Luxor looking for me."

"Don't flatter yourself," I can't resist putting in.

"This is it," Davies calls out to Mr. Hendricks. "Under the mosaic."

Mr. Hendricks waves at the hired thugs. "Get going."

Davies uses the barrel of Father's pistol to nudge Tess and me away from the mosaic. We scoot backward on our knees as the mustached stick walks forward with a pickax.

"If I may." He's British and, judging by how he's hoisting that axe, not terribly strong. "I'm not one to shy from manual—"

"Get on with it!" William's father shouts at his pocket watch. "Grab the snake so we can get to Alexandria and use the damn thing."

"Righto," says the Brit and smashes the floor.

Alex lets out a wordless cry, reaching for scattering tiles. My heart aches for him, my dear preservationist. This must feel like his own skull has been impacted. "Alex."

He gives a bare shake of his head, a bead of sweat running down his jaw.

Another swing, followed closely by another blow. The chapel floor jolts beneath us.

Tess's fingers wrap around mine. I want to hug her but don't dare move.

Another smash rattles the ground.

"I see it," the lanky Brit shouts. "I see, er . . . Perhaps not."

"Then keep at it," William's father barks.

William leans down toward Tess, glancing behind him. "Listen, the past is behind us. All that matters is that we're safe, and we're together—"

"'Together'? There is no together." Tess's composure breaks, her voice a roar. "You've undone everything Annie risked her life for. She won't want to know you when she gets out. She'll be as disgusted by you as she was by her husband."

"Careful." Davies looms over us now, bending so low his head nearly touches Tess's. "You seem to forget who holds the cards in this situation, younger Miss Ford. There's a fine line between gumption and stupidity. Don't cross it."

Davies grips Alex's thick hair, forcing him to look at him. "Or our bastard friend here will pay in your place."

"Stop," I choke out. "Please! Stop!"

William looks queasy. "Theo. You gave your word they wouldn't be harmed."

Davies whirls on him, letting go of Alex to grip William's chin. "Silence. Unless spoken to. And from here on out, you'll address me as Mr. Davies. I'm not your brother. Never was."

"Enough! Who the hell do you think you are?" Mr. Hendricks steps forward, grabbing Davies's shoulder, wrenching him to the side. "This is my show. Fall in line."

Davies eyes William with strange delight, hand resting on my father's gun as if longing to fire it again.

Satisfied with his desecration, the British toff backs away from the great gaping hole in the ground where moments ago a great shining serpent slept.

Belot peeks in with his lantern. He waves for one of the hired goons to come forward with a rope.

I glance at Tess, watching to see what she's about to do. Typically she's brash, quick on her feet and, I'd estimate from various scrapes in our childhood, about 40 percent effective in situations like these. Right now I would be happy to accept those odds, but my sister isn't doing anything except staring down Davies, utterly ensnared by fury.

"Please." I start by begging. It's worth a try. I widen my eyes like a waif in a moving picture. "You are better men than this; I know you are. Men of such high standing, accomplishment, of . . . of great daring. I cannot believe you to be wholly bad."

"Why, we are not bad at all, Miss Ford." The Brit looks shocked. "We do this for the betterment of mankind."

With a nod from Mr. Hendricks, Davies connects the revolver to Alex's head.

"Enough. Chatter." Davies's voice is quiet, in the manner of someone who is about to start screaming. "The translations, Miss Ford. Hand them over. Now."

Alex closes his eyes, slowing his panicked breathing with such visible effort that I feel my own breathing completely stop.

There's only one solution. A simple calculation. I pull out the notebook.

"Don't," Alex whispers. "Don't let them win."

"Oh, darling," I say, fighting to keep my face from crumpling. "They've already won."

Tess tugs on my hand as I stand. "Lila, wait."

She stops there. She knows we're plum out of options.

I turn to Davies, drawing back my shoulders, the last scrap of my dignity.

"As you've obviously surmised, we only needed the first scroll to find this place. The rest are for what's to come: trials, I assume, puzzles or traps." I laugh, like Tess might, like this is a game and we're winning. "Are we all present and accounted for, by the way? You don't happen to have additional armed men patrolling outside, do you?"

"None at all," the mustached British man calls out jovially.

I can tell by the way Davies closes his eyes and exhales through his nostrils that that was the truth.

"Wonderful," I say, heart hammering. "There you have it. I'll give you my notebook; you let us go, all three of us. With our camels."

William flinches slightly when I say the word *three*, as if he actually believes we would welcome him back into our party.

"We shall bid you adieu, take our chances in the desert, and wish you good—"

"You're overplaying your hand." Davies smiles blandly at me.

"Ah. Another gambling metaphor. How charming." My skin flares hot, itchy. "Well, of course, you're holding a gun. My father's gun. Aptly demonstrating through both threat and reference that although I have what you want, you could simply take it, as you did with him. Do forgive me. I'm new to these sorts of games."

I hold out the book.

Davies reaches for it.

But for once in my accursed life, I am faster.

It requires only two half-stumbled, half-sprinted steps for me to reach the lit brazier, where I dangle the notebook over the raging flame.

"You will find, however, that I'm a quick study," I get out, ever so cool and collected apart from the lock of hair that's just glued itself to the corner of my mouth. I blow. The hair stays put.

A storm gathers behind Davies's eyes. I watch his finger twitch against the trigger.

Alex's pulse judders in his throat.

"New game," I call out. "I am going to count to ten. If by the time I reach that figure, you drop all your weapons and allow us to go, I will leave this notebook behind. If we're not released by ten, I'll burn the book and its contents, the only clues to the sure-to-be-challenging trials ahead, and wish you all very good luck getting the Crown without it. Yes, you'll get angry and shoot us, but you also won't get what you want. Might even get stuck down there, or die, perish the thought. Everyone clear? Good." My hand shakes around the book. "One."

"Land's sake, Lila, he will shoot Alex!" William blurts.

"Quiet, boy!" his father snaps.

311

But Davies smiles. "No, he's right, I will shoot. I dispense with scruples in moments like these."

Davies may not have scruples right now, but that doesn't mean he's not scrupulous. Davies knows that if he shoots Alex, I'll drop the book, and their schemes and machinations will have ended in cinders and ruin, quod erat demonstrandum.

"Two," I say.

Everyone stares, frozen, a tableau vivant.

"Three."

Belot steps forward, shrugging wide. "Ah, but we both know you won't burn it, *ma petite*. All that work. Your mind in that book, your passion. Hours upon hours of painstaking work."

"Four. Oh, I'd hardly call it work, Professor, more of a pleasant pastime, an alternative to needlework. Five."

Mr. Hendricks shoves Belot aside, barreling toward me. "Give me the book, dammit!"

"Six." My knees have begun to tremble like jellyfish. "This game is ever so much fun, don't you agree?"

Mr. Hendricks cocks a fist. "I am telling you right now, if you do not do exactly as I—"

I let the book dip, singeing both the binding and the tips of my fingers. "Oops. You startled me. Seven."

"Listen to them!" William pleads, white teeth gnashed.

"Eight."

I shoot Tess a wild glance. She nods at me, tears glistening. This is no bluff. She knows it. Despite everything, she knows me.

At ten, I will drop it. And we will die.

"Nine!" I shoot them all a celebratory grin. "And . . ."

It all happens so quickly. Davies removes the gun from Alex's head and I nearly cry out with relief, when, from the shadows behind me, I sense movement and turn with a gasp to see some burly ruffian coming at me full tilt.

As Tess screams, "Do it!" I release the notebook into the fire. The charging brute slaps it away from the flames, then plows into me. My knees hit the ground with a *crack*, but I still grab for the notebook, snatching only air as it soars past.

Davies looks utterly unsurprised, simply scoops up the notebook from the tiles and turns away, flipping through its lightly toasted pages.

"You stupid, stupid girl," Mr. Hendricks barks, his face beet red beneath his beard. "You nearly cost us everything!"

"We're not done yet," Tess snarls back.

"No," Davies says idly. "As a matter of fact, you're not."

At a small motion of Davies's hand, the bald man grabs Tess's arm and drags her to the edge of the hole in the ground, while my personally assigned brute hauls me beside her. Of the mosaic, only a tiny triangle remains, one cobra's eye peering up at us, impassive, and beyond it, what can only be described as a drop.

Someone heaves a rope beside us, letting it fall. I glance back to see that it's tied to one of the stone columns.

To my surprise, Davies hands me back my notebook. "Impressive work, Miss Ford."

"As if you had time to read it," I scoff.

"I saw enough. Waste of a good mind, but it can't be helped." He squints at me, then into the chasm below. "And who knows? Maybe you'll even survive."

My stomach bottoms out. "What do you mean?"

"They're sending us into the tomb," Tess says flatly.

Davies smirks. "And here I thought you weren't the clever one."

"You can't do this," Alex shouts. But his voice is instantly muffled by a blow to his cheek that sends him sprawling.

I reach for him, but Davies trains his gun on me, clicking his tongue, while William jumps into the fray, hands raised as if to direct Park Avenue traffic.

"Theo—Mr. Davies, surely you can let them go now. I'll leave with them, ensure they don't interfere." He whirls around, gripping Mr. Hendricks's shoulders. "Father, this is madness; tell him to stop."

"I will do no such thing." Mr. Hendricks pries William's fingers off his arms in the manner of someone removing fleas from a pelt. "Theodore is doing exactly what I directed him to do, as family should. You and your traitor of a sister never learned loyalty. Fealty! Kings don't fight in the vanguard. Leaders know when to delegate."

Delegate.

"You want us to solve these riddles for you." I rifle through the notebook, but the words blur like a flipbook. "I translated them, yes, but I don't know the first thing about Egyptian tombs."

"This one does," Belot says, leering at my sister now like she's an interesting artifact. "Very astute in her own way. *Et sinon*, if you girls get it wrong . . ."

He pulls a sad face.

"We'll be the ones to suffer the consequences," Tess says.

William steps forward, resolute. "I'm coming with you."

"Absolutely not." Mr. Hendricks shoves him backward, hard. "Have some dignity."

"Yes, darling, do as Daddy says," Tess snaps, then folds into a wild curtsy, grips the rope, and plummets into the hole.

"Tess!" I scream, stumbling forward to once again grab at nothing.

When I peek over the edge, half the Fraternitas leaning over with me, she's already a good way down, jauntily dangling.

"You coming?" she shouts up. As if she's left me with any other choice.

I look behind me, reassured to see Alex standing again, no worse for wear, apart from his livid cheek.

He nods, solid. "You can do this, Lila."

Mainly to avoid disappointing him, I clutch the rope and lower myself gently into the gaping hole, ten feet or so above my sister. This is madness. The rope convulses against my clenched hands and knees as my sister continues her descent. Before I even attempt to adjust my grip, I feel it loosen beneath me and hear a muffled *thud* below.

"Made it." Tess's call echoes strangely.

I drop in small jerks, the rope slicing my palms, terror numbing my skin, as I struggle to hang on. My thighs strain together, desperate for a grip on the rope. I don't dare breathe or look at anything apart from the awkward, careful movement of my hands. When at last my toes scrape ground, I let out a sob of relief, let go, and stumble backward. The darkness down here feels thick.

Warm breath grazes my ear.

"*Si shon chis shora mun ek zit,*" Tess whispers in Fordish. "*Zo chis tik lei. Ek uru felta pall. Uru ba shossa i starne.*"

I know it doesn't seem like it, but this is good. It buys us time. We'll find a way.

"We'll require some lanterns," I shout up.

Tess screams, "And a picnic lunch! We work best on full stomachs, you know!"

Through the defiant veneer of her words, I hear a catch in my sister's voice.

"Oh, Tess." I breathe out the words shakily. "I'm so sorry about William."

"Don't even say his name." She pulls away from me with a shudder. "I'm furious, murderous. I wish like hell I'd wrung that son of a bitch's neck like a dishcloth up there."

315

"Well, it wasn't a very good idea for you to trust him, was it?" I blurt, then immediately clamp my mouth shut.

Why, oh why did I say that?

"You actually can't stop acting like Grandmama, can you?" Tess turns the heat of her anger onto me. "It's incredible. These past few days I've been thinking you've changed, but—"

"I thought you'd changed too," I snap, not even sure where I'm taking that insult.

"Changed? From what? The person I was a decade ago? You haven't paid the slightest bit of attention to me since—" Tess glances sharply upward.

Someone has swung his legs into the oculus above us, bellowing, "Lanterns! As requested!"

I have to grant this British fellow some measure of respect. He somehow manages to dangle three lanterns on one arm while climbing down that rope at an impressive clip.

"*Quu chep tik?*" I ask.

"The Earl of Tembroke," she answers in English.

"They've sent an earl down with us?"

He hears me as his boots touch bottom but doesn't seem to catch my meaning. "Your astonishment does me honor, young lady, but I insisted. I've grown tired of being the fifth or sixth to enter these tombs after their discovery. They don't even mention you in the newspaper if you're not one of the first three, and this time I intend to be number one." He draws a headline in the air. "'Earl of Tembroke Discovers Tomb of Legend.' And about bloody time!"

I'm guessing Tess and I don't factor into this queue of discoverers. We're the ponies in a mineshaft. And not the only ones. Above us, I see a pair of familiar field boots descending the rope into the wavering shadows of this chamber.

"They sent you down too," I cry. "Oh, Alex."

316

"I volunteered," he says, touching ground. "Cited my New Kingdom expertise."

I lift my lantern to see a rueful smile dance over Alex's chiseled face. "Found I couldn't bear the thought of being apart from you for even a moment."

A sob gathers in my throat, of some plaintive muddled emotion—gratitude that I'll have him close to me during these trials, mixed with heartbreak, knowing he faces the same slim odds of surviving them.

Tess strides past me and Alex to pat the earl, of all people, on the shoulder like old chums. "Let's get started, shall we?"

As the earl strides onward, Tess whispers, "*Tik lei. Tik i nomi ku'zit li shemin.*"

This is good. He's the most harmless one of the bunch.

"Remind me to learn Fordish when we get home," Alex mutters, and oh, I could kiss him for his implied optimism.

Instead, I raise my lantern and Tess raises hers in the other direction so we might gain our bearings. We appear to be at one end of a short, somewhat wide corridor, unornamented apart from two rather haphazardly placed rectangular hangings set farther down the chamber.

No, not hangings, I see, as the earl's lantern light reaches them—inlaid panels, possibly doors, one bright gold, the other dark as obsidian.

Tess glides past me, transfixed, while I stand in place, determining our immediate options. Worst case: we find the Serpent's Crown and give it to them, then they shoot all three of us and leave us to rot in the desert.

Best case: similar.

Tess's fingers hover over the walls as she continues down the chamber. "Tomb architects often created false doors to disguise actual entryways into secret antechambers, hoping to foil thieves, but there's nothing here to indicate a hiding spot."

I feel a headache blooming. "I do hope you're as much of an expert as you think you are."

"Alex," she calls past me. "How you put up with my sister for even a day is a mystery for the ages."

Alex is too absorbed in the mysteries of the chamber to pay any mind to Tess's bait. "The floor may offer a clue. You take the eastern end, Tess. I'll check here."

He gets down on one knee, feeling for changes in texture. Ahead of me, Tess follows suit, while I trace the walls, feeling nothing of note.

It does occur to me that there are three of us down here against one earl. We could overpower him, with no one above the wiser, if we're smart.

"Remarkable!" the earl shouts.

I turn to see him staring at the panel on the opposite wall, the dazzling one, decorated in glittering gold leaf in the shape of a sun disk, to indicate Aten, perhaps. He's not talking to me, though, nor Alex, I see now, but rather a third man who's appeared at the end of the corridor where we first came in.

It's Davies himself, still armed with Father's pistol.

So much for my slipshod hopes.

Mid-corridor, Alex slowly stands. Whenever Davies moves, he moves, and I realize with a keen ache that he's putting his body between me and danger.

I cradle my lantern, flip my notebook quickly to my translation for the second scroll, and, to drown out the sound of my hammering heart, announce, "Perhaps my decryptions might help?" I read aloud, "'On following with faith as Aten lowereth his face: the worthy knows not and fears not that which—'"

Tess cuts me off. "I certainly hope we can trust in *your* immaculate expertise, while we're at it."

Far behind us, Alex clears his throat. "May I suggest we postpone this debate?"

"Thank you," I snarl. "As I was saying, 'As Aten lowereth his face—'"

"Aten," the earl cries out from beside the gold panel, like a child in a lesson. "The sun disk."

I force myself to beam as Tess is doing, like we're all colleagues down here. "Precisely."

"Jolly good," he says and presses all his weight against the panel.

"Don't touch anything!" Tess and I cry out as one, whirling round, arms outstretched to intercept him.

But he's already hit the disk on the left panel. With gusto.

Above us, we hear a grinding roar, a mechanism long dormant growling to life.

On the other end of the corridor, Davies jolts alert, gun trained straight at us, like *we've* done something wrong. His eyes dart upward and widen. He backs away, then grabs the rope.

To climb.

The earl scratches his chin, peering up. "What the dev—"

And from the darkness tumbles rubble. Tons of it.

Dust shoots outward from the rockfall like a toxic cloak.

Tess wrenches me back just in time and holds her arms tight around me.

I hear nothing for a moment but a high whine, my ears deafened by the crash. Our lanterns flicker and revive, weaker, but enough to see that the corridor has been blocked, floor to ceiling, by a wall of ancient debris, punctuated by one gangly arm jutting from the bottom.

Tess kneels, touching the earl's wrist. "Dead."

We look at each other, then stand and press our faces to the obstruction.

"Alex!" I scream.

Faintly, beyond the rocks, I hear his voice, and relief floods my veins. "I'm all right. Are you?"

"We're unharmed!" I shout back, gripping my lantern. "We're . . ."

Tess turns in a slow circle. "Completely . . ."

Neither of us says it. Neither of us needs to.

We're trapped.

CHAPTER 28

TESS

❦

THE WALLS ARE LITERALLY AND METAPHORICALLY closing in. The earl was just here, alive, shouting about his bloody name in the papers, and now he's gone. William, turns out, is a vile traitor, we're separated from Alex, the end of this madness keeps retreating like a desert horizon, and now Lila and I are trapped in a tomb and—

I blink. I'm seeing things. It has to be a trick of the light.

Lila's voice is a cracked whisper. "Was that mound of sand there a moment ago?"

I snatch one of the earl's lanterns, dimmer now in the chamber's constricted air. I scan the corridor's perimeter, look up. And wince.

A dozen small apertures have slid open around the ceiling of the chamber. From the top edge of every wall, torrents of glittering sand cascade in long, thick, golden waterfalls down to the floor. The sand crunches beneath our boots as we back up against each other.

"It's clearly some type of mantrap," I whisper, glaring at the ten-foot-high stone ceiling; the three walls lined with sashes of sand; the fourth wall, a barricade of rubble. "The rockfall too. The earl must have triggered it when he chose the wrong door."

Lila nods toward the gilded panel, its dramatic sundial now partially obscured by the fallen rocks.

"If the golden door doesn't lead to the Serpent's Crown," she says, "it stands to reason that the black one does. Perhaps there's a levee behind it to stop the cascade."

She trudges through the mounting sand and shoves her hands against the black door.

"My Gooood!" She whirls her arms backward like a deranged windmill, teetering. "It's a Gad . . . darned . . . cliff!"

Dashing across the space, I pull her back.

We both sink to the sand-smothered floor.

She scuttles crablike away while I scoot closer to the onyx panel. Slowly inching forward, testing, sliding my foot across the chamber's floor until I reach what we'd only assumed to be a second door. My foot reaches a clear drop, my heel flapping over the ledge like deadweight.

I flip around and inch forward on my hands and knees, careful, face hovering close to the ridge. Wafting from below is the pungent smell of dank, deep earth. Frigid cold, churning up like an undercurrent. There's thick silence, too, so boundless, so laden, that I feel it on my skin.

"You're right," I whisper. "It's a pit."

"A pit." Lila lets out an incredulous pop of a laugh. "Of course. A pit!"

"Maybe we can push the sand over its edge." I shove a pile in demonstration. "Here, help me."

"A Sisyphean task. The sand is filling this chamber at a rate of five cubic feet per *second*."

"But—"

"We're doomed. Hope your flirtation with the son of our enemy was worth it."

"'Flirtation'?"

But Lila says nothing, her boots slipping as she flails away from me, attempting to stand. Finally upright, she huffs her way toward the wall of fallen rubble.

"I fell for him, Lila. You saw us; it was real!" I hurry after her. "You cannot blame me for this. I was wholly blindsided."

She shakes her head. "Only because you didn't want to see it."

"You honestly believe this is my fault?" I snap a laugh. "For falling in love? For being human? Although maybe a walking abacus would frame that as a weakness."

"In lieu of engaging further with you, I am herewith devoting my energy to more productive efforts, thank you very much." With a ridiculous, unearned battle cry, Lila yanks a five-pound brick from the blockade of rubble and tosses it onto the sand.

"So digging out *brick by brick* is better than my idea? You just said we're moments from being buried alive!"

"Between nine and eleven minutes, assuming a constant rate," she concedes, as she cleaves another small stone from the wall of rubble.

I twist my sweat-soaked curls behind my back and wildly look around. The gold door equates to getting crushed by rocks, while the black door leads to a long plunge and certain death. Staying would amount to eventual suffocation, seeing as the torrents are quickly covering the chamber in a thick swath of sand, despite the narrow opening to the pit. And yet going up the way we came down is no longer an option.

"Wait!" I grab her shoulder. "The other scrolls after the first are puzzles to solve, tasks to complete. Quick, give me those translations again."

"No." Lila whacks my hand away. "Start digging. I've entertained your suggestions for far too long."

"My suggestions have resulted in actual solutions." I suck in another wasteful breath. "Lila, think. Even if we manage to dig our way out in ten minutes—"

"Nine." Lila glances at one of the sandfalls, keeps digging. "Eight."

"Fine, eight, the Fraternitas will still kill us if we don't come back with the Crown. As I said, I need those translations, and now!"

"Don't bother doing your impression of Father. I'd say no to him too."

"Oh, I'll give you a Dad impression."

I lunge full-throttle for the notebook, but she spins away, nearly tripping on a sand mound. She presses herself against the wall, bumping into the dead earl's dangling arm with a horrified yelp.

Our eyes meet. I give a flustered laugh, lurch for her once more, and manage to pry the book straight from her fingers. She shrieks, lurching to take it back, but I block her with a stiff arm and victorious smile.

We both know she's no physical match for me.

"Fine, take it and go." Her eyes brim and overflow. "Jump down your trapdoor and leave me here to waste away . . . *again*."

My smile falls away. She wipes her eyes, placing her hands on her hips, but her lips keep quivering.

"What do you mean, 'leave you again'? Is this still about Queen's College?"

She turns away.

I cough from the sand's chalky billows, skittering around the nearest cascade. "Please. You barely spoke to me in those days and even less since, so stop pretending you care that I left, other than my decision's financial implications."

She shakes her head. "You ran away and left me."

"Because you acted like I didn't exist!" I blurt. "You're the one who ignored me every time I came back to New York. You're the one who barely wrote in the past seven years—"

"Because I was jealous!" She tries to stomp her foot into the sand, but it's past our calves now. "You've built an entire life. Managed what I couldn't, made your own way, regardless of expectations."

"But how many times did I beg you to join me? What I would have given on those digs—"

"And was I supposed to forget my duty to Grandmama, to Mother?"

"Hardly looked like duty to me," I say. "All those beautiful dresses. Your life was like a painting I could look at but never walk into."

"I thought I was saving you from it." She lets out a helpless laugh. "I estimated that only one of us had to play Atlas. Keep it all from falling apart."

The entire room rumbles. A teetering pile of bricks on the far side breaks off, tumbling from the pressure of the sandfall.

My eyes fly to Lila's.

A new, loaded silence resounds through the room.

"All right." I take a low breath, risking another glance down. Hell's bells, the sand is to our knees. "We've got some things to figure out. I want to. I think you want to. But we're never going to get the chance to do so if we don't manage to find a way out of here first."

Lila looks back at the brick blockade. Nods.

I thrust the notebook at her. "Out loud, please. Your writing's atrocious."

She flips the notebook with trembling fingers while I perch the lantern over her shoulder. The pages transform into soft orange, carved dark with the scrawl of handwritten notes.

"'Make offering to the light.'" Lila tucks a sweaty thread of hair behind her ear. "'Then let fear quicken in your loins, for the unworthy will perish.' Yes, we're well aware."

She flips another page.

"Here: 'The worthy knows not and fears not that which he does not know.'" Her voice takes on a primed tone as she reads the *Ba* scroll translation. "'Aten sinketh nightly beyond waking grasp into darkest chaos, fearless in his fall. But the small man craveth light, unseeing in his seeing, feeble in his strength. Earth embraces the small man.'"

We both glance at the earl's limbs, protruding from the tower of fallen rocks.

"How literal," she says with a swift clearing of her throat.

"Never say the ancient Egyptians didn't have a sense of humor. Is there more?"

"One last line: 'The cobra, old as earth and yet more patient, awaits the great.'"

The words rearrange in my mind, teasing out stories from Dad's library's texts, scholarship, books on mythology. Passages from the *Book of the Dead*, legends from the Eighteenth Dynasty. *Fearless . . . darkest chaos . . . unseeing in his seeing.*

It's there, our escape route, rippling beneath the words; I can sense it. Still, it's too slippery, impossible to fully grasp.

Lila hurries to read the next scroll's translation. "'On readiness of heart for passage through the underworld. All that is brought into the beneath—'"

I startle. "What did you just say?"

"'All that is brought into the beneath.'"

"Before that. 'Passage *through* the underworld.' That translation feels—"

"Flawless?" she hisses through gritted teeth.

Her pride might be obnoxiously admirable, if not for the

pyramids of sand rising like spires around the room. We're square in the middle of the tight space and the gritty current enfolds our thighs.

I heave myself above the sand tide, clambering to mount it, and offer Lila a hand to do the same.

"My understanding of this scroll sequence is that it mirrors a traditional ancient funerary text," I hurry to explain. "Where the passages describe the deceased's challenges passing *into* and *out of* the underworld. It's the same in the *Book of the Dead*. Egyptologists all agree on these translations. Are you absolutely sure the translation is *through*? *Through* the underworld?"

She cocks her chin. "This time I'm positive."

Adrenaline trills through me.

"That means there's an exit." I thrust a thumb at the rock wall caging us in. "And it's not that one. Quick, give me that book."

She hands it to me, taking the lantern, and I let the words crest over me once more. *The worthy knows not and fears not . . . darkest chaos . . . fearless in his fall . . .*

"Chaos!"

Lila's eyes widen. "Is that a general observation?"

I grip the wall, scrambling once more to ride the rising sand. Lila follows suit.

"The ancient Egyptians called the force of all life *Chaos*. Chaos is the catalyst for the beginning, the end, what all life springs from and will return to." My words practically trip over one another, terror eclipsed by the sweet thrill of discovery. "Chaos was always depicted as a dark, shadowy unknown, a . . . a place where the serpents of life were first created. Don't you see? All we have to do is pass through the tomb's darkness, claim the snake, and get out another exit. It makes complete sense!"

It doesn't appear as crystal clear to Lila. "Meaning what? There's some type of trapdoor?"

I point to the narrow black panel across the chamber, errant sand sliding off the mounting spires into its opening. "The pit. We have to leap into it."

"What?"

"The worthy '*fears not.*' '*Darkest* chaos.' 'Fearless in his *fall.*' We have to jump, Lila."

"No." Lila shakes her head vehemently. "Not on your life."

"The guardians of the Serpent's Crown wanted to cull the small-minded from the worthy, the terrified from the bold. We have to be brave if we ever want to see the other side of this."

"I've done loads of brave things, thank you. Disguised myself as a boy on a ship full of louts, fallen off a camel, walked through sprained ankles and shin splints and blisters, but I draw the line at jumping into a pit!"

I climb higher, then flinch when I bang my head on the ceiling.

I take her hands, pulling her upward. "I'm as terrified as you are, but look at this place; it's jump or die."

Lila peers at the narrow black portal, frozen, panicked . . . but doesn't let go.

I take that as tacit agreement.

Without another word, I drag her across the sand, toward the opening, then pull her down with me, scaling the slopes until we reach the opening's edge, no wider than the space of the two of us standing shoulder to shoulder. Swift tendrils of sand run around our feet into the narrow entrance to the pit, scattering into the dark like unraveling constellations.

"This . . . this is insane, irrational," Lila sputters, "jumping, blindly, without a clue as to what's below."

"But I'm right here with you, Lila; we're together." I steal a few sharp, staccato breaths. "That's all I've ever wanted for years, by the way."

The depths below appear hungry, primed to swallow us whole, so I look at her. "Just my sister."

Her face softens.

I grip her hand, raising our interlocked fingers. "On the count of three."

I could be wrong, epically wrong, but the truth is, I've never felt more right, capable, than I do right now, standing here with Lila beside me, trusting me to lead the way.

"One."

"I wasn't fully set." She gulps. "Would it be a nuisance to start again?"

"Two."

"Half counts, do half counts, Tess!"

"Three."

We leap. The world, upended; our lantern, extinguished. My stomach lurches and my head swims . . .

But only for a second. Before I can even think, we slam into something flat, cold, and padded by a layer of sand.

Lila sits up as I rub my aching side, the cascading sand from the chamber above still raining down upon us.

With an appalled face, Lila scrapes sand from her tongue. "I don't understand—"

"It was another illusion," I gasp, feeling around in the dark. "This is some sort of platform, camouflaged under the chamber."

I hurry to brush away the sand until my fingers hit something: a raised, cylindrical stone. I press the protrusion, following a hunch. Sure enough, the stone shrinks downward, away from my fingers.

"Wait, what was—" A grating echo roars over Lila's words. "Goodness!"

The platform gives way. Lila's body slams into mine. My stomach plunges and we're on our way down again. But not falling. No, we're sliding down a chute, some ancient bunco, tumbling, spiraling. I can't see, understand, make anything out.

"I beg your pardon!" Lila shouts. "Would you kindly watch your feet?"

"Sorry—ow, that's my hair!"

"I do not like this!"

And then, somehow, we're both laughing, fear and rage and relief boiling over into absurdity. Against all odds and hurdles, the Fearless Fords are barreling ahead.

And down.

We collapse, a tumbleweed of arms and legs, onto a cold stone floor.

I stand, woozy, elated, collect my bearings, and peer around . . .

At absolutely nothing.

CHAPTER 29

LILA

WE PICK OURSELVES OFF THE FLOOR OF A ROOM.

Just a room. That is all one can say for it.

Tess retrieves a flint from her pocket and strikes it against the floor, relighting our fractured lantern. I kick the sand off my bootlaces, taking in the walls, floor, ceiling constructed of white limestone slabs, their edges so fine that in the flickering glow, the effect is seamless. This chamber boasts no ornamentation whatsoever, providing nary a clue as to how to proceed—no deceptive sun disks, no cobras, and aside from the hole in the ceiling we've dropped through, no door out.

I jump for the ceiling to reassure myself we could retreat, if needed, but it's too high to reach. I turn to Tess, ready to suggest she clamber onto my shoulders, and hear a low grinding noise.

I look up in cold awe as a stone slides over the hole we just issued from, sealing it into as impeccably hermetic a design as the rest of this chamber.

"H-how?" I sputter. "How?"

Tess dusts off her gallabiyya. I stare at her.

She stares back, shrugging wildly. "Go ahead and blame me again if that's—"

"You? No! Ha!" My eyes will not stop blinking, and not just because of the last bits of sand still lodged in them. "I can blame only myself. I was wrong. My translation . . . not *through*; there is no *through*. It's a mistake, another mistake!"

Tess cups my shoulders. "You're going pale, Lila. Take a breath."

"There's nothing here, Tess. What if the Five Ladies didn't finish building this tomb? What if all the unpleasantness with Akhenaten happened too quickly for them to complete construction? Or what if they never intended for anyone to find the Crown? This was all a trap, designed to kill off anyone who sought it, and we're the first suckers to get here."

Tess lets out a surprised snort. "Lila Ford, *suckers*? Such language."

I grab her wrists tight and feel her pulse beating as rapidly as my own. "This is going to be our KV55, *our* tomb, except there aren't even any sarcophagi to lie down in!"

"Hate to interrupt your conniption fit with something even more alarming, but . . ." Tess holds her lantern high.

I blink away my terror and see what she's looking at. Something is issuing from the four corners of the room, a strange sort of vapor. It's thick, an eerie lilac in the lantern light. It trickles downward and curls like incense, painting purple patterns against the stark white of the walls.

Hope seizes my heart. "It's illuminating something. Like the golden walls at—"

"I don't think so." Tess's body is rigid beside mine, like she used up all her swash and buckle jumping down that chute. "It could be another trap."

I inhale deeply before I realize what she means. The vapor smells like crushed flowers, heady and sweet, not unlike the potpourri Grandmama keeps in a bowl in the sitting room back in New York. It makes me feel a bit funny, ticklish in the stomach, dizzy in the head.

It's some type of chemical agent. This could be very bad.

"Lila, quick, focus." Tess covers her mouth with her kufiyya. "The next scroll!"

Of course. The room might not bear clues, but the scrolls will.

I pull the notebook from my jacket and scrabble for the correct page.

On readiness of heart for passage through the Underworld

"'On readiness of heart for passage through the underworld . . .'"

My voice wobbles on the word *through*. I cough, taking in more of that strange, fragrant mist. It takes rather longer than usual for my eyes to focus on the words on the page.

"'All that is brought into the beneath is brought in offering: the fish, the cattle, the fowl, the shining and the base.'" I glance up. "Oh dear, were we meant to bring a gift?"

Tess blinks hard, reeling where she stands. Her face is blurry in the halo of her lantern. "I hope not. Go on. Quickly, please."

I rub my eyes and force myself to get the rest of it out in one go, racing ahead of my dizziness. "'Aten seeth all that is laid before him and knoweth its cleanliness and weight, but if small man should cling tight to the shining or the base, not of offering but of fear, the one god shall turn him asunder and he will sleep as still as the cobra in the earth.'"

I suck in sweet air and pick out a rectangular outline on the far wall, limned by that strange purple smoke. After another blink, it blurs and disappears, everything a cloud.

"We're meant to surrender something," Tess says, somewhere a few feet away, her voice strange in my ears. "We need to be lighter . . . to pass through . . . the Hall of Maat."

"'Maat'?"

"The goddess of justice decides whether you're light enough. She weighs your heart against a feather."

"And if it's too heavy?"

Tess swallows, unsteady. "Ammit will eat it. She's a lion-crocodile-hippopotamus."

"Fantastic." I let out a wild laugh and see it sizzle away in sparks. "Lighter how, Tess? Surely you're not suggesting we take off our clothes."

"Why would I ever suggest such a thing?" Mother coos from her chaise longue.

I squint. Hard.

She's here. How curious. Alive again, older than I remember her, but so close my heart beats madly, sending ripples through the whole room.

"Don't tell me you've become bohemian, Lila."

"Of course not." I laugh. "That aesthetic wouldn't suit me."

She pats the space beside her and I cross the room to join her.

My mother, oh heavens, how I've missed her. How strange that I thought she was dead, when she's been here all this time. My blue gown matches her white one so nicely today. We're a matching set of porcelain figures, made to sit perfectly still like this, day after day. Grandmama sits in a brocade chair in the corner, needlework in her lap, but she doesn't stitch or even move, only gazes at Mother and me with a rare smile fixed on her face.

It's morning outside, the city bustling cheerfully past, but I find I can't focus on the view through the windows. Are we in the new house on Riverside or back on Madison?

I rub my temples.

"Oh, my darling, don't scrunch your face like that," Mother says, but dotingly. "You'll get wrinkles and you're far too young. You must be fresh-faced to attract the very best."

"You're right." I reach for the bell to ring for tea, but something stops me. I look at my hand and the bell is gone. "I already have, though. And he loves my worry lines. He kisses them away."

She stares at me, frozen, a stopped frame from a moving picture, before she smiles again. "He's only practice, that boy. Your father's assistant, for goodness' sake? There will be others more suitable. You must learn from my mistakes, dear Lila, and think of the future practically, dispassionately."

"Alex couldn't be more different from Father," I say, and with those words, fresh anger rises in my chest. "And I don't exist to correct your mistakes, Mother, or to restore your family's legacy. I am my own person entirely. Not to mention that your marrying Father can hardly be counted as a grave error, as it resulted in two daughters. Tess is not a mistake, nor am I."

"Tess," Grandmama echoes, familiar contempt ringing in that one tutted syllable.

I stare back at her. "Tess is remarkable. She is the future, and you cannot stand that. You with your parties and pretenses and memories of wealth. You spend our money like you're still that pampered little girl, Grandmama, and I will not bear the burden of your profligacy any longer!"

With a look almost of astonishment, Grandmama fades, leaving the armchair empty.

"Now look what you've done." Mother's eyes glint with tears. "And what of me? If I can't guide you, my darling, serve as a model for you, then I am truly gone, as dead in memory as I am in body. Please, Lila. I am not ready to leave you."

Her face turns wan, gray-tinged, her breathing labored as it was at the end. Her forehead beads with sweat, and I long to cling to her as I did once, years ago, waiting for the doctor to arrive, but instead I hold her hand in mine, feeling its soft solidity for the very last time.

"You'll never leave us, Mother. I will love you forever and always," I say.

Her hand tightens into a fierce claw around mine. I feel my knuckles pinch together and let out a cry of pain. Mother, unblinking, grips me even tighter.

"Let me go," I gasp through the pain, my heart hammering. "I must live a true life, a free one, guided by my own principles. I can't be a paper doll anymore."

I stare at the sitting room and realize now what's wrong with it. It's as if it is all made of paper, an illustration in a storybook. Every flower is perfect, not a single wilted petal in sight. The noise of the city is glittering and polite. The smell isn't potpourri but rather something native to another continent, something grown and ground fine ages upon ages ago.

The room becomes blurry, shimmering with unreality. I wrench my hand from my mother's and stand. My lungs feel tight.

"I won't do it anymore." I bend to kiss her forehead, my tears streaming in rivulets as she clutches at my elbow. "I love you, I do, and I miss you so very much, but I cannot live for your memory. You have to let me go."

With those words, she does. She stares at her hand and it disappears, the rest of her fading fast.

I don't grieve. I know what's happening now, and I see the door at the far end of the hall, outlined in purple.

My tears glitter dry against my cheeks as I stare at the blank space where my mother sat a moment ago.

I'm still extremely likely to die here, but at least I'll die wholly myself.

The truth is, William's not to blame for my sad fate, and neither is Tess. I landed here because I chose to, and goodness, the realization does make me feel lighter.

"Goodbye, Mother," I whisper. "And goodbye and good riddance to Lila of the Veltin set. Right. What's next?"

The real room has returned, a dizzy cloud, but stars are gathering at the corners of my vision, and my lungs clench tight, like I'm wearing a too-small corset. I stagger forward, hands outstretched, and push on that rectangle. It slides a few inches, but not nearly enough. I'll need help to move it.

Where is my sister? This trial should have been easy for her. She's the proverbial rolling stone. What moss could she possibly need to shed?

I can make her out, vaguely, in the middle of the hall, draped in violet smoke. "Tess! Over here!"

I cough. The room is turning acrid and my eyelids are growing heavy.

"He will sleep as still as the cobra in the earth . . ."

My heart hammers. "Tess!"

She glances over her shoulder but not at me, scratching at her arms with her fingernails. "Bring me back, bring me back!"

What horror is she imagining?

"Let go, Tess!" I scream. "Follow my voice! It's not real!"

I step forward, deeper into the smoke, but it's too much. Reality starts to melt again. I step back and press my mouth to the crack in the panel, summoning fresh air. I'm not sure if I discern a substantive chemical difference, but I draw enough oxygen to turn and find her again.

"Look at me, please, please, *please*, Lila." Tess has turned to the left, sobbing. "I'm faded, but I'm not gone; you have to help me. I'm right here; can't you see me? Dad, look at me!"

"This is a dream, Tess!" I call. "He's not real, but I'm here. Come find me!"

For a breathless second, I could swear she's heard me, but then she turns away again, whirls around as if possessed, hands grasping at air.

"Grandmama, can you see me? Please tell me you can see me." She stalks forward, as if following a specter, calling out, "I'm home. I'm not in London; I came back. Lila, why can't you hear me?"

She pauses, as if lost in frantic thought, then paws at herself in a different way. "I'm a ghost. No, they've all forgotten me. I have to remind them, I *have* to."

Oh, Tess.

All those letters I discarded, all the ones I never wrote, out of stupid, pointless pique. All these years that she's believed I didn't care. That I forgot her. Forgot *us*.

Tess turns again, grabbing her head. Her eyes are closing, even as she screams. "No! No! Dad, stop walking. You're going so fast. Why can't anyone see—"

"I can see you!" I shout, stretching my hands out. "Clear as

338

day, Tess! Come find me, and quickly. We haven't got much . . .
time . . ."

I'm too woozy to stand. I slump against the panel until I'm
sitting.

Her voice is growing faint. "Please, I'll do whatever you
ask me to, Lila, just don't forget me. I'm real, I exist. You must
believe me."

She sobs convulsively, then crumples to the ground, her
knees buckling.

I draw one more stinging breath, unable to open my eyes.
With the last strength left in me, I cry out, "*Si duren sta uru!*"

I believe in us!

Even with my eyes closed, dots are gathering, big like marbles,
blotting out thought, action. Rendering impossible any breath.

But then, despite my body's numbness, I feel two cool hands
on my cheeks, slapping me gently.

And again. *Not* gently.

I wrench my eyes open. Tess stands inches away.

She kisses my forehead, hard.

"*Si duren sta uru,*" she croaks. "Now let's get the hell out
of here."

Holding each other up, we plant our feet against the smooth
white floor and, with everything we've got left, push on the
panel. It barely budges.

"Once more!" Tess shouts.

We both let out feral roars this time. Pain rips through my
shoulder as I push. I've torn something but can't fully feel it.
Then I experience something else, the entire world slipping, the
dimensions changing. Is it a hallucination, or have we shoved our
way out?

A narrow gap has appeared beside the huge block of
stone. The air shooting from it smells stale, dusty, unfragrant,

deliciously clean. We exchange a nod and line ourselves up for one more push.

That does the trick. The gap widens enough to allow us to slip through, one at a time.

"Ladies first," Tess jokes, motioning me forward. I can see pain lingering in her eyes. That last test took its toll on her, and not only physically.

"Then go ahead," I say.

She positively beams. "Get your translation ready. There's one scroll left, and for all we know, this one will hit us quickly."

I hasten to read the last page of my notebook. "'On proper bearing in entering the presence . . .'"

But Tess has already slipped through and out of sight. As I shimmy sideways into the narrow corridor to meet her, my body tingling back to life as clean air courses through it, I hear my sister call from the next chamber, "Ah, Lila? We've got some company."

Fresh panic roars through my veins as I emerge into a dark, narrow hall, where . . .

"Jiminy Christmas!"

Tess winces. "Not the liveliest company."

Scattered along the long, narrow chamber lies a decorative quartet of corpses, each charred into a lump of coal the exact size and shape of a man, contorted in agony for all eternity.

Behind me, I hear an ominous rumble.

We both turn with a start to see the stone block we moved slide itself back into place. I'm fascinated by the ancient mechanisms resetting all these chambers to their original state. It's remarkable and terrifying, and we've still somehow made it this far.

A redoubtable feat, but by the looks of it, we're not, in fact, the first suckers to accomplish it. Whoever these adventurers were, their exploits ended here.

I feel Tess's hand slip into mine.

"All right." She draws a tight, determined breath. "What were you saying about 'proper bearing'?"

SHEUT

On proper bearing in entering the presence of the cobra

CHAPTER 30

TESS

❧

OUR CHANCES OF PERISHING HERE?

Well, Lila must have calculated exact probabilities, but I'd wager on a million to one. I nearly thank the charred mystery men for the heads-up. Their baleful warning is blunt but effective.

Still, I raise my lantern to flash Lila an assured smile, muster my sapped energy to feign a swagger forward . . . then regret it.

Something's wrong. Something other than the corpses littered around the room. The stone floor shudders underneath my weight, and I lurch, unsteady, as if I've stepped onto a floating barge.

"What the thunder?"

The entire corridor rumbles. Then comes a groaning creak, followed by a strange hiss and a snap.

We flinch in unison as a tall, narrow fire jumps to life on the left side of the corridor. A breath later, a second ignites on the right, its mirror image.

Oh gods, here comes the end. I cower from the jumping flames, Lila burrowing into my side.

Except . . .

"Wait." I straighten cautiously. "These fires are contained. Maybe they're just meant to illuminate the chamber. We must have activated them by stepping into this hall."

Now that the towering flames enable us to see, we crane our necks around in shared wonder.

Spanning the walls behind the fire columns are two mammoth, matching, detailed panels—identical images of emerald cobras curving out of black waters. The huge murals coruscate under the firelight, while the rest of the corridor remains cloaked in shadow.

"Tess, look at the ground," Lila whispers, rubbing her shoulder. "It almost resembles a . . . game board, yes?"

As I lower the lantern for a better view, I realize I'm standing on a small, square block of gray stone. And before us unfurls a grid of similar squares. A sprawling, decorative stone checkerboard, just as Lila said, like the ancient game of Senet, except every one of these blocks is adorned with a different detailed symbol. Some of the squares display simple hieroglyphs, others bright images of desert sunsets, scarab beetles, the Nile depicted in shimmering turquoise. There must be dozens, if not hundreds of them.

"Each square is eighteen inches," Lila whispers. "There're six squares across, so the hall is nine feet wide by . . . I can't see how long it extends." She straightens. "Though none of that matters unless we figure out the point of the game."

"At least we know the stakes." I try not to glance again at the corpses as I offer her my hand. "Step *directly* beside me, onto my block. Who knows what a misstep triggers in here."

She tiptoes into position beside me, gingerly opening her notebook. Light and shadows dance across her translation of the *Sheut* scroll.

"'On proper bearing in entering the presence of the cobra . . .'"

The words take on new meaning under the watchful eyes of the eight-foot snakes, looming above us like ancient gatekeepers.

"'Aten, who shineth upon all, knoweth all that is thought and done and all that will be. His passage is perfection, and a man cannot follow. The mind of man is small, yet the small man thinketh himself great in body and thought. He reacheth only for light and that light shall devour him. But he who walketh with care and in care he helpeth to walk may find the footsteps of the one god and pass worthy before the snake of snakes.'"

I try to parse the cryptic words, look around for clues, and yet all I see is looming fire and endless stone retreating into shadows. Charred bodies, failed attempts. Lonely adventurers left to rot.

I wipe my brow, now damp with perspiration, inadvertently knocking into Lila's shoulder in the process. The corridor feels smaller, tighter now that those fires have ignited.

And am I imagining things, or are they climbing higher?

"Maybe the fire spreads past the pits if the player is unable to solve the riddle in time." Lila whispers what I'm thinking. "It takes more than ten minutes for someone to die by fire, I read once. Which surprised me. I would have thought asphyxiation would kill before immolation, or a heart attack from the pain."

"Will you just"—I hold up my hand—"read the scroll again?"

As Lila does so, I close my eyes, letting her words envelop me once more.

Aten . . .

The mind of man is small . . .

Light shall devour him . . .

I blink away tears, and when that doesn't suffice, wipe my eyes with my sleeve before Lila can spot them.

My facade is crumbling. Seeing those visions of my family in the last chamber nearly did me in. But underscoring the exhaustion and terror is pure fury, because I know it, I feel it. I'm focused on the wrong things. An Egyptian game board stands between us and the serpent, death and freedom, and I can't for the devil figure out why.

"'A man cannot follow.'" Lila frowns at her notebook, wiping her brow with her gallabiyya. "Not *man* but *a* man, singular. Don't you find that odd? As if they were expecting a woman all this time?"

"Wouldn't that do the Fraternitas in. Bigoted louses." I force a laugh. "Two bits of jam, meant to hold the key to man's future . . ." Trailing off, I stare again at the corpses.

One, near the right-side firepit, wears the tattered remains of a Roman legionary uniform. Another, on the left, charred Ottoman livery from the Crimean War era; I can just make out the arma. The one farther down the floor, right where the firelight surrenders to darkness, the remains of . . . peasant clothes most likely, probably a seeker from the Middle Ages.

Men from all different eras, far-flung locales. United only by their desire for the Crown.

Lila surveys them, too, nose crinkling. "How did they get here? We had to have been the first ones to find that illuminated map."

"Maybe there were other paths leading here." I shrug. "Perhaps there were rumors of an oasis in the east, a church covered in cobras. Or one of the monks let something slip. Three thousand years is an awfully long time to keep a secret as big as this one."

"We'll never really know, will we?" Lila asks, a bit sadly.

"A little late to inform their relatives anyway." Something connects, realization dawning as I pinch out a stunned breath. "They're alone!"

"Indeed." Lila sighs. "We all are in the end."

"No." I pull her notebook between us, thrusting my finger at it. "Not a *man* but *a* man, because *a* man cannot follow! Only the one who 'helpeth' is worthy!"

Lila considers me carefully. "Are you still suffering from the silly gas?"

"Gad's sake, Lila—this trial is meant to be performed by more than one person!"

I steal a breath and explain. "Little is known about Akhenaten's reign, but what we do know is that he was despised by his people. After he died, his temples were defaced and destroyed, and he was branded the heretic king because he came in and forced the Aten on his constituency, with no respect for their traditions, no empathy. That's why Akhenaten is considered a tyrant even by pharaonic standards."

I pause for a breath, glancing at the flames. Indeed, definitely climbing.

"The Five Ladies would have known the power of the cobra firsthand, that it could be a tool or a weapon. They'd want the next holder of the Crown to understand people and their needs, to be altruistic, collaborative, to put the group before themselves—"

"The opposite of a tyrant."

"Exactly!"

Lila gulps beside me. "So what precisely must we do to prove that we're worthy and, ah, not alone?"

My smile fades. "Your guess is as good as mine."

Arms linked, we pivot carefully on the stone block, surveying the firepits, the cobra wall panels on either side, the decorative stone grid before us.

"Tess. Look. Where the official lies, over there." Lila points four blocks down and two blocks over. "The gentleman with the gold buttons. See where he fell?"

"The stone's image," I whisper, peering up. "It's an exact match to the cobra panel."

"That has to mean something, yes?"

I scan the rest of the victims, then perch to get a closer look at the soldier corpse on our left.

"Careful, Tess," she murmurs.

My skin prickles, even in the heat. "Lila, he's near another cobra block."

"Walketh with care and in care he helpeth . . ."

"We're supposed to step on the stones that match the panels at the exact same time," I blurt. "Coordinated steps, like a dance!"

Lila's face falls. "Do not tell me that our future rests on my two left feet."

"It's not the waltz," I assure her. "More like skipping, or even jumping—the synchronized landing must quell the fire triggers under the floor."

"Could it really be as simple as a matching game?"

I arch an eyebrow. "Not so simple if you're alone."

She lets out a whimper.

"You'll be fine." I carefully slide past her on our cramped stone island, my body thrumming with anticipation. "We just need to time our leaps. You jump to the cobra block on the left; I'll move to its match on the right. Yours is closer, a small hop, but make sure to account for the skeleton."

"'Account for the skeleton.'" She presses her fingers to her temples. "Tess, you do realize that your cobra is four and a half feet down, four and a half feet over? You're jumping a hypotenuse of over six feet. That's Olympic-worthy."

"You wouldn't doubt me if you'd seen the record-breaking leap I made from Belot's window," I say, resisting the urge to tell her that her calculations are tearing my papyrus-thin resolve apart. "And don't forget, you're no slouch yourself. A mere hour ago you hurtled into an abyss."

The feeble jokes do nothing to lighten the mood. Lila continues shaking her head, rubbing her temples, then her shoulder again. Perhaps she hurt it in the last room.

"Listen." I take her hands. "Those stories you told me in the desert. Maybe they don't have to stay fantasies. Maybe it's not too late for the Fearless Fords after all. Because we're about to finish this, together. Indeed, I wouldn't have survived the last chamber were it not for you."

I look at my feet, still holding her tight. "And I really am sorry, Lila. For everything."

She gives my hands a squeeze. "*Sha*, Tess. *Si ti em.*" Oh, Tess. *I am too.*

I warily glance at the fire on the left. "Besides, if we're wrong? If we do end up like these sorry louts? At least we'll go down together."

Lila nods, her eyes drifting again to the stone checkerboard. "Okay. *Si duren sta uru.* Let's finish this. One leap at a time."

I nod, releasing her hands. Crouching now, ready to pounce.

"Or rather two simultaneous leaps at a time," she corrects. "All right. Ready."

"Count of three again?" I ask.

This time, we count together. "One . . . two . . . *three*."

I push off the stone landing with all my might, legs scrambling to stay aloft. The moment extends into a lifetime.

348

I land on the cobra block with a wild skitter. "Blazes!" I wheel my arms to keep from falling forward.

Balance restored, I turn to find Lila one row behind me, four blocks away.

"Made it!" She clucks proudly and arranges her filthy desert disguise. "Though I almost lost it there— *Whoooooooa!*"

A geyser of flame shoots up beside her.

My heart nearly stops. "Lila!"

"My boot," she cries, "my boot, my boot." She stumbles back, stamping her foot.

"Lila, stop moving. You'll set off another trigger."

"Shall I just let it burn then?" she screams.

"Roll your foot. Smother it out on your block!"

I watch, helpless, as Lila stomps, slides, rolls her foot until the flame pinches out, disappearing.

She raises her leg slowly. The tip of her chocolate boot has turned a tarry black.

Before I can ask if she's all right, a grumble rolls through the corridor. Another *hiss* and stuttering *snap*.

A second set of firepits ignites next to the first.

"It worked," I whisper.

Newly illuminated behind the second set of firepits are two new massive panels, rendered in hard onyx lines and incredible detail. In the murals, worshippers crowd, bowing on their knees. A glistening jade snake slithers at their heels.

"I see a block with the worship scene," Lila calls, still rolling out her boot. "Up ahead of me. Slightly longer jump but . . ."

I scan the floor until I find its match. "Got mine. Close to the middle!"

Lila shakes her foot once more and squares off. "Another count?"

I nod.

"One . . . two . . . *three*!"

We both leap, bounding through the air, and land on our blocks with *thumps*, close to each other this time.

"I'm not steady!" she blurts, but I lean across the block between us and grip her shoulders before she can teeter any farther. She lets out a cry of pain but gets her bearings.

Together, we slowly creep to standing until we're facing each other, eyes locked in giddy terror.

"Maybe I was wrong," I whisper, still gripping her. "It does feel a bit like a waltz, doesn't it?"

Another rumble resounds through the room. A crack, a hiss, and then a third set of firepits ignites on either side. In moments, two new wall panels glimmer to life—this pair spectacular in their simplicity.

Matching golden sun disks.

I turn to locate the disk blocks on the floor and begin to quake with excitement.

The entire hall floor is now illuminated. There are only three rows of blocks standing between us and the end of the corridor.

"Lila, look, we're nearly there!"

She clasps her hands in glee, then points two rows in front of us. "Sun disk!"

I find its match a few columns away on the right. "And the other!"

We share a delirious giggle. Despite these ominous fires and the corpses littered around us and the pervading, relentless smell of death, I've honestly never enjoyed playing a game as much as this one.

"One," I call out.

Lila nods. "Two."

"Three!" we say in unison, leap, and land on our twin sun disks.

This time there is no earth-shattering rumble. This time there's just the gritty whisper of sliding stone.

We watch in wonder as the corridor's back wall glides open, warm light coiling around its corners.

We leap with triumphant shouts beyond the stone game board and onto the corridor's solid ground. A quick dust-off and we rush toward the door.

"The Fearless Fords, dashing to victory," Lila whoops as we round the entrance. "Onward, to claim our . . ."

Her words fall away as we slide inside.

The alcove is a huge, glittering, torchlit treasure chest. Lined, floor to carved ceiling, with tightly packed shelves.

Gold and silver baubles. Statues carved from ruby, sapphire, and jade. Trinkets hammered out of onyx and sculpted from Nile clay.

Lila and I exchange a long, loaded look.

They're all cobras.

CHAPTER 31

LILA

I STARE AT THE PILED WALLS OF SNAKES AND THEY SEEM to move, contort, slither, but when I blink with decisive force, I find it stops. *All right, then. Which of you has been calling us?*

My mind numb with panic, I leaf through the notebook. "Let's see what the next scroll says."

Tess peeks around my shoulder as I flip to the last page.

An empty one.

"Oh right. *Sheut* is the last one. We appear to have reached the end of our clues," I say, straining for chirpiness.

Turning back a notebook page, I find my final set of decipherments.

"'Snake of snakes,'" Tess reads, squinting at the page. "That refers to the Crown. Which means this is where it lives . . . along with several thousand of its friends."

"A veritable nest of friends." Why did I say that? It only makes them more ominous. They're not actually moving; that would be ludicrous. They're only objects.

SHEUT

But he who walketh with care and in care he helpeth to walk may find the footsteps of the One God and pass worthy before the snake of snakes.

One of which is said to be extraordinarily powerful and deadly to both those who seek it and those who fall victim to its use. Sought by armies and powerful rulers, and now here we are, two girls from New York, on the brink of one of the greatest discoveries of the ages. The Crown cannot hold actual supernatural power, and yet, can any of this be considered rational? The fact that we're here at all?

I blink hard, steeling myself to the task at hand. We may yet join the ranks of all those failed questers, dead and gone and lost to time.

"So which one is *the* one?" Tess asks, stepping farther into the small chamber.

I follow, joining her in dizzied silence as we orient ourselves.

The chamber is domed and ovoid, aside from a dark dead-ended tunnel extending from one end. It's unlike any other room we've seen thus far, shaped like an egg on a spoon. Aten only knows why. All I know is that this space is absolutely chockablock with priceless treasures, cobras of every description, coiled, unfurled, hissing, shining, sleeping.

While I scan the notebook, I press my hand against Tess, aiming for her chest but smooshing her mouth instead. "Don't touch anything."

"Obviously I'm not going to touch anything. Who do you take me for?"

I lower my arm, but my shoulders stay tight. "Given what we've seen so far, a wrong choice will send the ceiling caving in on us or insects crawling from every hidden crevice. Scarab beetles. Is that what they call them?"

"It is indeed," Tess says tightly. "But we're more likely to simply get trapped in here forever. I don't see a way out."

Tess peeks down the tunnel, the handle of the spoon, so to

speak. "It just ends." She groans. "Which must mean there's a secret exit."

"Well, it would certainly be in keeping with the theme." I turn back to the notebook. "Perhaps we don't have any new clues, but I'm willing to bet there are heaps of old ones hiding in the text." I flip back to my first translation. "'Light will shine upon the tomb where sleeps the snake of the gods.' So that's good. We can safely eliminate at least three-quarters of these objects."

Tess shakes her head. "Care to elaborate?"

"Every single description of this snake points to it being asleep. Nowhere does it indicate that we're going to wake it up."

We stand side by side, shoulders touching, silently pointing at each uraeus that looks like it might be asleep.

"Thirty-seven," Tess says.

"Hmm, I had thirty-six."

"Shoot, I think I counted that one twice."

She motions to an earthenware cobra buried among the others, but my eye has been drawn back to the very first one I counted, on a low, tiered shelf near the center. It shines so brightly in the torches' glow that it seems to form a sort of core, all other snakes orbiting in its gravitational pull. It's made from purest gold, by the looks of it, not just the uraeus attachment but a *full* headdress, fit for a pharaoh of any epoch. The snake in its crown is elegantly coiled, eyes closed in a slumber that looks less like peace, more like expectation. It's waiting to be worn. It's ready. It's exactly what I pictured when I was a child.

It's clearly a trick.

I turn to Tess. "What do you suppose will happen when we choose the right one? A door will open up? Or the ceiling? Not another pit . . ."

"*When* we?" She grins. "I applaud your optimism, dear sister.

Right. *When* we successfully choose the right serpent, I'm not sure how, but I expect we'll be politely shown the way out of this hellhole." She winces. "No offense intended to any gods or ghosts still in attendance. Your home is lovely. I can see why so many choose to stay."

I stifle a laugh, bracing myself for an offended spirit to actually pop out from the pile of snakes and recite us one last arcane riddle, but if anything, the room seems to shine a bit, like the snakes share our sense of humor.

Yes, *our* sense of humor, mine and my sister's. I shouldn't be so amused. I'm on tenterhooks, facing the likely prospect of either sudden, terrifying or slow, agonizing death, but Tess is with me, finally, truly with me, and I feel such relief, such life rushing through me, that I cannot see how anything will top this moment for me ever again. Me, Tess, at the end of a quest.

If we must die, we'll do it proudly.

But not unless we absolutely have to.

"Would you mind terribly giving me one more primer on the mythology?" I ask. "Serpent's Crown, sacred uraeus, emblem of . . ."

"Supreme power," Tess supplies, her eyes distant as she rifles through inner volumes of historical knowledge. "In other contexts, the serpent on a pharaoh's headdress is tied to the goddess Wadjet, but I'm not sure here. We don't know enough about Aten to know whether his followers recognized any of the other gods or subsumed them. You know the Crown legend, though, right? Isis created the first Crown out of earth and sunlight for Osiris to wear as the first pharaoh. But as for Wadjet herself . . . Let's see. She was the protector of Lower Egypt, the Nile Delta, the land . . ."

"'Old as earth and yet more patient,'" I recite. Interesting.

"When Egypt was united, she was joined on headdresses by

a vulture depicting Nekhbet, goddess of Upper Egypt, and they were known as the Two Ladies."

"Quite a lot of powerful ladies." I stare at Tess and she stares back and my skin begins to tingle as if magic is swirling all around us.

This is it, the first time I've felt it completely, all those clues, hopes, positive signs combining into a singular sensation of rightness. We're two mortal humans, flawed and incomplete and often foolish, but better together, and better still with those we've met along the way.

We were meant to be here, not by virtue of being worthy— but maybe, as Samy said, because we know ourselves not to be.

Tess looks at the serpent, *the* serpent, and then at me.

I nod. It's obvious. Among the bright faience, vibrant lapis lazuli, basalt, copper, gold, and silver ornaments, the snake of snakes calls to us now like a beacon.

I help her balance, wincing away the pain in my arm as Tess stands on tiptoe to reach without touching the others. But an inch away, she hesitates, looking back at me. "Shall we do it together?"

Excitement courses through me. "Together it is."

We reach, four hands stretching, until we touch it with our fingertips. It doesn't bite. It's even somewhat warm. Together, we lift.

As predicted, a small hidden square beneath our chosen serpent waggles in answer. The entire chamber begins to rumble. I hold my breath. Here comes the verdict.

Tess draws her hands back from the snake as if it were poker hot. I cradle the serpent, eyes darting for what's next.

The ground begins to quake, and I turn to Tess in wild alarm, but as I register my sister's exultant expression, I find myself laughing along with her. I don't mind this particular feeling one bit. It renders every moment of struggle, filth, and fear worth the living of it.

I pull Tess tight, legs braced against the shaking earth, until we see it, an oval of light shining against the floor of the dark tunnel. A *widening* oval, now a full circle of light, a spotlight on the ground.

We tiptoe out of the chamber of snakes and down the narrow, dead-end corridor, closer, closer, peeking up.

"Son of a . . ." Tess trails off in sanguine awe.

I gawk at the newly revealed tower above us, the blue of the sky beyond piercing my eyes. "It's a secret exit to the well we found when we got here."

"The *dry* one." Her voice echoes strangely, like more than one shout is joining in. "It didn't look all that deep from up there. How—"

Answering her question before she can ask it, another grinding noise resonates throughout the tunnel. We watch, wonderstruck, as steps emerge in a spiral around the tower's walls. They shudder outward, then click into place with a resounding, absolute silence.

The Tomb of the Five Ladies has finished its show. And what a spectacular one it was.

"Thank you," I say to the snake in my hands.

"Do you think I can kiss it?" Tess does the happy dance she used to do as a child, pretending to be a buccaneer. "I'm going to kiss it."

As I step forward to offer it up, something catches my eye—a movement on the floor, I think at first.

But no.

Moving shadows, marring the circle of light.

"This is where the noise came from," someone mutters, his voice distorted against the stone.

Someone else: "Anybody down there?"

We freeze, recoiling together, as something falls in front of us. A rope.

"Answer me!" a fresh shout echoes down the well. This voice is all too familiar. Mr. Hendricks.

Tess's face goes pale. "They found us. I'd forgotten. I was so focused on this that I'd . . ."

"Yes." I can barely hear my own voice. "Me too."

"Do you have the Serpent's Crown?" Davies shouts.

"Tell us now!" Mr. Hendricks bellows over him.

At the threat in his tone, the bravado, the sound of an insecure man backed by many guns, my heart flutters like a baby bird fallen from its nest.

I look to Tess. What should we do? Lie? Keep silent, pretend we're not here?

But as I turn, she's already calling back up, "Of course we have it. We wouldn't dream of turning up to a party empty-handed."

Her defiance is electrifying—her perfect society smile tinged with just the right dose of venom. Alas, it lingers all of an instant. Her face crumples, but I don't want those scoundrels to witness her capitulation. I pull her back into the chamber of snakes, out of view.

"Oh, Lila, all of this, for nothing." Tears fall thick down her cheeks. "Worse than nothing. They'll take this and they'll kill us and . . . we've lost!"

"No," I say firmly, stepping back to motion down at the two of us, dusty and slightly singed and incredibly unwashed and hungry and thirsty, but intact. "We're here, Tess. We're alive, so alive, and we're together. We did it, by any measure."

"You're right." She sniffs hard, smiling through the last of her tears. "We did! And so what do the Fearless Fords do next? Tell me our happy ending."

"We do what we always do." I lift my chin. "We survive to adventure another day."

We both stare down at the prize cradled in my hands. My palms start to sweat, as if the serpent is stirring.

"We could try it out," I blurt. "If anyone needs their minds bent, it's this lot."

"It's too risky." Tess squints upward. "If it doesn't have any power, they blame us. If it does . . . Well, that carries its own risks, doesn't it? All those tests, I believe, were designed to ensure that whoever finds the crown would not be the type of person who would use it."

"Not necessarily," I hear myself arguing. "They wanted someone to wear it, in the end. Otherwise, surely they would have destroyed it."

Tess raises her eyebrows. "Destroy a sacred object created by Isis? It would have been sacrilege."

"We're worthy. We've proven ourselves." My hand is gripping the snake far too tightly. "We'd use it well."

"The only way to use it well is not at all." Her eyes catch on the snake. She, too, is wavering. "But if you disagree . . ."

"*No*," I force out, and with my next breath, I feel the mounting pressure within myself release, the snake cool in my hand, my reason restored. "You're right."

I pass her the Serpent's Crown before I can change my mind again.

She clasps it tight. After a long beat, she whispers, as if stricken, "Davies is the worst of them."

I reach for her. "Oh, Tess."

"No, I'm thinking." Intensity burns in her eyes. "I've learned a thing or two about him. Mr. Hendricks assumes himself to be the leader. In his arrogance, he hasn't bothered to notice what a wild card Davies is."

"And how does that help us?"

"I may know a way to use this and escape with our moral virtue unscathed." She glances behind her. "I'm going to grab another, ah . . ."

"Keepsake?" I offer, wincing.

"Keepsake." She winces back. "Yes. Which will destroy the chamber, no doubt, so we'll need to be quick. Did you notice the very shiny one in the middle?"

I laugh, helpless. "How could I not?"

"That's the one I'll give Davies." She pockets the real snake—small, clay, unassuming. "And let us hope he's hoisted on his own petard."

She pulls me into a fervent hug. I grip her, eyes closed and teary, trying to conjure some of what we've lost to the last seven years.

"We'll make it," I say to her, to myself. "And if we don't . . ."

"*Sta ruska sint uru ribben,*" Tess recites. *We go out in glory.*

I kiss her cheek, sealing the deal.

She glances back at the chamber one more time, capturing a final memory of all that splendor. And then she runs inside to trigger the trap. Too nervous to watch her, I peer up at the cluster of heads gathered around the opening of the well, far above us, all those men of industry, title, power, desperate to see whether two young women have managed what they could not. I can feel their greed, their ambition laid bare, even from this distance.

They wouldn't have lasted three minutes down here.

Tess sprints to my side, the golden ornament in hand, heaving a steadying breath. "I'll go first and bring the decoy up with me," she whispers. "Follow my lead, okay? We'll need to move quickly. I don't mean to be bossy, just—"

"No." I smile. "I trust you."

She beams back. "Likewise, sis. More than anybody else in the world."

The words make my eyes fill. They sound like *I love you.* They sound like *goodbye.*

With no more than a resolute nod, she starts up the steps. I draw a breath and follow.

"Have you got it?" Mr. Hendricks calls again, his voice pitched high with desperation. "Come on, girl, answer me!"

"We're coming up with it," Tess shouts back. "Tsk-tsk, gentlemen. Let's show a little decorum. This is a coronation, after all, not a frontier hoodang."

I snort and it echoes, blending with a new sound, the chamber below us starting to shudder and crumble, the walls cracking, the floor caving.

Tess triggered the trap. And she was right—we'll need to be fast.

My sister is quick as a lemur, every bit as limber as she was climbing park trees and garden trellises when we were children, and I scramble to keep up, clinging to the side of the well, spiraling up, up, up, hand on the handhold, foot on the next step, and repeat, trying not to get dizzy from my torn shoulder or so distracted by the chaos below that I fall into it, focused ever upward, until the sun hits me square in the face and I devour clean desert air and haul myself painfully over the well's raised edge and down onto cracked ground.

I don't care that I've fallen on my face. I don't care that my arms feel like they're about to fall off. I kiss the earth before I pull myself to standing. I made it out. Alive.

And speaking of survival . . .

My heart leaps. I see Alex, on his knees, three guns pointed at his back, suggesting that one proved previously insufficient. He fought back while we were down there, judging by the state of his shirt, the bit of blood on his lip, and the blooming bruise on his chin, but he doesn't look pained as he takes me in. He looks rapturous. I let my eyes linger on him for one blessed blink.

Then I take in the greater party.

There's a clear division between these two disparate groups. To my right, Mr. Hendricks waits with a deflated William and a frothing Belot, plus a handful of other well-dressed, puffed-up men hovering two steps back. Several yards to my left stands Davies, with a ragged band of hired goons clustered behind him as if unwilling to get too close to the toffs.

I do a quick count of both groups and arrive at fifteen in total. Including William, whatever he wishes us to believe. Next I count myself, Tess, and Alex, just for the sake of rigor, but alas, the total remains the same: three. Fifteen is decidedly greater than three.

Behind me, the well lets out a surrendering, clattering roar, then sinks a foot deeper into the earth, smoke spewing out of it like a volcano erupting. Everybody jumps except Davies.

Mr. Hendricks steps forward, as if propelled by his over-puffed chest. "The Crown. Show me."

My eye is drawn past him to Davies. I recognize the look on the younger man's face. It's the same telling expression that gambler wore back on the *Stoat*. The one who was cheating.

Wild card.

Tess glances at me, but what can I say? I'm following her lead, as promised, and there's no way out but forward.

Slowly she lifts what she's holding, tilting the headdress so that it catches the light.

Everyone draws in a musical gasp, including me. It's golden, clearly everything they dreamed it would be: glorious, precious, shining with the glory of the Aten, rich with the lore of the ages. It's their ritual come to life. It's their dream.

363

Mr. Hendricks reaches greedily with both hands, smug child-like satisfaction in his eyes. He deserves this treasure; he knows it in his marrow. He, of all men, should have the Serpent's Crown.

But Tess steps straight past him.

"Mr. Davies," Tess whispers, holding the golden headdress out before her. "You're not like the others. Are you?"

Mr. Hendricks's mouth falls open as he watches her ignore him.

Davies's eyes grow wide, almost innocent. "No. I'm not."

She smiles like a goddess descending. He extends his hands, a child at Communion. She slides the headdress into them and steps back.

Mr. Hendricks spins around, spitting mad. "What in the hell do you think you're doing? This is for us. The Fraternitas de Nodum!"

"Of which I am a member." Davies smiles down at the shining snake headdress, then lifts it high in the air. "You haven't forgotten my initiation, have you? Yes, my mother was a seamstress, my father a drunk, as you so tactfully remind me at every opportunity. But I am equal to you now in every conceivable way. More than that. I'm *worthy*."

I catch William's eyes going wide as his father's face turns purple. And yet, even as Mr. Hendricks splutters, his eyes, *everyone's* eyes, remain tethered to that headdress, watching Davies lower it firmly onto his head.

"Put the guns away. You won't need them now," Davies says softly, his eyes unblinking like he's walking across a circus wire.

The goons glance at one another, confused, before pocketing their weapons.

Davies takes them in with apparent satisfaction. He turns to Tess next, eyes narrowed, a cat with a cornered mouse. "Kneel before me."

Tess, oh, my dear, proud Tess, stays upright for a full two seconds, letting out a defiant cry before her knees crumple, her back falls flat, and her arms stretch out along the earth in supplication to a pharaoh, a god, to Theo Davies, not even remotely worthy, mad with power within seconds.

As a question of logic, I know that Tess is only playacting, but my heart still feels like it's being cleaved in two, watching my vibrant sister behave like a vacant puppet.

As I knew he would, Davies points to me next. "Kneel."

For a moment I'm stunned solid by worry, resentment, resistance. Then my knees fold.

I kneel.

CHAPTER 32

TESS

❦

SILTY WIND PUMMELS MY EARS, SINGES MY EYES. THE
blinding sun is merciless. Still, I manage a peek at Lila through
the glare and the grit. She has collapsed into a heap beside me,
her long arms out in front of her, her head bowed in worship. My
mirror image.

Relief surges through me, a warm current. *Your performance
is perfect*, I long to assure her but do not dare.

My sister's playing her part as brilliantly as Sarah Bernhardt
in her farewell tour.

Davies lets out a cold, satisfied laugh, adjusting the gleaming
cobra on his scalp. "Rise," he commands, his hazel eyes glittering
like that garish headdress.

In unison, my sister and I slink upward to sit, as if we are his
pawns, our faces blank, docile, unassuming. I resist the urge to
meet Alex's eyes across the square; withstand, too, my desire to
gaze upon William again, or else he might look right through me
and spot this charade for what it is. Against all odds, thus far,

this ruse is working. I knew Davies wouldn't resist the grab at absolute power. Now I just pray for his faith to hold fast.

Davies looks at Mr. Hendricks and says flatly, "Shoot yourself. In the head."

Mr. Hendricks sputters like a boiling teapot. "What?"

William abandons Alex's side, rushing forward. "Theo—*Mr. Davies*, rather—"

"Kill yourself!" Davies shouts. "*Now!*"

Mr. Hendricks's face sunsets into a deep crimson, his eyes bulging with rage, disbelief. He begins pointing and shouting at his squadron of tycoons and pasty thugs in desert gear waiting in the wings. "Seize him!"

Davies pushes the headpiece tighter on his head, his shaking hands betraying him. "I said, shoot—"

"Take that lowbred traitor down!" Mr. Hendricks roars as a trio of goons step past him, drawing their guns.

Davies is sweating, his eyes raised to the heavens. "Gods above, Aten, show them my power! Force them to obey their new master!"

And then time slows down, the scene before us unfurling like a scroll; chaos, as I suspected, the nonpareil catalyst:

Davies, glancing at Mr. Hendricks now, terror and understanding at last crashing over him as two of Mr. Hendricks's goons barrel into his chest, pummeling him to the ground, the headdress flying and rolling across the dirt toward Ty Avondale's feet.

Belot, squeaking in distress, scuttling away—though in his hasty escape, he trips over Edward Fane's boot and lands in a balloon of dust.

Mr. Hendricks stomps forward, red face twisted viciously, shouting, "Stop! The bastard's mine!"

He steps on Davies's chest, spits in his face, as Davies twists and writhes, in vain.

Mr. Hendricks draws his gun and—

A boom rattles the sky.

Davies's face bursts open, his body shivering in shock on the ground.

Lila and I cry out, clambering back.

"Drop your weapon."

We turn toward the voice. Across the square, Ty Avondale now wears the headdress, gun drawn, Carl Randolph and two other goons flanking his sides.

Mr. Hendricks snorts. "Not damned likely!"

He turns and shoots Avondale in the chest.

The impostor crown rolls free. And with it, full war breaks out. Carl Randolph darts to grab it while Edward Fane yanks Randolph's shirt collar, pummeling him in the spine.

Alex dashes out of nowhere and slams into Mr. Hendricks. Mr. Hendricks and his gun go flying to the ground.

"Alex!" Lila cries.

"Grab the gun, Tess!" Alex shouts.

Without hesitation, I duck and roll toward the pistol, though I'm not quite fast enough. Belot is already hobbling straight for it like a mad gargoyle, hands clawing outward to claim the weapon first.

"Lila!" I shout.

My sister, closer to the gun now, lunges for it, marvelously scooping it up. As she does, she barrel-rolls into Belot midstep, knocking him off-kilter. She barely looks ruffled by the scrap . . . until Belot staggers backward.

He stops fitfully, arms flailing; pink, wretched face frozen in terror, though it takes me a breath to understand why. He's teetering on the cracked edge of the well, balancing, heaving, struggling . . .

He slips and disappears.

"Mademoiselllllllllle . . . !" Belot's echo plunges like a sinking stone into the well, so far we don't even hear a thud.

I let out a cluck of relief as Lila's hands fly to her cheeks. "Did I—I . . . I didn't mean—"

"Oh, take credit where credit is due," I crow.

But as I hoist myself up to go to her, I meet the hard end of a pistol.

Wincing, I blink. Mr. Hendricks, still huffing, sweaty, leering, digs his gun into the middle of my forehead.

I slowly raise my hands. Open my mouth to say something. Anything.

Mr. Hendricks's blue eyes narrow with purpose.

"Father!" William calls across the square. "No!"

My eyes strain sideways to find Lila's.

"Your charade is finished," Mr. Hendricks seethes. "No more playing, no more lies!"

My blood pounds. I nod, frantic.

This is it. We have no weapons, no alternate escape plan; we're done for.

"I know you didn't activate it."

I suck in a long, slow breath as, with his free hand, Mr. Hendricks places the golden headdress onto his own thinning scalp.

Across the square, Carl Randolph now lies in a heap while Fane and two henchmen engage in fisticuffs. Alex fends off one advancing goon just as another attacks from the side.

"Make it work," Mr. Hendricks roars. "The scrolls gave a code word, yes, an ancient command? Say it!"

I'm too shocked to form an answer.

Mr. Hendricks thrusts the gun barrel into my brow again, this time so hard the world's edges singe black. "Speak it or I'll kill you," he growls. "I swear on my name, I'll skin you alive!"

I feel the boom more than I hear it.

Mr. Hendricks's face twists into quiet shock before he collapses into a gnarled heap.

I squawk, scampering back, sand and sky swirling like an angry kaleidoscope . . . until I spot William.

Our eyes meet, wild. He pockets his gun and dashes across the square toward me, athletically landing a hard jab to an onrushing goon. Then he grabs my hand and Lila's and pulls us along with him.

He yanks us behind the collapsed well's remains, a temporary barricade. His hands are still shaking, tears streaming like rivulets down his sandy face. His haunted eyes dart between me and the field beyond.

"William." I swallow. "Oh, William, I . . ."

"You need to run," he says emphatically. "There's no time—you must go. I can cover you both."

A chorus of gunshots drowns us out, shattering the desert air.

"Alex," Lila says. "I can't see him from here. Did he escape? I think he's—"

"Getting the horses," William finishes.

I shake my head. "How do you know that?"

"Because it's my plan," he croaks. "There are no words, Tess. I was only trying to save Annie, save us all—"

"Time to surrender, Junior Hendricks," a distinguished voice trills out above the melee.

Huffing, I peer between the cracked stones of the well. Ed Fane, the King of Coal, wears the false crown now. He advances across the square, gun in hand. He catches my eye through the rubble and laughs viciously, opening his arms like a deranged circus conductor.

"The Old Guard is dead. It is time for me to lead the world into a new—"

He collapses from a bullet fired from somewhere across the square.

The golden headdress rolls once more along the sand.

"Alex is waiting by the gates," William pleads, steering my gaze toward him, away from the carnage. "I know I ruined everything, but I'll be damned if you're not surviving this!"

He stands and pops off a quick round before collapsing once more, pale as death.

"Get to the far side of the church," he says. "There's another exit set into the fortress wall, beyond the gardens."

Lila primes herself to run.

"No," I blurt at him. "No, you absolute dolt, I'm not leaving you to die here. I—"

He pulls me in, hard and desperate, his lips meeting mine, the heat of him hurtling through me, leaving behind a searing ache as he draws away. He fumbles to remove a derringer from his ankle holster and thrusts it into my hand.

"You deserve a better story." He pushes Lila and me forward. "Now go!"

He stands once more, firing his pistol beyond our barricade.

"Come on!" Lila grabs my hand.

"You first—I'll, um, I'll cover you!"

Lila races toward the church, me backstepping after her. The space beyond the well is littered with corpses, though still there rages an all-out brawl. Partner betraying partner, accomplice against accomplice, all desperate, frenzied, hungry for eternal power. One of the goons must spot our getaway, as his eyes widen in shock.

Lip curling, he raises his pistol in my direction.

With a yelp, I pull the trigger of my derringer, and the little silver weapon bucks in my hands with a roar.

The goon doubles over, gripping his leg.

Reaching the back wall of the church, I whirl away from the chaotic scene, pressing my back against the stone, digging into my garment pockets for the small clay trinket. My fingers brush the cool, earthen clay. Such a small thing, to cause so much deceit, betrayal, agony.

Hugging close to the church, Lila and I scale the building, boots sliding against the packed earth. As we round the building's back wall, Lila lets out the loudest, most primal shout I've ever heard.

Alex, dear Alex, stands waiting twenty paces away at a hitching post in front of the settlement's mill, just as William promised. He's loaded Mr. Hendricks's horses with saddles and the Fraternitas' trove of provisions and supplies and holds their reins, ready to ride.

Lila crashes into him. He hugs her tight before pulling away to beam at her. "Quite the performance you two gave back there." He lets out a pained laugh.

"We only gave them what they deserved," I say, pulling the real uraeus discreetly from my pocket. "And nothing more."

At Alex's astonished expression, I add hastily, "We'll fill you in on the journey."

Lila nods. "If this whole Egyptology path proves unfruitful, Tess and I have a future in theater."

"Helena and Hermia?" I say as Alex tosses us the reins.

"And who's who?" Alex asks, breathless.

"I'm Helena," Lila and I claim in unison.

He shakes his head. "Another thing we'll sort later."

I help Lila mount our gray Arabian while Alex hurries to untie the remaining horses from the post so they'll be free to scatter.

"Escape through the desert is hard enough," he mumbles as he works the knots. "At least this way we won't have pursuers."

Lila glances toward the tumult, then at me, eyes softer now. "Could we leave just one?"

"Yes, let's. *Semper callidus*," I say, recalling William's family's motto. "Let's hope William is infinitely resourceful."

Saying a prayer aloud might jinx it, but William *must* survive this. He simply must. Despite everything, he deserves his real family, reunited. He deserves a better story too.

We ride away from the church, toward the rolling green gardens calling to us like an emerald flare. Shots still echo behind us, but I dig my heels into our mare, keeping my eyes trained forward.

As we pass the working well, the penned animals, the mill, Lila calls ahead, "Where are the rest of the monks? Do you think any of them survived, Alex?"

"I reckon we aren't the first travelers to have come looking, judging by that fissure on the mosaic floor." As we ride, Alex points toward the mill's top floor, where shadows undulate across its windows. "I'd say they have this routine down pat by now."

We cantor onward, the fortress wall looming larger and higher with every gallop.

"William said there's another door on the other side of the oasis," I call to Alex.

He glances back at me, nodding, steering us east.

We ride until we find ourselves along the bank of the oasis's gurgling stream. It draws a sparkling line beside us before cutting and disappearing belowground in the distance.

My hand fumbles into my pocket again, feeling once more for the small clay Crown.

I am still astounded we found it.

"This cannot fall into the wrong hands," I say, hoping that Alex and Lila can hear me over the wind.

Alex eyes the relic queasily. "And it will never be safe in a museum."

"Nor does it belong in one." Lila tightens her grip around my stomach, signaling her adamance on the matter. "Not a Western one, anyway."

Alex glances back once more, his shoulders relaxing an inch. "Egypt is its home."

I pull on the reins, our horse slowing in turn. The stream below us grows wider, its indigo waters churning deep and dark.

"Should we toss it here?" Lila says. "Into the water? Let the current carry it?"

"It's clay," I protest. "The water would erode it. And the Five Ladies considered this sacred; they wouldn't want it destroyed."

"Is this decision even ours to make?" Lila leans around me. "Alex, what do you think?"

Indeed. Alex is the one who grew up playing in Cairo's streets, paddling in the Nile. Whether or not he has ancient *baladi* blood running through his veins, he's a good sight more Egyptian than either of us.

Alex squints into the setting sun.

"I think we trust in our friends." He throws us both a warm glance as we ride onward.

We soon reach the monastery's fortress door. Alex quickly dismounts, shoving off the plank of wood locking the exit with a groan of exertion, and swings the heavy door open.

We canter in silence into the limitless desert. Vast, shifting sands that have stood witness to thousands of years, hundreds of generations, millions of lives moving through time like a river, ebbing and flowing, carrying us forward like a current into the wonderful unknown.

"So we're headed straight for Cairo?" Lila asks, her words quivering like a sail in the wind.

I laugh. "Maybe best to set our sights on Luxor first."

"Agreed. I think we're all entitled to a day's rest," Alex says. "And, might I suggest, a bath."

He gives his horse a dig and dashes ahead of us.

Still laughing, I snap the reins as Lila lets out a cheeky guffaw. She whoops behind me and squeezes my sides while we gallop after Alex.

He's right. After weeks in captivity, battling henchmen, tussling with sinister titans, solving ancient puzzles, I daresay it's high time for a rest. A breather. The adventure is done after all.

Still.

As the changing winds flutter over the rippling dunes, I have the most distinct and delicious suspicion that Lila and I are only getting started.

Search Continues for Pioneering Sorbonne Professor Edwin Belot

World News

Cromer, the Maker of Egypt, Resigns;
Announcement Entirely Unexpected

DAILY NEWS

World - Business - Finance - Lifestyle - Travel - Sport - Weather

Issue: 240   THE WORLDS BEST SELLING NEWSPAPER

First Edition

SOCIETY SHOCK AS BUSINESS MAGNATE JAMES HENDRICKS AND ATTORNEY THEODORE DAVIES BOTH DIE IN DESERT PISTOL DUEL

CHAPTER 33

LILA

❧

LIGHT SPILLS OVER THE SITTING ROOM OF THE *HARAM-lik* in fractal patterns, here an intersection of diamonds in a ratio of four to seven and then a shift to longer rhombi, four to nine, as the sun reaches a lower part of the glass. I could sit here all day and watch it in perfect peace, rest and read, sip tea and eat little fragrant cakes, help with the children, chat in Arabic with our hostess, join the men for dinner, steal fleeting kisses with Alex when we're sure no one is looking.

But after three weeks housebound, no matter how lovely the house, Tess has had enough. Every day, she paces the corridors of the *haramlik*, the *maq'ad*, the courtyards, like a lion testing the borders of its cage, peering outward through every oculus, desperate to widen her world. Small wonder, given all she's been through.

Right now my sister sits beside the window that overlooks the courtyard. I'm not sure whether she's actively eavesdropping or just trying to feel less sequestered, but I see her toes sliding restlessly back and forth along the burnished floor and rouse myself to join her.

She shoots me a wink, tapping her lips to signal silence, and then whispers, "He's just read the papers."

As if in answer, our father's familiar thunderclap of "Ha!" echoes along the colonnade. "Nobody's going to buy this load of hogwash."

"Oh, they will." Samy chuckles. "If there is one thing I have learned about polite Western society during my time working with the Agency, it's that they adore nothing more than watching decorum explode. They will *want* to believe that it all happened exactly as the papers have described."

I peek out to see Father trying to shove himself upright, only to be persuaded back into his plush chaise by Alex. Father leans past him with a wince. "Don't get me wrong, no love was ever lost between those two bastards, but a full-fledged shoot-out in the middle of the damn desert over no more than a family spat?"

"'Then see how was the end of the criminals,'" Samy quotes from the Quran. He picks up one of the papers and strolls away with it, singing a jolly song under his breath.

Tess and I share a satisfied glance. We perused the latest stories with breakfast before passing the papers along to the rest of the house, as per Nura's usual morning routine. Rather incredible to get our hands on the *New York Times* all the way in Cairo, but our hosts do enjoy reading widely. Even so, this printing is four days old, and the news traveled slowly, so it makes for a veritable compendium of scandal. Everyone in Manhattan must be positively beside themselves by now. Talking about my role in it all, no doubt, clueless as to what it truly was.

I read William's name in the society pages, but only in brief, describing his return to New York alongside his now-widowed sister. They've shocked society, apparently, by refusing to receive their mother at Annie's Hudson Valley mansion. My name, meanwhile, was all the more glaring by its omission. After all, it was Lila Ford's shocking engagement that triggered the cascade of events leading directly to the death by pistol of not one but two New York millionaires, with several other notable obituaries thrown in for good measure.

Which means I shall have to play the role of jilted ingenue when we go back. I've already written to Grandmama, and she back to me, via telegram. She's stunned, appalled, but above all, enormously relieved I did not inextricably link myself to that dreadful family. Mrs. Hendricks is in such disgrace that Grandmama has had to cut her off entirely, but the rest of Mrs. Hendricks's former intimates have proven great bastions of support to our family, popping round Riverside daily to share tea and gossip and sympathies for poor lovely Lila.

I do not relish the prospect of maintaining the ruse in person, though after waiting the tactful amount of time, far more wonderful, and accurate, news will overtake all the foul false gossip.

Just as soon as Alex gets around to asking my father for his blessing.

When we returned to Cairo, bedraggled and ready to come clean, Father was ready to throw punches at his old protégé for stealing his daughter out from under him. But Tess and I told him the rest of the story before he could so much as rouse himself from his settee, and he was for the better part of an hour too astonished to speak.

When he did pipe up, his first question was, "Where's the Crown? Can I see it?"

There was a familiar hunger in his voice. A pleading in his eyes.

"Lost, alas," Alex said quickly. "To the desert sands."

Father recovered from his disappointment by dinnertime that night, having us regale him with stories of our puzzles, our close shaves, our brilliant partnership.

"My girls," he said, beaming so proudly. Then he laughed so hard he nearly tore his stitches. "Can't believe I fell for that engagement line. As if you two would have each other."

We've been searching for a delicate way to bring the subject back around to our impending nuptials for the past several weeks, to no avail. In a way, it's both prudent and diverting to keep this secret close for as long as we can.

It distracts, after all, from the larger secret we're keeping from him.

The night we arrived, after Father retired to his bedroom, we presented the uraeus to Samy, expecting . . . we weren't sure what. An outburst of amazement, exhilaration, a speech about what this would mean to the nationalism movement, a flurry of plans.

Samy smiled dotingly at it, cupped in his palms. "Hello, little friend."

Then he passed it straight to Nura, who shepherded it away.

"A powerful object, powerful symbol, no question," Samy explained as we stared at him, incredulous. "But perhaps more powerful as a myth. A mystery. Egypt will determine its own destiny. But not like this."

I'd glanced at Alex in consternation. What was Samy suggesting? No announcement of its discovery, no public exhibition, no recognition of Alex's scholarship?

But Alex positively glowed with relief. "We'll take the secret to our graves."

I've mulled it over since that night, thinking of Egypt and the world beyond, all those dizzyingly disparate manners of living, faces, voices, minds. Surely the beauty and strength of a culture lie in that variety. The idea of anyone, however well-intentioned they may seem, rising to power to force everyone to speak in a single voice, a one-note chorus, chills me to my marrow.

But I set aside my worries for the future. At least we've secured the Crown, ensuring that this particular bit of history does not repeat itself.

I peek between the lattice now and see Alex—my own future—staring up into the window, eyes twinkling as if he can see me clearly. My entire body twinkles right back.

"I need a change of scenery," Father grunts.

Alex clears his throat and reluctantly turns away. "What you need, Dr. Ford, is to recuperate."

"Hey, pea!" Dad shouts up at the window now. "I know you're spying. Get down here and finish this chess game with me. Save me from my boredom."

My sister bites her lip to keep from laughing.

With a grimace, she calls down, "Won't be a minute." Then adds to me, in a grinning undertone, "He's gotten better at losing, don't you think?"

I snort. "Maybe slightly."

The maids slide past to greet Nura, back from her errands. Tess and I rise along with them, eager to help, or rather, to maintain the pretense of it. We know what Nura was really doing at the market.

"Well?" Tess asks, skipping into step beside Nura as she unwraps her dark hair from her veil.

Nura draws a tight breath, suddenly looking no more than our age. "It is happening! We will begin with a series of lectures while we secure a campus. We hope to open next year. And yes . . ." Nura turns to me, now exultant. "Women will be admitted."

One of her maids lets out a shocked squeal. Nura laughingly shushes her, then draws her into our giddy, dancing embrace.

We hurry into the courtyard to share the exciting news, to celebrate with the children, with Samy, with Father and Alex. A litter of kittens was born to a neighbor and the children have taken three, who sit in our laps and crawl on Father's chest, and he pretends to be annoyed, but everything is sun-dappled and full of hope and about to irrevocably change.

"Last day in Egypt." Tess sighs, guessing at my thoughts as we stroll upstairs to dress for dinner, along the corridor that displays Nura's family treasures.

"We'll be back," I say, slipping my hand into hers.

Without strictly planning to, we both slow our steps near Nura's jade figurines. They've found an unobtrusive companion on their shelf, a small, dun snake carving. It looks happy here. And no one will ever glance twice at it.

Tess and I share one last secret smile and continue to our room.

⤧

Reality, such as it is, doesn't really begin to hit us until we've departed our Thomas Cook steamer, bidding farewell for now to the River Nile and hello to the SS *Heliopolis*, which will take us to Marseille, where we'll debark and hop aboard the *Neustria*, and honestly, it would all feel so much less exhausting if New York were not the final port of call.

Tess joins me at the bronze second-class railing of the *Heliopolis*. Stout against the wind, her straw hat sits smartly pinned into her stylish pouf. In her newly purchased travel dress and jacket, she looks like the cover of a summer issue of the *Delineator*, whereas I've let my own hair down, their ends scraggly from the spray of seawater. The contrast startles a laugh out of me. Tess looks at me askance, thinking I'm poking fun, but I just throw my arm around her waist and kiss her hard on the cheek and soon she's laughing right along with me.

"What if . . . ," Tess says as the ship hits the first Mediterranean swell, sending a salty smattering into our upturned faces. She swipes it away, peevish. "Now, hear me out, Lila."

"Was I interrupting?"

"You were about to." She squints up at me. "What if we didn't get on the *Neustria*? But instead stopped off in Marseille. Stayed with Alex for a bit."

"What, in France? In his château?"

"Look at you, tossing these terms off so lightly, Lila to the manor born." Tess's twinkle holds indulgence rather than malice.

I glance over my shoulder and see Alex helping an old lady across the deck to an indoor table set for tea and cannot picture him amid his supposed inheritance. Moneyed or not, he's still my Alex. Sensing me looking through the window, he grins haplessly over his shoulder, almost shoving the poor woman off his arm in the next lurch of the ship, and my whole body turns to pointillist tingles.

"We don't have to stay long," Tess goes on. "I was thinking we could spend some time together in England after that. I still haven't sat for my maths exams, you know."

"*Maths* plural?"

"They say *maths*. And it's *sport*, singular. Don't worry, I'll teach you the language."

I shake my head, ignoring her smirk. "I thought you were dropping all that. 'Pursuing your career through other avenues,' isn't that what you said?"

"Better to have options, don't you think?" Her mouth quirks

the way it always does when she's almost but not quite telling the truth.

My glare grows yet narrower. "And what about your debut ball? The next spring season will swing around more quickly than you think."

"Yes, well." Tess looks even more pleased by this turn of conversation. "I was thinking we might just hold it in England, since you're keeping your engagement under wraps for the moment."

We share a quick glance through the windows behind us, seeing Father inside holding court at the bar, Alex still trapped in conversation with the sweet old lady, who must have invited him to sit with her for tea.

"Loads of American girls come out during the London season after all," Tess goes on.

"*Loads*," I echo, dubious.

"It isn't as if I can't order a Worth gown from there."

"A Worth gown, is it?" Now I'm grinning. How can I help it? She's planned it in her mind so clearly already that I can start to see it myself.

"How long are we staying in England under this proposal?" I laugh.

"Long enough to keep Grandmama out of our hair as *we* plan my ball . . . and to give me time to decide whether to include William Hendricks among the guests."

I gawk at her, appalled. "Tess."

Her apple cheeks go pink, but she lifts her chin, determined. "He did get us out of a very bad spot in the end."

I do not put in, "That he got us into in the first place," but it is a challenge.

Then I notice a little muscle working in her jaw. I lean closer. "All right. What's really going on?"

"I thought you'd never ask." Eager as a puppy, Tess produces a rolled-up piece of parchment from deep in her jacket pocket.

I gasp with anticipation, but it's not what I thought. It's written in English.

"A letter." I take it from her.

"And before you ask, yes, it was sent to Dad, care of Samy, and yes, I managed to squirrel it away first, and no, he hasn't read it. Yet."

Apparently my confusion has made my fingers too sluggish in unrolling the letter for Tess's liking, because she snatches it back and does the reading for me, in her own fashion.

"'Blah blah blah, hope you're recovering, ghastly business in Cairo, et cetera . . . something that may be of interest once the doctor deems you fit to travel.'"

She glances back at me, exultant. I lean over her shoulder and pick up the thread.

I frown. "Do you know this person? Sir Neville Standish?"

"Not yet." Tess readjusts a lock of her hair. "But I'm sure an introduction could be arranged. And we know where he lives. Upper Tump."

"At least it's not the lower one," I quip, but then suspicion strikes. Tess looks altogether too pleased with herself. "Father won't be ready to take on something like this for months."

"Honestly, I wouldn't agitate him by even telling him about it. Not yet anyway, not until we figure out the full story and essential players. He'd insist on leaping into action, but we both know he'd rupture something and be straight back in the hospital in days. Far better for him to hole up in Oxford and return to his long-languishing academic responsibilities while we do what all young women are meant to do—glide our way through polite society and secure ourselves suitable husbands. And if a

The object in question is of Celtic origin, perhaps older, mentioned in the Roman correspondence we discussed, all of which point to that runic code no one's yet managed to crack. Select members of that society I shall not stain the pages of this letter by naming have been making enquiries of some of my colleagues at the university about so-called ley lines, similar to those Nazca Desert markers you delved into early in your career. Only a hunch. Feel free to correct me, as I'm but a humble dabbler.

My connections in the southwest tell me that Lady Leona Tembroke, in particular, has taken to spiritualism in the hopes of locating the missing earl, certainly not in and of itself a thing of note, if it weren't for the fact that she's been arranging outings to various Iron Age hillforts and Neolithic circles alongside others of quite questionable affiliation, and I fear they may be homing in on a goal I would much rather they never achieve.

Once you're up to it, old chap, and back to your Oxford duties here on our fair island, why don't you pay me a visit here at Upper Tump and I'll lay out all I know and crack the Macallan I was gifted upon my retirement from academia.

I must confess, I'm itching to get back into the hunt, and I wonder if you are too. Especially considering the abysmal moral calibre of the people who stand at odds with us.

Yours as ever,
Sir Neville Standish

few misadventures were to befall us along the way, why, we can scarcely be blamed for that, can we?"

Tess shrugs, cheeky as an alley cat, but there's truth in her words. If Father were to get this letter, he'd answer it immediately, recklessly, foolishly.

Even so, this is too far, shockingly bold, thrillingly brazen.

It's something the Fearless Fords would do.

We gaze along the ice-white hull of the newly built ship, this sea of legend, a great sapphire swell before us, humbling in its expanse. Tess waves for Alex to join us, while I breathe it all in, sea salt and possibility and ancient runes and maths . . . then I squeeze my brilliant sister's hand and seal the oath with a single nod.

For all her bravado, even Tess looks a little stunned by what we've just agreed to.

Alex, ever the hero, appears behind us laden with a champagne bottle and three saucers dangling from his fingers.

"You star!" Tess says.

"Courtesy of Dr. Ford," he explains with a nod to the bar.

Father pauses his confab to shoot us a wink and a rascal's grin, then returns to the throng hanging on his every word.

"To what shall we toast?" Alex asks.

Tess's eyes twinkle, and I think for one pained moment she's about to divulge my secret wedding engagement to the entire ship.

Then she hoists her sparkling glass. "To misadventure!"

"Hear, hear," seconds Alex.

And with that, we all happily drink.

A NOTE FROM THE AUTHORS

IN WRITING *THE ANTIQUITY AFFAIR*, WE WANTED TO craft an adventure novel that pays homage to the best parts of stories like *Indiana Jones*: the twists and turns, the puzzle solving, the world travel, and the romance. At the same time, we also strived to write a socially conscious story that examines and grapples with the sexism and racism inherent in those types of franchises, the notion that archaeologists have the right to plunder other cultures for the sake of "fortune and glory," and that rugged, individualist, gun-toting males are the only heroes who can save the day. Our two sister protagonists, Lila and Tess, are by no means perfect, but throughout the course of the novel, they learn to question and challenge their reckless archaeologist father, fashion their own approach to the profession, and ultimately form their own nuanced opinions on the times in which they live—times that are in many ways not so different from our own.

Delving into the early days of archaeology meant grappling with real history—which is, of course, one of the great joys of writing historical fiction. Our story hops between New York City, Paris, and Egypt in the spring of 1907, a time of robber barons, colonialism, deeply entrenched racism, and misogyny, but also huge social change. We've included within these pages real historical figures, from the mysterious heretic pharaoh Akhenaten to famed archaeologist Howard Carter, seen here in his early career, years from the discovery of Tutankhamun's tomb, working under the tutelage of Gaston Maspero, the curator of the Egyptian Museum. We've imagined greater intrigues for Maspero in *The Antiquity Affair* than he likely encountered in real life—though one never knows!

Some of our fictional characters have been based upon historical figures, such as Theodore Davis, the real New York attorney who financed Howard Carter's later expeditions. We should in good conscience note that there is absolutely no evidence that Davis was in any way villainous. As a prominent businessman, however, he may very well have been a member of a real secret society such as the Freemasons, as was, anecdotally, Lord Cromer, the controversial Consul-General of Egypt, who appears in the periphery of this story. The real Cromer was driven out of office in the summer of 1907, as he was unable to quell rising outrage following an episode of British occupying forces enacting gross brutality against Egyptians in the Denshawai region. In our story, we've imagined that Cromer would be all too eager to have a mind control device at his disposal in order to stay in power. The Fraternitas de Nodum, thankfully, was our own nasty creation.

We also borrowed from history for story settings and locales. Our scenes that take place in the Louvre and Egyptian Museum, for example, depict the layouts and collections as they existed at the time. General Samy Pasha's home, too, was inspired largely by real-life Cairo palace Bayt al-Razzaz. And while the Serpent's Crown and the myth surrounding the relic are fictional, KV55 is an actual tomb, still considered by scholars to be the hasty burial site of Akhenaten. We've maintained the tomb's layout, its date of discovery, and the artifacts contained within . . . with a few added touches of our own, fanciful answers to some of the mysteries of KV55 that archaeologists still puzzle over today, from the anachronistically bare walls of the burial chamber to the odd, elongated shape of the pharaonic mummy's skull. While we've slipped between the cracks of the historical record to take factual liberties in service to the story, perhaps our imaginings may spark your own theories and research.

ACKNOWLEDGMENTS

THE WORK OF CREATING THIS BOOK HAS BEEN A LONG, epic adventure of its own—and since the very beginning, our superb agent has been by our side, supporting us with stellar insight, cheerleading, and a whole lot of tenacity. Katelyn Detweiler, you are our hero! Thank you also to Sam Farkas, Denise Page, and the rest of the hardworking team at JGLM. We're so happy to have you as our agency family.

Kimberly Carlton, our editor extraordinaire, you saw what we were trying to accomplish with this story, challenged and encouraged us, and made the voices of the Fearless Fords come alive. We are incredibly grateful for your brilliance and support. Working with you has been a dream in every sense of the word!

Julie Breihan, our exceedingly clever line editor, we greatly appreciate your keen eyes and dedication to making this story shine. Thank you, too, to Amanda Conway, whose expert analysis and sensitivity read feedback were invaluable.

Many thanks to the rest of the Harper Muse family who not only have made this book possible but have made us feel incredibly welcomed into the fold: Amanda Bostic, Caitlin Halstead, Margaret Kercher, Colleen Lacey, Nekasha Pratt, Kerri Potts, Savannah Summers, and so many others. We're also grateful to the art and design teams, with special thanks to James W. Hall for designing our book's gorgeous cover.

We'd like to thank our community of writers: our fellow Harper Muse authors, old Freshman Fifteens (how we met each other!), our Fearless Fifteeners, the writers and faculty at VCFA, the Alliterati, and the *mediabistro* crew. Thank you for your continued support, friendship, and camaraderie over these many years. We are beyond lucky to call you all our writing squad.

From Lee: Through ups and downs, writing peaks and valleys, my family has *always* been there. In particular, a huge thank-you to my parents, Joe and Linda Appicello, who've read every draft, who have kept my hope alive, and who've taught me to never, ever stop dreaming. Thank you, too, to my sisters, Jill and Bridget: my lifelong confidantes and the reason I love reading and writing sister stories so much. A big thanks as well to Penn and Summer, lights of my life, for being infinite sources of joy, laughter, and motivation. And finally, my endless love and gratitude to my husband, Jeff. You've been behind this story—every story—since the beginning. *Principesco!* My best friend, champion, self-declared publicist, and partner in crime: "You're simply the best."

From Jenn: I'd like to express my gratitude to my whole family, but especially my husband, Rob, who makes everything work, who cares about the things I care about simply because I care about them, and who teaches me more about romance every day. Thank you to my parents, the unofficial Jenn Thorne Book Club, whose love and encouragement keep me going. And thank you to my two sons, Oliver and Henry, for your ongoing patience that I have yet to write a book about Pokémon. And extra appreciation goes to my dearly missed mother-in-law, the great reader and all-around most wonderful person Pam Thorne, who loved

ACKNOWLEDGMENTS

even early iterations of this book and who always championed me
more than I did myself.

And last but certainly not least, thank you to our readers.
Having this book in your hands is well worth all the trials, puzzle
solving, and strenuous effort we've faced along the way—the hap-
piest ending of all!

DISCUSSION QUESTIONS

1. Several families are featured in *The Antiquity Affair*, including the Fords, the Hendrickses, and even Akhenaten's family—the "Five Ladies" of myth who brought about the pharaoh's downfall. In what ways are family bonds life-affirming in this book, and in what ways are they harmful? How are the characters affected by the roles they've been assigned within their families? How do they break free of them?

2. Lila and Tess are both talented heroines, though in different ways. In what ways are they using their particular skills as the story opens? How does that evolve as the story progresses? Are there ways in which you feel women's talents are still constrained by societal expectations and pressures today?

3. In their authors' note, authors Kelly and Thorne discuss the inspiration for the tomb at the heart of the novel, as well as provide historical context about the field of archaeology and the political situation in 1907 Cairo. Did anything in the note surprise you as being true? Is there any aspect of the story you see in a new light after reading the authors' note?

4. *The Antiquity Affair* includes many nods to the *Indiana Jones* franchise while also subverting its notions of heroism, particularly through the character of Warren Ford. In what ways do Tess and Lila challenge the trope of the rugged individualist hero? How does the novel's depiction of the world of archaeology differ from what you've seen in classic adventure films?

5. Central to the myth of the Serpent's Crown is the idiom "The serpent calls the worthy," and yet, as General Samy says, "To be worthy is to know oneself unworthy." How is the notion of "worthiness" explored throughout the story and tested through the trials of the Serpent's Tomb?

6. The Fraternitas de Nodum, like Akhenaten before them, craves the mind-controlling power of the Serpent's Crown. Discuss the ways in which imperialism and other political systems have historically relied on limiting freedom of thought in order to maintain control.

7. The promise of the Serpent's Crown resonates strongly for each character in this story in ways that are tied to their deepest wishes, beliefs, and worldviews. What does it represent to Warren Ford, Lila, Tess, Uncle Samy, Alex, and Theo Davies, among others?

8. In recent years, the Louvre, the British Museum, and other venerable Western institutions have removed several artifacts from their collections, returning them to the nations from which the artifacts originated—often under duress, after public campaigns and protests. Do you agree or disagree with these campaigns? Has this book caused you to question any assumptions you held about how the excavation and preservation of antiquities were handled in the past?

9. Perhaps the most morally gray character in *The Antiquity Affair* is William Hendricks. What's your opinion of him as the story closes? Are his actions in any way excusable? Do you feel he's redeemed himself at all by the end?

10. Lila, Tess, and Alex are presented with several options for safeguarding the Serpent's Crown at the end of the novel. Do you believe they made the right decision in the end? Would you have made another choice?

ABOUT THE AUTHORS

LEE KELLY

Heidefinition Photography

LEE KELLY IS THE AUTHOR OF *CITY OF SAVAGES*, *A Criminal Magic*, and *The Antiquity Affair* (co-written with Jennifer Thorne). Her short fiction and essays have appeared in *Gingerbread House*, *Orca*, and Tor.com, among other publications, and she holds an MFA from the Vermont College of Fine Arts. An entertainment lawyer by trade, Lee has practiced law in Los Angeles and New York. She currently lives with her husband and two children in New Jersey, where you'll find them engaged in one adventure or another.

JENNIFER THORNE

Verity Rivers

JENNIFER THORNE LIVES IN A COTTAGE IN Gloucestershire, England, with her husband, two sons, and various animals. She is the author of folk horror novel *Lute*, picture book *Construction Zoo*, and, as Jenn Marie Thorne, YA novels *The Wrong Side of Right*, *The Inside of Out*, and *Night Music*. *The Antiquity Affair*, co-authored with Lee Kelly, is her first work of historical fiction.

From the Publisher

GREAT BOOKS

ARE EVEN BETTER WHEN THEY'RE SHARED!

Help other readers find this one:

- Post a review at your favorite online bookseller

- Post a picture on a social media account and share why you enjoyed it

- Send a note to a friend who would also love it—or better yet, give them a copy

Thanks for reading!